MARY, MARY

A phone call late on a hot Dublin evening. An anxious mother, enquiring about her daughter. Then a week later, the dreadful truth begins to unfold. The policeman, McLoughlin, watches as the green cover is pulled back from the mortuary slab. The young woman's battered, mutilated body is exposed, and for Margaret comes the dull, aching realization that this is not – can never be allowed to be – the end. Margaret is a psychiatrist, recently returned to Dublin to nurse her dying mother, and now her daughter Mary is dead...

Please note: *This book contains material which may not be suitable to all our readers.*

MARY, MARY

MARY, MARY

by

Julie Parsons

Magna Large Print Books
Long Preston, North Yorkshire,
BD23 4ND, England.

British Library Cataloguing in Publication Data.

Parsons, Julie
    Mary, Mary.

    A catalogue record of this book is
    available from the British Library

    ISBN 0-7505-2513-4

First published in Great Britain 1998 by Pan Macmillan Ltd.

Published in Large Print 2006 by arrangement with
Pan Macmillan Publishers Limited

Magna Large Print is an imprint of Library Magna Books Ltd.

Printed and bound in Great Britain by
T.J. (International) Ltd., Cornwall, PL28 8RW

To
Harriet, Sarah and John,
with all my love

PERMISSIONS

ACKNOWLEDGEMENTS

My special thanks to:

My mother, Elizabeth Dobbs, who taught me how to tell a good story.

My sister, Gay Johnson, and my brothers, Simon Parsons and Rory Parsons, and their families, for their help and comfort in good times and bad.

My stepfather, Peter Dobbs, for his kindness.

Lorelei Harris, who told me to do it.

Mary O'Sullivan, who I tried it out on first.

Renate Ahrens-Kramer, Phil MacCarthy, Sheila Barrett, Cecilia McGovern, and Joan O'Neill, who listened and gently told me what was wrong.

Alison Dye, who showed me what was right.

Carole and Alexandria Craig for the alternative view.

Paula O'Riordan for her loyalty and friendship.

Dr Ursula Barry, Dr Kevin Strong and Karen O'Connor, BL, for their help with the medical and legal elements of the story.

My friends in An Garda Síochána who were so generous with their time and expertise.

Dr Art O'Connor, Central Mental Hospital, Dundrum, for the interesting conversation one bleak winter's day.

Treasa Coady for her leap of faith, and Charles Pick and Martin Pick for their expert help.

Suzanne Baboneau, who showed me the loose ends and gave me the means to tie them up.

And last but not least the Cadens, the Morrisseys and the Flahertys for all the parties.

PART
1

1

You could say it began with a phone call. After all, that's the way most cases begin. And you'd wonder then, looking back, whether there was anything about it that warned you, that reached out and grabbed you, that said, Hold on a minute, this is serious.

But at the time it was just another anxious mother. Worried, embarrassed. Not sure she should be phoning. Not sure if she was doing the right thing. Her fear turning to anger.

'If she'd said she wasn't coming home, if she'd rung, if she'd let me know.'

He'd heard it all before. Regularly. He doodled on the margin of the newspaper. Ice-cream cones with pointed creamy peaks and pints of stout in old-fashioned glasses with the little bulge three-quarters of the way up the side. He wrote the time in the phone log. Twenty-one forty-eight. Twelve minutes to the end of his shift. Sunday, 6 August 1995. The middle of the bank

15

holiday weekend. Still hot at this late hour. Too hot. Damp patches under his arms and an itch in his crotch. The hospitals would be filled with cases of sunstroke, and God knows how many fights there'd be in the couple of hours after the pubs closed. All those tempers, stoked by bare brown skin, arm against arm, thigh against thigh, hopes raised, desire rushing to the surface like the bubbles in a pint. And then the bright white neon light, flashing on and off. Time, gentlemen, ladies. Please. Cigarette butts scattered across a pockmarked floor. Lipstick smeared. Sunburn itching, already beginning to peel. His hand on her leg. You cunt, you. What the fuck do you think you're at? And that single moment of pure rage that brings the glass crashing onto the table.

'Are you listening to me? Are you writing any of this down?'

He sighed, and stretched his aching back. He had a pain, midway between his neck and his waist. He thought he'd done it playing golf a couple of months ago. Not as fit as he used to be. Too much desk work. Not like in the old days. Stationed in Belmullet, rowing out into Achill Sound, the pale blue of the Iniskeen Islands, hazy shadows on the horizon, and the mackerel

16

jumping into the boat. Bank holidays were different down there. It was always suicides. Someone would hear a shot. Bits of brain everywhere, strewn across the old dresser, and the dog whimpering in the corner.

'Have you tried all her friends? Rung round, asked them if they've seen her?'

That did it. He held the phone away from his ear.

'Look. You don't seem to be taking this in. We're visitors here. My daughter doesn't know many people. I've told you this already. She went into town yesterday evening to meet a couple of kids from her ballet class. She's been gone for over twenty-four hours. I wouldn't be on the phone to you if I didn't have a reason.' And the voice rising in pitch and in volume. 'There's something wrong.'

'And how old did you say she was?'

'For the third time she's twenty.'

He'd have to tell her. Not that she'd want to hear it. They never did – parents, that is.

'There's just one thing. At her age she can, if she wants, leave home. There's not much we can do about it. She isn't a minor. I'm sorry, but people disappear all the time.'

Silence. Then a deep breath. He screwed up his face in anticipation. He looked

17

around the room. In the far corner, doddery old Pat Byrne lounged with his cap still on, reading the *Sunday World*, and biting his nails. Systematically. Crunching his way from finger to finger. Through the open door to the kitchenette he could see Nuala Kenny brewing tea. He waved in her direction, miming a drinking motion with his free hand.

'Look. I know what you're saying. But I'm worried. I want you to take down her details and do whatever you can to find her. Do I make myself clear?'

Fuck it. More paperwork. He pulled himself up off the high stool, feeling the catch in his back as he stretched for a missing person's form from the shelf above. His trousers were too tight. When he undressed at night there was always a red X-shaped mark from his belt buckle just above his belly button. How had it happened that he'd put on so much weight? Where was that skinny young fella who'd graduated from Templemore thirty years ago?

He sat down again, cradling the phone between his shoulder and his ear. 'OK, let's start at the beginning. Name?'

When he'd finished, he drank his tea. It was lukewarm, the sugar a thick layer, like fine river sand, at the bottom of the mug. He looked back over the page. He tried to imagine her, to conjure up the girl from his carefully printed words. Tall. Five foot seven and a half. Thin. Eight stone two pounds. Dark. Black curly hair, sallow skin with blue eyes. The form didn't have a space for pretty or plain or downright ugly. You didn't ask. But in this case he could guess. He knew how he'd feel if she was his child. The statistics for the year were frightening. Eight women murdered, nearly two hundred reported cases of rape, five hundred sexual assaults. Too many. Too many unsolved. He was glad, suddenly, that he was a desk man, that all he had to deal with were the black marks on the white paper, not the flesh and blood.

He filed away the report, and cleared off his desk. He had reassured her, told her not to worry. Said to leave it another twenty-four hours. If she hadn't come home then, to bring in a photo, and they'd get going on some publicity. He stepped out into the warm night and walked through the car park. He could smell chips from the van that was always outside the big pub on the corner. But he didn't feel hungry. He looked up at the moon, two days to go until it was full, still as beautiful as it had been when he was a kid, when it had followed him home down the lane, on nights so dark he could feel the blackness touching his face.

She was out there, somewhere, under the grey blue light. Mary Mitchell, aged twenty. Black hair, blue eyes, slim build. When last seen she was wearing a black T-shirt, a red suede miniskirt, and a black denim jacket. Speaks with a New Zealand accent.

He started up the engine and drove slowly out of the car park onto the main road. Forget about it, he told himself. There's nothing you can do. And he sighed. Deeply. A long sigh of regret.

2

You could say it began with a phone call, but which call was it? The one she had just made to the Garda station or the other one, four months ago, dragging her out of her sleep, the red numbers on the alarm clock showing 01:02? She had put out her hand automatically, the years of being on call still dictating to the tendons and ligaments of her arm, the nerve-endings in her fingers. She picked up the receiver, the hard plastic cold against her ear. She stated her number. Her voice was steady, matter-of-fact, all traces of sleep gone. There had been a pause, and then the hiss like the sound of the sea from the inside of a shell. And the voice, querulous, but unmistakable.

The same voice called to her now. 'Margaret. Come here. I need you.'

She put down the receiver. She looked at herself in the dusty gilt mirror, still hanging as always above the small table in the hall. She shook her hair loose from its wooden clasp, smoothed it down with both hands, then clicked it neatly back into place. She wiped away an imaginary smudge from the fine lines between her eyebrows. She tried to smile at the reflection before her, but her mouth trembled and the bright shine from her eyes hinted at the tears that lay just beneath the surface.

'Margaret.' Again the voice, louder. She turned away from the mirror and walked into the large room to the right just off the hall. A woman sat in a rocking chair beside a high bed. She was tiny, her body shrunk inside the red silk dressing gown, which was tied around her waist. Her white hair stood up around her heart-shaped face. She was rocking relentlessly, her slippered feet arched against the floor, the chair's wooden runners drumming loudly through the silent house.

Margaret walked to the bay window. She looked out at the sea. High up, to the east, the moon turned its shining face towards the earth. Low down near the horizon Venus flickered. She leaned her head against the glass. Behind her, the voice continued. A series of complaints. I have a pain in my back. Why don't the pills work? When is my nice doctor coming? I don't like the nurse from the hospice. I'm not dying. Why does she have to visit me? Can't you do something? That was why I asked you to come home. To help me. I thought you'd help me.

She turned away from the dark night. She leaned against the window sill and looked around her. When she was a child this had been their sitting room, bright and pretty, with pale yellow wallpaper and flowered curtains to match. Now it was her mother's sanctuary and lair. Newspapers were piled in tottering stacks. Cardboard boxes covered most of the floor. She had tried a couple of times to tidy them away, but her mother had snapped and snarled, so now she left everything as she found it.

Pushed into the corner was the bed her parents had once shared. It was covered with the same pink eiderdown, faded now and lumpy, the goosedown settled in clumps beneath the tattered satin. She remembered the smell of that bed. Her mother's perfume, Ma Griffe, wasn't it? and her father's hair oil, and another smell that she only came to name many years later. She had crept into it on nights when the east wind banged against the windows and monsters from the sea threatened to rise up and invade the shore. She had slipped her cold body up against her father's warmth, curving into him, making herself as small as possible. Always against him. Never against her mother. She would have sat up, switched on the bedside lamp and told her not to be silly, to get right back to her own bed, not to be waking them up at this ungodly hour. But he just wrapped his arms around her, his breath on her face.

'Where's John? Why isn't he here? Why won't you let him in?'

Dead and gone, my beloved father.

'You're not listening to me, are you?'

'What?'

'I told you. The pain. It's bad.' Tears

slipped down her wrinkled face, and a thin sound, like that of an injured kitten, came from her mouth. Still she rocked, backwards and forwards, her tiny hands holding tight to the arms of the chair. Margaret felt the same sound welling up in her own throat. She stood up and took one last look at the moon. Then she pulled down the blinds and shut out the night.

3

'You have beautiful hair,' he said, winding a long strand around his fist and draping the end across his mouth like a moustache. 'You'll miss it.'

The kitchen scissors with the orange plastic handle stroked her cheek. She kept her eyes fixed on the floor. The black curls dropped like feathers. Swansdown, she thought. Like Odile in *Swan Lake*.

'Here,' he said, when he had finished. He held her head tight with one hand and with the other pushed her face up against his cracked pocket mirror.

'Why?' she asked him, forcing the word

24

out through a mouth sour with his taste and the taste of blood.

'Why not?' he replied, pushing her to the floor.

'Let me go.'

'Why?'

'Because...' Her voice broke, the words drying up, as her throat closed around her vocal cords.

'Because you're mine,' he sang in a loud falsetto.

'Please.'

'Ah.' He sat back in his chair, crossed his legs and folded his arms. 'Begging now, are we?'

'No.' She pushed herself up, looking into his eyes.

He kicked her then, his foot driving into her stomach. She fell back, silent, the wind knocked out of her. Then she whimpered, lying like a baby in the womb, arms and legs crushed together.

He threw the scissors across the room. They landed with a loud clang on the stone-flagged floor. A shaft of sunlight glanced across the open blades and winked invitingly at her.

He got up and went over to the large enamel sink. He turned on the tap. Water gushed out. He filled a cup. He walked back and squatted down beside her. He cradled one arm around her shoulders, lifting her up until she could drink. Now she began to cry, the salt of her tears burning her lip where it was cut and swollen.

'What do you want? My mother, you know she'd give you anything. She'd do anything you asked.'

He pulled a tissue from his pocket and dipped it into the water. He dabbed gently at the blood caked around her nose and mouth. His breath was heavy on her face.

'Anything now. Would she? And would you? Do anything I asked?'

A long sigh, which ended in a sob. 'Do I have a choice?'

'Oh, we all have a choice. That's what separates us from the beasts of the field. Makes us human.'

'Human.' She struggled to get to her feet, pushing herself up with her manacled hands, but her legs buckled beneath her and she fell back, her naked knees banging on the hard floor, bringing more hot tears to her eyes.

He prodded her with a bare foot, scraping the soft skin of her cheek with his toenails. 'On second thoughts, you don't look very human so maybe, after all, there is no choice for you.'

She tried to pull away, but he grabbed her hair and dragged her down beside his chair.

'Now. Your mother. A pretty lady. A very pretty lady. And plenty of money too, is that right?'

She nodded, her eyes closed.

'And did she make it all herself or is she like one of those in the song?'

'The song?'

'You know.' He let go of her hair and she fell once again to the floor. He stood up and took a deep breath, miming holding a microphone. He closed his eyes and swayed. His voice rang out clear and tuneful.

'Them that's got shall get,
Them that's not shall lose,
So the Bible says and it still makes news.
Mamma may have, papa may have
But God bless the child that's got its own, that's
got its own.'

He bowed deeply towards her as he finished. 'Hey, what about a bit of applause, a bit of appreciation.'

She raised her hands and tried to clap, the metal of the handcuffs catching and pinching the skin of her wrists. 'Take them off. Please, Jimmy. You know it's been much more fun without them.'

'Fun, is it? For who, or should I say for whom?' He grabbed hold of her wrists and pulled her, dragging her behind him as he walked towards the other, smaller room. He lifted her onto the bed, pulling the cuffs up and over the brass post.

'You know what, little Mary, I think I'm going to give your mother a present. You say she's a psychiatrist. She helps people with problems. People like me. People with psychoses and neuroses. So I'm going to give her a little puzzle to solve. And it's all to do with the word "why". Why do I do what I do, and why do I do it to you?'

A sound filled the room. The sound of a cornered animal, a rabbit screaming as the ferret squeezes its narrow muscled body down the hole. A rabbit, frozen, immobile, its eyes unfocused, as the ferret bares its pointed teeth, and the darkness spreads. Slowly.

4

The phone rang loudly through the silent house. Margaret listened but didn't move. Twice already that morning the phone had rung, but when she picked it up there was no one there. So she sat where she was, on the floor in Mary's bedroom, a pile of coloured leotards on her lap. Mary had left them, discarded, when she rushed out of the house that evening. 'I'm late, I'll tidy my room tomorrow,' she had called back over her shoulder as she grabbed her bag and slammed the front door.

Margaret had picked up the scraps of cotton and Lycra. Red and blue, purple and green. Like the flowers that Persephone gathered the day Hades stole her away to the Underworld, she thought. Six months before Demeter saw her again. Six months of every year that the world mourned the loss of her daughter.

Four days since Mary had gone. Margaret buried her face in the soft pile of clothes. Mary's familiar smell surrounded her. She

29

breathed in deeply. How long would it be before the smell would fade, before all trace of her would be lost? She slipped sideways onto the worn carpet and curled into a ball, conscious suddenly that the phone had stopped ringing and the house was silent once again.

A new routine had taken over her life. Normal time had been suspended. She measured her days now in accordance with the change of shift in the Garda station. She allowed herself one phone call for each eight hours. Six a.m. to two p.m. Two p.m. to ten p.m. Ten p.m. to six a.m. She played games with herself, worked out ways of delaying, set up arbitrary rules. I'll have a cup of tea first, then I'll phone. I'll read the paper, then I'll do it. I'll make sure Mother takes her pills, then I'll dial the number. She ate sparingly, intermittently. Cups of coffee and pieces of bread and cheese were her staple diet. Sleep was haphazard, snatched in minutes rather than hours, never in bed, sometimes at the kitchen table or on a bench in the garden. Once in the rocking chair in her mother's room. Outside the sun shone, a perfect ball of fire glittering in a sky that mirrored the cornflower blue of the sea below. The little beach at Seapoint was packed. They straggled down the road past her windows from the DART station, the mothers and children, friends and lovers, a brightly coloured caravan of happiness. She stood at the gate and watched, so close she could have reached out and touched them, yet a million light years from the cold dark world in which she was living.

Around her flowed the business of the house, dominated by her mother's illness. She had cancer, first diagnosed eight years ago and treated. A radical mastectomy followed by six months of chemotherapy. Now it was back. A tumour on the spine. The first time a letter had sufficed, but this was different. She had lain in her bed, twelve thousand miles away, listening to Catherine's sobs, and thought, it's time to go back. To say goodbye properly, to lay the ghosts.

Now her cheek rested against the floor. She closed her eyes. She could feel the movements in the rooms below, travelling up through the house. The Hoover trundling backwards and forwards over the faded rugs set up the steady, rhythmic vibration that rattled Mary's jars and tubs of makeup on the dressing table. Nellie must be here, she thought. Poor old Nellie, as Catherine called her, not realizing that Nellie who had worked for them since she was fourteen was considerably younger and healthier than she. The doorbell rang twice. She lifted her head slightly, then dropped it back again. The familiar rumble of the doctor's voice. Catherine's favourite. The youngest recruit to the local practice. Came to see her every day. Sometimes brought her flowers or chocolate. Flirted with her, responded to the coquettish glances she gave him through her sparse eyelashes, pretended not to notice her smudged and smeared lipstick and powder. Who else would come on this bright morning? Perhaps Father Lonergan, with his gracious smile and long, well-tended hands. Maybe one or other of the neighbours who remembered when Catherine was the best-dressed woman in the parish with her hand-made shoes and tailored suits.

Margaret rolled onto her back, and folded her arms tightly around the bundle of clothes. Sunlight moved and shifted across the room. As it had when she was a child. An apple tree grew up the back of the house, right against her bedroom window. Many times she had crawled out over the sill and scrambled down its arthritic branches, jumping the last few feet to the lawn below. Mary had done it too, in the first week after they arrived. Just to see, she had said, if all the things you told me were true. O ye of little faith, Margaret had chided her, as she stood on the grass looking up at the window. Be careful. You don't want to hurt yourself. But Mary was as light and lithe as she had been, landing on her toes on the mossy grass, then spinning away from Margaret's outstretched arms, her feet placed precisely, her body aligned perfectly, a succession of jetés carrying her effortlessly onto the stone terrace where Catherine sat, a large gin and tonic in front of her on the slatted table.

Margaret sat up, slowly. Beside her was a wooden bookcase. She turned her head and checked the titles. All her old medical texts. Vander, Sherman and Luciano's *Human Physiology*. Davidson's *Medicine*, *Gray's Anatomy*. How to fathom the mysteries of the human heart she thought, as she pulled them out one by one, flicking through the yellowing pages. Her handwriting, surprisingly childlike, decorated the margins. Passages underlined, further references to be consulted and then, sandwiched between a line drawing of the inside of the knee and the muscles of the thigh a scrap of cardboard torn from a cigarette packet. 'I love you' was printed in careful capitals, the black ink faded.

Tears came then, running down the creases beside her nose, gathering in the corners of her mouth, dripping onto her hands. Silent tears, and again, another sound, insistent. The phone, ringing. Again and again. No longer a summons she could ignore. She got to her feet, folded the cardboard carefully in two and pushed it into her pocket. She walked down the stairs to the hall, wiping her face with the back of her hand. She picked up the receiver. She held it to her ear. Beside her the grandfather clock chimed midday.

'Hallo,' she said. Silence. She spoke again. 'Hallo.' Still silence. Then the sound. An intake of breath.

'Please, speak to me.'

And another sound. Whistling, high, clear. A tune. For the first few moments the notes seemed unconnected, disjointed. Panic flooded her body. What did it mean? What was it? Then a voice rose up from the silted layers of her memory. Her father calling her to his side.

Listen, Maggie, listen to this. My mother, your granny, loved this record. Listen. Hands fumbling with the crackling brown cover on the hard black disc. Be careful, Maggie. If you drop it it'll break. Careful,

now. Put the needle down very gently.
And now the same tune, whistled.

Bring flowers of the fairest, bring blossom the
 rarest
From gardens and woodland and hillside and
 dale,
Our poor hearts are singing, our glad voices
 bringing,
Our praise of thee, loveliest Queen of the May.
O Mary, we crown thee with blossoms today,
Queen of the Angels and Queen of the May.

The whistling stopped. Silence again. And coldness, sweeping over her body. The muscles in her legs weakening. Sweat breaking out on her palms, on the soles of her feet. Hairs standing up on the back of her neck. And a sudden pain, deep in her heart, forcing her down onto the floor, to bang her head, again and again and again, until that was all she could remember.

5

She had asked him to phone her mother. So he had done it. As simple as that. Driven into town. Found an empty box. Put the money in the slot. Punched up the numbers. And bingo. The first couple of times he hadn't said or done anything. Just stood there in the sun, listening. He liked the sound of her voice. She had a funny mixture of accents. It was mostly Dublin, south side, but her vowels were a bit different. More like her daughter's. Kind of spread, wider, looser, if that was a way you could describe them.

He'd never done anything like that before. Well, not since he was a kid, anyway. And then it had been random, haphazard, names picked out of the phone book. So he'd never been able to imagine properly how they'd look when they lifted the receiver and listened, and began to feel frightened. But this time he'd taken Mary's little photo album with him, and he flicked through it until he found the picture he liked best. Her

36

mother. Margaret. Sitting on a beach. Wearing a bikini. Leaning forward to pour tea from a flask. One small breast about to fall out of her top. He stroked the picture with his index finger. One day he'd feel the skin itself. Not just the silken skin of the emulsion covering the print, but the real thing.

He had been tempted to bring Mary with him. He had thought he might let her speak too. Maybe she could have persuaded Margaret to come and meet them. But prudence overcame impulse. Too difficult. Too dangerous. Better this way. Less messy. So he left Mary handcuffed to the ring in the wall. She'd told him she wouldn't scream or shout, but he didn't believe her. So he got out the sticky tape and covered her mouth. Tears had burst from her eyes when he finished. Silly girl. She should have realized by now that he wasn't susceptible to them. They didn't move him at all.

The third time he phoned was the best. He'd known it would be good, but not how good. He stood in the phone box on O'Connell Bridge. The one on the south side of the river, at the point where Westmoreland Street curves around onto Aston Quay. It was so hot the chewing gum all over the footpath was beginning to melt.

There were people all around him. Tourists in silly summer clothes, baggy Bermuda shorts and loose shirts decorated with palm trees and blue waves. Flocks of Spanish students shrieked like angry parrots as they clustered around the poster shops, buying cheap CDs and gimmicky souvenirs. A couple of guards stood by the traffic lights. A man and a woman. He was tall and bulky. He rocked back and forth on his rubber-soled shoes, his hands in his pockets, his sleeves rolled up over brown arms. She was small, her fair hair scraped up under her cap. She was looking up at him, smiling, almost flirting. Then turning away to look at the map that a tourist had shoved under her nose.

An old man came and leaned against the phone booth. His hair was long and grey, streaked with nicotine, matted. He was wearing a dark overcoat, far too heavy for the hot weather. As the rough material scraped against the glass, Jimmy saw himself reflected, smiling, his teeth very white. He looked like the picture that his mother hung framed in the hall. His confirmation photo. Red rosette and grey suit, and a smile, his mother said, that would make the angels happy. He turned back to the phone, waiting. When he put his lips together and began to whistle that song he felt such intense excitement. It burst out of him, pleasure like nothing else he'd ever known. He couldn't understand how no one else seemed to notice.

It was his mother's favourite. She loved the way they always played it on *The Gay Byrne Show* on the first of May. For days afterwards she'd be going around singing it. Out of tune. Her voice mangling the words. He'd always hated it. Until now.

And when he'd finished and put down the phone, he went for a wander. Up to Grafton Street, looking at the pretty girls. And then he saw her. Mary. A bank of televisions in the window of the Sony shop. He stopped for a moment in the street, and stared at the face on the screens. A woman eating an apple stepped in front of him. He could hear the crunching of her jaw, and see the little bubbles of juice that were collecting in the corners of her mouth. He waited for her to move, but she didn't. So he went into the shop. It was the lunchtime news. A missing-person report. Four days since she'd been seen. An interview with the girl's mother. Standing in the garden, a mass of roses behind her. Wearing a simple white T-shirt and a pair of blue jeans. She looked straight at the camera. She looked straight at him. Please, she said, please, if anyone knows where my daughter is. Please tell the guards, or tell me. She lifted her hand as she spoke, and smoothed down her hair. Dark brown, shiny, straight, pulled back from her pale forehead. He put his face close up to the screen. She disappeared, broke up, into lines of light and dark. He stepped back and there she was again. Perfect, beautiful, his.

6

The black bull twisted and turned. Blood coated its back, a slick of red, and dripped from its wide-open nostrils. The matador stood, his body bent like a crescent moon, the red cape stiff, held out to the side. The bull came at him, his head down. The matador jumped back. He dropped the cape. The bull kept coming. The matador fell, his face buried in the sawdust. The crowd roared. Two men rushed in towards the bull, distracting him, teasing him, turning his attention away from the small man in the tight blue and gold suit, sprawled now, clumsy, inelegant, on the ground. The bull's heavy, wounded body lumbered away, the lances tearing at his skin, dragging at his flesh, slowing him down, so he swayed and staggered, his head drooping low.

Margaret watched in spite of herself. She wanted the bull to stay his ground, to deal with his tormentor, to catch him on his curved horns, toss him in the air, make blood pour from his wounds too. But now a doctor was kneeling beside the young man, explaining in French, too fast for her to understand, the nature of his injuries. She stood up, uncurling herself from the hard upright chair on which she was sitting and stretched to the top shelf of the dresser. She lifted down a bottle of whiskey and placed it on the table with a glass. The room was dark, apart from the flicker from the small television set. It was sometime in the early morning of the seventh day.

He had phoned again. Yesterday evening, just as the angelus bell was ringing. Again he said nothing, but she had known neverthe-less who it was. She phoned the guards in Dun Laoghaire about the calls. They sent someone to talk to her. A young man, dark-haired, polite. He stood on the doorstep

41

beside her, his gaze fixed on the Kish lighthouse on the horizon. He took down all the details in his notebook, his handwriting precise, neat. He asked for permission to put a tap on the phone.

'Why not?' she said. 'Although he's hardly likely to call from anywhere significant.'

'You don't think so?' he replied.

'Well, do you?'

He shrugged and looked at his watch. 'We can't be certain that whoever is phoning you has had anything to do with your daughter's disappearance. There are a lot of people out there who are quite capable of doing something like this, just for fun. It could be kids, anyone.'

'And where would they get my phone number from?'

'Look,' he said, 'we'll keep an eye on the house. Our lads will patrol past here every hour. If you need anything, we'll be with you in a couple of minutes.'

She unscrewed the cap on the bottle and poured the yellow liquid into the glass. She drank and poured again. Then she leaned down and picked up the heavy black book from the pile on the floor. The cover was embossed to make it look like crocodile skin. The word 'Photographs' was inscribed on the front in flowing gold script. Dust clung to it, and to her fingers. She had found the albums under her father's desk, tucked into the bay of the window in the room that had always been his study across the hall from where her mother now slept.

She remembered. The feel of his bony thighs underneath her. The books spread open on the shiny desktop.

'And that's my mother, your grandmother, and that's my father, your grandfather, and that's Uncle Peter and Auntie Bridie.'

One neat finger, the inside edge of the nail stained dark yellow, tracing the family. Who was who and what was what. Big houses covered with Virginia creeper. Shiny horses held at the bit by small boys with flat caps and lace-up boots.

'And look, Daddy, here you are. With Mammy.'

'That's right, Maggie mine. And what were we doing?'

'You were getting married.'

'That's right. And we were very, very happy.'

Standing together outside the church. Mother in a long white dress, with a scoop neck edged with flowers and a train that flowed in folds and frills and ended up beside her small white shoes. Father in a grey suit with tails and a top hat held in one gloved hand. His brown hair was slicked down over his head and he was smiling as he stood arm in arm with his young bride.

And then her favourite picture.

'Where's that, Daddy?'

'You know, Maggie, think.'

'Is it when you were on your honeymoon, Daddy?'

'That's right, my pet.'

'And is it the tower that has the funny name? The Eye-full tower, is that right? I wish I'd been there. Why didn't you take me too?'

And his laugh vibrating through her back, warming her up.

'I couldn't take you, my sweet. Because you weren't even thought of then.'

'Wasn't I, Daddy? Why not?'

She looked at the photograph now. He was standing, framed by the tracery of the tower's iron legs, a cream linen jacket hanging from his thin shoulders, a panama hat pushed back from his forehead. His hands were shoved in his pockets and he was laughing.

She turned over the stiff black pages slowly, peering at the faces, wondering, seeing her own face looking back at her. And Mary's

44

too? Sometimes here and there. Not in the colouring, or the shape, but occasionally a hint, a touch, an expression, a set of the jaw, an angle of the shoulders to the breast, a turn-out of the foot.

She poured more whiskey and picked up the remote control, flicking through the numbers. The satellite channels were still transmitting, pictures of children in a feeding station in central Africa, and refugees, a straggling, desperate band. She watched for a couple of minutes, the alcohol soothing, calming, drowning the cries. Then she picked up another of the albums. Baby pictures, the same baby all the time. Held stiffly in her mother's arms. Sitting in her high chair, waving a silver spoon. Smiling broadly, showing the gaps in her front teeth. Riding her first bicycle and her first pony. Standing in her bathing suit, long legs skinny and knock-kneed, hair trailing rats' tails over her shoulders. First communion and confirmation, the perfect angel. More signs of triumph and success. Winning rosettes and cups at the local shows. Prize day at school. And then. Nothing.

She turned over the rest of the pages. All of them were empty, except for the rough patches marking out the perfect squares and rectangles where the photographs once had been, showing where they had been torn from the stiff black paper. She got up slowly, her glass in her hand, and walked out of the kitchen, feeling her way up the uneven wooden stairs in the dark. She pushed open the door to the study and switched on the light. Once there had been other photographs, framed, on the mantelpiece, on the wall. Graduation Day in Trinity College. A sketch he had done of her for her sixteenth birthday. Her first trip to Greece, standing in front of the Acropolis wearing a long white dress. He had loved that photograph. He always kept the original in his wallet and she'd got it enlarged and framed as a surprise one Christmas.

She stood in the middle of the room and looked around. Nellie had been sent in to pack his books and papers into the tea-chests that were now lined up along one wall. She knelt down beside them and reached in, scrabbling through their contents. The metal lining, exposed along one edge, cut into her arm, scratching her skin just above the elbow. Still she searched and hunted, pulling out handfuls of loose typed pages, bundles of notebooks, old diaries. Finally she sat back, her knees stiff, her hands covered in grime.

She stood up and walked out of the room. She opened the front door. The air outside was warm, thick with the smell of the salt from the sand and mud, exposed now in the low tide. She leaned against the railings at the top of the steps, and drank deeply from her glass. A large black car passed slowly, weaving its way carefully through the other cars parked on the narrow road. She watched its red tail-lights as it continued to the end of the cul-de-sac. She listened to the sound of the engine as it stopped, reversed, and drove back again. She couldn't see who was in it. One, maybe two people. The police, she thought. It slowed, and stopped. Just for a moment. Then it moved on. She turned and watched its lights as it swung round the corner past the Martello tower and up the hill to the main road. Then she walked back into the house and closed the door.

7

The dog whined. He tugged at the worn leather lead, his breath struggling in hoarse gasps from his open mouth. It was Sunday, 13 August. The eighth day. Seven-thirty in the morning. Cooler than yesterday or the day before, but bright sunshine angling down through the chestnut, the ash and the oak, warming the white fronds of meadow-sweet, so that even at this early hour its honey smell hung in the air.

The dog pulled and jerked again, burying his nose underneath the tussocks of rough grass that grew on either side of the path running along beside the canal. He stopped, his head down, his feathery black tail pointed, tense, draughts of air filling his nose with the scent of a thousand possibilities.

The elderly man with him bent down slowly, his knees creaking, cartilage and bone scraping painfully against each other in the quiet morning. He steadied himself with one hand on his stick. With his other hand he caught hold of the dog's collar, forcing his shaking fingers to release the lead's metal catch. The dog licked his hand, his long tongue curling around the swollen arthritic knuckles, then rushed away down the track, his tail sculling now, like a short black oar, behind him.

The man followed slowly. He spoke quietly to himself as he paused here and there, poking his stick into a pile of old tin cans, pulling down a large bunch of elder-berries, hanging dark purple, almost black like small overripe grapes, watching the dragonflies whose petrol iridescence darted over the canal's murky water.

Ahead, twenty feet away the dog had stopped, poised on the bank. Excitement ran through his small body, waves of tension rippling along his shiny black back. His feet scrabbled in the dry, dusty grass. He moved from right to left, twisting and turning, then he whined again, and barked. The old man caught up with him. There was a piece of elder branch in his right hand. He held it up above the dog's head, waving it from side to side, then threw it in a looping arc into the water. The dog barked again, braced himself, and leaped in, his head breaking the surface, ripples spreading out on either side from his paddling front paws.

'Jude,' the old man called. 'Here, boy.' And he whistled, a thin quavering sound.

The dog grasped the branch, his lips drawn back, his white teeth exposed. He turned and began to swim towards his master.

'Good boy. Good dog,' the old man called. And then the small black body disappeared, under an ash tree that was hanging out from the bank. Afterwards the old man wasn't sure, couldn't be certain when he realized what was in the plastic bag that Jude had found, had begun to tear, had ripped open. It was only after he had called and whistled, and Jude had climbed up beside him on the grass, his wet tail flopping from side to side, that he noticed the dog had something caught between his teeth. And when he prised open his mouth and pulled out the black strands, it was then that he saw the shape of what was lying beneath them in the water, and it was then that he began to run, crying out for help, the dog rushing and jumping along beside him, leaping up to pull at his jacket and lick his face.

8

She would dress for the occasion. She would take off the jeans and T-shirt that had become her uniform. She would wear her favourite cream shift, with the crimson linen shawl that she and Mary had chosen together. She would wrap around her neck the string of coral that Mary had given her on her fortieth birthday. She would brush her hair and put on makeup. She would do what had to be done.

Two of them had arrived just after eleven that morning. She had been helping Catherine to have a bath when the doorbell rang. She ran downstairs still holding the towel, dark patches of water all over her shirt. The older man introduced himself. Michael McLoughlin, Detective Inspector. He held out his hand, but she didn't take it. She stood there in the sun, drying herself, hearing the words but not listening to their meaning. The younger man took the towel from her as they walked into the hall and closed the front door. He draped it over the banisters.

'Not there, don't leave it there,' she said. 'Hang it on the washing line. In the garden. That way.' And she pointed to the stairs that led to the kitchen and the back door.

'We'll wait,' Inspector McLoughlin said. 'Take your time.' And he sat down on the chair by the phone, and unfolded the newspaper that was sticking out of his jacket pocket.

The body was on a trolley covered by a green surgical sheet. They hadn't said much to her as they drove into the morgue in Store Street. The younger man, Finney she thought he was called, was at the wheel of the unmarked car. He drove fast, too fast, overtaking anything that got in front of them, barely making it through the amber lights. She had to brace her feet on the floor to stop herself falling from side to side on the shiny back seat. Beside her head swung an air freshener in the shape of a little green fir tree. It tapped out a neat rhythm against the glass of the window as the car wove through the heavy Sunday traffic. Just like the sound of a pencil tapping on a piece of paper, she thought. Mary's favourite colouring pencils. Lakeland. In a beautiful tin. Mary kneeling up on a chair at the kitchen table, drawing laboriously, carefully. Making the exaggerated zigzags of the Christmas tree. Colouring it in methodically, her little hand gripping the green pencil, forcing it to stay within the thick outlines, the sharpened end bursting through the flimsy paper. Outside it was the hot southern-hemisphere Christmas. Inside she was decorating the tree with snow, pieces of cotton wool stuck on with flour-and-water paste. She sat back on her heels to examine it for any imperfections. Tap, tap, tap, the pencil on the paper. Look, Mummy, isn't it lovely?

She wanted to tell him to slow down. She wanted to savour these last few minutes of not knowing. So far, nothing had really happened. She was just going for a drive on a hot sunny Sunday in August, like all the other people in all the other cars that crammed the stretch of road from Blackrock to Ballsbridge. But already he was swinging around from Pearse Street into Townsend Street, the traffic lights green all the way, the river water yellow and shining as they crossed the bridge and slowed to a stop outside the small, unobtrusive brick building, in shadow now behind the bulk of the city's bus station.

She stood beside the trolley. The policeman, McLoughlin, was talking to her. The

53

mortuary attendant would lift the sheet, just for a moment. He would ask her to look at the body. He would ask her then if she could identify her. He would need her to speak out loud, 'for the record you understand'. She nodded. She knew what had to be done. There was a summer, years ago, when as a student she had worked in this morgue. Cleaning up, preparation, routine work. It was a good job. She had liked it. The only problem was the smell. Formaldehyde, which clung in the strands of her hair and in the folds and wrinkles of her underwear, seeping beneath her green scrubs. And the other smells that stayed, lodged in the mucous membranes and the imagination. Her eyes moved around the room from the covered trolley to the bone-white enamel sinks. All the surfaces were hard and gleaming. Stainless steel, ceramic tiles, glass jars and containers. The only soft things that came in here were the bodies that lay like this one, passive, waiting.

McLoughlin cleared his throat. Behind him stood Finney, running one hand through the lock of dark hair that hung down over his right eyebrow, catching her eye and smiling, deep dimples cutting wedge-shaped holes in his cheeks.

'If you're ready, Dr Mitchell.'

She stepped forward, closer to the body. She braced her feet against the cold chequered floor. She uncurled her hands from the fists they had become and smoothed them down against her dress. She nodded.

Afterwards she always remembered that her first reaction was relief. This couldn't be Mary. Mary had thick, boisterous, black curls. Hair that had a life of its own, that resisted brushes, combs, rubber bands, ribbons. Hair that flowed like water, always finding another way to escape. Not this, sparse and patchy, hacked, the white skull showing through, like an old doll that's been forgotten and thrown to the back of the cupboard. She put out her hand and touched it, and as she did, a tendril of black sprang out, curled up and around her finger. Like the side shoots of the sweet peas her father had planted every summer, springy, twisting themselves around the wire, clinging on even when summer storms pulled and tore at them. And then she felt shame, that she had not immediately, instantly, undeniably recognized her. Despite the blackened eyes and bruised cheeks. Despite the small triangular tear in her forehead where the dog had ripped through her skin. Despite the hugely swollen lips and bent and twisted nose.

McLoughlin spoke again. 'Can you identify this person?' She supposed afterwards that the right words had come out of her mouth. She didn't remember. But she had turned on them all then, and screamed at them to get out, to leave her alone. And the policeman McLoughlin had turned to the other men, the mortuary assistant and Finney, and put his finger to his lips, stopping their complaints, and backed them out into the corridor.

They watched her through the round window in the door. She had turned away from the trolley. She walked around the room. She opened drawers and closed them. She took down the jars of chemicals and read the labels. She put them back neatly, carefully, on the shelf, in order of height. She opened the stainless-steel sterilizer, her index finger pointing and moving as she checked its contents. She inspected a pile of X-rays, lying on the bench, holding them up in front of the light box, leaning forward to examine the ghostly remains of others who had passed through here. She paced from one side of the room to the other, her feet keeping carefully to the marking of the black and white floor. Her lips were moving but they could hear nothing. She took off her shawl and dropped it, a spreading crimson stain. She sat down, her back against the wall, and rocked herself backwards and forwards. She put her hand in her pocket. She pulled out a rose, yellow, full-blown, and held it to her nose. She stood then, and went back to the trolley. She lifted the sheet up and away. Beside McLoughlin, Finney gagged, a small choking sound, loud in the quiet of the corridor, then made as if to push open the door. McLoughlin put out his hand and grabbed hold of his arm. He shook his head.

They watched her again. She was standing at the top of the trolley. She placed her palms on either side of her daughter's face. Then she walked around and stood beside her, running her hands down the girl's beaten body, marking the pattern of the bruises, green, yellow, brown and black. She bent down and kissed each stiffened finger and tried to twist her own into the rigid palms. Then she went back up to her daughter's head. She leaned over and kissed her on the lips, placing the rose so its petals nestled into her neck. Then she turned away.

9

And so the wheel is put in motion, thought McLoughlin. A rock drops into a mountain lake and the ripples spread. A shot bursts from the barrel of a gun and a flock of crows wheel into the sky. A butterfly flaps its wings and on the other side of the world a tidal wave roars in from the sea. A girl is murdered, and throughout the city the stain of the crime disturbs, awakens, shuffles the deck of past anger and suspicion.

He stood at his kitchen window high up in the Dublin mountains and watched as the natural glow of the sun faded and was replaced by the artificial brilliance of hundreds of thousands of lights, orange, yellow and white. Somewhere down there, he thought, we have all the answers to all the questions. Who and why, how and where, the basic tenets of the investigation of crime. Often, at the beginning of a case, he would stand here, a glass in his hand, and rummage through what he already knew. Then he would let his imagination drift and float, slipping like the elusive incandescence of a candle into all the corners which were, as yet, dark and gloomy. Obscured by the cobwebs of ignorance.

This is the best time, he thought, as twilight turned to night. He toasted his reflection in the window. A time of anticipation, excitement, hope. No decisions had been made, no mistakes had been committed. It was all out there, waiting for him.

He turned away and busied himself with the task of the evening. He would prepare dinner. He would eat something simple and cook it the way his father used to. He opened the fridge and took out a piece of meat in a plastic bag. It was fillet steak that he'd bought yesterday. He'd gone into town for a haircut, and afterwards, still with pinpricks of hair caught between his neck and his collar, he'd wandered around Grafton Street in the sunshine, drifting in and out of the shops in the narrow side streets, buying odds and ends of food. The steak, a bag of new potatoes, a couple of heads of dark green York cabbage, and a punnet of late-season raspberries, which he dipped into as he drove home. Good stuff. None of your overpriced 'food as fashion accessory', he thought, as he laid the meat on the counter and tipped the spuds into the sink to wash, and then into a large saucepan with a close-fitting lid.

Janey wouldn't be home until late, so the note on the dining-room table said. What was it tonight? He sifted through the week. Mondays was yoga. Tuesdays was enlightenment through meditation. Wednesdays was reflexology. Thursdays was poetry for beginners. Fridays was dinner with her mother. Saturdays she tried to keep free for him. Tonight was Sunday. That meant a get-together with the women from her group in some pub in town. Did he care? He opened the fridge again and took out a couple of cans of Guinness. He poured them into a pint glass, standing back and watching the transformation, like alchemy, as the cream-coloured liquid swirled in tiny whirlpools and finally settled. He drank. The cold sharpness hit his tongue. A wonderful sensation. Always surprising in its intensity. Like the way it was in the early days when he kissed Janey, when the taste of her mouth traveled through his body. In the days when they still made love. It had been a long time since he had wanted her like that. Sometimes he would wake in the night, pressed up against her back, his face buried in the nape of her neck. Once he would have driven halfway across the country to smell her particular smell, to feel her softness under his mouth. But now she would grunt and shift away and he would roll over and go back to sleep very quickly.

He chopped the cabbage roughly and put it into a pot with an inch of water and a couple of shakes of salt. He lifted the lid on the potatoes, stepping back quickly as a geyser of steam threatened to envelop him, and prodded them with a knife. Another ten minutes or so, he reckoned. He bent over and sniffed the moist piece of fillet. Perfect. Perfectly tender. Just the faintest fleshy tang. It would take only a couple of minutes to cook. Best to wait until the vegetables were nearly ready.

He laid the table, taking from the cupboard a cream linen cloth. Handmade. Part of their wedding present from Janey's mother. He stroked the material with his fingertips. The same kind of stuff that woman was wearing this afternoon at the identification. He was still glad about the way he had handled it. Afterwards Finney had gone on and on about 'procedure'. Fuck procedure and fuck these smart young guys who think they know all about it. He had lost count of the number of times he had watched mothers, fathers, uncles, brothers, sisters gaze at the body of someone close. He'd take a bet with himself. Nine times out of ten he was right. He might never get the evidence to prove it, but he could tell straight away if they were involved in the death. In all the years, though, he'd never seen anyone respond the way she had. Stripping the sheet off the girl. That took something. Guts, madness, or a combination of the two. He'd watched her face as she looked at her daughter. At the purple bruises across her stomach. At the cuts, bites, and burns eating into her skin. He had to turn away, to rest his eyes on the neutral white tiles on the floor. But she didn't.

He got up and went out to his briefcase, lying where he'd dropped it in the hall. He took the file from it that the lads in Dun Laoghaire had given him. He opened it. All the missing-person stuff. There was a photograph clipped to the top cover. He picked up his glass and drank deeply. She was a little beauty. Heart-shaped face, dark blue eyes, white teeth, with a little gap between the front two. Such a smile. Involuntarily he smiled back at her. He thought again of the woman they had picked up from the old house down by the Martello tower in Monkstown. He had angled the wing mirror as they drove in along the sea road, and watched her. The same shaped face, but thinner, sharper. High cheekbones, grey eyes, full mouth. She reminded him of someone you'd see in a pre-Raphaelite painting. Something by Burne-Jones or Dante Gabriel Rossetti. A bit smaller, maybe, and thinner, but with that same perfection of features. She must be well into her forties but she didn't look it. Except if you looked closely. Then you'd notice the looseness in the skin of her neck, the lines that underscored her eyes, the slackness of her breasts as they flattened under her dress, and the narrow streaks of grey in her sleek brown hair.

He drained the potatoes and left them to dry in the colander. He turned off the heat under the cabbage, and set the frying pan down on the ring. He poured in groundnut oil and waited until a wisp of smoke signalled its readiness. Then he dumped the steak down, quickly, first one side then the other, searing it, then cooking it more slowly for another couple of minutes. He put the meat on a warmed plate in the oven, and added a spoonful of mustard and a dollop of cream to the pan, stirring slowly until all the flavours were mixed and the sauce flowed smoothly.

Here, Michael. Taste this.

A large hand holding a wooden spoon in front of his face.

No, Da. It's mustard. I don't like it. It's too hot.

Not like this, Michael, taste it.

A tongue licking, tentatively, then quickly as his saliva began to flow. That's lovely, can I have some more?

Looking up at the tall man leaning over the stove, a flowery apron tied over his uniform shirt and trousers and a grin of anticipation for the feast to come.

He sat down at the table, poured the sauce over the meat, piled potatoes and cabbage onto the plate, added a large pat of butter and plenty of salt and began to eat. Janey wouldn't eat like this now. She'd given up animal fats. The fridge was filled with tubs of soya-based spreads. He told her that he couldn't eat food made without the proper ingredients. You have to have fat, he said. It's a flavour enhancer. It makes it taste. But she didn't want to know. She'd gone right off cooking. All she ever used was the microwave and the kettle. Instant meals eaten standing up. 'Like a horse,' as Anthony

Quinn said, once, in that great old film *La Strada*.

He stacked his dirty plates in the dishwasher and put on the kettle, cleaning and tidying while he waited for it to boil. He put three large spoons of coffee into a heavy jug, poured the water onto it, then stirred briskly. While he waited for the grounds to settle, he got out the mop and bucket and washed the grey lino. Then he sat down again, pouring coffee into a mug, and brandy into a glass. He picked up the file and began to read.

Simple story, really. Or so it seemed. The girl had gone out with some friends on the Saturday night. They'd been drinking in the Globe in George's Street. She'd left just before eleven. Said she had to get the DART home because her mother was by herself with her grandmother who was ill. The guards in Dun Laoghaire had spoken to the friends. Three girls and a boy. All aged between eighteen and twenty. She'd met them at a dance class in Digges Lane. They said they liked her, she was fun, but she wasn't involved with any of them. Not really. After the reports on the news and in the papers last week, a TV shop at the bottom of George's Street had given the guards a video. They'd a camera mounted in their window, and a playback facility to a large monitor. And they'd a tape running. They'd checked it. And there was the girl. She'd stopped to look at herself. The tape was time-coded. It was exactly 23.01. She could have been going that way to Pearse or Tara DART station, but the more usual route would have been along Wicklow Street. Still, it was something. He hadn't seen it yet. Finney could dig it out tomorrow, and check any of the other CCTV cameras in the George's Street area.

He turned over the pages. There was something here about the mother. Margaret Mitchell, doctor. Aged forty-four. Widow. Had lived in New Zealand since 1975. Nothing he didn't already know. And a log of her calls to the station. Persistent. He could imagine. A lousy job, trying to fend off a frantic mother.

He looked up suddenly. There was a bang, glass and metal rattling together. A woman's voice, sharp and accusatory, chimed with the insistent whining of a Siamese cat. Cat and woman arrived in the kitchen together, legs and feet entwined.

'You didn't feed him.'

'I didn't know he wanted to be fed.'

'Well, if just occasionally you thought about

his needs, about anyone else's needs.' Her voice slithered and slurred. She smelt of the pub. Cigarette smoke and the sweetness of lager. She pulled out drawers and slammed cupboard doors, finally finding a tin of cat food and an opener. She piled a plate high and slopped it onto the floor; cubes of brown meat and orange jelly spilling everywhere.

'Careful,' he said. 'I've just washed that.'

'Makes a change.' She squatted beside the purring cat, her movements awkward, uncoordinated. She stroked his cream body. The cat arched beneath her touch.

'Nice pussy, good pussy, sweet pussy, Mummy's baby,' she chanted into his pointed brown ear. She looked up at McLoughlin accusingly. 'You didn't tell me you were in-volved in that case.'

'Which case?'

She stood up and helped herself to brandy, slopping the liquid carelessly into a tumbler. 'Which case,' she mimicked. 'I saw you on the nine o'clock news. In the pub. Everyone was talking about it.'

'You were out when I got the call. Hill-walking, wasn't it?'

'You should have come with me. Then they'd have had to find some other star to lead their investigation.'

He sat back and looked at her. When had it all happened? That they had stopped loving each other. No magic turning point. No single incident. Just the slow, sad accretion of contempt and dislike leading to revulsion and despair.

She finished her drink and stood up. 'I'm going to bed. Are you coming?'

'In a while.'

There was a photograph on the mantelpiece in the sitting room. He'd bought the silver frame for it for their first anniversary. It had been taken the summer before. Janey on the pier in Dun Laoghaire. She was wearing a long loose dress covered in small pink and white flowers. Her hair, iron grey now, stood up around her face in blonde curls. Her blue eyes were crinkled up against the sun and her cheeks were flushed with happiness. They had gone that day on his motor scooter to the pier and then to Killiney for a picnic. They had found a spot on the hill with nothing between them and the sea but the gorse and the bracken, and they had made love. It had been his first time to go all the way, but not hers. He felt then that he had never touched anything as wonderful as her full breasts. He lay with his head between them, and when he was ready she pulled him into her. He came, he remembered, almost immediately. But she had smiled and kissed him and told him she loved him. He got up now and walked down the passage to the bedroom. He opened the door. The sound of gentle snores drifted towards him. He closed the door, quietly.

When next he looked up from the file it was very late. He poured himself another brandy and opened the french windows that led out onto the tiled patio. The city was laid out below, glittering, shining. The streets and roads ploughed deep furrows of light through the dark. Roundabouts glowed like magic symbols. Further away to the east, the twin chimneys of the Pigeon House pointed their totem signs into the sky. He moved his gaze westward, upriver. Down there, moored, safe from harm, lay the real love of his life. A thirty-two-foot gaff-rigged ketch. *Sea Horse*, her name written in flowing script along her port bow. Norwegian pine and oak. Bought for a song as a wreck ten years ago. Lovingly restored, rotting plank by rotting plank. He thought of her now. Rocking gently on her chain, keeping time with the undulations of the tide.

He sat down on the ground, his back against the wall of the house, the day's sunshine trapped in the stone, warming his back and his thighs. He would, he decided, drink until he fell asleep. Out here, where the air was fresh, on his own.

10

The girl and the dog sat on the stone steps outside the house, waiting. The girl rested her head on the dog's golden shoulder. It was very hot. The, dog panted loudly. Strings of saliva dripped from his pink and black lips. The girl smoothed her white T-shirt down over her plump little breasts and carefully tucked it into the elasticated waistband of her blue and white gingham skirt. She crossed and recrossed her legs, swinging first one foot and then the other. She put both feet on the ground and leaned over to admire the shine of her patent-leather shoes. Her face smiled back at her. She began to sing tunelessly.

'When the red red robin
Goes bob bob-bobbin'
Along, along.'

She got up and dragged the toe of her shoe through the gravel on the drive, making the shape of hopscotch squares. She hopped awkwardly up and down, still muttering the words of the song

'Red Robin,
Bob-bobbin
'Long, along.'

The dog followed her, jumping up to catch her attention, scraping her plump white arm with its long claws.

'Ow, stop it, Bella, don't.' The girl pushed the dog away, and sat down again to inspect a scratch on her upper arm. 'Sore, Bella. Not nice.'

She put the thumb of her left hand in her mouth and sucked hard. Spit gathered in the corners of her mouth. The index finger of her right hand twisted and untwisted a lock of her fine, mouse-coloured hair. The dog lay down and rested its head on her feet. The girl's heavy-lidded eyes lost focus and half closed, then opened suddenly as she heard the sound of a car. Her thumb came out of her mouth with a loud plop. She wiped the spit away from her chin and stood up quickly. She had been told many times that she must not run towards the car when it came around the corner past the big bushes. She had been told that she must stand very still, like a statue, until the car stopped. Then and only then was she allowed to move.

But today she could not wait. She didn't remember how many days it had been since she had seen her brother. It seemed like a very long time. The last time he had come he had brought her red ribbons decorated with little white cats. He had plaited her hair in two pigtails and tied them with the ribbons in big bows. She had refused to take them out even when she was going to bed. She had gone to sleep chewing the ends. The next morning Mammy had taken off the sodden ribbons and thrown them in the rubbish. She had cried and screamed and when Mammy wasn't looking she had tried to lift the heavy lid off the bin to find them, but she couldn't manage by herself.

He knew she would be waiting for him, that she would run out into the middle of the gravel circle in front of the house. He crouched down low over the steering wheel as he swung the big black car around her, once, twice, three times. She waved and waved and blew kisses. He pretended to drive the car straight at her, but nothing he could do would dampen the welcome she gave him. It had always been that way. He remembered the day they had brought her home from hospital. He was thirteen. He didn't want her, a sister, a baby, someone who needed to be looked after, someone they might love more than him. But they left her lying in the carrycot in the hall. He knelt beside her and looked at her screwed-up face. And then she opened her eyes and smiled, right up at him. He put out his finger and touched her lips. She opened her mouth. Her tiny tongue, pink, kitten-like, lolled out and licked him. He put his finger in her mouth and she sucked it, hard.

He stopped the car suddenly and as he opened the door she rushed to him, scrambling up on his knee and flinging her plump arms around his neck.

'Hey, hey. Calm down, Molly. It's OK. I'm here now.' He unwrapped her arms and cradled her against his chest. She was getting far too grown up for this, he thought. She had, he noticed, a faint black down on her upper lip and her body gave off an adult, oniony smell. Her checked skirt had ridden up her heavy white thighs, and he smoothed it down again, carefully.

'Nice skirt, Molly. Is it new?'

She nodded, her thumb back in her mouth.

'Hey, my girl, you're not supposed to suck your thumb, are you?'

Again the silent nod. And then the lips opened and the childlike voice said 'But I like sucking my thumb. It makes me feel nice.'

'Well, I have something else that will make you feel nice. Here.' He manoeuvred her off his knee onto the passenger seat, and reached over to open the glove compartment. 'Now, look in there and see what you can find.'

She knelt up on the seat and clumsily shoved her hands into the small space.

'Careful, Molly,' he warned.

'Look.' She had something in both hands. In one was a small cardboard box, shaped like a swan, and in the other a large glossy brown shell decorated with small cream circles all over its humped back.

'Presents for me,' she crowed, 'lots of presents for Molly.'

'Put that back.' He grabbed at the shell. 'The chocolates are for you, but not that.'

'Aaah.' Her voice rose. 'That's not fair. You said look in there and see what you can find.'

'But the chocolates are for you. See.' He carefully opened the little box. 'They're all your favourites.'

Her fingers hovered over the selection. He made to prise the shell out of her other hand.

'No!' She pulled her hand away. 'No. I like this. It's pretty. And, anyway, you know Mammy says I'm not allowed to eat choccies, only at my birthday party.'

'Mammy doesn't have to know, does she, Mollser?'

'I'm going to tell her, I'm going to tell her, it's not fair. You said there was a present for me. I want this.' And she waved it in front of him, then hid it behind her back, tears pouring down her round red cheeks.

'OK, OK. Shh.' He took a tissue out of his pocket and dabbed her face. 'Look, you can have it, but you can only play with it in the car, because it's called a shell, and shells live in special places, deep down at the bottom of the sea, and they have to be kept in the dark most of the time, except when special people are playing with them. So I have to keep it here in the glove compartment, to make sure it's safe.'

'But I want to show Mammy. Why can't I show Mammy?' Her voice rose in a whine.

'You can't and that's that. It's our secret and if you tell her I'll tell Mammy that you didn't stand like a statue, that you ran out before the car stopped, and you know what Mammy will do, don't you, Molly?'

'She'll be cross.'

Yes, he thought. You could put it like that. But the word didn't really express the glacial withdrawal of affection, the retreat into anger and recrimination.

Molly reached into the box of chocolates and helped herself. The shell lay abandoned on the seat. He picked it up and held it against her ear.

'Do you hear that, Molly-moo? That's the sound of the sea and all the whales and dolphins and the other big fish that live deep down where the shell has its house. That's the sound they hear all the time.'

'When they wake up?'

'When they wake up and have their cornflakes and just before they go to sleep at night. That's the last thing they hear, the sound of the sea.'

Molly sighed, a shuddering goodbye to her tears, and laid her face against his arm.

'Jimmy, I love you. When I grow up will you marry me?'

'Of course I will.'

'And I'll have a white dress with a white thing on my head. And I'll look so pretty just like Barbie doll.'

No, he thought. You'll never be pretty, with your flat features and your mouth that's always open and your tongue that hangs out, and your squat little body. And you'll never grow up. You'll always be the same silly little Molly, even when your hair is grey and your features are wrinkled. And who will look after you then? He pulled her face close to his and kissed her gently on the lips.

11

Margaret woke. She was lying on her back, the sheets and blankets tucked tightly around her. She didn't remember going to sleep, but she knew she had woken in the night, her face wet. She had lain quite still and cried very quietly, the tears seeping from her eyes and trickling down into her ears. Then she had fallen asleep again and dreamed, strange unconnected scenes of mountain tops covered with snow, of fantastical birds with snakes' heads and elephants' feet, of tables covered with luscious tropical fruits, heaped high on pewter platters. She was sitting at the top of the table eating a feejoa, a silver-grey fruit from New Zealand shaped like a large acorn. She had sliced it in half with a penknife and was scooping out the soft flesh with an elegant silver spoon. Catherine, her mother, was seated at the other end of the table, and John, her father, was midway between the two. Margaret had reached out and taken his hand, and he had reached out and taken Catherine's. A warm current flowed between them. Even now, after she woke, she could still feel the tingling in her fingers.

She had no idea what time it was. Sunlight flitted around the curtains and winked in the bevelled edge of the pier glass in the corner. She got out of bed slowly, testing the strength of her legs before she stood up. Her body felt weightless, insubstantial, disconnected. Only her memory was real, and with her memory, her pain.

She stood in front of the mirror and pushed her tangled hair away from her face. I have aged, she thought. I feel as old as my mother, as sick and as near to death as she is. Why does my heart keep on beating? Can

I not will it to be still? She picked up a hairbrush from the dressing table and turned it over. Trapped among its bristles were fine black tendrils. When she was a child Catherine had made her brush her hair one hundred strokes every night before bed. 'You will regret it in years to come if you don't look after your hair properly,' she had warned. 'Look.' And she sat down beside her on the long stool in front of her dressing table and uncoiled her own shining plait. It was, Margaret recalled, one of the few things they ever did together. She still maintained the daily ritual. It was a time for reflection. She started now, counting the strokes under her breath as the brush sliced through her thick locks.

There are, she thought, two ways of looking at this. As a doctor I understand death. I have seen it many times. The easy death where the patient slips away, slides into uncon-sciousness and then into that further stage beyond, and the hard death where the patient struggles and cries, is frightened and con-fused, refuses to give in and let go, knows exactly what is happening right until the end. I have seen the young and the old die, the good and the bad. I have even, she thought, been responsible for hastening death. At least twice. The first was a man who had tried unsuccessfully three times to cut his wrists. He told me what he wanted to do. I showed him his mistake. He was assuming that the protuberant blue veins running from his hand along his arm were important. He didn't realize that he needed to cut through the radial artery, which lay deeper along the lateral aspect of the wrist. I showed him how to do it, exactly where to put his blade. The second time a woman in her mid-fifties came to me with the early symptoms of Alzheimer's. I did all the tests and confirmed her suspicions. The woman said she did not want to continue her life. She knew the decision had to be taken quickly. So I wrote her a prescription for sleeping pills and cautioned her about the dosage. She thanked me and kissed me goodbye.

I understand, thought Margaret what happens when the heart stops pumping oxygen through the body, pushing its sweetness into every blood vessel. But I don't understand the loss of being, the negation of existence. It must be the reason why so many people believe in an afterlife. To make sense of the essentially meaningless. I know it in an abstract way, but I can't accept it. All I have is the knowledge that I will never see Mary again, that she has been taken from me and I will have to live with that. Until I, too, die.

She reached one hundred strokes. Her hair hung on her shoulders, gleaming, sleek. She twisted it into a knot high on her head and clipped it in place with one of Mary's slides. Wooden, in the shape of a sea horse. She knotted the belt of her dressing gown and crossed the corridor to the bathroom. Narrow stained-glass windows cast lozenges of yellow, bright blue and scarlet on the black and white floor. A large bath stood on gnarled lion's feet. The walls were white ceramic and the pipes were chrome. Between the two windows hung a gilt-framed mirror, and above the rectangular washbasin was a round shaving mirror on a retractable arm. Margaret had always loved it here. When she was small she used to perch on the side of the bath watching her father shave. The morning ritual was always the same. He would wear his old tartan dressing gown. He would take his favourite razor out of its leather case. He would fill the basin with hot, hot water, load up the worn bristle brush with lather and transform his face into a Christmas card Santa Claus. Then scrape, scrape, scrape, metal on skin. Splash, splash, splash, the razor in the basin. Scrape, scrape, scrape again. Finally he would turn to her and say, 'Now, Maggie, feel that.' And she would run her hand over his cheeks and his chin. 'What do you say?' And they would chant together, 'Smooth as a baby's bottom,' and laugh, while Catherine rattled the door handle and fretted.

Margaret turned on the taps and water spat into the bath. The pipes rumbled and gurgled. Steam rose, misting the windows and the mirrors. She drew her finger down and across the glass, drawing trees and flowers, dogs and cats, stick figures of women and children, houses with curling tails of smoke coming out of chimneys. Then abruptly she wiped them all away with the flat of her palm. She dropped her dressing gown to the floor and lowered herself into the water.

In the old days scalding hot baths were used as treatment for the bad and the deluded. The elemental powers of heat and water brought together as a purgative. Another way to drive out the devils.

She remembered. A row of baths in a huge tiled room. Light flooding in through lunettes in the ceiling. Shackles hanging from the walls. The slim dark man, his hand heavy and proprietorial on the small of her back, looked at her over his half-glasses. 'Of course we don't use them these days,' he said. Dr Ian MacDonald, Medical Director, Bethany Lunatic Asylum, Kowhai Creek, North Island, New Zealand, 28 December 1975. Midsummer. Her first day at the hospital. She had decided she would walk the two miles from the small town. It might take her mind off Mary, nearly five months old, her face scarlet, phlegm and tears covering her cheeks, cries turning to screams as Margaret handed her over to the next-door neighbour.

'Don't worry, dearie. She'll be right as rain. As soon as you're gone. Wave bye-bye now to your mum. There's a good little girl.' And the screams retreating behind the faded front door.

The narrow road climbed steeply. The cracked and rutted footpath ended after a quarter of a mile. Sticky clay embankments closed in on both sides. The surface of the road turned to dust and rubble. There was silence apart from the crunch of her shoes on the stones, and her breath, coming in gasps as the road got steeper. A car passed, hooting. Sweat dripped down between her breasts. Her hair was hot and heavy on the nape of her neck. When she reached the top of the hill she paused to catch her breath and look back. Red corrugated-iron roofs sprawled haphazardly along a winding riverbank. Grey-green fields spread in every direction, sprinkled with sheep, like sugar frosting on the top of a cake. Somewhere in the distance a dog barked, insistent. Below, she noticed the tiny figure of a man on a horse approaching the large flock. As he got closer the individual specks of white came together, coalesced, became one huge irregular shape, moving and flowing like milk spilt on a linoleum floor. Another car passed. Curious faces pressed against the windows. A hand gestured. Two fingers upright. She tasted bile in her mouth.

A high barbed-wire fence ran along the road for as far as she could see. Then a gate, open, with a long drive curving in front of her. On either side were lawns and flower beds. She was reminded suddenly of the flowers in the park in Dun Laoghaire on a hot summer's afternoon. Hybrid roses with huge red blooms, red-hot pokers, Calla lilies, bedding geraniums in lurid pinks, and gladioli, sheaves of them, white, yellow, orange, standing to attention in the hot sun. Ahead of her, a man in dungarees pushed a creaking lawnmower. A group of men were on their knees, weeding. Their movements were slow and uncoordinated. As she walked by one of them shouted, a garbled collection of syllables strung randomly together.

Past the men was the house. Four storeys, wooden, painted dark green. A fairy-tale turret topped it off. She walked up sagging steps onto the wide veranda. The woodwork was trellised and ornate. She stepped out of the sun into darkness. Her footsteps echoed on polished wooden floors. The smell of Jeyes Fluid tickled her nostrils and eyes. The sweat on her back was suddenly cold. Dr MacDonald took her by the elbow as he escorted her past large rooms where silhouettes sat still, heads bowed, or stood rigid in corners. Nurses bustled like flocks of seagulls, chattering, laughing. Upstairs the rows of beds were pristine, ordered, sheets and blankets precisely folded. Men and women in corridors pushed mops and brooms. Their clothes hung off them like damp washing on a line. Their feet shuffled in felt slippers.

She sat in the doctor's large office. The matron, Miss Blackman, wielded the shining silver teapot, and offered slices of jam sponge.

'This is a place of confinement.' Dr MacDonald stressed each syllable equally.

His Scottish accent was clipped and precise. Miss Blackman nodded in agreement. 'Control is our watchword.'

'Not cure?'

'Cure?' He raised his eyebrows. 'Miss Blackman, how many years have you worked in this hospital?'

'Let me see now, Doctor. It must be twenty-five, maybe thirty.'

'And how many of your patients would you say have left here cured?'

Miss Blackman smiled. She placed her manicured fingertips together and rested her cherry lips gently on them. Then she spoke. 'I'm afraid, dear Dr MacDonald, that they don't usually leave.'

The water had gone cold. Margaret hauled herself up out of the bath and wrapped herself in a towel. She dried quickly and dressed. She ran down the stairs and out into the garden. She sat on the wooden bench and turned her face up to the sun. She wanted to keep her eyes open and let the brilliance cauterize her irises, burn out the pictures that played over and over again. She would need, she knew, to find her own way to do it. To replace the pain with another emotion. She would reach that point she knew, soon, but not yet.

12

'So. Tell me about Mary.'

'What do you want to know?'

'Everything and anything.'

'Why?'

'Well.' McLoughlin paused. The sun was hot on the back of his neck. He loosened his tie and opened his top button. 'So far the only piece of concrete knowledge we have about this case is that a twenty-year-old girl called Mary Mitchell is dead.'

'Not dead.' Margaret took off her dark glasses and looked at him. 'Not dead. Murdered.'

McLoughlin had arrived in Monkstown at five-fifteen. He had spent the morning in the station at Swan's Nest. His team had been assembled. Twenty men in all. He had gone down through the list of jobs to be done. Joe Fisher was the book man. It was up to him to keep a note of who was assigned to what. The usual routine. They wouldn't have the pathologist's report until late tonight or maybe first thing tomorrow morning. But he

87

didn't expect there'd be much in it. Seemed pretty obvious how she died. Her injuries looked consistent with rape, both vaginal and anal, and violent assault, It was probably the beating around the head that actually killed her. Anyway, it didn't seem as if they were looking for a murder weapon as such, other than a pair of fists, although they would want the knife that caused the nasty cuts around her nipples. But first things first. Where had she gone when she left the bar and who had she met? He sent Finney to re-interview the people who had last seen her, and to see what he could find from all the CCTV cameras in the George's Street–Dame Street area. The other lads were given the questions, questionnaires, knocking on doors, all the humdrum, boring, tedious, can't-see-the-wood-for-the-trees legwork that constitutes the bulk of policing.

That just left the mother. He had phoned ahead to say he was coming. To ask if it would be convenient. She was cold, precise. She told him not to come before five o'clock. 'The hospice nurse visits in the afternoon.' That was fine. It would give him time to go back and have another look at the canal, at the place where Mary had been found.

He drove west out through the traffic,

which clogged the main street of what had once been just a pretty little Georgian village on a bend in the Liffey. He remembered how pleased his mother had been when he was posted to Swan's Nest, An easy life, she had predicted. Nothing but the odd drunk farmer and a bit of sheep-stealing. Not for long. The city had spread out and engulfed the acres of lush farmland. Now it was a suburb. A drab, cold, featureless suburb where lawlessness flourished.

He had driven down the steep hill from the bridge at Hazel Hatch and parked his car where the road ended, just in front of the metal barrier that prevented anything other than bicycles, children's prams or buggies or pedestrians proceeding down the narrow path beside the water's edge. Ahead he could see, hanging limply in the still air, the yellow crime-scene tape. A uniformed guard leaned against a tree. The whole area on either side of the canal had been searched thoroughly, but they had found nothing. No footprints in the hard, dark earth, nothing in the dusty grass, no tracks, no trails, no spoors to follow.

He bent down under the plastic cordon, saluting the guard on duty. He walked along beside the water, the sun hot on his back, until he came to the spot where Mary's body had been found. She had lodged in the branches of a submerged ash tree. It wouldn't have been visible in the dark, and although the body, wrapped in black plastic sacks, sealed with bands of grey sticky tape, had been weighed down with concrete blocks tied around the neck and the waist, somehow the whole thing had stuck. There was a moon that night, on the wane, heading towards its third quarter, but it would still have been very dark out here, away from the bloom of the street lights. He, whoever he was, must have had a job getting her body up the narrow path from the car. He would have stood with his bundle, and flung her out as far as he could. Not easy to do, with a dead weight. Maybe he had something with him. A plank, an oar, to push her away. Whatever. Maybe he began to panic, to lose control. He heard the splash, couldn't see exactly where she was, didn't want to make too much noise. Didn't want to waken any of the people sleeping in the three or four barges tied up along the bank. McLoughlin stopped to inspect them. They weren't his cup of tea. Too top-heavy, bits added on here and there. Floating caravans, really. None of the grace and style of the classic sea boats he loved.

He turned away and walked back towards his car. He used to come out here blackberrying when he was a kid. He and his sister. Under strict instructions not to eat all the fruit. It's for jam, not for you, his mother would say, grabbing him by the ears and forcing him to stick out his tongue to be inspected for the tell-tale purple stains. Too soon for blackberries now. The berries were hard, just beginning to redden on the prickled stems. I'll come back in a month or so, when this is all over, he thought.

'When will this be all over?' she asked.

McLoughlin shrugged. 'It's hard to tell. We could get lucky. It could be a few days, a week, or...' He stopped and picked up the jug of lemonade on the table. 'May I?'

She nodded. They were sitting in the garden behind the house, the sun still hot on the stone terrace. The house was in a perfect position, right in front of the sea. There were only about ten others on the little road. Early Victorian, he reckoned. Deceptively large. He had driven past them slowly, looking for a name written in faded white paint on the gate post. Inis Arcáin. Sherkin Island. The island of the sea pigs. Called, he guessed, after the beautiful little place just off Baltimore in West Cork.

He had rung the doorbell a number of times when he first arrived. The old woman had answered. He hadn't met her before. He held out his hand and introduced himself. She was very small and thin, her hand a loose bundle of bones in his. She was dressed even on this hot day in an Aran cardigan, buttoned up to her wrinkled neck, and a pair of thick tweed trousers.

'She's in the garden. You can go round by the side gate.'

Margaret was sitting on a wooden chair on the terrace. Her eyes were closed, her head leaning back, her face turned towards the sun. He stood for a moment looking at her. Today with no makeup, her hair pulled back in a knot, she looked younger, sweeter. He wanted, suddenly, to kiss the small hollow in the centre of her collarbone, visible now where her shirt was unbuttoned. She opened her eyes. He felt his face go red. Caught in the act, he thought.

He sat down in the seat facing her, the wooden table between them. He drank the lemonade. Bitter-sweet.

'Why did you go to New Zealand?' he asked.

'I thought you wanted to talk about Mary.'

'Well, the two are related, are they not?'

'Are they?'

Oh dear, he thought.

'Look, Dr Mitchell, I know this is very difficult and painful for you.'

'Do you? How do you know? Has this ever happened to you?'

He moved his chair slightly, the wooden legs grating on the stone flags.

'Dr Mitchell, I am a policeman. For the past twenty-five years I have been investigating the practice of violent crime. You are not, I'm sorry to say, the first mother whose only daughter has died in a horrible and brutal way. And I'm equally sorry to say that you will not be the last. I am, I'm afraid, only trying to do my job. As efficiently and successfully as I can.' He paused and leaned towards her. 'Do I make myself clear?'

She nodded. 'Clear as day, Inspector.'

'Good. Now. As I was saying. Why did you go to New Zealand?'

She stood up and walked away from the table. She sat down on the small wall that bounded the terrace.

'I had been planning to go there with my husband but he was killed in a car crash, a couple of months before we were due to leave. Anyway, after a bit of thought I decided that I might as well go by myself. I had a job waiting.'

'And when was that?'

'Twenty years or so ago.'

'Before Mary was born?'

'No. Just after. But my husband died before her birth.'

'And his name was?' He opened his note-book

'David Mitchell, but,' she held up her hand, 'all this happened in London. It was a long time ago.'

He looked at her. 'So let's get this straight. You were living in London. You had got married and you and your husband were going to New Zealand together. Then he died, and you went by yourself after the baby was born. Is that it?'

She nodded.

'You didn't want to come back here to your family?'

'Look,' she stood up again, 'I've told you what happened. What is this? Am I a suspect?'

'What?'

'A suspect.'

He laid his pen on the table. 'What makes you say that?'

'Well, it's fairly common practice, isn't it?

In cases like this for the police to assume that those closest to the victim are most likely to have had something to do with the crime. Isn't that so?'

He nodded, slowly.

'And in fact,' she stood over him, her face pale, her eyes red, 'even as we speak I imagine that one of your underlings is faxing the New Zealand police about me. Isn't that so? So why you're bothering to ask me these questions is beyond my comprehension.'

He shrugged his shoulders, feeling damp patches spreading across the back of his shirt.

'Correct me if I'm wrong, Inspector, but as you will soon know, if you don't already, I worked in an institution for the criminally insane for a number of years, and I understand that combination of passion and proximity. It's lethal.'

He smiled at the way she put it. He must remember it for his next lecture in Templemore.

'And as you pore over the pile of stuff from the Auckland police, you and your fellow officers will be saying, "We know she's a widow, but does she have a boyfriend, a lover? Someone who's been working up to doing this. Does she know about it? Has she turned a blind eye to it so far? Maybe she's jealous of the girl. Maybe they're both in love with the same guy? Is that it? Good old-fashioned jealousy. So let's poke around, see what dirt we can dredge up on the mother. Make our job as easy as possible." Isn't that the way, Inspector?'

He took out a packet of cigars. Half coronas. He lit one, the blue smoke hanging between them. It was quiet in the garden, except for the constant thrum of the traffic on the road above, and the clanging and rattling every few minutes as the DART rushed by. She had turned away from him. She was hunched over, her arms wrapped around her shoulders. He could see the individual vertebrae of her spine through the thin material of her white shirt. He felt intense pity for her. But pity was the wrong emotion at a time like this.

'Mitchell, Margaret Mitchell.' The name trickled out of his mouth with the smoke. 'I loved *Gone With the Wind*. It was my favourite book for years.'

'Christ almighty.' She turned on him, her voice harsh. 'Why aren't you out there looking for that bastard who destroyed my daughter, instead of sitting here with me? What do I know? I know nothing about this.

I've never gone through this before. I've never felt pain like this before. I don't know what to say or do. Except that I know, my reason tells me, what kind of person we're dealing with. I've seen them all. I've interviewed them, sat in their cells and shared their dirty little secrets, their disgusting fantasies. I've heard them lie and cheat, twist the doctors and the courts. Offer up their own abuse as some kind of excuse. Exploit the generosity of jurors. And I've seen their victims. The little girls who will never be able to love and be loved, the old women who will never leave their houses again, the countless pathetic creatures who sit with their faces to the wall, rigid, inert, lifeless with fear.'

McLoughlin stood up. He closed his eyes and held his face to the sun. Then he turned back towards her. 'Passion and proximity. As you say, a lethal weapon. Are you sure your daughter didn't have a boyfriend here?'

She began to cry then. An ugly sound, her body jerking, her hands over her face. A black cat jumped down from the apple tree. He ran over to her, pushing his face into hers. She stretched out and pulled him close. McLoughlin got up and went into the kitchen. He opened cupboards and ran his hand along the dresser shelves until he found a bottle of whiskey. He walked back into the garden and poured some into one of the lemonade glasses. He handed it to her. She drank it quickly. He sat down again on the wooden seat and waited.

She put down the glass. He handed her a handkerchief from his pocket and she wiped her eyes and nose.

'That phone call you got, do you have any thoughts about it?'

She shook her head. 'I haven't heard that tune for years. New Zealand is a very secular society. Religion doesn't play the same role that it does here.'

'No?'

'It's a strange place. On the surface very beautiful, very peaceful, very green.'

'Lots of sailing I hear.'

'That's right. The beautiful Pacific Ocean. Outside the window, like an extraordinary sleeping sea creature. It makes people very agoraphobic. It stretches for thousands of miles. In every direction, nothing but water. And people do the most appalling things. Every few years. Madness seeps out of the earth, the way the steam, the geysers, the boiling mud escape through the fault lines. Whole families massacred, wiped out.

Dreadful anger.'

'Like this?'

'Maybe.' She held. out her glass for more. 'What about you? Are you not drinking? On duty I suppose.'

'Well,' he drained the last of the lemonade from his glass, 'why not? My mother always says it's bad manners to let someone drink alone.'

'A sensible woman.'

'So,' he poured from the bottle and saluted her, '*why* did you go to New Zealand?'

13

The shutter opens. Light pours from the object in the frame onto the piece of film. The shutter closes. The image is trapped, an insect caught in amber. Light from the enlarger saturates the sensitive paper. Waves of crystalline sodium sulphate, mixed with potassium bromide and water, release the image. Slowly, gradually, as the paper rocks in the solution, it swims back up to the surface. Light meets light again.

The row of damp prints hung limply from

a piece of cord. They twisted gently in the draught as the door opened and then closed quietly. A woman in a garden. Black and white reducing everything to its simple constituents. Her dress is white, her hair is black. She is picking pale roses. The foliage around them is ebony. The woman's face is milky, her lips and eyes dark shadows. She turns towards the camera. Her gaze is distant, remote. She sits on a white chair, a book open on her lap. A sable cat sits beside her. One bleached arm rests on his back. The same woman is seen through an open window. She has something in her hand. Her hair is loose. Her hand has moved. She is brushing, brushing. Click, click, click. Her hand moves from the top of her head down through her hair.

Jimmy inspected the prints carefully. He was pleased. It had been worth spending the money on the telephoto lens. His father was right again. He had gone on with all the usual crap about taking things seriously. He kept repeating, 'If a thing's worth doing it's worth doing well,' like a mantra. He suggested photography classes. Jimmy complained and moaned and thought about refusing them point-blank. But if the old man was going to pay what was the point in looking a gift horse in the mouth? After all, he'd bought him the Mercedes to get the chauffeuring business off the ground. And it wasn't as if he couldn't afford it. All those fucking awful townhouses he was putting up all over west County Dublin.

The classes had surprised him. They were difficult. The word, he thought, is 'challenging'. Completely unlike school. What a waste of space that had been. Even thinking about it made him chafe with boredom. The rules, the discipline, the creeps you had to spend time with. The work was never a problem. He could, he knew, have been one of the stars if he'd wanted. But what was the point? He hated all the teachers. They were either brothers who leered, or lazy arseholes, time-servers, only interested in rugby or their nice wives at home in their nice gardens.

The photography teacher, now, she was different. She was English, from somewhere down south, some boring provincial town. She had an obsession with the west. She wanted to go to Connemara and shoot stacks of turf and stone circles. Apart from that she was fine. She knew her stuff. She could answer all his questions, and she was very pretty. Small, with a neat little waist and glossy brown hair, cut like a little boy's. The last night of the course the whole class had gone for a drink in Temple Bar. Little Miss Teacher got completely pissed on tequila. She was like something out of a 1950s Doris Day movie. Transformed. She took off her glasses and began to sing. All that old Billie Holiday stuff he loved. She was amazing. She sashayed up and down the bar, sticking out her little tits, practically shoving her cunt in his face. So, of course, he had to give her a lift home. He fucked her in the car, and again in the hallway of her house, and that was before he managed to drag her upstairs to the bedroom. He had a lot of fun that night. She was so drunk she didn't make a sound.

He unclipped one of the prints and put it down on the light box. He picked up his magnifying glass and moved it slowly and methodically over the surface of the paper. The image of the woman grew and shrank. He liked it when one side of her face was huge, the other tiny. It made her ugly, distorted. He examined the photograph for technical imperfections. As far as he could see there were none. It had been a particularly good negative and he had made it into an equally good print. No scratches, no blemishes. Just a nice sharp image, well composed, and well printed.

He kept his favourite photograph in one of the little pockets in his wallet. He took it out now. It was small, perhaps three inches wide by two inches long. The white border had been trimmed with a guillotine that cut with a fancy rippled edge. The photograph was of a girl with a baby. The girl was very young. She looked like she might have been twelve or thirteen. Maybe the same age as Molly was now. She had a fringe and long straight fair hair. Her nose was slightly turned up. She was wearing a nightie, with a frill around the neck. The baby was wrapped tightly in a blanket. Although it was very small it looked too big and heavy for the girl's skinny arms. The baby's mouth was open, and one tiny hand had escaped from its shawl. The hand was waving. He held the magnifying glass up to it. There were deep dimples over its knuckles. Its thumb curved back, the nail long. The baby had a birthmark on its tiny wrist. Brown, like a smudged ink blot. He held the glass over it and then over the mark on his own wrist. Bigger now that he was fully grown, but exactly the same shape.

He had found the photograph years ago. In the shed at the bottom of the garden, in a tin trunk filled with old crockery, battered saucepans, bits and pieces of kitchen rubbish. It wasn't long after they had come back to live in Dublin. The trunk had come with them. He remembered it being unloaded from the big truck with all their other furniture. All the stuff from their flat in Manchester.

It was cold in the shed. It was November. Through the little window he could see the washing line, the sheets and pillowcases hanging wet, grey smoke from the chimney drifting down with the mist, and piles of leaves that his father had raked together. When he got out he'd smash through them, scatter them across the garden so his father would have to start all over again. He kicked the door. It rattled and shook but didn't give. It was no use. It was bolted from the outside. His mother had done it. He had listened to her footsteps, the click of her high heels on the concrete path getting fainter as she walked quickly away. He had screamed after her, I hate you, you're a bitch and a cow, but she didn't answer.

It wasn't fair. He wasn't the only one who'd been stealing at school. Everyone in his class did it. But he was the one who got caught, taking the senior infants' lunch money in the playground. The head teacher, Brother Miley, had phoned her and she'd driven to collect him. She was wearing her new fur coat, the mink she was always telling everyone about. She hit him when she got him outside, away from the teacher's knowing gaze. Her diamond ring cut into his ear and made tears jump into his eyes. But he wouldn't cry. Not in front of her. And when they got home she caught hold of his tie and dragged him out of the car and through the house, yelling and screaming, calling him all kinds of names, not caring who heard, and then she shoved him into the shed.

She'd done this before, but she wouldn't do it for much longer. He might only be twelve, but he was tall. Already his head was level with hers. Soon, if she tried to hit him he'd hit her back. But meantime it was cold. He was hungry and it was getting dark. Perhaps there might be something to eat in the trunk. A box of biscuits they'd forgotten about. So he knelt and scrabbled among the piles of newspaper-wrapped cups and saucers and chipped vases, until he reached the bottom. An old apron was bundled in the corner, probably put in as wadding for the breakables. He held it up, shaking out the damp material. There were patches of mould all over the pattern of yellow sunflowers. He put his hand into the square front pocket and felt his fingers slip over something small and shiny. He took it out and held it up in the fading light. He looked at it closely. Then he put it carefully in his pocket. And he kicked the door again. Harder this time, his big toe hurting against the wood, until the bolt gave and the door swung open, banging back against its hinges.

Upstairs, warm and safe, he lay in the dark under Tina's bed. She wasn't home from work yet. But she'd be here soon. He could imagine her legs coming towards him, her calf muscles big and strong underneath the fine nylon of her tights. When she got close enough he would be able to see the dark hairs trapped beneath the mesh. He wanted to reach out and stroke them, but he wasn't allowed. Not any longer. When he was little she had always taken him into the bath with her, and into bed, snuggling him close, hiding him under the blankets. But when he started going to secondary school she told him he was getting too big, that she didn't have room any longer for him. That it wasn't right for sisters to sleep with brothers of his age. But he discovered that if he kept really still and was very quiet she didn't notice when he hid under the bed, or in the big hot press in the bathroom. And he could peek out through the little split in the boards and watch her washing herself, the soapy water running down her white body, dribbling into the deep fold between her breasts and the creases in her tummy, trickling through the thick black curls, and onto her heavy thighs.

The light came on, and he watched her feet walking across the carpet towards him. She sat down on the bed, the springs sagging over his head. He took the photograph out of his pocket and put it down on the dusty floor where he could see it. Why was she holding him like that? He was very small. He must have just been born. And why was she wearing her nightie?

He had wondered and wondered. And he, too, had hidden the picture, in a wooden pencil case under a loose board in his bedroom. A couple of times he thought he would ask her, but when he tried to sit on her knee, or hung over the back of the sofa and put his arms around her neck she always pushed him away. And then he found out all about it. At school, in the playground, one break-time. Just after his thirteenth birthday.

It was that snotty-nosed creep Peter Cooney who told him. In front of all the others. Came straight out with it. Of course he didn't believe him. How could Cooney know that his big sister was really his mother? Because I heard my ma talking about it. On the phone to her friend Mrs O'Brien. Crap, crap, crap, he had screamed, and he'd gone for him, with his head, so Cooney fell back on the tarmacadam, blood pouring out of his nose. But still he wouldn't shut up. It's true. Fitzer is a bastard, Fitzer is a bastard, Fitzer is a bastard. He was still shouting it when Jimmy kicked him in the balls, as hard as he could. And then the others joined in, pulling at his hair and his sweater, and shouting, together, as if they'd been practising, as if they knew already, until Mr Linehan who was on yard duty came running over, and grabbed Jimmy, and held him down until they got the ambulance for Cooney.

He never went back to that school. He never told her, the woman he had called his mother, what had happened. And soon after they moved from the pebble-dashed semi in Booterstown, to the big house in Killiney where they lived now. And not long after that Molly was born. They sent him to boarding school, where he daydreamed his life away. He didn't talk to any of them very much any more. Except Molly. And he still kept the photograph, hidden, a secret. Tina didn't come with them when they moved house. She got her own flat in town. Sometimes at the weekends and during the school holidays he'd follow her as she went from work to the pub to meet her friends, and back to her flat. He was very good at it. She never spotted him. And then she got engaged.

Now he held the photograph between his thumb and index finger, rubbing it, smoothing it. Then he put it back in his wallet. He plugged in the little kettle he kept here in his darkroom. He was thirsty. He took a brightly coloured packet off the shelf. It was Red Zinger herbal tea. He had taken it from the English girl's kitchen, that night when he had gone in to get himself a glass of water. It was on a shelf with all kinds of strange foods. Glass jars bright with coloured beans, and herbs and spices. The packet caught his eye. It was so cheerful. He read the ingredients. Hibiscus flowers, lemon zest, cinnamon, rose-hip. He said the name over and over. It jumped off his tongue like sherbet. He took out a tea bag and put it in his special mug, pottery, dark blue, with a big J scratched into the glaze. Molly had given him the mug and a jar of honey last Christmas. She had been going through a Winnie-the-Pooh phase and the jar had a picture of a bear on the label, the word honey spelt 'hunny'. He chanted softly to himself,

'Isn't it funny how a bear likes honey?
Buzz, buzz, buzz I wonder why he does.'

Steam curled from the kettle's spout. He switched it off and poured the boiling water into the mug. He dunked the tea bag up and down and dropped it neatly into the pedal bin. He stirred a teaspoon of honey into the dark red liquid. As he waited for it to cool, he unlocked his filing cabinet and began to leaf through its contents. He had read in a photographic manual that for really efficient work a proper filing system was highly desirable. The book recommended an album for negatives, a picture file and an index. He had followed this prescription to the letter. Now he had a perfect record of all his photographs. My family, he thought. My kith and kin. My flesh and blood.

Carefully he slid the negatives out of their envelopes and held them up to the light.

There was no doubt about it. He had come on in leaps and bounds. In the beginning he hadn't bothered about light, framing, depth of field. All he had wanted was the image, pinned to the paper. He was embarrassed now by some of his earlier work. He had been a fool to think it would be easy. But his mistakes had taught him about timing, control, preparation, follow-through. Every time he went out with his camera the end result was more perfect. The English girl had taught him well. She quoted the economist Schumacher, who had written a book called *Small is Beautiful*. This, she said, should be his motto when he was taking pictures. Getting the little details right. He had found the book beside her bed. He had photographed her that night with the jacket lying on her stomach. The flash had gone off right in her face, but even that didn't wake her.

He finished his inspection and locked everything away. He washed his mug and put it back on the shelf. He took one last glance at his latest crop of prints still hanging, drying. Then he switched off the light and opened the wooden door. Outside it was quiet, the only sound the stirring of the branches of the pine trees, the only brightness the pinpricks of stars flung across the sky, and a smell of the countryside, newly mown hay and damp earth. He fastened the heavy padlock and checked it again. Locked up tight. Until the next time.

14

The black cat rubbed the length of his body against and around Margaret's legs. Once, twice, three times, backwards and forwards. His tail felt hard and muscular, prehensile, unfamiliar as it rolled off her calves. She reached down and ran her hand along his gleaming back. He arched under her touch, then pushed his bony head against her, nuzzling her knuckles with his sensitive nose. Then he lay down on the kitchen floor and rolled over, wriggling from side to side to attract her attention. She rubbed her foot along his soft belly. There was a little tuft of white just in front of his empty testicular sac. As her foot got near it, the cat grabbed at her toes with his claws, then followed up with his sharp teeth. She pulled away, but not before he had drawn a thin line of red on her instep.

She looked at the small beads of blood strung like tiny corals along the line of the scratch. Already the body was taking care of its defences. The blood was coagulating, the white cells rushing to repel bacteria and in a couple of hours a scab would form, providing the protective armour beneath which new skin would grow.

The coroner's office had phoned that morning. They had suggested an undertaker. The arrangements had been made. Mary would be buried with her grandfather, the day after tomorrow. The funeral Mass would be at ten o'clock in St Patrick's Church in Monkstown. There would be no notice in the paper. There would be no fuss. Margaret repeated the words aloud and banged her fist on the kitchen table. No fuss.

'Dr Mitchell, are you all right?'

Margaret looked up. A large woman in a tight white uniform was standing in the door.

'I'm sorry, I don't want to intrude.'

'You're not, of course you're not. Please,' Margaret gestured to a chair and cast around for a name, 'Sinead. Sit down, have some coffee. Or would you prefer a cold drink?'

'Coffee would be lovely.' The nurse

slumped into the offered seat, dumping a bulging leather bag on the table beside her.

Margaret handed her a cup and offered chocolate biscuits. 'So,' she asked, 'how is she?'

'Well.' The nurse sipped slowly, then took out a tissue and wiped the beaded sweat from her forehead. 'The morphine seems to be making a big difference. She seems much more cheerful this morning, probably because she's sleeping a lot better. Although I'd say she's still having a problem with constipation. It's very common. It's one of the unfortunate side effects of the morphine. But you know how she is. She really doesn't like talking about it. In fact, whenever I try to raise it with her she just refuses to answer.'

Margaret nodded. 'Yes, bodily functions were never a strong point with my mother.'

'Nor for many of her generation. We see it all the time with older people. It's very difficult to help them sometimes, they just don't like talking about things that embarrass them.'

Embarrass, awaken, remind, provoke, challenge. All these and more, thought Margaret. Anything that disturbs the crust of accepted memory.

'And her prognosis? Can you give me a

better idea?'

Again the nurse wiped her forehead. She spoke slowly, carefully. 'Not really,' she said. 'It could be six months, it could be less. But it's better not to think about the length of time. We encourage people to concentrate on the quality of the experience. We do find,' she paused again and sipped her coffee, 'that for some people, these weeks can be truly wonderful. They can be full of emotional discoveries, revelations, ways of developing a true understanding of each other. They can be exhilarating, packed with insight, a time for parents and children to really come together.' She stopped abruptly, and picked up a biscuit.

The cat jumped up onto Margaret's lap and put one paw on the table. Margaret dug her fingers into the indentations behind his ears. Loud purrs vibrated through his body. He unsheathed his claws and gripped the soft material of her skirt.

'Dr Mitchell.' The nurse finished her biscuit and picked up the balled tissue from the table. She wiped her fingers carefully, and dabbed around her mouth. 'I want you to know how well we all think you're coping with this appalling tragedy. If there's ever anything that any of us can do to help, if you need time by yourself and someone to sit with your mother, please, you have my phone number. Please call me.'

Margaret tried to smile, to force the muscles of her face to move the skin into an acceptable shape. She opened her mouth to speak, to thank the woman for her kindness, but nothing would come out. She knew what words she should use. She could hear them in her head, but she couldn't find the way to make the connection between thought and action. She felt suddenly as if she was locked inside a glass case. The world existed somewhere outside, but within was darkness, cold and silence.

And then the phone rang.

The nurse stood up quickly. The cat jumped from Margaret's knee, its claws pulling at the skin of her thighs.

'I'll answer it,' the nurse said, 'on my way out.' But as she gathered up her bag and started up the steps to the hall, the phone stopped. 'I hate that,' she said, 'drives you mad wondering who it was.'

Mad. Wondering.

'Margaret, Margaret.' The stick banged against the floor. Catherine was seated, propped up in the armchair by the window. The stick banged again and again.

Margaret stood in the door. 'What is it?'

'The phone. Who was on the phone? Was it for me? It must have been for me. Was it John? Phoning from the office to say that he wouldn't be home for dinner. He's never home, these days. He's always too busy. He works too hard. Was that it? Was it John? Why didn't you tell me? I wanted to speak to him myself.' Her voice rose, an hysterical whine. 'Why do you never tell me anything?' She had put on her makeup. Bright blue eyeshadow was smeared across her wrinkled eyelids, brown powder scattered over her sunken cheeks. Scarlet lipstick wandered up and over her thin lips. A clown's sad Cupid's bow.

'It was nothing, Mother. A wrong number.'

She closed the door and stood looking at the phone. It was a new model, plastic, out of place on the Victorian side-table. It had all the latest gadgets, redial, call waiting, a stored memory, built in answering machine. And a light that flashed when the phone rang. It was flashing now. It would continue to flash until she answered. Like a tiny lighthouse, warning of dangers ahead.

'Margaret.' Again the anxious whingeing muffled by the closed door. 'Answer the phone. It's John. I know it's John.'

She lifted the receiver. There was a pause and a click. The line hissed. Then a girl's voice, familiar, happy, singing.

'I'm a little tea-pot, short and stout,
Here's my handle, here's my spout.
When the tea is ready, hear me shout,
Lift me up and pour me out.'

And again the voice. Mary's voice.
'Now, it's your turn, you do it.'
A whirr of a tape. Then silence.

A hot day. Margaret shifted uncomfortably on the hard upright chair. She had dressed up for Mary's first end-of-term concert. Her feet were swollen and they rubbed against the leather of her shoes. She wanted to kick them off and press her toes and the ball of her foot hard down on the cool of the lino tiles.

She looked out of the big windows that lined the school hall. The cricket pitch was dust, bare earth at either wicket. The playing fields stretched away, the green of the grass burnt brown, sloping gently towards the gorse and scrub that formed their natural boundary. We're not allowed to go in there, Mary had told her. Only the big boys when they lose their cricket ball. In the distance creeping up the other side of the hill were the neatly ordered rows of Mrs Begavitch's vineyard. The kids called her the Begabitch. So Mary said, whispering the bad word into her ear, and giggling at her daring. Margaret could just about hear the crash and clang of Mrs Begavitch's bird-scarers over the chatter of the children and the hum of their parents' conversation. Yards and yards of tin cans strung above the vines and when that failed she would patrol with a shotgun, a figure of fun in her shape-less print dress and rubber gumboots, her head wrapped in a voluminous scarf covered with pink and scarlet roses. She had come to this village by the Pacific Ocean just after the Second World War had laid waste to her village in Yugoslavia. And still an outsider, Margaret thought.

Silence crept across the audience as Mr Gibson, the headmaster, introduced the school choir. They sang a Maori song, their sweet voices denying the darkness of the language. Above the stage Queen Elizabeth spread her gaze benevolently, her blue cloak decorated with a huge diamond sunburst. The applause rushed round the room, like waves breaking on the rocks at high tide. Heads crowded together, commenting, praising. A handkerchief was passed down a row, a proud grandmother wiping her eyes. Boys and girls followed each other onto the stage. Each new arrival was greeted with cheers. Good-humoured comments and words of encouragement were shouted. There were exclamations of surprise at family resemblance. Younger brothers and sisters taking the places relinquished by their older siblings. A moment of sadness when prayers were said for a child who had died of leukaemia. Simple words, plainly spoken, Margaret noticed. No ritual mention of Our Lady or the Saints. Just an appeal directly to God. Then Mary was on stage. Margaret felt a sudden apprehension. Her palms prickled. A ripple of enquiry gathered momentum around her. The little girl curtsied. Her curls bobbed in their red ribbons. She held the corners of her pinafore. One small foot, its white sock and shoe snowy perfection, pointed in front of the other. She began to sing and mime the gestures, carefully, precisely. When she opened her mouth one of her front teeth was missing. Margaret knew there was a bright shiny coin in the little pocket in the bib of her dress. The tooth fairy had left it the night before. As she finished Margaret began to clap. Her palms burned and tickled and tears filled her eyes. Mary looked suddenly the image of her father. Margaret had never seen it so clearly before. It wasn't just the curls or the colouring. It was her composure, the set of her tiny face, the attention to detail, her awareness of every part of her body. Tears had stung her eyes, and her throat had closed over. As it did now.

Mary, she called out to her. Why, tell me why? What have you done?

Again, the voice, peevish, complaining. 'Why do you never tell me who calls? This is still my house, you know.'

Margaret wiped the tears on the back of her hand. She pulled herself up off the floor, and opened the door again.

'It was John, wasn't it? Don't lie to me.'

Margaret heard her own voice asking from somewhere in the distance, 'Mother, tell me. Why did you not want me to come to Daddy's funeral?'

Catherine looked up at her, lucid now, her eyes clear. 'Because I didn't. I looked after him. I loved him. When he was alive he only wanted me. Why should it be different when he was dead?'

Margaret stepped back, away from that voice, that anger, and turned towards the stairs. One foot in front of the other, carefully, precisely, she walked up to Mary's room. It was as it had been left that Saturday. They had brought the bare necessities from New Zealand but Mary had squirrelled together a collection of postcards, pictures torn from magazines, dried flowers, cheap jewellery, dog-eared books. She had always been a hoarder. When she was small Margaret had regularly purged her school-bag of its accumulated clutter, ignoring her protests as she dumped stones from the beach, chewing-gum wrappers, her beloved shells, notes from friends, dried-up apples, crusts from her sandwiches. She had also gone through her pockets from time to time, until Mary had accused her of being nosy and bossy. But she felt no guilt now as she searched her clothes. Opened all her books, shaking them by the spine, pulled cassette tapes from their boxes, ripping apart the cardboard of the labels. Clothes tumbled from the wardrobe as she dragged them from their hangers, dumping the contents of the drawers on the carpet. She ran her hands underneath the yellowed newspaper that lined the shelves. She ripped the carpet free of its tacks and tugged the curtains from the rails. She stripped the bed, tearing at the sheets and hauling the mattress onto the floor. Finally she pulled the pillow out of its cotton case. As she did so a handful of something white poured out. She knelt and gathered it up. She held it to her nose. White lavender, that was all, just white lavender.

She lay down on the tumbled bedclothes. The smell of the lavender mingled with the smell of the dust. She rolled over on her side, one hand between her thighs, the other holding the pillow. She wanted someone to hold her too. Mary's father. She wanted him. She closed her eyes. She had known the night she had conceived. Her medical training told her this was impossible. But her medical training was wrong. Afterwards her body felt different, heavy, not her own. Every pore gave out his smell. When she looked in the mirror he looked back at her. When she looked at her hands she saw his. A blue bruise, in the shape of a butterfly, decorated her right breast. She had begun to kiss him, she remembered, from his ankles to the top of his head. She had stopped when she got to the marks on his right thigh. The three little red circles in a straight line. The same three

123

filling the sails, and the salt air filling our lungs with goodness.

He watched Dave Finney weaving his way through the crowd at the bar with a tray of pints. He was a nice lad, when he wasn't being a pain in the arse. Good-looking. Charming. Parting the drinkers like Moses at the Red Sea, his smile at the ready. Clever. Knows just when to flirt and when to play the mammy's boy. Just like I did once. Once long ago.

All around him the rest of his team were seated. He'd brought them here for a drink. They'd had their first proper case conference this afternoon and they'd covered a lot of ground. Important, he always thought, that the guys felt they were part of whatever was happening. Good for morale to shoot the breeze, jolly them along, share some gossip, have a bit of fun as well as all the slog.

He put out his hand for the pint that Finney was passing over to him. He waited until Finney had handed around the rest of them and was seated, then he raised his glass in salute. He drank. A long swallow. He needed it, and another and another. Too many, he knew, but too bad.

'So,' Finney put down his glass and took

out his cigarettes, 'what do you reckon?'

'About what?'

Finney lit up, blowing out the match with a jet of air from the corner of his mouth.

'Him, her, it, whatever.'

'Him, judging by the force of the blow that killed the poor girl.'

The pathologist's report hadn't made pleasant reading. Not, you could say, that they ever did. Someone had smashed her skull, probably with a fist. The blow had lacerated the middle meningeal artery. She would have lost consciousness more or less immediately, then come to for a couple of hours. But death had been inevitable. He tried to imagine the pain she was feeling from her other injuries. Lacerations and bruising to the vagina and anus. Something solid had been inserted into her, possibly a broom handle, possibly a knife. She had cigarette burns to her thighs, breasts and stomach, and circular cuts had been made around her nipples. Her pubic hair had been trimmed as well as the hair on her head. Probably with ordinary kitchen scissors, the pathologist said. Big blades, not too sharp. The other cuts had been made with something like a razor blade or a Stanley knife. Her wrists and ankles were cut and bruised.

She'd been handcuffed or tied with some other kind of metal chain. McLoughlin had pinned the photographs of her body to the noticeboards around the incident room. The colours, scarlet, black, white, purple, stood out vividly against the drab monotony of the grey walls, ceiling and floor. A reminder, he thought, of what we're dealing with here. Never forget that this is what this bastard has done.

'An unlucky bollocks, wasn't he?'

'How do you mean?'

'Well, he couldn't have been expecting that she would have been found so quickly.'

God bless the old man and his nosy little dog, thought McLoughlin.

'Not that it makes that much difference,' continued Finney. 'We didn't find anything useful at the canal.'

'So what does that tell us?'

'Either he's very clever and well planned, or he's just lucky.'

'And how long do you reckon it had been since he killed her?'

Finney smiled, the dimples in his cheeks deepening. 'Well, boss. It's like this. Rigor mortis sets in six hours after death. The body is stiff within twelve hours. Rigor mortis lasts for thirty-six to forty-eight hours. So either he dumped her within six hours, or after thirty-six. And there's no way that she'd been dead that long. Not by the look of her. So, I'd say, she was probably about four hours dead.'

'Good boy.' McLoughlin raised his glass to him. 'Now a more difficult question. What do the girl's injuries tell us?'

'He's a nutter?'

'Yeah, I suppose. But they also say that he's not afraid to get up close. Not afraid to get his hands dirty. He could have killed her with a piece of rope, or a tie or a stocking. He could have killed her with his knife. But he didn't. He chose to do it with his fist. Bone on bone.'

'Maybe he didn't mean to do it at all?'

'Just having a bit of fun, you mean?'

'You know what I mean.'

McLoughlin did. Unfortunately. But he didn't know why. He'd given up trying to fathom the reasons for the cruelty that men inflicted on their women. This morning before the conference he had sat down with the files on all the other known sex offenders. There were about three hundred in all. Rapists, murderers, child molesters, makers of obscene phone calls, purveyors of pornography. He flicked through the photographs and details of their crimes. He held up each picture and looked at it closely. After all his years in the force he still expected to be able to tell something about a person from the way he looked. God knows why. His naïve expectations were never borne out by reality. None of these men looked like anything in particular. He could imagine having a pint with them or a game of pool on a wet Sunday afternoon. But he could never quite understand how that could be. When he looked at himself first thing in the morning, as he dragged his razor through the shaving cream, he was sure he could see an accumulation of bile and badness, sins of omission and commission. Did all these men have portraits in their attics that registered the agony for which they were responsible, the damage they had done?

'Who was it who said to know all is to forgive all?' he asked.

'Jesus, I don't know,' Finney replied. 'Was it your woman, the girl's mother? She's an intellectual type, isn't she?'

'Intellectual, maybe, but forgiving never. We had the most interesting conversation yesterday.'

'Oh, yeah?' Finney smirked. 'I was wondering why you went out there on your own.'

'Piss off.' McLoughlin picked up his pint and held it over the younger man's head in mock anger. 'She was absolutely adamant that there is no rehabilitation for sex offenders. She was telling me, she worked in a hospital for the criminally insane in New Zealand once, and she says that all these fancy notions about therapy and group sessions and treatment leading to cure are complete crap. Punishment is the only answer, she says.' The look on her face, the anger, the hatred. He could understand anger and what it might make you do. And the double-edged sword of passion. Delight on one side and despair on the other. There had been a stage in his life with Janey when he had wanted to hit her, to hurt her, to pulverize her into silence. He had balled his fists and pounded the table. Once he had thrown a large cast-iron pot at her head. Fortunately it had missed, but it still had a dent where it had crashed into the kitchen wall and bounced back onto the tiles.

But there was a difference between that kind of violence and the slow systematic brutality that so many men meted out. Or so he reasoned. Of course, when he thought about all the domestics he had been called to, usually by mothers or next-door neighbours who couldn't stand the uproar any longer, it was nigh impossible to separate the rage from the sadism. The penis used as a weapon, like the fist or the boot. But none of the men they had in their files had ever shown quite the level of calculated brutality as the guy who had killed Mary Mitchell.

'So tell me, boss, what else did she say? Did she tell you anything about the girl?'

McLoughlin shrugged. 'Not really. She was absolutely certain that she didn't have a boyfriend. That she wasn't seeing anyone special.'

'That's what those kids said. The ones she was with that night.'

McLoughlin had read their statements and compared them with the statements the Dun Laoghaire police had taken when Mary was still officially a missing person. There were virtually no discrepancies. One girl said Mary had been drinking Malibu and pineapple. Another that it was the new alcoholic lemonade. The boy, Gary Palmer, said it was after eleven when she left the bar, The girls all said it was a bit earlier, around five to. The only real difference in the state-ments was that in the second of the two, those taken after she was dead, they were less inclined to say that they liked her. A bit more honest now they knew she wasn't coming back. It wasn't that they had anything against her, that they said she was unfriendly or arrogant or unpleasant. They just seemed to think that she was a bit too introverted, hard to talk to, remote, as if she was thinking about something else. We thought, said the girl called Aoife, that it was because she was a foreigner. That was all.

He wondered about the mother and the daughter. He wondered about the father. A marine biologist, she had said. An orphan, brought up in a Barnardo's home. Very talented. He was doing research into oyster production.

'Dave,' McLoughlin finished his pint, 'get us another, and a whiskey chaser.' He handed over a wad of notes, and gestured to the others to throw in their orders. A couple of them were leaving. Bertie Lynch and John Casey. They were going to do another round of questionnaires in the George's Street area. And they'd keep on going back, daytime and night-time, until they got somewhere. Someone must have seen something. Finney had got the videotape from the TV shop and he'd made a couple more finds. The camera in the Central Bank had shown her standing on the steps between 23.05 and 23.20. And even better, the camera from the traffic lights by the Bank of Ireland showed a dark girl and a fair man in what looked like a black Mercedes.

He thought again of the photographs on the noticeboard. The close-ups of her head had showed that her ears were pierced, the tiny holes clearly visible in the fleshy lobes. She had been wearing, according to her mother, silver earrings inset with paua shell in the shape of fish. They were, so her mother had said, her favourites. She remembered, she told him, Mary standing in front of the mirror in the hall fiddling with them just before she went out. She was wearing the earrings and a gold ring with a tiny diamond on the little finger of her right hand.

'Where did she get it?' he had asked.

'From me, of course,' her mother replied.

'Was it an antique?' he had continued.

She shrugged. 'Depends what your definition of antique is. It was a piece of Edwardian costume jewellery. Not worth much.'

'And where did you get it?'

She paused and said, 'Why do you want to know?'

'It could be important.'

'It was a present from my father for my sixteenth birthday. It had belonged to his mother. But my fingers got too big, so I passed it on to Mary. And in case you want to know I also gave her the earrings for her last birthday.'

Both ring and earrings were missing. They were doing a check of the second-hand jewellers and pawnbrokers. So far nothing had come up.

Her bag was missing as well. Her friends had said she was carrying it when she left the bar. And her mother had confirmed that she always took it with her, no matter where she was going. It had been given to her by her favourite ballet teacher in Auckland. It was very heavy, brown leather, like an old-fashioned school-bag with two big straps and a buckle. She kept everything in it. Her ballet gear when she was going to class. Makeup, her address book, family photographs, her diary, bits and pieces of curiosities she'd picked up.

'I was always telling her it was going to do dreadful things to her posture, wearing it the way she did, slung off one shoulder, but she just ignored me.'

'And did she often ignore you?'

'That's none of your business, Inspector. None of your business at all.'

She didn't realize. He could see. She still

hadn't taken it in. Everything was his business now. Every detail and nuance of her life. Except that it wasn't 'her' life any more. It was their life. Collectively. And part of him. And would be until all this was over.

He looked around, aware suddenly that the pub was half empty. Finney had dumped the glasses and a pile of change on the table. He was standing up, fiddling with his car keys.

'I'm off, boss. Things to do.'

'Are you not joining me?'

'No, not now.'

'Hot date, eh?'

Finney grinned, his white teeth showing, suddenly predatory.

'Ah, go on, see you tomorrow.'

McLoughlin sat down again, the pint in his hand, the glass of whiskey beside it. Thinking time, that was what he needed. Thinking time and drinking time, and for him the two always went together.

16

The rose trailed down the graveyard's crumbling stone wall. Margaret lifted a branch, studded with thorns. The flowers were of the creamiest pink. She pulled a bloom towards her and prised open the petals to reveal its golden heart. Scent as sweet as strawberries with a hint of lemon filled her nostrils. She breathed deeply, closing her eyes as the petals brushed against her cheek. As she let go and stepped back they dropped in a soft fall, like pink-tinted snowflakes.

Behind her Catherine stood, still, silent, gazing around, lost.

'Can you remember, Mother, where Daddy is buried?' Margaret took her hand.

She had seemed much more lucid earlier. She had slept, had some clear soup for lunch, and taken her pills without any protest.

'Would you like that, to go to the graveyard? You could show me Daddy's grave, and we could see where Mary will be buried. Will we do that, Mother?'

And Catherine had nodded and smiled.

She had allowed Margaret to dress her, and brush her hair. It was such a warm day that Margaret had persuaded her to wear a dress, a pretty print with big white buttons all the way down the front. Don't worry, she said, I'll bring your shawl in case it gets cold.

The caretaker had shown them his map and pointed out the corner where he thought they might find John's grave. He had warned them to watch their step, looking them up and down, his glance resting a fraction too long on Margaret's bare legs. Vandals, he said, had done some terrible things here. He didn't want to upset her, but she should stick to the main path. She had thanked him, pressing some money into his hand. He watched them walk away, the old woman, her eyes vacant, her body frail and feeble, and the younger woman, thin, but strong, who looked at him with grey eyes, like her mother's, her skirt moving against her legs. As he lifted his hand to take the cigarette out of his mouth he smelt the scent of lavender from her skin.

The cemetery was overgrown and neglected. Long grass swayed and swooned over slabs of stone and marble, The white of cow parsley, the pink of willow-herb and the astringent splash of ragwort made it look like a country meadow, interspersed with strange outcrops of rock. Outside the walls the traffic hummed like a large spinning top. Inside the only sound Margaret could hear was her heart beating rhythmically and the cackle of an aggravated magpie, which danced stiff-legged from branch to branch in front of them.

They turned to the left at the end of the main path. On either side were large tombs and monuments, interspersed with yew trees, whose formal conical shape had long been abandoned. A stone angel stood on top of a sarcophagus decorated with stone rosettes. His wings were unfurled, ready to fly. In one hand he held a sword. In the other a shield. His hair curled softly around his face, but his nose was chipped. Such a pity, Margaret thought. It made him look like an illustration from one of her medical books showing the effect of syphilis on the nasal cartilage. Her father would have laughed at the association. Suddenly she missed him so much that she felt breathless, a pain circling her heart.

She stopped to look at the tomb. It was covered with faded inscriptions. She traced the worn lettering with her fingertips. The family name was Purefoy. All seven children and their parents had died within fifteen years of each other. The youngest, named only 'baby boy', had died on the same day as his mother, whose dates of birth and death made her barely thirty-three. What a waste, she thought. These days antibiotics would probably have saved the lot.

The rose had caught her attention. As she picked her way towards it her foot hit something hard and angular. She hesitated for a moment then bent down and scrabbled in the grass. She held in her hand a wrought-iron wreath, acanthus and laurel, tributes for a hero. Further down the path a newly dug grave was a raw gash of colour, the heaped earth covered with wreaths of carnations and lilies. One spelt out the word 'Mam' in pink and white. She tried not to think of what lay beneath but the images came unbidden.

'Help me, help me, please.'

Margaret turned quickly. Catherine was standing with both hands to her face, terror written in her hunched shoulders. A marmalade cat, dishevelled, neglected, his coat staring and matted, was in front of her on the path, seated, unmoving. He miaowed, a long desolate sob, then as Margaret clapped her hands and shouted he slunk behind a tussock of dry grass.

Margaret took her mother's hand and led her on, in the direction the caretaker had suggested. They walked slowly, stopping from time to time to check the names inscribed on the headstones.

'I know this place.' Catherine looked at her, lucid again. 'I remember,'

John's grave was at the end of a row. His headstone was a large slab of white marble. John Patrick McKenna, 1910–1990 it said, and below, Beloved husband of Catherine. Rest in Peace in the Arms of the Lord. Beside him were the graves of his parents, Margaret and Thomas, and his two brothers, Michael and Eamonn. A large evergreen oak spread its dark green branches over the graves. It was cool and dark here. A small breeze kicked up a miniature tornado of dust, and stirred Catherine's thinning hair. Nearby a blackbird, perched in a crabbed weeping wych elm, sang.

'Do you hear that, Maggie?' John pointed to the bird. 'He's practising. He's doing his scales. He must be giving a big concert tonight in the blackbirds' favourite theatre. They'll all be there, the spotty thrushes, the bossy sparrows, the crows in their best suits, and even the tiny little wren who never has anything decent to wear.'

'Can we go too, Daddy?'

'No, I don't think so. We're too big and fat to fit in. But if we keep very still we'll hear all the best bits right where we are.'

She couldn't remember why they had come here. But she remembered that they had brought flowers, a bunch of red roses. It had begun to rain. Slowly, first little spatterings of water, then big drops that made dark patches on her white blouse. John took off his jacket and held it over his head. He pulled her in underneath close by his side. The grass had just been cut, and was lying in loose cocks everywhere. She wanted to run and kick her feet through the piles, the way she would have done at home, but it didn't seem right, not here, with all the dead people lying just under the ground.

'What does it feel like to be dead, Daddy?' she asked.

'Oh, sort of tired, sleepy. Like when you've been down on the beach all day, swimming, and you come home and have your tea and then I make you a big cup of cocoa and when you get into bed I come to read you a story. And you can't keep your eyes open. That's what it feels like to be dead. But, of course,' he stopped and looked down at her, 'of course, I don't really know. Because guess what?'

'What?'

'I'm not dead,', and he pulled away from her, twirling around, miming an umbrella above his head, and began to dance up the path.

'Mother.'

'Yes?'

'Were you with Daddy when he died?'

'Of course I was.'

'Did he say anything about me?'

'It was very sudden. He just collapsed, at home, after dinner. He was lucky, he didn't have pain.' And she began to cry, little girl's tears dropping down her cheeks.

Margaret put her arm around Catherine's thin shoulders and drew her close. She kissed the top of her head, and stroked one frail arm as they walked slowly back to the car. She had stopped blaming her for her indifference, her coldness, her lack of love. Her father had been forty when she was born. Her mother was thirty. Catherine had told her once, in a fit of rage, that she had never wanted her. I would, she screamed, have got rid of you if I could. But there was no way. There was no doctor here who would do it. I tried, I truly tried. There was one man I went to. I offered him money. But he said no. I made myself sick having you. I hated the sight of my body, fat, swollen, ugly. And it was worse when you were born. I watched the way you took your father's love from me. You took his gaze from me too, I watched him when you came into a room. His eyes followed you everywhere.

She had been so scared that she would feel that way about Mary, her own daughter. That she would resent her, hate her, be jealous. That she would feel she was a parasite, feeding off her own life's blood. And it was such a relief that it wasn't like that when she was born. It was love, pure and simple and unqualified. She had told Mary that there were no 'buts', no 'maybes' in her love. No matter what. Mary had just laughed and kissed her, and buried her head in the hollow of her shoulder. Silly Mummy, how else could it be? she had said. And Margaret was so grateful that her daughter would never know the terror of the other way.

Beside her the old woman was still sobbing. 'I want to go home,' she cried. And Margaret soothed her, and shushed her, and tucked her into the car, wrapping the soft shawl around her arms as if she was swaddling a baby. And didn't look at the other car, the one with the silvered windows, that was parked beside them. And didn't notice the man sitting, reading a book, resting it against the steering wheel. The man with the fair hair who lifted his eyes as they came through the gate, and watched behind his dark glasses.

17

The address book lay on the passenger seat beside him. He picked it up and looked at the cover. Flowers, fruit, foliage and birds entwined in a repeating pattern of muted blues, reds, ochres, dark greens. Thrushes with sharply defined speckles of colour on their breasts held strawberries in their beaks. He turned it over. The blurb on the back said, 'Strawberry Thief, Chintz 1883, designed by William Morris'. Jimmy knew he recognized it. He remembered his mother's hands, holding a tapestry needle, clumsily stabbing at the canvas. The pattern book with all the William Morris drawings lay on the hearthrug with the bag of brilliantly-coloured wools. Soon abandoned like so many of her crazes. Passed on to Molly to take to school for her craft classes.

He sat in the car and turned over the pages. Every letter had its corresponding flower decoration. Acanthus, Bachelor's Buttons, Columbines, Daisies, each one prettier than the one before. Childlike writing straggled over and under the narrow lines. On the page for M, written in adult script was 'Catherine McKenna, where Margaret and Mary Mitchell are staying in Ireland', and an address and telephone number. And under that again, in the writing he now knew to be Mary's, 'Our home from home, until we go home again, boo hoo.'

He looked at his watch. He was parked outside the Shelbourne Hotel. His passengers today were a wealthy American couple. He was to take them shopping, then drive out to Wicklow, through Avondale, up through the Vale of Clara to Glendalough, then home by Powerscourt Waterfall, in time for dinner at Patrick Guilbaud's. He had a cool box packed in the boot, with a couple of bottles of champagne, and brown bread, smoked salmon, picnic bits and pieces. He looked at his watch. He had been booked for 10 a.m.

sharp. It was now 10.22. He shifted uncomfortably on the leather front seat. Sunlight bounced off the car's polished bonnet. The air was heavy with petrol fumes from the traffic, which flowed and stopped, flowed and stopped, around Stephen's Green and down Baggot Street. Already it was very hot. The weather forecast had said maximum temperatures of twenty-four degrees, and it must be close to that now.

He was wearing his full uniform. Crisp white shirt, dark jacket and trousers, and peaked cap. He had got up half an hour earlier this morning to get it all ready, standing in his underpants in his little kitchen, ironing his shirt, then pressing the creases in his trousers with a damp cloth. Nice smell, the steam rising from the material, reminded him of freshly baked bread from the oven.

He drummed his fingers on the steering wheel, then pushed the buttons on his radio, flicking from station to station. He had heard the news a couple of times this morning. Nothing more about Mary. In one way he was pleased, in another disappointed. It had been such a strange feeling when he had heard the news items about her, and seen her photograph all over the papers. His first reaction was that it was an intrusion, a violation, of his privacy, and hers. And then as he had listened to the speculation about who might have done this 'terrible crime' he felt a certain sense of satisfaction. There was excitement in the voices of the reporters. He watched them on television, listened to them on the radio. Some of them were young, his age, but they wouldn't have been able to do what he had done.

He slipped the address book into his pocket and opened the car door. He slid through the hotel's revolving door, into the cool of the lobby. He walked quickly past the porter's desk and round to the public phones. He pulled a card out of his pocket and stepped into the dark of the booth. He punched in the number. As the electronic tone burbled in his ear he thought of its corresponding ring pulsating through the quiet house. He could see it now, the faded red door and peeling paint around the bay windows. The rusting wrought iron of the gate. The yellow rose, which climbed along and over the front wall. He had picked a bud to press between a stack of books, to preserve, to keep.

Where might she be? What might she be doing? Sitting with her mother, or in the kitchen making coffee. In the garden, fiddling about, as Mary described it, lying down with her nose in a book. She will, he knew be thinking about me.

'Hallo?' The voice was questioning. He didn't answer.

'Is that you?'

He let out his breath slowly.

'I can hear you. I know what you're thinking.'

No you don't, he responded silently.

'Speak to me, please. Tell me who you are.'

His hands were slippery with sweat. His breath came from his throat in gasps.

'I'm trying to imagine who you are, what you are. What kind of a thing you are.'

He closed his eyes, the blood rushing through his veins like rain in a storm drain.

'You're not a human thing, are you? Not a person like me or my daughter. You're some kind of a disgusting beast that lives in the dark, aren't you? Ugly, dirty, revolting.'

The hairs stood up on the backs of his hands, and his blood surged. He rocked slowly backwards and forwards.

'Was she easy to kill?'

He opened his mouth. He wanted to speak, but no words would come out.

'And what did she say, before she died? I want to know. Tell me.'

Jimmy heard her scream then, no words, just noise. He shoved his fist in between his teeth, again that indescribable feeling of power and pleasure. Then there was silence. No, he wanted to shout. Come back, don't leave me. But instead he slammed down the receiver and stumbled out and into the men's toilets.

They were waiting for him beside the car when he walked back into the sunshine. A mismatched couple. The man looked like he was in his fifties. He introduced himself as Rod. His hair was white and long but pulled back from a domed balding forehead in a ponytail. His skin was very brown and wrinkled. Black-rimmed glasses with tinted lenses obscured the top half of his face, exaggerating the power of his fleshy mouth. He was wearing an expensive grey tracksuit, which fitted snugly over his barrel chest. Jimmy watched them in the rear-view mirror. The woman's name was Liza. She, too, wore dark glasses. Her hair was short and silver blonde. She wore pink Lycra leggings and a short pink top, which showed off her brown stomach. And a gold chain looped around her neck which slithered against her skin as she moved.

They sat close together in the back of the

149

car. The man's hands were large and finely formed. One of them played with the knobs and buttons on the inside of the door. The other fiddled, smoothed, pinched and caressed the woman's hair and skin. Jimmy watched the long, manicured fingers resting on her shoulder, dangling down, just above her nipple. He tried to keep his concentration on the road. He couldn't see where her hands were. He watched the man's mouth, the thick lips parting with pleasure.

Skip the shopping, Rod had said. So he headed out along the Bray Road, keeping his foot on the accelerator. Occasionally the man would lean forward and ask a question, nothing demanding, just the names of villages, hills, rivers. When they passed the signpost for Avondale, he said, 'Oh, yeah, right, Parnell,' and began to whisper in the girl's little ear. Jimmy watched his pale pink tongue flicking, probing, the way she turned her body into his. He wondered. Should he? Could he? He could veer off the main road. They wouldn't notice. They wouldn't know until it was too late. He could fake a flat tyre. He could open the boot, take out the jack.

'Hey.' Rod was tapping him on the shoulder.

150

'Yeah?' He part-turned his head to hear what he was saying.

'Pull over here. This'll do fine.'

He watched them walk into the forest, the girl with a tartan rug slung over her shoulder, the man swinging the cooler by its handle. He waited until he could barely hear the sound of their voices. Then he locked the car and followed, slowly and quietly.

They had stopped only a couple of hundred yards from the road and spread the rug in a small clearing thickly covered with pine needles. Thin shafts of sunlight illuminated the man's white hair, the girl's gold jewellery. Jimmy found himself a comfortable spot on a fallen tree trunk and waited. At first there was only the sound of the champagne cork and laughter. Then there was silence. He crept closer and watched the scene unfold. Without her clothes the girl was extraordinarily beautiful, her breasts paler than the rest of her skin and pink-tipped, and the man, despite his age, was muscled and strong. Jimmy's heart began to beat faster and faster. Keeping time, he thought, with them. He groaned, softly, slowly at first, then, like his pounding heart, faster and faster, as they too groaned, then screamed, calling out to each other, shattering the forest's drowsy peace.

Their brown bodies were wrapped one around the other, arms and legs entwined. He could barely tell them apart. Yes, yes, yes, he wanted to scream out to them, but all he could do was shove one hand into his mouth and stop his cries with his clenched fist. He had never seen as much as this before. Bits and pieces, snatched through windows, or glimpses of couples in parked cars. But this was different. And absolutely complete when he saw that the girl's eyes were open and she was looking across the clearing towards him as she pulled herself up onto the man and arched her body, and offered Jimmy her breasts, and her mouth.

When they got back to the car, their bodies slack and indolent, he was waiting. He opened the back door, and put the remains of their picnic away in the boot. Rod smiled and patted him on the cheek as he handed him a bundle of notes.

'I guess we might as well have a look at this waterfall you people are always talking about,' he said, as he settled himself into the back seat. And as they drove north towards Enniskerry Jimmy watched them again in his rear-view mirror, taking pleasure in their pleasure, and reflecting on chance and happenstance and their part in his life. He had come very close to blowing it today. Planning was the key to success, his father was always telling him. He could see now that he was right. If today he had acted purely out of desire he would have been finished. He had planned Mary. He had taken his time. He had wanted to do it as soon as he met her. The afternoon of the thunderstorm, three weeks ago. He laughed when he thought about it. Talk about heavenly portents. The sky had opened and bolts of lightning had crackled in huge illuminated Ys against the black of the clouds. Swollen raindrops had drilled into the roof of the car. And a girl had held out her thumb to him. She was standing on the kerb, her T-shirt and skirt sticking to her body, her hair in dripping hanks. And she was laughing. He remembered the look of her nipples through the wet cloth, like those hard, crunchy, pointed sweets that kids eat at birthday parties. He had wanted to sink his teeth into them immediately. But he didn't. He gave her a towel to dry her hair. He offered her coffee from the flask he kept in the glove compartment. He brought her home and he asked her for a date.

'Did you enjoy your day?' he asked Liza, as he dropped them back at the hotel. She smiled at him, and nodded towards Rod's broad back.

'Anything to keep him happy,' she said, resting her hand on his for a moment.

'Would you like my phone number?' he asked her quietly.

'Why not?' she replied.

He put his hand in his inside pocket and pulled out a wad of paper. He shuffled through it, looking for one of his business cards.

'Hey, who's this?' She pulled a photograph out of his hand. A woman and a girl.

'My mother and my sister.'

She studied the picture. 'Real cute,' she said, looking from him to the two faces and to him again.

He took the photo from her. Written on the back in a childish hand was 'Me and Mummy, Christmas 1995'. It was creased and crumpled, one corner folded over. She shouldn't have left it loose in her bag like that, lying in the bottom with her lipsticks and her comb and all the other bits and pieces she carried around with her. He was surprised at how messy she was. When he went through it after she was dead he'd found a half-eaten apple smeared all over a battered paperback book. He'd cleaned the brown goo off its cover. William Blake, it said, *Songs of Innocence and Experience*. And inside on the flyleaf was printed, neatly in black ink, 'David Mitchell, London, 1972'.

'My dad's,' she had said. 'His favourite poet. I like him too. Listen to this.' And she had read to him. Not the first time they'd gone out together, but maybe the second.

> *'To see a world in a grain of sand,*
> *And a heaven in a wildflower,*
> *Hold infinity in the palm of your hand,*
> *And eternity in an hour.'*

'Isn't that neat? I love it.'

The photograph should have been in her little album with all the others of her mother and the one of the man with the long hand-some face, and the black curly hair.

'My dad, that's him,' she had said. 'It's so sad that he died before I was born, that I never knew him.'

'I never knew mine either,' he told her, and she kissed him on the mouth and said, 'Well, that's something else we've got in common, isn't it?'

He had gone through the bag looking for her house keys. And in the inside pocket he had found the shell. Suddenly he wanted to

155

hold it up to his ear and listen to the sound of the sea, the faraway sea that she had told him about. 'It's warm,' she said, 'and dark blue and when you lie on your back with your face in the sun and the water lapping up over your ears you think you've died and gone to heaven.'

'Hey, Liza, what's keeping you? I'm getting hungry.' Rod stopped at the revolving door, and beckoned to her, his manner suddenly petulant, impatient. She folded Jimmy's card in two and pushed it into the waistband of her leggings.

'Gotta go,' she whispered. 'Hope you enjoyed yourself today as much as I did.'

If she only knew, he thought. Only knew.

18

McLoughlin stood in the doorway of the long, high-ceilinged room. A bunch of white chrysanthemums hung limply from his right hand. Guilt tugged his face into a dutiful smile and dragged his feet slowly forward. In front of him was a large wooden table and seated around it were six women and two men. White heads were bowed, pink scalps stretched tightly across old bones. Plates covered with cabbage, mashed potatoes and slices of meat were laid out before them, the food congealing into a mess of green, grey and light brown. The smell made saliva trickle into his mouth and his stomach twitch and flutter. He took another step into the room. Sunlight barely made it through the smeared windows. Three 60-watt bulbs suspended over the table did little to help. Their white glass shades were greasy and fly-spattered. A dusty cobweb, long since abandoned, looped from light to light.

No one spoke. A knife scraped across the surface of a plate. A glass was filled and water gulped noisily. A spoon dropped from an arthritic hand and bounced to the floor. A trolley laden with bowls, butter-yellow custard slopping over their rims, pushed through the swing door from the kitchen. A burst of radio chatter followed, competing with the rattle of its uneven wheels. On a bracket high on the room's end wall, a television flashed pictures silently. Children, dark-skinned and dirty, mouthed at the rest of the world. Then a girl, seated on the case of a cello, peeled the yellow wrapper from a chocolate bar and sucked it greedily into her red mouth. McLoughlin ran his tongue around his lips. He could feel the crumbs of sweetness, clinging.

Another sound competed with the bang of the crockery on the wooden table. A trickling, slow and hesitant at first, then more insistent. McLoughlin's eyes found the puddle, spreading out round the red rubber stoppers on the feet of the chair nearest to him. The woman sitting on it began to shift awkwardly, moving her slippered feet out of the wet. She banged her spoon on the table and began to cry. Tears rolled down her white cheeks.

The woman next to her got up, slowly, pushing herself to standing with her stick. McLoughlin went forward, holding out his hand to her. She took it, grasping his fingers as strongly as her twisted joints would allow, and pulled herself upright, planting her feet carefully. He leaned forward and brushed her cheek, still soft, with his lips. Close to, her skin smelt of Chanel No. 5, keeping at bay the stench of cabbage and urine.

'Come on,' she said, 'let's go somewhere we can smoke.'

'What a surprise. I thought you'd be far too busy to come and see me for weeks. Even more weeks than usual.' She watched closely while he fitted a Sweet Afton into her amber cigarette holder. He placed one end in her mouth and held a light to the other. She sucked hard, until it glowed a satisfying red. As she exhaled, yellow smoke from her lungs mixed with the pale grey, which curled and floated like scraps of water vapour up and around her head. She took the holder from her mouth with a hand that trembled. For a moment he thought the cigarette was going to end up on her lap, but she managed to hold on to it with the tips of her fingers. Then she put it back between her lips and drew the smoke deeply into her lungs again.

Cigarettes and his mother. Never the one without the other. Wherever she went through the house she was preceded by a series of ashtrays and followed by a collection of butts. He'd tried to get her to give them up, but he supposed now there was no point. They were her one real pleasure.

'You're looking well,' he said.

'Really?'

'How's the pain?'

'The pain is the pain. It doesn't change.'

'I thought the doctor was going to try some new drug or other.'

'Michael,' she tapped the ash onto the floor, 'I don't know what other old woman you've been visiting, but I've told you a million times, there is no new drug for me and my arthritis. Now,' she leaned back in her chair, 'do me a favour. Tell me something about the world outside. Please.'

He leaned towards her and carefully unbuttoned her grey cardigan. He smoothed the wool down and began to fasten the buttons again, making sure that each fitted neatly into the hole opposite.

'There,' he lined up the two edges of ribbing, 'that's better. Whoever dressed you this morning wasn't looking at what they were doing.'

'For a change,' she snapped, pushing him away.

He put his hand in his pocket and pulled out a naggin of Paddy. He poured a large tot into her bedside glass and picked up the carafe of water.

'I'll have it without,' she said, as he carefully placed the whiskey between her two disfigured fists.

'You don't have to live here, Mam. You could come and stay with me,' he said.

'For God's sake.' Her lip curled incredulously. 'You. You must be kidding. What you

160

really mean is live with Janey. You're never at home. And you know how she would just love to have me to look after.' She drank deeply from her glass and nodded at him for a refill.

'Well, if not me then what about Clare? She'd have you.'

'I don't want to live in London. I don't want to be "had" by you or your sister. At least here I get a minimum of pity every day. Now, will you either shut up or talk about something that's a bit more interesting than me and my bloody illness?'

They sat in silence. He watched her over the rim of his glass. She must be in her mid-seventies, he thought. Roughly the same age as Catherine McKenna. Not that she'd ever tell him exactly how old she was. But while the McKenna woman was tiny and frail, as insubstantial as a dandelion gone to seed, his mother had got bigger as she got older. Once she had been strong and solid. Now her fat was soft and flabby, her breasts pendulous under the shapeless woollen sweater. Her legs were swollen too, her ankles falling out over her black-laced shoes. But she still had the same beautiful brown eyes, and thick hair, pure white, caught up in an elegant pleat at the back of her head.

'Who does your hair, Mam? It's lovely.'

'A gorgeous young nurse. New. Very sweet. She's mad to meet you. We saw you on the news last night.'

'Oh, yeah?'

'So, tell me. Who did it?'

'Your guess is as good as mine, I'm afraid. We haven't a clue.'

'Ah. I was wondering.'

'What?'

'Why the visit.'

He laughed. 'Yeah, you're right. Propitiation of the gods, isn't that it? One good turn deserves another.'

'And have you, what's the saying, "rounded up all the usual suspects"? Your father always did that. A good beating and you'd be amazed what you'd get. That's what he'd say.' And it was her turn to laugh.

He filled her glass again, noticing the way the stiffness had gone out of her jaw, the tension had seeped from her shoulders as the whiskey did its job.

'Yeah, well, things were a bit easier in his day. Not nearly as many rules and regulations, safeguards for people's civil liberties.'

'Civil liberties. That's a joke. What about the victim's civil liberties, the victim's rights? Eh? Tell me that.'

He took a deep swallow from his glass.

'It's unbelievable. I sit here day after day, listening to the radio, watching the television, and all I hear, from *Morning Ireland* until the last news bulletin of the night, is excuses. What about some action? Remember de Valera, how he dealt with the IRA in the forties?'

'Hang on a minute, Mammy. Times are different now.'

'Different? Really? All that's different is the response. The killing and the maiming in the name of a united Ireland still goes on. And what about all the rapists, the child molesters, the wife beaters, the drug addicts, the vigilantes? Do you know what I have, Michael? I have what they call, nowadays, compassion fatigue. I'm fed up to the back teeth with the way the weak are terrorized by the strong. I'm sick of watching everyone fall over backwards to help the criminals and do absolutely nothing for those who have been hurt and abused. Do you know they brought a woman in here the other day? Eighty-two years old. Older than me. She was raped in her own home by some little bastard with a syringe. Raped, beaten, terrorized. She'd been well able to manage on her own up until that. But now she's had it. She lies in her bed crying, night and day. What about her rights? But of course it's not "politically correct" to say that, is it? Not among all you younger people.'

'Actually, Mam, I met a woman, a "younger" woman, the other day who agrees absolutely with you.'

'Oh, yes?'

'Yeah. The dead girl's mother. Margaret Mitchell. A real toughie.'

'Is she? We saw her on the news too. She didn't look tough. Beautiful, I thought. But destroyed.'

'Not yet she isn't.'

'And what about you?'

'Don't worry about me, I'm grand.'

She looked carefully at him. Her gaze was knowing. It made him feel like a ten-year-old again. A naughty ten-year-old. Caught with his hand in her purse.

'You were lucky, you know, to get away with it. In your father's day you'd have been transferred somewhere cold and remote with only a handful of sheep for company.'

He looked at his shoes. They needed a polish. They were good leather. Brown brogues. Expensive. But worth it, he always thought, to spend money on clothes. He poured the end of the bottle into his glass.

He had blamed the drink for what had happened. The affair. He shouldn't have messed around at work. Not with a girl who was his junior and was married. To another guard. There had been a scandal. He was out of order. They'd held an inquiry. He had thought he would be busted. Lose his job. He checked himself into an alcohol rehabilitation clinic for six weeks. It got him out of the way until the gossip died down. Except that it never really had. He was still suspect. That's why he needed a good result in this case. To redeem himself. To show that he was a good guy. That he was on the right side.

He looked at his mother. She was tired now. Her face was grey and sweaty. She tried to behave as she always had. In control, at the centre. As she was when his father was alive. The household revolving around her. But all that had ended the day he died. Shot in the head during a bank robbery. In the main street in Dundrum. Everyone said he was a hero, but he should have stayed out of it. She brought home the tricolour from his coffin. Kept it with his uniform in the cupboard in the bedroom. But nothing was ever the same again after that day. For any of them. Ever again.

19

Six o'clock in the morning. Thursday, 17 August. Midsummer long past and the northern hemisphere inching away from the sun.

It had been growing lighter for the last couple of hours. The sky was the colour of a homing pigeon's wing, shades of grey overlapping, light trapped between layers of cloud as the bird's feathers trap air. The sun hung just to the east of the Kish Bank. It was due to rise at six minutes past six. The Fraser Bank and the Muglins would feel its warmth first. Then it would spread, slowly and steadily, over Sandycove, across Scotsman's Bay, setting the mica in the granite of the East Pier a-sparkle, as it began its measured track across the country. Yellowing fields of wheat and barley, grey lakes with glinting metallic waves, mountains of purple and blue, silver stone pavements all turning on their axis towards the sun.

At six in the morning it was already warm. Throughout the city, sleepers lay with arms and legs splayed, bedclothes scattered. Skin against skin was damp and clinging. Light pushed through the curtains and blinds left open to make the most of the night air. A cat paused on a doorstep, a mouse limp in its mouth. A robin circled, its tet-tet-tet a shrill proprietorial proclamation, before settling on a garden fence. In ponds and streams water lilies' pink and white buds, mitred like the nose-cones of rockets, waited for the first rays of sunlight, their cue to open. A hand reached out to a radio, then fell back limp. A burst of music, the brisk chatter of the news headlines and finally the weather. It will continue dry with mainly sunny skies. Light, occasionally moderate, south-west winds and becoming very warm with maximum afternoon temperatures of twenty to twenty-six degrees.

Jimmy lay on his side. His cheek rested against a ragged teddy bear. Both hands were buried between his legs. His eyelids fluttered, stopped, fluttered again, his eyeballs rotating and rolling from side to side, following the pictures that played across the fine skin. He opened his mouth and grunted out a couple of syllables. Sweat beaded his forehead. His top jaw clamped down on the bottom jaw, grinding tooth upon tooth.

'Aaagh.' The cry burst out of him. He rolled over on his stomach. His breathing was slow and deliberate. Muscles softened and released as his body relaxed. The teddy bear dropped onto the floor beside the bed. Its brown eyes stared at the ceiling. A fly landed on its button nose and perched, cleaning its proboscis with its feet. The bed creaked as Jimmy rolled over again. The fly tensed. Its movements ceased. Then it fluttered its transparent wings and rose, circling around the bed before heading for the open window.

McLoughlin's eyes opened slowly. The alarm had just gone off. Beside him Janey snored softly. He felt as if he hadn't slept at all. His mouth was filled with acid and his eyes with grit. Fragments of dreams stayed with him. He ran his tongue around his bottom teeth. Some time in the night he had woken in panic. His teeth were crumbling, shards of enamel sticking to his tongue. He tasted the metal of his fillings and gagged.

Now he sat up and took a mouthful of water from the glass on the bedside table. It was stale and tepid. He swished the water around his mouth, checking that there were no gaps, and spat it back into the glass.

Janey stirred and turned towards him. She was wearing her usual T-shirt and cotton leggings. Her breasts sagged against the faded cotton. As her head slumped sideways on the pillow he noticed that her hair was thinning around the crown. He suddenly felt sorry for her. She hadn't aged well. He used to wonder how different things might have been if they had had children. He didn't think about it that way any longer. Mostly he tried not to think about it at all.

He got out of bed and walked through the house onto the terrace, picking up a pair of binoculars on the way. The city sloped beneath him towards the boundary of the bay. Sunlight sparked off the bonnets and windscreens of the hundreds of cars already beginning to crawl towards the centre. He sat down on the wooden bench and scanned the view. In a garden a few hundred yards away a woman was hanging washing on a line. He fiddled with the focus to get a better view. She was young, probably in her twenties. Her hair was short and blonde, unbrushed. A cigarette drooped from her mouth. She worked methodically. Children's bright T-shirts pinned together, then a row of men's shirts, white and blue. Next, little girls' dresses, hung by their puffed sleeves, and socks in bunches, like overripe fruit. Underwear, bras, black with lace, and an all-in-one kind of thing, like an old-fashioned corset, but without the bones, and finally pants, pale pink and white like scallop shells edged with sea foam. He could feel their softness against his cheek and smell the silk and nylon. I shouldn't be doing this, he thought. But he didn't put the glasses down.

The woman finished her task. She stood for a moment looking around her. She turned towards his gaze. McLoughlin felt a sudden panic, but her face was distracted, expressionless. She flung the cigarette down on the parched lawn and gathered up her plastic laundry basket. The cigarette smouldered, a pale blue ribbon of smoke curling. One slippered foot crashed down, grinding it into the brown grass. Then she disappeared from his view.

McLoughlin got up and went back into the kitchen. He made coffee, strong, and switched on the radio. A familiar voice filled the room. The chief Garda press officer was answering questions about the Mitchell murder. He assured the interviewer that on this, the day of the girl's funeral, the gardaí were confident that an arrest was imminent.

Bullshit, thought McLoughlin. The smooth voice continued. On behalf of the gardaí he wanted to extend his condolences to the young woman's family and to reassure them and the rest of the community, particularly women, that everything that could be done was being done to catch the culprit. And, of course, he appealed to the public to come forward if they had any information, no matter how insignificant it might seem.

Dappled sunlight ebbed and flowed across the black and white tiled floor in the kitchen in the old house in Monkstown. The voice continued, rising and falling. Margaret reached out and yanked the plug from the socket. The voice stopped mid-sentence. She got up from the table and walked down the hallway. She opened the front door. The sky and sea were the palest blue, the merest hint of the colour they would be at midday. She sat down on the granite steps, pulling her dressing gown around her. She had stayed awake all night, keeping vigil. Mary's body lay half a mile away in the church. It had been taken there yesterday at five o'clock. The coffin had been closed at four-thirty. Margaret had kissed her daughter over and over again. She had gently combed what remained of her curls, carefully shaping them around her bruised and battered face. She had talked softly to her, explaining what would happen next. She told her about the graveyard and her grandfather who would be near. Then she had taken Mary's hands in hers, and turned them over, examining each palm, tracing the life-line, looking for signs.

How could I not have known? she thought. I should have known. I should have known something. She slid her index finger along Mary's right palm, folding her limp fist over it, willing her to cling, to latch on the way she had when she was a newborn. She remembered. Lying stiffly in a high hospital bed in London. Her stitches were tight. She felt as if she would never walk easily again, but she knew that already she had begun to heal, her skin renewing itself. They had done an episiotomy just before she had begun to push. The doctor looked up from between her legs. He was wearing small round glasses and thick sideboards crept down his cheeks. He said brusquely, 'Pant, pant hard.' A nurse held the mask over her face and told her to breathe. She felt gloved hands, fiddling, poking, and the sharp sting as the scalpel sliced through her taut perineum. After that it was easier. She gritted her teeth, her fingernails making red crescent moons on the forearm of the nurse who held her up. And at last that sensation. The big fish rippling out in a gush of salty water. She would have done it all again, just for that moment.

'Let me see,' she demanded, and the doctor held the baby up, genitals towards her. She saw the swollen red mound of her vulva and the strength of her legs, bent and kicking, testing the open space after nine months in the muscled womb.

Later when she had been stitched and washed, and the baby swaddled in the hospital's green towelling blankets, Margaret hauled herself out of bed. She took the baby from the scratched metal cradle and laid her out, carefully unwrapping the layers that surrounded her. She observed her movements. She stroked her cheek and watched how her tiny open mouth turned towards the physical contact, seeking the nipple. She ran her finger down the wrinkled sole of her foot, watching the downward curl of the toes. She turned her over and stroked her spine, checking the responses, the way she curled and moved from the pressure. Finally, she put her two large index fingers into the baby's tiny fists and pulled back, waiting to see how well she clung, so tightly that her whole body lifted from the bed, her head falling back.

'You've a perfect baby, a little beauty.' She looked up. A young man was standing at the foot of the bed, her chart in his hand. A small gold cross was pinned to the lapel of his black jacket.

'It's Mrs Mitchell, isn't it?'

She turned back to her task. 'Dr Mitchell, actually.'

He glanced down at her chart. 'Yes, of course, I'm sorry. I'm Father Pat Kinevane, the hospital chaplain.'

She didn't reply.

'I just wanted to let you know that I say mass at ten every morning in the chapel. It's on the ground floor.'

Margaret concentrated on dressing the baby. She fiddled with the nappy pins. They seemed so large and clumsy, so man-made, in comparison with the baby's small exquisite body. As she struggled with the spring her fingers slipped and she pierced her own skin.

'Ah!' She sucked her finger, annoyed.

'Here. Let me.'

He came around beside her and picked up where she had left off. He took the pin from her hand and carefully stuck it through the heavy cotton nappy. He held the baby up with one large hand and gently eased the tiny vest and nightgown over her dark head. He did up the small white buttons and wrapped her tightly in the towelling blanket.

'There. All done.' He held her out to Margaret.

'Thank you, Father. I'm impressed.'

'Nothing to it,' he replied, 'at least, not when you're the eldest of ten. I've wiped more bottoms and changed more nappies in my short life than most women these days will ever get near.'

Margaret sat gingerly on the side of the bed, suddenly conscious of the shortness of her nightie. She pulled it down with one hand and awkwardly cradled the baby to her.

'I take it you're from Dublin,' she said.

'That's right. And you?'

She nodded.

'I understand that your husband died recently.'

She said nothing. Her throat was tight and sore.

'Perhaps you would like to pray.'

'No.' Her voice was harsh. 'I wouldn't.'

The noise of the ward reverberated around them. A radio played loudly. Stevie Wonder singing 'Isn't She Lovely' was punctuated by the clatter of a trolley laden with aluminium teapots and plain white crockery, pushed carelessly by a nurse who bumped against the end of Margaret's bed. She winced at the pain of the stitches. A group of men swung through the glass doors, laden with bunches of flowers and boxes of chocolates, elaborately wrapped. Loud congratulations and cheers were exchanged. The priest jerked his head in the direction of the noise. 'You wouldn't want to be feeling tired with that lot around.'

'Listen.' Margaret reached out and touched his sleeve. 'There is something you could do for me.'

'Yes?'

'I don't have a priest and I'm emigrating to New Zealand in a couple of weeks' time.'

'Yes?'

'Would you baptize the baby for me, here, before I leave the hospital?'

'Well.' He paused, and ran his hand lightly over the baby's downy head. 'Don't you want your family with you?'

'I just want it done. As soon as possible.'

The sign of the cross made with water.

176

The giving of the name, Mary. The bestowing of the blessing.

And now it has come to this. Margaret knelt in the front pew, the coffin covered with flowers just out of reach. The words of the priest guaranteeing protection, the love of God and everlasting life, bounced from the high-panelled ceiling to the worn brown tiles of the aisle. St Margarita's stained-glass look was serene, the lilies in her hand unfaded, untouched by time. The cry of anguish from the mouth of the dying God filled her head.

Eloi, eloi, lama sabachthani? O God, O God, why hast thou forsaken me?

Beside her, Catherine gazed open-mouthed at the altar. Behind her was a throng of the curious. As she left the church she noticed Inspector McLoughlin and Sergeant Finney. They both looked anxious and unhappy. McLoughlin took her hand. His palm was damp. She wiped her hand down her skirt. Most of the people milling around outside the church were strangers. A TV news camera turned its long lens on her, A woman with big teeth and a red suit tried to ask her questions. Men called her name and pointed cameras at her. She turned away, her features rigid. One man in particular caught her attention. His hair was very fair, almost white. When he took his camera away from his face he was handsome. He reminded her of an angel from a Botticelli painting, golden, pure. He looked at her and smiled. It was such an open, joyful expression that she found herself responding. Her face creased into his mirror image. Appalled, she put her hands up over her mouth. How could she smile today of all days? When she looked again he was gone.

I have gazed into the abyss, she said to herself. I have looked and the worst of it is that there is nothing to see.

20

The address was Tritonville Road, Sandymount. The name was Anne Brady. Finney had found her. He had checked the list of the mourners at the funeral. And at last come up with someone other than her mother and her neighbour, who had known Margaret Mitchell, McKenna as she had been, when she was young.

McLoughlin drove slowly down the road

checking the numbers. He stopped outside 186. It was Victorian, two-storey over basement, paved front garden with a boat trailer parked at an angle across it. There was a brass plate below the doorbell on the pale pink front door. Dr Anne Brady, General Practitioner.

She made him coffee, offered him slices of home-made ginger cake. They sat in the kitchen, the door to the garden open, so, she said, she could keep an eye on the children. There were three of them. All girls. Aged six, four and a year. The older two were having a doll's tea party on the grass, while the youngest slept, face down in her playpen.

'How do you find it,' he asked, munching on the cake, 'working and having such young children?'

She shrugged. 'It's made a big difference. I've really cut back on my hours. I take surgery here in the mornings, but I try to get everything done before the girls come home from school.'

'And your husband, what does he do?'

'He's a surgeon. Orthopaedic. Does a lot of sports injuries. Cruciate ligaments, cartilage jobs.'

'Big business, these days.'

'And how. He spends as much time on his

mobile phone as he does in theatre.'

'And was it medicine that brought you together?'

She smiled. 'You could say that. We were students at the same time. Barry was in the year ahead. I seem to remember borrowing a lot of his lecture notes.'

'And Margaret? She was in the same class as you?'

'Inspector,' she leaned over and filled his cup again, 'explain to me again exactly why you want to talk to me about someone I haven't seen for years.'

There was more than one reason. He could tell her that it was customary in a murder investigation to try to learn as much as possible about the victim and the victim's family. They usually did this by interviewing friends, neighbours, colleagues at work, school, college, wherever. But it was a bit difficult with the Mitchells. They hadn't been living in Ireland. Their one close relative, Mrs Catherine McKenna, was extremely ill. So the guards had to try to build up a picture of Margaret and her daughter some other way.

That was what he would tell this pleasant-looking woman, with her short blonde hair, her neat pink shorts, and her spotless pine kitchen. The other reason he would keep to himself, like the contents of the file that had landed on his desk this morning. It was the log of the calls made to the Mitchell phone since Thursday, 10 August. Bertie Lynch had gone through them, checking off the numbers. Most were from the hospice, the doctor, the guards. A couple were from Nellie Walsh, the cleaning lady. Two or three from Father Lonergan in St Patrick's in Monkstown. There were a number of calls from New Zealand. And then there were the rest. All made from public phones scattered around the city centre. She had told the guards of three that had been made to her. She hadn't told them about the tape of her daughter singing the nursery rhyme, and the bizarre one-sided conversation that she had had. With whom? He couldn't begin to understand what was going on in her head. When he showed the log to Finney his response had been brutal and immediate. 'Bang her up in a cell, boss. We'll soon find out what the fuck is going on.' But that wasn't his way. Better to wait and see. Watch and listen.

And then there was his own personal reason for being here, for sitting in the sun, drinking this woman's good coffee and eating her even better cake. He knew the feeling of old. He'd had it before a number of times, but not recently. The desire to use and hear a particular name, to hold it in your mouth, on your tongue. A way of getting in touch, of knowing, of being close.

'So, Margaret Mitchell, née McKenna. When did you first meet her?'

'We went to school together. The Holy Child, Killiney. I can't remember the first time I ever saw her. I must have been five and she'd have been just a little bit older. I got on the train at Blackrock and she got on at Seapoint.'

'And what was she like?'

She rested her chin on her hand for a moment. 'She was always quite something. Even as a very small girl.'

'Pretty?'

'Not just pretty. I think the word is charismatic. In its most powerful and awful sense.'

'So you didn't like her?'

She looked at him with surprise. 'Oh, I did, I was mad about her. Or else I was mad with her. With Margaret it was either one extreme or the other.'

'So she had friends and enemies?'

'Not enemies as such. More like people who felt hurt, or left out, or neglected.

Everyone wanted to be in Margaret's orbit. And if you weren't, well, you felt as if the sun had gone in.'

He pointed to the cake. 'May I? It's delicious.'

'Of course.' She cut him another slice. 'It's the fresh ginger. It makes a big difference.'

'So she did well at school.'

'Star pupil. Prizes all the way. Not just academically either. She was a great swimmer. I'm sure she could have been a champion, but she wasn't interested. She played hockey too, like a demon.'

'Oh?'

Dr Brady smiled, her mouth curving into an engaging half-moon. 'She was wicked, ruthless. I remember saying to her once that her decision to become a doctor must have come from some sense of guilt for all the injuries she caused on the pitch. Actually, she didn't deny it.'

'And did she have boyfriends at school?'

'No. None of us could understand it. She was absolutely gorgeous. Small, delicate-looking, lovely hair and eyes. But not a fella in sight.'

'Until university?'

'Not even then. No one special anyway. She'd go out with the gang, drinking, dancing. And, needless to say, there were always loads of guys around her, but no one in particular. Except the lovely Joe Macken.'

'Oh?'

'Yeah, I'd forgotten about him. He had a huge crush on her. They used to spend quite a lot of time together, but I don't really think she was interested in that way. If you know what I mean.'

McLoughlin took out his notebook. 'Joe Macken, did you say?'

'Yeah, but he doesn't live here any longer. He's in the States, Los Angeles, I think. Plastic surgeon, making a fortune.'

'And how did she do at college?'

Again the smile, and the slight shake of the head. 'Need you ask? Top of the class again. All the lecturers were mad about her and, of course, when we started going into hospital she got on brilliantly there too.'

'Any area in particular?'

'Well, we all thought she'd go for surgery. She had that fantastic concentration, that ability to shut everything else out. Wonderful hands. And, of course, you don't need many, what they call, "interpersonal" skills.'

'Her weak point?'

'Weaker I'd say. She could be wonderfully charming, thoughtful, kind, if she felt like it.'

'And still no romance, no lover?'

'Well, if you're asking me, did she have a sex life? Is that what you're asking?'

Of course, of course he wanted to know. 'Yes, I suppose so.'

'I'm sure she did. We all did. It was in the days before you had to be worried about safe sex, you know. The Pill generation. Sex, drugs and rock and roll.' She giggled. A pretty sound. 'Hard to believe now, isn't it? We're all so bloody respectable.'

'Tell me about her parents. Did you know them?'

'Not well. They were older than the others in our class. She was very close to her father. I met him a few times. He was a lovely man. Very handsome, charming, bright. He always came to any of the dos in school. I remember the Reverend Mother fluttering around him, bringing him extra cups of tea, that sort of thing.'

'And her mother, what about her?'

'She was very good-looking too. My mother always used to comment on her clothes. Handmade suits. Always wore very high heels and lots of makeup. I don't think they got on that well. Margaret didn't really talk about her.'

'So you must have all been surprised when

she disappeared to New Zealand?'

'Not the going away. I never thought she'd stay here, But what did surprise me, really amazed me, was that she went into psychiatry. Of all people. She could have had her pick of the plum areas.'

'And is psychiatry not one of them?'

She looked at him, her eyebrows lifted in surprise. 'Psychiatry? Bloody bottom of the barrel. Messy, difficult, unscientific, hard to quantify results, long-term care, badly funded. Just the kind of thing ambitious young doctors hate.'

'I see.'

'But then I heard. A friend had been over there on a visiting lectureship. Obs and gynae, six-month job. And he came back and told us that she'd become something of a media star. Now, that didn't surprise me. Not one bit. Here, look. I got it out when I heard you were coming.' And she stood up from the table and picked up a newspaper cutting, which had been lying folded on the counter top.

He'd seen it before. It was in one of the pile of faxes that the Auckland police had sent last week. A profile from the *New Zealand Herald*. All about how attitudes to mental health, in particular women's mental health, had changed because of her pioneering work. There was a photograph. Head and shoulders. Smiling, efficient. The perfect embodiment of the successful woman.

'Now,' Dr Brady continued, 'that's more like it. Still the star of the show.'

'And your friend, did he get to see her when he was there?'

She shook her head. 'No. He said he tried a couple of times. She was working for television at the time. Doing a series on women's health. He said he phoned her at work, and eventually got through to her. She was polite, just about, he said. But that was it.'

'Were you surprised?'

'No. Not really. Margaret was always very focused. If you were part of the picture she'd be focused on you too. But if you weren't...' She raised her hands in a gesture of resignation.

'And have you seen her,' he asked, 'since all this happened?'

'Only at the funeral. Of course I tried to speak to her when I heard about Mary. I phoned. But she was abrupt to the point of rudeness. She said she didn't want any visitors. So I wrote to her. I'll wait a week or so, then I'll try again.'

'And you never met her daughter?'

'No. I didn't know she was home until this happened. What was she like? Oh.' She paused, embarrassed. 'Of course. You didn't know her either.'

But it didn't seem like that to him. It was a funny thing, the policeman's intimacy with the victim. He had seen Mary's body from every angle. He knew her physically inside and out. If he'd seen her walking down the street he wouldn't have been surprised. She was alive to him, as much alive as her mother. And she would stay like that until the case was over. That was what made it so difficult when a murder was unsolved. The dead were never buried. Not properly.

He stood and thanked her. The baby had woken and was pulling herself up, reaching over the top of the playpen, her face red and streaked with tears. Her mother bent and picked her up, soothing her, kissing her, making her happy again. She walked him to the front door. He stood for a couple of minutes, talking to the little girl in her mother's arms, tickling her under the chin, playing 'Incy Wincy Spider' up and down her pink towelling suit.

'You're good with children, Inspector

McLoughlin. You must have had practice.'

He stepped back, smoothing down his tie. 'No. I don't have any of my own, I'm afraid.'

'Ah.' She was embarrassed. And a bit anxious. He said a final goodbye and walked down the steps, his feet crunching across the gravel. He looked back at her as he crossed the road to his car. She was still standing in the doorway. She was wondering, the way they all did. What had she told him, what had she said? What meaning did it have for him that it didn't for her? He could have comforted her, told her that she had said nothing he didn't know already. But he would have been lying. So he left it, left her standing in the doorway, the baby on her hip, and that strained and puzzled expression still on her face.

21

The postcard was lying face down on the doormat. Margaret bent to look at it. Her name and address were typed to the right. There was no message on the left. She picked it up. It wasn't made of the usual stiff cardboard. It was flexible and soft in her hands. She turned it over. Her own face stared back at her. Wearing her striped dressing gown. Sitting on the doorstep in the clear blue morning of the day of Mary's funeral. Her hair loose on her shoulders, deep shadows under her eyes, and one long leg sliding through the gown.

She dropped the photograph, sweat breaking out on her fingertips and palms. It floated slowly, caught in the draught from under the hall door. She sat down quickly on the hard-backed chair by the telephone table, her legs feeling strange, as if they weren't quite her own. The cracked leather seat creaked and groaned. Gouts of horsehair, as bristly as wire wool, pushed through the covering and pricked her thighs. Her gaze travelled over the faded Persian rug, the once rich reds and blues dulled further by a thick layer of dust. What is Nellie up to? she thought. Catherine would be appalled if she could see how shabby everything has got since she's been sick.

She bent down again, her fingers trailing across the rug's stipple and sliding onto the slick surface of the photograph. She turned it carefully around on the floor with one finger. It wasn't a bad likeness. Better than a lot of the pictures she'd posed for. Must have been the spontaneity, the fact that she didn't know it was being taken. She was completely herself. No sense of being watched. Unconscious. She turned the photo over and looked closely at the postmark. It had been sent yesterday from the city centre. Baile Átha Cliath it said, and the date 23:08:95. She tried the words, stumbling over the unfamiliar combinations of consonants and vowels. It had been a long time since she had spoken Irish. Once she had been nearly fluent, summers spent learning the language in Connemara, honours in the Leaving Certificate. But it had slipped from her memory, like sand dribbling through a clenched fist, to be replaced by the names, lists, facts, quantities, connections that make up the study of medicine, Sometimes the odd word or phrase would broach the surface of her consciousness. 'An bhfuil cead agam dul go dtí an leithreas?' Or 'Dún an doras, más é do thoile' remembered as a chant, learned by rote, like a prayer said so often that it has lost its meaning.

She picked up the card and turned to walk towards the kitchen. Unbidden the words filled her head, and the music that went with them.

Sinne Fianna Fáil, atá faoi gheall ag Éirinn,
Buíon dár slua, thar toinn do ráinig chugainn,
Faoi mhóid bheith saor, sean tir ár sinsear
  feasta,
Ní fhágfar faoin tirán ná faoin tráill.

Mary had been so surprised the first time she had heard her sing the national anthem. They had been standing on the footpath in Queen Street, Auckland. St Patrick's Day, 1980. It was autumn. It had rained heavily in the morning, but now the sun shone brightly in the slack pools in the road. She had taken Mary into town to buy her new winter shoes. She didn't realize what day it was until the parade began to pass. A ragged collection of floats straggled by. They were decorated with green ribbons, and shamrocks and Kiwis entwined. A large woman with an elaborate red bouffant, her solid white flesh squeezed into a green sequined jacket, sang 'If You're Irish Come Into the Parlour' from the back of a truck, throwing handfuls of wilted shamrocks at passers-by. Her accordion accompaniment struggled against the drums and pipes of the band who followed. They droned 'Seán South from Garryowen' with the monotonous intensity of the fundamentally unmusical. Boys played tin whistles and bodhráns and girls marched in step, green boots laced up their calves, short green and orange kilts flicking rigidly from side to side as they moved. A group of women, wearing red flannel skirts with lace blouses and black shawls, posed in a tableau in front of a plywood cut-out of a thatched cottage. The wooden curl of grey smoke from the chimney shook as the lorry struggled over the tramlines and looked as if it might get tangled in the telephone wires that criss-crossed the street. Three rows of men wearing black berets marched with jackboot precision behind the floats. They were holding placards that said 'Brits Out' and 'Free the Prisoners'. Friends waved and saluted from the footpath, gesticulating with their bottles of Guinness and glasses of beer, coloured a sickly pea green. Then another truck with little girls, Mary's age and size, wearing dresses embroidered stiff with shamrocks, harps, Celtic crosses and beasts from the *Book of Kells*. Their ringlets and ribbons jerked up and down as they pranced and danced, and kicked up their skinny little legs, arms stitched to their sides, Mary gasped and screamed to be lifted up, her mouth wide open, desire lighting her eyes, her feet already twitching and arching. As Margaret held her close, Mary's peach-soft cheek caressing her own, she remembered feeling herself swinging up and onto her father's tweed-covered shoulders. The delicious, precarious excitement of it all.

She had twisted her fingers through his hair to keep her balance and drummed her heels against his chest, until he pinched her calf and said, 'Careful, Maggie, not so hard.' And she put her two hands around his forehead to steady herself, and looked over the crowd and down at all the other children who weren't as lucky and didn't have such a lovely daddy who very soon would take her to buy a stick of candy-floss and a big balloon. While all the time Catherine sighed and looked at her watch and said plaintively, 'It's so cold, John,' and 'Haven't you had enough, John?' and 'My bladder, John, it's weak.' And finally, and most effectively, 'You'll overexcite her, John. She'll never sleep tonight.'

'Look, Mummy,' Mary's small hand pinched her cheek, 'what's he doing?' A tiny boy, his uniform black with red and silver trimmings, a mace at least twice his size, twirling and whirling around him, up and over, throwing it, catching it, just before it hit the ground. And behind him a large banner held by two older boys, green and silver shamrocks, and in old Irish script, 'The Takapuna Celtic Silver Band'. Seven rows of instruments, the onlookers' faces reflected, distorted in their shiny surfaces. Tubas, trombones, trumpets, saxophones, clarinets and the drums, small round snares played by boys as small and tense as their instruments, their sticks drilling holes in the tight leather lids, and the big bass drums, huge sides vibrating, slowly, loosely, boo-oom, boo-oom, boo-oom. As each row passed in turn, the tune came and went, melody separated from harmony, followed by rhythm. And then she recognized it for what it was. Instantly the words formed in her head, and she stood straight, in spite of herself, feet together, head back and up, one hand holding Mary, the other stiffly by her side. And a sudden gagging homesickness, a longing that took her twelve thousand miles away, across the warm blue of the South Pacific, to the cold grey-green of the Irish Sea. To where? Home?

'What's that, what's that?' Mary had yelled, pulling Margaret's hair to get her attention, and putting her two small hands on both of Margaret's cheeks to turn her face around to her own. 'Tell me.' And later when she had worn herself out with leaping and jumping and twirling, and practising 'madra' and 'bainne' and 'fír' and 'mná', she demanded and whined and sobbed and sucked her thumb until Margaret gave in and found out where the dancing classes were held. The man who answered the phone in the Irish Centre had greeted her with a 'Top of the morning'.

'What?' she said. He repeated the greeting, unaffected by her incredulity.

'Your name's on the mailing list, mavourneen,' he assured her. 'You'll never be homesick again.'

Margaret dropped the photograph on the kitchen table. She opened the middle drawer in the dresser and took out a small paper folder. She emptied its contents and spread them in a circle. Mary in her dancing costume, toes pointed, arms by her side, looked up at her. A toy doll, not a child. Her face regulation solemn, her curls tied with green ribbons.

'Wasn't I cute?' she had said, when she found the pictures in the kitchen in a pile of old gas bills. 'Should I have stuck to the Irish dancing? What do you reckon, Ma?'

'Don't call me Ma,' Margaret had answered

from behind the *Irish Times*. Then she looked at her over the paper and said, 'Do you remember your teacher, Mrs Curtin?'

'Kind of.'

'Remember,' Margaret persisted. 'She had a little girl the same age as you. She used to come and play sometimes, and sometimes she'd stay with us.' When her mother couldn't go out until the bruises on her face faded. When her mother couldn't stand it any longer and had run away to stay with her sister in Wellington. When her mother overdosed on Valium, and went to hospital to be pumped out.

'What happened to her? My teacher. She died, didn't she?'

The coroner's verdict was death by drowning. Accidental. But there had been no accident about it. She had walked out of her front door and down the quiet road to the beach. And then she just kept walking. Into the sea, out of her depth until the weight of her clothes and her waterlogged lungs pulled her under.

Poor Ellie Curtin. Pretty, frail Ellie Curtin. The beginning of Margaret's crusade. She wrote her first book about her. She owed her, skinny little Ellie Curtin.

The first time she had come to Margaret's

front door, her nose smashed. Margaret had brought her in and cleaned her cuts and bruises, and said to her, 'Leave him. You're crazy to stay. Come here, with me. Bring the kids. I've plenty of room.'

But Ellie just sat on the sofa, her arms crossed, rocking backwards and forwards, the tears burning the raw skin on her face, and said, 'I can't. You don't understand. I love him.'

And she had seen them a couple of months later, Ellie and Mick, and the four kids, on the beach. One Sunday. A picnic basket and a cooler of beer. The kids making sandcastles and playing rounders, and Ellie and Mick lying on a blanket, their arms around each other, their legs entwined. She had sat up and watched them, jealousy burning a hole in her stomach, until she couldn't bear it any longer and she had called Mary and walked along the beach, as far away from them as she could. And had come home later that day, and got drunk herself, sitting on her own on the verandah, watching the stars. Until the doorbell rang, and it was Ellie, screaming, holding her side. And underneath her dress, a burn where he had held the iron to her skin, until it smoked.

Ellie had taught her about love, and

dependency, and cruelty and desire. Taught her everything she knew, and died for it.

Now Margaret stood in front of the small rectangular mirror, which hung on the wall by the clock. I look like the same woman that I was three weeks ago, she thought. But this isn't Margaret. This is a changeling. The fairies have stolen away the real Margaret and replaced her with this thing with the same colour hair and eyes, the same mouth and teeth, the same hands and feet. This thing is weak, passive, a victim. This thing is reduced to nothingness by the attentions of a madman. It is the starling that the cat has trapped in a corner. It shrieks and shrieks, its sweet voice transformed into harsh ugliness. This thing will never allow the real Margaret back into its skin. Not unless the real Margaret does something about it.

She walked back up the steps and along the hall. She could hear her mother's voice, faintly, the rise and fall of a conversation. She walked into the room. The blinds were down. The room was dark and cool. Catherine was lying propped up on her pillows. Her eyes were open, and she was looking up, at something, at someone above her. As Margaret watched she smiled, coquettishly, from under her eyelashes. Then she puckered her lips, and held up her arms. 'Now John, now, do it now. I want you now. John. Please, please.' Her head rolled from side to side, her eyes closing, then opening again. She opened her mouth and cried out, her withered body moving underneath the thin quilt.

'Mother.' Margaret stepped back.

Catherine turned her head. Her eyes slid past her, darting around the room, expressions flickering across her face, like the images from the projector playing across the cinema screen. Madness, thought Margaret, is tapping on my shoulder. I should know what to do. I have looked into the eyes of the deranged. I have heard what their voices have said. And I have been the voice of reason, of responsibility, of common sense. But I know nothing. Of life, of death, of good or evil. I am become as sounding brass or a tinkling cymbal.

And then, the phone. Ringing. She picked it up. She waited. The hiss of the tape.

The Lord is my shepherd
I shall not want
He maketh me to lie down in green pastures
He leadeth me beside the still waters
He restoreth my soul;

He leadeth me in the paths of righteousness for
his name's sake.

Her own voice, echoing, distorted by the size
of the church. A cough, the disturbance of
air as the congregation moved, settled itself.
Her own voice. The reading at the funeral.

Yea though I walk through the valley of the
shadow of death
I will fear no evil
Far thou art with me;
thy rod and staff they comfort me.

Lies all lies, no one comforts me.

Thou preparest a table before me in the presence
of mine enemies;
Thou anointest my head with oil;
My cup runneth over

With pain and bile, the smell of vomit and
the taste of bitter aloes on my tongue.

Surely goodness and mercy shall follow me all
the days of my life;
And I will dwell in the house of the Lord for
ever.

There is no room in the house of the Lord for me. Goodness and mercy are anathema now.

And the words repeated, distorted.

I will dwell in the house of the Lord for ever
Dwell in the house of the Lord for ever.
in the house of the Lord for ever.
For ever.

Then silence.

22

The crystal ball revolved slowly, scattering light like handfuls of silver coins over the heads of the dancers packed onto the floor. McLoughlin felt mournful. He had drunk far too much. Depression had set in. He looked around the huge ugly ballroom with a mixture of despair and contempt. Once, he would have been out there lurching from side to side, forcing his unwilling feet into a variety of dance steps. Now he sat, heavily, a half-empty pint glass by his hand, the remains of the turkey and ham dinner cold on his plate. Another retirement do, another set of dreary speeches, tearful reminiscing, drunken confidences. In fifteen years, maybe, it would be his turn. He would sit at the top table, Janey on one side, the Assistant Commissioner on the other. The presentation would be made. They'd find it difficult to know what to give him. He didn't play golf, or make home videos or go on trips to England to follow his favourite football team. They knew sailing was his passion, but they'd hardly come up with enough cash for a boat. And they all knew he was a good cook. He'd made them plates of chips often enough in the station kitchenette. He stifled a laugh. He couldn't see it somehow, the retirement subcommittee in the cookware department of Clery's picking out the latest deep-fat fryer.

He slipped his hand into the inside pocket of his jacket and carefully extracted a cigar. It was a big fat Havana in its own metal tube. He'd wandered into Fox's at the bottom of Grafton Street a couple of days ago to treat himself. Janey didn't approve. He didn't care particularly, but he didn't like it when she harangued him in front of other people. Fortunately at the moment she was deeply engrossed in conversation with the girl Dave Finney had brought along. The noise was too loud for Mc-Loughlin to eavesdrop successfully, but the odd word that drifted his way alerted him that Janey was delivering a lecture on alternative medicine.

He slowly unscrewed the tube and slid the cigar out onto the table. It lay like a thick golden finger, unsullied, perfect against the stained white tablecloth. He touched it gently, rolling it from side to side, then picked it up, holding it against his nose and inhaling deeply. Strange to think of the metamorphosis of scents, from the powerful sweetness of the tobacco plant's flowers to the aromatic spice of the dried leaf. As he was about to put the cigar to his lips he noticed that Janey was watching. She began to lean towards him, her hand tapping the table, her mouth opening to speak. He got up quickly, and pushed his way through the crowd towards the bar.

Familiar faces surrounded him. There were many he knew nearly as well as his own he'd spent that long looking at them over cups of steaming tea and early morning fries in stations like Castleblayney, Elphin, Letterkenny. Some had aged badly, their bald heads sprinkled with brown spots and sweat, bellies falling in heavy folds over their belts. There were a few who still had the leanness and lightness of their youth, the wiry elegance never affected by bad diet, long hours and too many pints. Here and there he spotted casualties. One man in particular who had seen his best friend gunned down by a Provo active service unit. It had been whispered that he had run, crouched behind the car while his mate took the fire. Who could blame him if he hadn't been brave and noble, a guard in the best tradition? A dead hero, like McLoughlin's own father. He wasn't alone. McLoughlin knew that courage, like self-confidence, was an elusive quality. Some days you had it, most days you didn't. He was profoundly relieved that he had never really been tested. He had woken many times, cold sweat sticking to his skin, terror hanging like a muslin curtain around the bed, knowing that the fear was not of the bullet but of the failure to measure up. As he manoeuvred his way through the heaving, shifting mass, nodding to some, ignoring others, he felt the sadness and loneliness of the one who finally knows he doesn't belong. Most of these men were intrinsically good. They did their job, they loved their families and friends, they had their networks of loyalties and responsibilities. They knew who they were and what they wanted. They were the lucky ones.

He leaned his elbows on the bar avoiding the pools of beer and ashtrays overflowing with butts. He found himself a bit of space and lit the cigar, puffing hard to get it going. Thick smoke filled the air around his head. He looked through it to his face reflected in the smudged mirror behind the row of spirits bottles. He was tired, the bags under his light brown eyes heavy, the lines on his forehead scored deep. He raised his glass and drank.

'That's a great smell.'

McLoughlin squinted sideways, then turned in the direction of the voice. 'Hey, Tony. How are you? Where've you been hiding? I didn't see you earlier.'

Tony Heffernan eased his tall body into the small space beside McLoughlin, a pint already in his hand. 'We've only just got here. We drove up from Cork this evening. We're staying over night. Breege wants to see her mother tomorrow. She's in the Mater Hospital.'

'Serious?'

'She's had a stroke, but they say she'll be out in a couple of weeks.'

'Out and in your tender care, I suppose.'

Tony grinned. 'No, thank God. Breege isn't able for the strain.'

McLoughlin looked at his friend, suspiciously. 'You're looking well. Things going OK in Community Relations?'

Again Tony smiled his big cheerful grin. 'Couldn't be better. How about you? Busy, I hear. Is it good?'

'McLoughlin sighed, looking into his pint. 'It's not that great, really.'

'Oh? Having problems?'

McLoughlin lifted his glass. 'Ach. You know the way it is. Everyone wants instant answers. Quick solutions, like TV dramas. Solve the mystery before the final commercial break.'

'Not happening, no?'

'No, I'm afraid not. But let's not talk about it. It'd spoil the evening.'

'Can't be that bad, then.' Tony looked around him. 'I'd forgotten what these things are like. Are we the only people here not talking about football?'

'And hurling and golf handicaps.'

Tony signalled to the barman for the same again. 'How are things with you and Janey?'

McLoughlin shrugged. 'Why do you ask?'

'Just wondering.'

'Well, the answer is same as ever.'

'No way to live, is it?'

Again the shrug.

'Well, Michael, I want you to know. I've made a decision. I'm forty-six. I've had enough.'

'What?'

'I'll tell you the way it is. I get up every morning at half seven. I make breakfast for the kids, and I take them to school. Breege doesn't stir. I get home around six. I make the dinner and clean up. We have to eat either before seven or after eight. Because Breege can't miss *Emmerdale*, *Fair City* and *Coronation Street*. On Mondays we can't eat until after eight thirty, because of *EastEnders*. We never talk, not really, about anything that's to do with us. Instead we have these bizarre, virtual-reality style conversations about pregnancies and affairs and abortions and gangland killings. I've had it, up to here.' He gestured with his hand six inches above his head.

'So she's still taking all the dope?'

He nodded, the gaiety gone, misery turning the corners of his mouth down. 'But I've decided. I'm leaving.'

'So,' McLoughlin chomped on his cigar, 'who is she?'

'What makes you think there's someone else?'

'Come on, Tony, you've been living like this with Breege for the last ten years, at least. I know all about it, remember?'

Tony leaned his head on his hand. 'Her name is Janet Simms. She's a widow.'

'A Protestant widow by the sound of it.'

'Headmistress of St Columba's Church of Ireland National School, just outside the city on the road to Bandon.'

'How d'you meet?'

'I went to give a talk to her sixth class about drug awareness, and it went so well she invited me back to talk to the fourth class about cycling road safety, and then we were running weekend workshops on drug abuse, and she came along, and somehow one thing led to another.'

Christ, I hope you know what you're letting yourself in for, McLoughlin thought, as he swivelled around, watching Breege making her way from table to table, shaking hands with senior officers and their wives, greeting old friends, finally sitting down beside Janey, their heads together, their arms linked.

'You haven't told Breege about this yet?'

'I'm going to tell her tomorrow, when

we're driving back to Cork. After she's seen her mother. Then I'm giving it two weeks to sort everything out. I've already been to a solicitor. It's not going to be easy. Financially it'll be a disaster for a while.'

'And the kids, how will they take it?'

'I'm hoping they might decide to come and live with me. They're old enough to do without their mother. Peadar's going into transition year and Stephen into second. They'll like Janet, I know they will.'

'Well, all I can say is good luck to you. I've never had the guts to go through with it.'

'You've never met the right woman.'

'I dunno; I wonder.'

'Word has it that you've a bit of a crush on the girl's mother, am I right?'

'Jesus, don't talk to me, the gossip machine is in overdrive already.'

'Well, as they say, no smoke.' Tony smiled, putting an arm around McLoughlin's shoulders.

'Actually, I've a bit of a problem there. Any advice would be gratefully received.' And he told him about the phone calls, about the transcripts, about the surveillance he'd set up. 'It's around the clock. I haven't told the boss yet, but he'll know when the overtime bill comes in.'

'It's a gamble. And it could be dangerous.'

'Yeah, but she's made herself a ready bait. She's not co-operating with us. Makes life difficult for everyone.'

Tony grinned. 'Tricky business, watching people. You're never sure you're going to like what you find out, are you?'

McLoughlin caught the barman's eye. He ordered brandy. He looked at his friend. He could see the hope, the energy, the excitement. He envied him.

'And you're sure Breege doesn't know anything about it?'

Tony shook his head. 'Did Janey ever?'

McLoughlin smiled. 'Funnily enough, no.' He picked up the glass of brandy and raised it. 'Let's drink,' he said. 'To passion.'

To the passion that dragged him out onto the dance floor, falling from body to body, refilling his glass endlessly, until he staggered out into the warm summer night, and drove, somehow, from the hotel beside the sea at Killiney Beach, around the coast to Monkstown. To the passion that made him stand in the road, watching the house, dark now, the faintest glow coming through the fanlight above the front door. To the passion that got him to climb, hauling his reluctant belly, carefully and quietly over the wall from the laneway, and creep around the back, to where he could watch her as she stood in the kitchen, drinking a glass of water, then upstairs in the bathroom a shadowy figure against the stained-glass windows and finally through the window of her bedroom, in the soft lamplight as she stood for a moment looking out into the dark before finally pulling the curtains.

He woke the next morning slumped in the front seat of his car. It was parked outside the closed gate. Janey must have shut it when she came in, long before he got home he presumed. His mouth tasted sour and dirty. He craned his neck to look in the rear-view mirror. His lips and tongue were stained berry red. He looked down. His fly was open. He didn't remember driving home, but he did remember, just about, the club he'd gone to, the woman for whom he'd bought the bottle of expensive wine, the fumbling in the street outside. He remembered it just enough to feel sick, disgusted, angry and sad.

To passion, he thought, as he climbed stiffly from behind the wheel, and prepared to face the day.

23

She stood on the doorstep and went through the checklist. Keys, money, what else did she need? A small hand pulled at her skirt. Don't forget, Mummy, your hankie. She felt in her pocket. It was there, folded, ironed, folded again, embroidered with their initials, M.M.

'Maggie, are you off out?'

Nellie stood at the top of the kitchen steps, the broom in her hand.

'Yeah, that's right.'

'Will you be late?'

'I'm not sure, I'll probably be back around six. Can you stay till then?'

The older woman nodded, her double chin shaking. 'Where are you going?'

'Nowhere special. Just into town.'

'And if anyone phones what'll I say?'

'Say I'm not feeling well, that I've gone to bed and can't be disturbed.'

'Fair enough.'

Margaret turned and went into Catherine's room. Her mother was sitting up against the pillows, the television flickering in front of her.

'Mother,' she said, 'I'm going out for a bit, but Nellie is here.'

Catherine didn't move. Margaret bent to kiss her cheek. Catherine pulled away, a fraction, but enough.

I'll remember that, Margaret thought, as she let the heavy door slam behind her. She paused at the top of the steps, conscious of the brightness, of the gleam and glitter of the outside world. She felt suddenly fearful. I don't need to do this, she thought. I could go back inside. Upstairs her bed was waiting, unmade, the quilt lying where she had left it when she crawled out just an hour ago. It would be so easy to take off her shoes and sneak back into the warmth and the dark. Even if she didn't sleep she could lie with her eyes closed. But that wasn't good. To lie in the dark without sleep was to call back all the bad things. The things she had learned, been told, hadn't wanted to know.

She put on her dark glasses, comforted by the protective shield that slid down over her eyes. She scanned the road in front of the house. The car was parked as always four doors away to the left. She walked down the steps, over the cracked and uneven surface of the flagged path and through the creaking wrought-iron gate. Three children came towards her with a black Labrador puppy on a lead. Its paws, too big for the rest of its body, flopped on the ground, malleable like Plasticine. The children pushed past her, talking loudly, quarrelling over whose turn it was to hold the dog. The youngest child, a little boy, straggled behind, trailing a blue and white towel, its edges already grimy. She watched as they crossed the road to the Martello tower and disappeared down the concrete ramp to the sea. Then she turned away and walked along the footpath towards the car. As always it contained two people. There was a woman in the passenger seat. Margaret had never seen her before. She had straight blonde hair with a fringe, and she was wearing a crisp white blouse. From behind her glasses she noticed how their demeanour changed as she approached, how in spite of themselves they straightened up and began to speak to each other very earnestly. Ten yards more and she would turn the corner to go up the metal steps over the railway line and along Seapoint Avenue to Monkstown DART station. She glanced back over her shoulder towards the

215

car. The two heads were facing neatly in front, no sign that they were watching her. But she knew that someone would be waiting when she came out of the narrow alleyway that led from the top of the steps to the main road.

She walked quickly up the stairs, the soft leather of her sandals making barely a sound. How many thousands of times have I left my footprints here? she thought. In rain and in shine, by day and by night, in despair and in elation. As a child and an adult. In sober black lace-ups polished for school, my dark red gabardine flapping in February gales. In platform-soled shoes, strapped around my ankles, skirt so short that anyone coming up behind me could see my knickers. I have run up these steps, taking them two at a time, the sound of the train getting louder by the second, and I have dawdled and dallied, puffing on the last of a cigarette before facing home. I remember necking here. Can't remember who the boy was, but I can still feel the ache of the mark on my neck where he sucked and sucked until the blood stood out, dark red and purple, dots of colour in a pointillist bruise. To be covered up in the house and displayed proudly everywhere else. And the flasher. Penis, white, dribbling from his fly, the moment's wonder then the giggles, 'Did you see that?', the mocking and ridicule. Looking back, the man's shoulders drooped as he turned away. And always the same smell. Piss and rotting leaves. Damp even now in the middle of the summer drought.

She paused again before she stepped out onto the wide footpath. I spy with my little eye, someone, someone, who will it be?

A young man was walking along the other side of the road. His step didn't falter as she turned parallel to him, matching his stride. Surveillance, she thought. That's what this is. Pronounced in the American way, sounding the double ll, as if it was English. She had looked the word up in her father's Oxford dictionary. When she realized she was being watched. From the French, it said, *surveiller* and the Latin *vigilare*. Meaning supervision, close observation, invigilation, specially of suspected persons. And how many of these young men who have had her under 'sir-veylance' have also been voyeurs? Enjoying her ignorance of their existence, her unconscious state of being in the shadow of their consciousness?

She turned down the lane to the DART station. There were footsteps behind her. It was mid-morning, way past the rush hour. She bought her ticket, pushed through the turnstile and walked quickly down the wooden steps to the platform. She counted the number of people waiting. A young woman rocked a crying baby in a buggy. Two teenage girls, twins, she noticed, were lighting cigarettes. Giggling as they manoeuvred the cigarette ends into the single flame. They were identical except for their hair. One was bleached white blonde, the other a natural brown. They still looked like children, despite their tiny skirts, Lycra tops and thick makeup, their faces round and soft.

She felt Mary's cheek against hers, her arm linked through her own, as they sat on this same bench. Mary's long legs stretched out in front, one thong sandal slipping on and off her arched foot. A young man walked past and she made as if to trip him. He smiled and she smiled back, pulling her legs back in under the bench, and whispered into Margaret's ear. She felt the warm breath and heard the words, 'Nice, eh?' and then the giggle and the sidelong glance, and the hand twisting the black curls away from her face.

She leaned back in the sun, ignoring the young man with the rolled-up newspaper who lounged against the end of the shelter. She rested her head against the warm granite, closed her eyes and waited.

McLoughlin was used to waiting. Once, he had added up all the hours that he had spent in cars, in bars, on street corners, on park benches, in chippers and cafés. In bus and railway stations, in hotel foyers, in stinking gents' toilets, and the grand total was something like four weeks for every year he had been in the force. Hours and hours balancing on the cusp between complete boredom and adrenaline-pumping alertness.

They'd got the call at 10.43 just as they were leaving Harcourt Square. He and Finney had been at a meeting with the *Crimeline* people. They were talking about featuring the Mitchell case on next month's show. Apparently Margaret had left the house, heading for the DART station. Brian Conroy had been with her on the train. She'd got off at Lansdowne Road. Stupid arsehole had assumed she was going to Pearse Station and had nearly missed her. Not that he said as much, but McLoughlin could hear it in his 'Fuck it, I nearly blew that one' tone, and his heavy breathing. A lot of these new guys puzzled him. It wasn't that they were stupid.

Far from it. Most of them were, in his opinion, overqualified, with their law degrees and management courses, sweated through by night and on their summer leave. But they lacked imagination. They didn't believe in any of the mysteries of life. Everything was cut and dried. Good and evil were concepts outside their range of knowledge and understanding. Brian Conroy's view of Margaret Mitchell was that she was respectable, middle-class, better-looking than his mother. She had got the DART into town. She was going to get off at Pearse or Tara Station, and go shopping. What else would she do?

McLoughlin reached into the glove compartment and took out his binoculars, They were parked on Wellington Road, just about twenty yards from the intersection with Pembroke Road. According to Conroy, Margaret had gone into number 378, the house with the red door, which was clearly visible from where he was sitting. He trained his glasses on the house. Three storeys over basement. Two windows on the top two floors. One window at hall level. Net curtains covered their lower halves. He scanned the blank glass above. Something was hanging in one of the smaller windows at the top of the house. It looked like a mobile, possibly the kind that hangs over a baby's cot, No sign of any of the occupants. A metal milk-bottle tray with six empty bottles was on the wide front step, beside the old boot-scraper. He couldn't see much of the basement. A straggly box hedge obscured his view. He focused on the front door. Only one bell. Unusual in this street where most of the houses had been in flats for years.

They waited. Another beautiful day. Warm now, hot later, the weather forecast had said. Finney fiddled half-heartedly with the radio and yawned loudly. McLoughlin got out of the car and stretched, then began to pace up and down the wide footpath. He had always thought that Wellington Road was one of the finest in the city. The houses were mostly two-storey, crumbly red brick, built in the second half of the last century, with high ceilings and good plasterwork. A few years ago they were full of cupboard-like bedsits occupied by students. Now most had been restored to their full splendour, front gardens rampant with designer growth. He leaned his cheek against the fraying bark of a cherry tree, part of the avenue planted along both sides of the road. Incredible in spring, pink and white blossom, frothing like a strawberry milkshake.

And then as he turned slowly back towards his car he saw her. Standing on the front step of the house with the red door. A woman beside her, holding a baby in her arms, and as he began to move in her direction she started to run. Down the stone steps, while the other woman first of all tried to restrain her, then stood back, watching until she had disappeared from view up Baggot Street.

'I'll go, I'll stay with her,' McLoughlin shouted back to Finney. 'Stay in touch.' And he waved his radio, as he ran around the corner onto the main road.

She was still walking quickly, and McLoughlin could barely keep up with her, but her cream linen dress was a beacon that led him on through the crowds past Quinsworth, the Waterloo House, the old red-brick hospital, now a drug clinic, whose shallow granite steps were littered with junkies, over Baggot Street Bridge and on towards the city. There was something about the way she moved that attracted him, gave him pleasure. He watched her from the other side of the road. She seemed to glide, negotiating smoothly around anyone or anything that got in her way. He noticed how both men and women responded. Heads turning as she passed, sidelong looks of interest. He watched, engrossed, imagining, then realized that she had stopped, still on the pavement, outside Doheny and Nesbitt's pub. She was standing looking at the window, the wide brass trim sending shards of light back out into the street. Reflecting her imperfectly. As he pulled himself up short a woman walking behind him cannoned straight into his back. He apologized sheepishly, and slunk into the nearest doorway.

Later his notebook said some of it, his memory told it all.

11.30 Sits in the snug in Nesbitt's. Drinks two cups of coffee. Asks the barman for the *Irish Times*. Speaks to him about the weather, the number of tourists in town, etc. (*I sat in the bar, and watched her through the half-open door. When she took off her dark glasses her eyes were swollen.*)

12.30 Bar is beginning to fill up with lunch-time trade. She pays and leaves. (*Looked uneasy, scanned the faces as they came in.*)

12.35 Walks west along Baggot Street, turns north down Merrion Street to Merrion Square. Enters National Gallery. Goes immediately to the Irish section. Stops for eight minutes in front of *Self Portrait* by

Robert Fagan and *The Conjuror* by Nathaniel Hone. Goes to the ladies' toilet. (*Gazed at the paintings as if they could answer questions for her. Seemed to take particular pleasure in Fagan's Italian wife, the French cap of Liberty on her Regency curls, her breasts bare and unadorned. Two French tourists, male, stood beside her. One tried to talk to her, I wanted to intervene, but she took care of them herself.*)

13.15 Leaves National Gallery. Walks west along Clare Street, turns north down Lincoln Place and goes into Trinity College through the Lincoln Gate. Walks as far as College Park. Sits on a bench for fifteen minutes. (*Hot, very hot. She took off her sunglasses and leaned back, her eyes closed. Letting the sun warm her, soothe her. Her legs were splayed out across the grass. Did she sleep? Possibly for a couple of minutes. When she opened her eyes again she looked confused.*)

13.55 Proceeds north through New Square and left Trinity College by the Pearse Street gate. Continues north up Tara Street, across Butt Bridge and up Gardiner Street. Enters Hill 16 pub. Contact Sergeant Finney to tell him of my whereabouts. Ask him to keep in touch. (*She walked like someone possessed. She looked neither to right nor to left. A group of kids begging on the bridge grabbed at her. She pushed them away. She began to run. They pursued her. She lost them in traffic. She stopped for breath. She checked her bag, her purse. She smoothed her hair. Then she turned and walked quickly up Gardener Street. She stood out like a pale narcissus, a beam of light on an overcast day. She crossed Gardiner Street at the Parnell Street/Sheriff Street intersection. She went into Hill 16. She ordered a gin and tonic. I stood outside and craned to see in through the windows. She drank it quickly. Ordered another. Does the barman recognize her? He speaks to her quietly. She smiles, he takes her hand. She squeezes it. I am filled with envy. I look at his ugly nicotine-stained fingers. I want to break them.)*

14.30 Leaves Hill 16. Continues north to Mountjoy Square. Turns on to the south side. Stops outside number 50. The last intact house. Restored by Desmond Guinness and the Georgian Society in the late sixties. Opens the door with a key. Enters house. (*What was she doing there? Did she live in that house? Why didn't I meet her then, know her then? I was working in Store Street when she was a student. I could have bumped into her, late at night. I'd go into Hill 16 sometimes. Funny crowd. Rough bunch. Locals, market traders and a few hippies. Afghan coats. Curly hair, all very pretty. Squatting, 'caretaking', they called it, the old houses. Living rough, I called it. No running water, rats in the basements, who cares about the plasterwork? Could have busted them all for dope, acid, magic mushrooms, but the Super never thought it was worth it. I stood back against the railing that bounded the park. I looked up at the second floor. Metal grilles over the windows. Couldn't see much. She was standing up against the window. Her palms were against the glass. She looked over me. What did she see? Come down here to me. Let me comfort you. Let me hold your sweet body against mine, let your heavy head droop on my shoulders.)*

15.40 Mitchell walks back down Gardiner Street, turns into Parnell Street, crosses O'Connell Street at the Parnell Monument, and continues east along Parnell Street. Enters Conway's pub. Sits at the bar. Drinks gin and tonic. Picks up an *Evening Herald* lying on the bar and reads it. (*She looked tired. Her dress was rumpled, her feet were dusty. Strands of hair escaped from the once neat coil at the nape of her neck. There were shadows under her eyes. She looked towards the dark corner where I was sitting, drinking a pint. Our eyes didn't meet. She shifted her weight on the bar stool. One leg rubbed against the other.*

She lifted her arm to smooth her hair. Her breasts moved underneath the soft material of her dress. She finished her drink, ordered another one. She moved from the bar to a seat from where she could see the television. The channel was SKY or CNN, one of those rolling news bulletins. I looked towards her. Tears were streaming down her face.)

16.45 Mitchell leaves Conway's. Crosses Parnell Street to the Rotunda Hospital. Enters. Sergeant Finney takes over. (*It happened suddenly. She had gone to the ladies'. I had just ordered another pint with a vodka chaser. I was paying the barman when she came back into the bar. She didn't stop, she practically ran out the front door. Hoped to fuck that Finney was outside. I ran out after her, just in time to see her going in through the Rotunda's old front entrance. Finney was behind her, thank God. I followed, along the old tiled corridors, up the stairs beside the lift. One floor, two floors. Women everywhere, swathed in floral dressing gowns, bare legs and fluffy slippers. The smell of babies, sweet, sickly. Nurses, sexy in their crisp white and blue uniforms. What the fuck is she doing here? A nurse tried to stop me. She pointed at the sign. Neo-natal care. I pushed her away. Doors leading off a wide corridor. Doors with glass windows. I peered through each one in* turn. Then I found her. She was standing over an incubator. Tears were falling down her cheeks, and splashing on its plastic lid. Inside a baby lay swaddled in cotton wool, its red face like a mouse from a Beatrix Potter story, peeping out from underneath its soft white bonnet. She sobbed, agony pouring from her body. Then she saw me. Go away, she screamed, pushing me with hands made fists. Haven't you done enough? I stepped back, dumbly, back and back, until I was against the door, while she screamed and screamed. Her pain, her rage. But what could I do? I'd had to ask her. I'd had to tell her. It was my job. I had to go to see her, sit in the garden with her, watch her disintegrate once more with grief and hurt. Tell her that the pathologist had said that Mary had been pregnant. Once. That the signs were there. The slit-like opening to her cervix, the change in pigmentation of her nipples. He couldn't say when. He couldn't say whether she had had an abortion or a miscarriage. But he could say that once she had conceived, and the embryo had become a foetus. How was I to know that she, the girl's own mother, didn't know? That she would turn on me, first of all deny that it was true, say that it couldn't have happened. Then stop and think, and wonder. That she would scream abuse at me, then tell me to go away,

*never to speak to her again, to leave her alone.
Pound on the table with her hands till they were
bruised and swollen.*

*They came, the doctors and the nurses. They
sedated her, laid her down on a bed where the
day before a mother and her newborn had lain.
And I went back to the pub, and finished my
drink.)*

24

*And I will dwell in the house of the Lord for
ever.*

There was something very satisfying about
the word 'dwell', Margaret thought. The
sound of the hard 'd' followed by the soft 'w'
gave it a strange contradictory ring that
appealed to her. It was like biting through
the crust of a crème brûlée and sinking your
teeth into the exquisite sweetness of the egg
custard underneath.

She leaned back against the hard wood of
the pew and put her feet on the low
embroidered kneeling pad. The church was
cool, almost cold in comparison to the hot
sun outside. Like churches in Italy or Spain,

man-made pools of relief against the torment of God's great sun. Around her, along the side aisles and in the small chapels, figures emerged from the shadows to light candles, kneel, sit, bow their heads, occasionally speaking to each other in harsh stage whispers. An old man at the back opened his newspaper, the fresh newsprint crackling loudly. Did my father come here to read the paper in peace and quiet? she wondered. After he retired when he no longer had the comfort of his daily routine. She ran one finger along the tarnished brass plate in front of her.

John Patrick McKenna 1910–1990
R.I.P.

His life had once been precise and ordered. He had liked it that way. She remembered the name-plate on his office in Merrion Street. Seán MacCionnaith, An Rúnaí, written in old Irish script, black gloss on a blue background. She had seen it for the first time on her tenth birthday. He had taken her to work with him that day, midsummer 21 June 1961. As a special treat, he said, because now you've reached double figures you're almost grown-up. They had caught the marmalade-coloured train, the one that came all the way from Rosslare. It was crowded by the time it reached Monkstown with no spare seats. He wedged her between his legs so she wouldn't fall as it shunted and lurched from station to station along the line to Westland Row. Other travellers, men with briefcases and newspapers under their arms, greeted him with varying degrees of familiarity. He introduced her to them, prefacing her name with 'and this is my beautiful ten-year-old daughter'. She smiled but said nothing. When they got out of the train she slipped her hand into his pocket and matched his pace as he walked briskly along Westland Row, past Merrion Hall, with its huge billboard proclaiming, 'I am the Way, the Truth and the Life', and up Merrion Square to his office in Government Buildings. The porter saluted as they pushed through the glass doors and marched along the corridor, its brown linoleum giving back the sharp slap of the soles of their shoes. Outside his office they stopped. Margaret tugged his jacket, pointing at the sign, and giggled. He put his finger to his lips, miming 'shh'. He opened the door. A large black typewriter faced them, and peering over the top was a small middle-aged woman with curly grey hair.

'Miss O'Connor,' he said, 'may I have the pleasure of introducing my daughter Margaret. Today is her tenth birthday.'

The woman stood up and held out a white hand. Margaret took it and squeezed the limp fingers. She looked around, at the piles of papers, the big black telephone with the row of switches on one side, and the shelves of books, bound in green, emblazoned with harps. They went through another door to her father's office. His desk was much larger, with a white blotter in a leather cover, a silver paper-knife, and in a silver frame a photograph of Margaret and Catherine. A portrait of Éamon de Valera hung on one wall, and the other walls were covered with more books. He sat her down in a leather chair in the corner and gave her a pile of newspapers to look at while he busied himself with his phone calls and correspondence. At twelve-thirty precisely doors could be heard opening and shutting all over the building. Miss O'Connor stood at the door and coughed.

'Yes,' he said, without looking up from the page in front of him, 'back at two as usual.' He tidied his papers together and put his pens and pencils in a neat line.

'Now, Margaret, it's lunchtime,' he said, and took her by the hand again. When he opened the door onto the corridor the smell of boiled cabbage surrounded them like a pale green mist. She remembered that she had suddenly felt sick but she had stood in the queue in the canteen, holding her tray and doing what he did. The meat was slabs of grey, cross-hatched with creamy gristle. She pushed it around on her plate until he gave her a disapproving look, then cut it up into tiny portions and forced it into her mouth.

The bones of her buttocks pushed through the cotton of her skirt. She shifted awkwardly on the hard seat. She had lost weight. The standard response to grief, she knew. Inability to sleep, inability to eat. She couldn't remember the last time she had cooked a proper meal. One with a profusion of tastes, a variety of elements, put together with care and attention to detail. Protein and carbohydrate. Vegetables and fruit. Colours and shapes and textures, instruments of pleasure and contentment. She existed now on cups of tea and coffee, scraps of bread, the occasional apple. And alcohol. The blessed balm of forgetfulness. She looked down at her hands clasped loosely in her lap. Her wrists were tiny and fragile. Her wedding ring slipped on her finger. She was pleased. She could understand the euphoria of the hunger striker, slipping in and out of hallucinations as the brain responded to a lack of glucose. She felt an extraordinary desire to deny the physical bounds of the body. Her daughter had moved beyond the confines of flesh and bone. Perhaps she could do the same. The books said that this was a phase she would go through. But she didn't want to leave it behind. She didn't want to be like everyone else who lets go of their pain, who moves from denial to anger and eventually to acceptance. She wanted to cleave her rage to her, feed on it, draw strength from it.

She looked around at the saints in the stained-glass windows and the Stations of the Cross, simple marble bas-reliefs. There were times when she had felt a physical pain as sharp and piercing as the pain of nails through the palms of the hand, through the bones of the foot. There were times when she felt her heart would break, would divide like the leaden heart of the Happy Prince, cracked in the terrible frost. And sometimes it was as if her heart was frozen solid like the heart of the Snow Queen, waiting for the kiss that would melt it, that would release some emotion other than this terrible consuming rage.

The bell of the angelus began to toll above her head. She put her hand in the pocket of her skirt and took out an envelope. Her name was printed on the outside. She knew it was from him. There was no stamp. It had been pushed through the letterbox some time during the night. She lifted up the unsealed flap. Inside were two photographs. She spread them out on the pew beside her and stared at them. One must have been taken on the day of the funeral. She was standing outside the church. Her face was blank with grief. The other was of a hand and a wrist stretched out against a neutral background. It was a right hand. A ring set with a small diamond was on the little finger. And there was a watch on the wrist. Cheeky, cheery Mickey Mouse. She turned the picture round to get a better look at it.

They had been standing in duty-free in Singapore. Margaret had bought perfume for her mother, and a large bottle of Scotch. She was trying to decide whether to buy a rather beautiful pair of pearl earrings. She looked around for Mary to ask her opinion. Her daughter was on the other side of the aisle.

She was handing over money and laughing. 'Mary,' Margaret had called out against the din of the cash registers and the 'Blue Danube' waltzing electronically through the loud speakers. 'Over here. Come and look at these.'

But Mary was only interested in the watch. 'Isn't it just di-vine?' she had cooed, delighted with the way Mickey's oversize hands pointed to the numbers. 'And it ticks,' she had said, holding it up against Margaret's ear. 'Listen.'

Margaret pulled away. 'It won't last,' she said, 'it's a piece of junk.'

'Don't be mean.' Mary pouted melo-dramatically, rubbing the clear plastic face against her T-shirt before strapping it on. 'She's an old spoilsport, isn't she, Mickey?'

Did she ever buy the earrings? She couldn't remember now. She looked again at the watch in the photograph. Mickey's white gloves were raised high above his head, the long arm on top of the short arm, like one of the traffic policemen who stand on all the Singapore roundabouts. Officious little men, waving white sticks, demanding obedience from the cars, motorbikes, buses that swirl around them. The big hand and the little hand together at twelve o'clock.

Showing the time. And the other photograph showing the place. A place and a time to meet? Did the watch say twelve noon, or twelve midnight? She wasn't sure, but the picture of her was in daylight, sunshine. And it was a safe place, a public place. Secure and protected.

The last note of the bell ebbed away. Margaret got up and walked to the back of the church. She stood just inside the porch by the rickety wooden table where the copies of the *Sacred Heart Messenger* were piled neatly. There was a constant stream of people in and out. She looked closely at all the faces as they went past. Who was he? Where was he? But there were no answering glances, no sudden recognition. Impatient now, she stepped outside into the sun. Cars moved slowly up and down from the main Monkstown Road, past the church and southwards to Mountown, Baker's Corner and Dean's Grange. Margaret twisted and turned in both directions, scanning the shoppers and the lunchtime wanderers. Monkstown as always was busy. A woman with two small children came out of the delicatessen holding a large plastic bag. The children had buckets and spades and a shrimping net on an awkwardly long pole. The woman grabbed them by their wrists, dodging cars as she dragged them across the busy road. One of the children fell, sprawling in a noisy, complaining heap. The woman dropped the bag. Oranges rolled in every direction, followed by a packet of sandwiches. The traffic backed up, hooting impatiently. The child got to her feet, sobbing. Hastily her mother tried to gather everything up, scooping child and lunch into her arms and lurching to the safety of the pavement. The traffic moved on, leaving an orange, burst open, pith, flesh and juice smeared on the tar-macadam,

A seagull swooped low towards an over-flowing rubbish bin, hanging, lopsided, from a lamp-post. It grabbed at a piece of bread, tearing it with its hooked beak. Crumbs and crust fell to the footpath. The bird dropped to the ground and picked at it. A dog ran up, barking. The bird hovered, reluctant to abandon its booty, then lifted again, beak open and a harsh cry bursting out. It flew up and up, beating its wings hard, and wheeled and banked away towards the sea, over the pepper-pot spire of the Protestant church across the street. The huge granite building, its twin towers like carved chessmen, the landmark that dominated the main road from the city centre.

Margaret followed the bird's flight with her eyes. Then she looked again at the photograph. Behind her, in the picture, was not this church, St Michael's, where her family had worshipped, where Mary's funeral mass had taken place, but the other one, its turrets looming dark in the bright sunshine.

Of course he would be in that church, empty at midday. Built at a time when there was a huge Protestant population here in this affluent suburb by the sea. Now its congregation was decimated by emigration and indifference.

She hurried down the steps, her heart banging irregularly under her left breast, chiding herself for not having realized before. She was in the wrong church. The traffic was backed up from the lights at the bottom of Monkstown Road. She darted out into the middle, weaving between cars, narrowly missing being hit by a motorist coming from the opposite direction. He blew his horn, waving his fist as he jammed on the brakes. She didn't appear to notice. She ran on, in through the open gate, past the noticeboard listing the times for Sunday Service and Holy Communion; her feet scattering gravel in her haste. When she reached the wooden door, shield-shaped, its handle a ring of brass, she hesitated and caught her breath. She had been given the chance of a reprieve. She could end all this now, decide that she would play no further part. She could go home. Apologize to the guard whom she had eluded so successfully by jumping from the garden wall onto the DART line and sneaking along the embankment to Salthill. She could give up. Step back. Leave it all to McLoughlin to muddle his way through. But that was not what she wanted. She thought of all the times in her life when she had taken the easy way out. She would not add this to the list.

The door creaked and banged back against the inside wall as she pushed it. She stood in the porch. Ahead were double doors, which led into the main body of the church. To the right, she knew, were the winding wooden stairs which would take her up to the gallery. She trembled. Cold, the hairs standing up all over her body to trap her warmth. Cold like Christmas. Darkness, candles, their golden flames wavering in the choir's hands. A boy soprano's squeaky voice.

'Once in Royal Daa-vid's city,
Stood a lowly cattle shed,
Where a mother laid her baby,
In a manger for his bed.
Mary was that mother mild,
Jesus Christ her little child.'

And the choir picking it up, carrying on the story. The service of Nine Lessons and Carols. Every year since she could remember. An act of ecumenism, her father had called it. They sat in the gallery, down at the front so Margaret could giggle and wink at Gillian, the rector's youngest, who slouched in the choir stalls, a reluctant angel, until she opened her mouth to pour forth all the passion of that doomed love. And Margaret had cried as the sweet voices told of prophecies and mystery, stars moving across the infinite blackness, of animals and men gathering to worship and praise. And the most exquisite sadness seized her, and the tears dripped down her cheeks and gathered in the corners of her mouth.

She put one foot on the bottom step. It creaked loudly. She looked up. The stairs turned away from her to the right. The walls were painted a sickly pale pink. She grasped the banister and hauled herself up. She stopped and listened. A car went by playing loud music. The beat pumped out then faded to a low rumble. A bird was singing, repeating over and over again the same two notes. Light filtered through the small stained-glass window on the tiny landing, and spattered across her skirt. Amethyst and gold. Shifting and dancing. A cloud passed across the sun, and the colours vanished. She could smell her own sweat. Bitter, rancid, laden with fear. She felt dizzy and light-headed. She calmed herself with slow deep breaths. Then she continued up the narrow stairs, one foot following obediently the other. The sound of the organ, rich and brown like Christmas cake, filled her ears, and the musty smell her nostrils. Old ladies, her father had said, moth-eaten fur coats, damp, giving off steam in the warmth of the congregation. She reached the top and turned again to the right. The gallery was in front of her. Ten rows of dark oak pews sloping down. At the far end the huge stained-glass window, a mosaic of blues, reds and greens. In front of it the altar, a simple white cloth, a brass cross, a vase filled with white lilies. She walked forward slowly, holding on to the end of each row for support. She reached the front. She looked down, saliva

242

filling her mouth. Below was the wooden pulpit, decorated with carvings of birds and animals. On the other side the lectern in the shape of an eagle, the ceremonial Bible open, in place. She raised her eyes and looked across to the wide gallery on the left. A figure, a man, sitting in the front pew, his legs lolling over the rail, both arms spread wide along the back of the seat. His blond head thrown back. A face she recognized, remembered. A smile that had called out to her. And she remembered her own face. That dreadful day. How her lips had widened, cracked open. And now as she looked across at him she saw his lips were pursed. And she heard that sound. Whistling.

25

McLoughlin opened the door to the interview room and walked in, Finney at his heels. It was a small room, no windows, walls that had recently been painted magnolia, and an off-white ceiling adorned with two long fluorescent tubes. Standard issue for all the new Garda stations, like this one in Blackrock.

There was a small veneered table in the centre. Seated on one side at an oblique angle to the door was a woman detective. Chris Murray was her name. Nice girl, good at her job. Didn't get too excited about some of the shit she had to take. It was she who had phoned an hour earlier. Said she had something that might interest them. Something about the Mitchell case. And the phone call couldn't have come at a more opportune moment. McLoughlin had just been in with his boss. Finucane had waved this morning's *Irish Times* under his nose, and snarled about lack of results, bad press, 'All those fucking feminist journalists ranting on about how the streets aren't safe for women. And what have you been up to, Michael? How have you been spending your day? Between pints, that is? You've twenty men working on this case. Guards and sergeants. Detectives and uniforms. How many man-hours so far? And with what result, eh? Tell me that. You'd want to watch it. There's a queue of people waiting to have your job.'

He had told Finney all about it as they drove through Tallaght. He was never sure how wise it was to confide in a subordinate.

On reflection he knew it wasn't wise at all, but he was so angry he had to get it off his chest.

'Well, are you surprised?' Finney asked him.

'What do you mean, surprised?'

'Aren't he and Declan Hickey good mates? Don't they play golf together, regularly every Saturday afternoon, come rain come shine?'

'Ah.'

'The penny, is it dropping, slow?'

No, it was falling in a cascade, like money from a slot-machine win. He winced. Sergeant Declan Hickey, husband of Aine, the beautiful, the desirable, the one who had nearly cost him his job.

'You're blushing,' said Finney, smiling broadly.

'Fuck off. Let's change the subject.'

They had just crested the hill at the top of Mount Anville Road. Ahead lay the bay, the horizon a narrow line of navy blue, and the sea striped light and dark green, like a block of Russian agate. Far out, beyond the South Wall, he fancied he could see the rust-coloured sails of a Galway hooker.

'You'll have to come sailing with me some day, Dave. When this is all over. I'm going to take a few days' leave, and I'm thinking about taking a trip up north, Strangford Lough, Portaferry, around there. Would you come?'

But really, would he want him? As a rule he didn't mix work with pleasure. Kept his boat separate from everything else. Untouched, uncontaminated, a place of safety.

Blackrock station had the look of a fortress. Red brick, solid. Riot-proofed, he thought. Not that they needed it out here. Far from the madding crowd of knackers, junkies, gougers that Swan's Nest had to deal with. The desk sergeant greeted him warmly, stopped to reminisce about his father and the old days, then showed them to the room where the girl was waiting.

She was sitting across the table from Murray. Sobbing. Murray pushed the box of Kleenex across to her, but she shook her head and took a handkerchief from the pocket of the denim jacket that was slung over the back of her chair.

McLoughlin walked towards the table and held out his hand. He introduced himself and Finney. She took his hand for a moment, then dropped it. Her palm was cold and damp. He pulled up a chair and sat down.

He cleared his throat. 'Well,' he said, 'what

have we here?'

Murray gestured towards the woman. 'This is Jenny Adamson. She is a photography teacher who runs classes in Temple Bar. She has come in to tell us about an attack that was made on her some months ago. She believes that the person involved may have had something to do with the Mitchell murder.'

McLoughlin looked at the woman. Mid-thirties, he reckoned, although she seemed younger because of the way she was dressed. Her hair was brown and glossy. It was cut in what he recognized as a pageboy style, a short fringe and a graduated fall down both sides of her face. She was wearing small gold-rimmed glasses. Behind them her eyes were red and puffy. The pallor of her face was accentuated by the harshness of the room's light. Her small mouth trembled uncontrollably. She was, McLoughlin could see, extremely frightened.

'Could I–' she began, then stopped, overtaken by another burst of sobbing. No one said anything. 'Could I have a cigarette? I don't smoke very often, and I don't have any of my own.'

'Of course.' Murray reached into her bag, which was under the table. She took out a packet of Benson and Hedges and held them out. The woman fumbled with the box, unable to control her hand. Murray took out two. She put them both in her mouth and lit them. Then she gave one to her, putting it between her index and second fingers.

The woman pulled hard on the cigarette. As she exhaled the smoke her shoulders slumped.

'Where are you from?' McLoughlin asked.

'Chichester, in the south of England.'

'Ah, yes, very nice. Good theatre, beautiful cathedral, lovely gardens behind the Bishop's Palace.'

'That's right.' She smiled.

'And you've been in Dublin for how long?'

She explained that she had come on holiday three years ago. She had read Synge's book on the Aran Islands and wanted to see them for herself. And she had decided to stay to do a book of her own on the islands and the sea. Photographs, mainly, with some text. Teaching was just a way of making a living, 'You know, keeping body and soul together,' until the advance from the publishers was finalized.

'So, perhaps, Ms Adamson, you wouldn't mind telling myself and Sergeant Finney why you're here.'

She had been watching the evening news. A couple of weeks ago. There was something about the funeral of that poor girl. The one who was murdered. And she saw him.

'Who did you see?' McLoughlin asked. She lifted her cigarette again to her mouth. As it touched her lips she began to cry. They waited. Eventually she spoke. It was him. The man who had raped her. He was there outside the church. He was with all the other photographers.

'And do you know his name?'

She nodded. 'His name is Jimmy Fitzsimons. He took one of my courses a few months ago.' And she began to tell them. She was sorry she hadn't before. She knew she should have gone to the police. That men like him will go on doing things to women like her as long as women don't stand up for themselves.

McLoughlin held up his hand. 'Listen to me,' he said. 'You have done nothing that deserves reproach. What's important is that you have been brave enough to come forward now. If you didn't feel that you could come to us before that's a sorry reflection on us, not on you. Do you understand?'

She bent her head.

'Now,' he continued, 'tell me what happened. From the beginning. When did you first meet him?'

'It had been...' She stopped for a moment to think. It must have been about the second week in January. That was when her post-Christmas course began. It ran for three nights a week for ten weeks. She usually had room for eight people. Jimmy arrived late for registration. She tried to tell him that she was full, but he wouldn't take no for an answer. She was about to insist that he would have to wait for the next course when he pulled out a bundle of photographs from a plastic bag.

'Look,' he had said. 'Look at these.' They were black and white portraits. All the subjects were women. They were very good. Technically they had faults but he knew how to pin down his subject, find the image he wanted. One was of a young girl with Down's syndrome. She was eating an ice cream, a large white cone. Her tongue was out, licking. Her concentration was completely focused.

'Who's she?' she asked.

'My sister,' he said.

'Oh, I see,' she replied.

'Do you? Do you really?' he had answered.

She felt awkward, suddenly very self-conscious.

'Did he tell you much about his family?' McLoughlin leaned forward to look at her more closely.

Not immediately. She felt that she had said the wrong thing about the girl, so she kept off the subject. Then one evening after the class he had stayed behind to help her clear up. She asked him to put away some of the large bottles of chemicals. He was very helpful, very obliging. But she still felt awkward with him. She found herself blushing when he spoke to her, talking too much. And then he took a parcel out of his bag. It was wrapped in shiny brown paper and tied with string. It was a photograph in a frame. It was of her. She was sitting in Stephen's Green. It had been snowing and she was wrapped in an old fur coat with a matching hat. A duck was standing on the frozen pond looking at her. She had bread in her hand, and she was just about to throw it. There was a wonderful sense of anticipation in the photograph, but it made her feel uneasy. She tried to remember. Had she seen him that day? He was watching her face closely. She could see that he would be quick to take offence.

'Thank you,' she said. 'It's very good. You must have taken it last Sunday. Why didn't you come over and say hello?'

'I didn't want to disturb you,' he said. 'You looked so content there, on your own.'

She ran her fingers over the pretty pattern of leaves and flowers on the frame. 'It's beautiful,' she said. 'Where did you get it?'

'It was my mother's,' he replied.

'Oh, I see. That was nice of her to give it you.'

'She didn't,' he said, as he methodically washed down the benches.

'So,' McLoughlin said, 'what happened after that?'

She paused for a moment and hid her face in her hands. The soft brown hair fell forward. Then she sat up straight and stared at a point in the far wall. She had begun, she said, to find his presence disturbing. She noticed that she was thinking about him a lot, anticipating the classes. She was extremely disappointed when after giving her the photograph, he missed three sessions in a row. When he arrived again the following week she was surprised by her feelings of relief.

'So this was more than just a friendship, the way you were feeling?'

She nodded.

'And describe this man to us. What does he look like?'

Again she covered her face with her hands before she spoke. He was, he is, very beautiful. Not handsome the way men are, but beautiful. He's about five foot nine or ten, very slim. He has hair the colour of butter and eyes the colour of the sea. His skin is quite brown and very clear. He has white teeth and a sweet smile.

No wonder, thought McLoughlin, that she couldn't come forward. It's the old story. Hard to believe that someone good-looking is a villain. Much easier to imagine if they're short, squat, acne-scarred and dirty. And so easy for a woman to feel that she's to blame, that her desire was the trigger for his violence.

'So, Ms Adamson, tell us what happened on the night in question.'

For a moment McLoughlin thought she was going to faint. She began to breathe very quickly. Her face flushed then the colour ebbed away completely, leaving her skin the blue-white of skimmed milk.

One problem, she said, was that she couldn't remember everything that had happened. Afterwards it was as if the night was a painting, still wet, that someone had smeared with their hand. The colours were vivid, but the content, the details, were blurred and indistinct. It had begun, she knew, with celebration. The end of the course. She had bought some champagne, cheap stuff, and they had opened the bottles with much cheering and laughing and clowning around. He had joined in. Usually he didn't really get involved with the other students. He was a bit aloof. But that night he had been laughing and joking too. There was a sense of excitement in the room, and everyone was affected by it. She had felt as high as a kite from the first drop of wine, but it wasn't just the alcohol. She remembered that he had smiled at her, his teeth very white and his mouth the colour of crushed raspberries, and she had felt so happy and alive. Then someone, it wasn't him, had suggested that they go and have a drink, somewhere local, like the Norseman.

'Will you come, Jimmy?' she had asked.

'Would you like me to?' he had replied. And she had giggled like a schoolgirl and linked her arm through his.

In the bar she ordered tequila.

'Look,' she said, 'this is how you drink it.'

And she swallowed the shot in one go, sucking hard on a fresh lime. He bought her another and another. Someone put money in the jukebox. Billie Holiday was singing. 'Lover man, oh, where can you be?'

'Listen. I can sing that,' she said, and sat up on the bar, her voice deep and strong, playing with the tune, letting the words trickle from her mouth. They had danced together. It was wonderful. He was very affectionate, very loving. He held her right hand lightly against his heart. The fingers of his other hand slipped down inside her collar stroking the nape of her neck. She drank more. She didn't remember how much.

'And what about the other people you were with, what were they doing?'

She didn't remember. When the barman called time and turned on all the lights they were alone. He took her by the hand and they walked to an underground car park. She didn't remember which one, or how long it had taken them to get there. He had been kissing her and touching her all the way. She remembered that his car was big with silvered windows. She remembered how her reflection had billowed in and out, making her feel dizzy and a bit sick. When she got into the passenger seat he had leaned over and locked the door, and he had said, 'Snug as a bug in a rug,' just the way her mother did when she tucked her in at night when she was a child.

'And where did you go?'

She hadn't been sure at first. She had fallen asleep in the car. Then she vaguely remembered standing outside her house. It was very cold and he had taken her keys from her bag and was opening the door.

'And then?'

She got up from the table. Murray half rose too, but McLoughlin waved her back to her seat. She began to walk around the walls. Corner to corner to corner to corner. And as she walked, she talked.

Darkness, pain, nausea, fear. The back of my head hit the floorboards in the hall. Jimmy's face is above me. Why is he shouting? Saliva is dripping from his mouth onto my breasts. Where are my clothes? I'm holding up my hands to push him away. He's hitting me. My mouth is full of blood.

It's dark again. I can taste and smell vomit. I'm lying on my stomach, my cheek is pressed into the stinking pool. I can't move my arms. Pain, shooting through me, a piercing agony. I open my mouth to scream, but he's pulled me over onto my back and he's forced himself into my mouth. I'm going to be sick again, but he's beating me. I give up. I close my eyes. Then. Look at me, look at me, he screams. But I can't see. I'm going to be sick. He's hurting me. I've never felt pain like this before. Why are you doing this, why? There's a dreadful, dizzying whirl of lights, sounds all mixed together, screams and laughter and a pathetic sort of mewing. Is that me? It can't be me, can it? Then more pain. The smell of burning skin. No, it can't be. Stop, please, please, please. Then nothing.

And when I wake I don't know if he's still there. So I lie where I am, face down on the floor. My arms are tied behind my back, my legs are spread apart. I listen. My breath is the loudest sound in the room. I stare at the dust between the floorboards. Is this what it's like to be crippled, to be helpless? I struggle to go beyond the sound of my own body. A minute passes. An hour, half the day. I begin to move. Very slowly. Sweat drips into the dust. Gradually I sit up. I pull my hands free. He has used my apron, the yellow one with the white daisies, to tie me. I try to stand, but my legs give way like a broken balsawood model. There is dried blood and faeces caked all over my thighs. I stand in the shower. The water stings as it washes over the cuts, the bites, the burns. The water is pink as it swirls down the plughole. I swab myself with disinfectant. My eyes water from the pain but I won't cry any more. I wrap myself in a blanket and lie on the sofa drinking brandy from a tumbler. When I can stand and walk again I get rid of everything that reminds me of that night. I throw out my clothes, the sheets from the bed, the white goatskin rug smeared with brown. I smash the pottery bowls in which he urinated and defecated. I break up the beeswax candles that he shoved into me. He has destroyed my home. I want to set fire to it. To melt my shame. I will never feel safe again. I feel as if my house is made of cellophane, transparent, flimsy. So I move. To an apartment building with video cameras, a spyhole in the door, a security guard with a dog. But I will never again feel sure that my body is my own. That I own it. I will never again take that for granted.

She stopped talking and stood with her face to the wall. Murray stood up and went over to her. She turned her round and led her back to the chair. She whispered to Finney. He left the room.

McLoughlin spoke. 'Have you told anyone

else about this?'

She shook her head.

'And have you seen him at all since that night?'

Again the shake of the head.

'And tell me, Jenny, if we can find him will you take a case against him?'

Once more she shook her head. Murray looked at him anxiously.

'We can't make you do anything, Jenny. It's completely up to you, but–'

The woman screamed the words. 'No, no, no. Don't you see? I couldn't. How do you think it's been for me here in this room with you? To turn myself inside out like a ripe fig, let you see all those bits which should be hidden. I couldn't do that in a court. I couldn't sit in the same room with him. I'd die.'

'But–' he tried again.

'No buts, no maybes, no might-bes. No. Nothing. I can't do it.'

McLoughlin leaned forward in his chair and stared at the flecked lino on the floor. Rape was such a peculiar crime. It took one of the most wonderful and pleasurable things in the world and turned it into an abomination. He knew that she wasn't telling them everything he had done, or made her do. He knew that the reason she wouldn't go to court was because she felt involved, responsible. It didn't matter that the law would be on her side. As he had forced himself into her body, embedded himself in her, so she would always feel that she was part of the crime. He'd seen it before so many times. They had thought things would be different when the law had changed. In the old days a barrister could rip a woman apart in the witness box. Now they did it more subtly but to similar effect. Tarred with the same brush. Victim and perpetrator for ever united.

He looked up at her. 'You've told us his name. Do you have an address?'

Wordlessly she pulled a folded piece of paper from her pocket and handed it to him. He opened it. The completed application form for the photography course. His name and address were printed carefully. Jimmy Fitzsimons, 22 Canal Lane, Dublin 4. McLoughlin spoke again. 'By the way, do you know what he does for a living?'

'Yes, of course. He has his own chauffeur business. That's why he has the big car. I think it's a Mercedes. He takes wealthy tourists on special trips around the country, Hidden Ireland weekends, race meetings, that sort of thing.'

The door opened. Finney came in with a tray with a metal teapot, mugs, and a plate of biscuits. He dumped it on the table. He poured tea, the colour of nicotine. McLoughlin sipped delicately. 'Disgusting stuff,' he said, putting his mug down. No one else spoke. He watched as the colour returned to the woman's face. She would, he *knew*, sleep well tonight. As well as she would ever sleep, with triple locks on the door, and the sounds of the night a constant torment. Once you've felt real fear, he thought, the world is a very different place.

26

Whistling. His mouth pursed, his head flung back towards the ceiling. As if she wasn't there. As if the only thing in the world was the sun pouring in through the stained-glass windows, the hollow throb of the traffic outside, the smell of floor polish and dust, and that wonderful feeling of power and control.

He didn't look at her. He didn't need to.

He knew she'd come. He had recorded her features, her mannerisms, her expressions. The receptors in his memory had soaked them up as the light-sensitive paper soaked up the images from the negative. Stored them so they could be taken out at night and played with. Imagined. In different settings, doing different things. Played games with them like the little Lego people he had when he was small. There now. This is the mammy and this is the daddy. And this is the big sister and I'm the little brother. Or should that be, this is the granddaddy and this is grandmammy, and this is the mammy and I am the son?

Pictures to play with over and over, that was what he wanted. To lay them out like the cards in a game of patience. Contrasting colours and shapes. An elaborate hierarchy of desire. This one goes on top of that one. This one fits with this one. Or like a jigsaw puzzle. This hand matches that arm. This face goes with that body. Maybe, let's try it another way. Let's put mother's head with daughter's breast. Daughter's leg with mother's foot. Until the puzzle is completed, the game worked out, the end has come.

He paused. Stopped. Listened. He had been in this church once before. A Sunday, how many weeks ago? He counted back. Three or four. Mary had brought him. They had been out driving. She loved sitting in the back. Protected by the silvered windows. Hidden.

'Isn't it great?' she would say, snuggling into the cushions. 'No one can see us. Drive on, my boy.' That evening she had got him to go past her house. They had stopped outside. It was still light. The front door was open. A large black cat was sunning itself on the top step.

'What's your mother like?' he asked.

She didn't answer for a while. She chewed her gum, then took it out and stuck in a piece of wrapper. She took a swig from the bottle of Coke mixed with vodka that he had cooling in the ice-box. Then she said, 'She's very beautiful. She's very clever. She's good at everything she does. She drives me fuck-ing berserk.'

'She must miss your father?' he asked, as he reached out for the bottle.

She shrugged. 'Nah, he died a long time ago.'

'No one else?'

Again the shrug. 'Who could she meet that would measure up to her high standards? Come on,' she said, 'let's go,' and she told him to drive to the church. She led him in and up the stairs to the gallery. Evening service was just finishing.

'Isn't this neat?' she said. 'I love it in here. It's kind of mad. It reminds me of *Alice in Wonderland* or something like that. The towers like chessmen outside. I'd like to come back here,' she whispered, 'in the dead of night, when stars are weeping, when there's no one else around. Wouldn't you?'

He began to whistle again. This time he leaned forward, looking down into the nave. He rested his head on one hand, gazing beneath him at the rows of empty pews and the chequered tiles of the central aisle, and then for the first time he turned and looked towards the gallery at the west end of the church. His heart fluttered like a butterfly trapped in a hand as he saw her there. She was standing, rigid, gripping the front rail. She was staring straight at him. She looked... He tried to find the words to describe her. She reminded him of the women in some pictures the photography teacher had shown him. They had been taken, so she said, during the Depression in the southern states of America. The women's white angular faces held no expression as they gazed at the camera. It was the same with photographs he had seen of prisoners liberated from the death camps. There was a complete lack of curiosity in their look. He supposed that when you've lived on the edge of survival, curiosity becomes a luxury you can't afford. But he wanted her to be curious about him, about what he'd done, what he was doing.

He was, after all, intensely curious about her. He knew what size dresses she wore, what fruit she liked, what books she read, what music she listened to. He knew the little things, like the colour of her toothbrush, how she liked her eggs boiled, that she took sugar in her coffee but not in her tea. And he knew the big things, that she had never been in love since her husband died, that she didn't love her mother the way she had loved her father. He knew all these things because Mary had told him.

He felt suddenly tired. He had planned this for a long time and now that it was here it was a bit like Christmas when he was a kid. He was worn out with the anticipation. He lay back on the pew and closed his eyes. He would rest for a while and then he would do what had to be done. He patted his pocket to reassure himself that he still had the knife. It was funny to see how people changed when you showed it to them. You'd expect them to respond as if it was a gun, but in some ways he suspected that a knife was more frightening. Guns could, and did, miss. But up close with a knife?

He opened his eyes. The church was suddenly dark. High above its slated roof towers of brilliant white, ice crystals gleaming, hung in the dark blue sky. Cloud piled upon gleaming cloud, drops of moisture freezing, melting and refreezing, layer upon layer, until hard and dense as golf balls they crashed with a huge burst of energy towards the ground. He was cold now. He sat up. She was still standing in the same place, but her eyes were fixed on the altar directly before her. He walked to the end of the row. She didn't move. He turned and went up to the back of the gallery to the stairs that led down into the nave. He looked over his shoulder towards her. Still she didn't move. He walked quickly down the stairs and came out at the north door. He tried the large handle. It was locked. He walked around behind the rows of pews, keeping out of her sight, to the front door. A heavy iron bar was propped against the wall. He picked it up and slotted it into place. He stopped to listen. The hailstones were beating an intricate dance rhythm against the windows. There was no sound from above. His heart began to beat faster, faster. He put his hand to his throat. He could feel the pulse jumping, evenly. He looked up at the ceiling, imagining her standing above him. What was she wearing? He had only seen from the waist up, but it looked like it was a long white skirt, with a plain navy blouse. Short-sleeved, round-necked. Was it buttoned up the back?

He moved down the nave and looked up. Now he was directly beneath her again. He began to walk backwards towards the chancel, step by step, arms open wide, head up.

Now she began to move. She turned and walked towards the stairs. She disappeared from view. He waited. The double doors from the porch opened. She came down the aisle towards him. When she was within four feet she stopped. She was smaller than he had remembered, smaller than her daughter. More delicate. She stood in front of him. Her white skirt hung like a drooping lily almost to her feet. He began to move towards her.

'Don't!' Her voice cut through the empty church, echoing, harsh, strong. 'Don't you dare touch me.'

He stepped back involuntarily, suddenly anxious. She lifted her head and straightened her back. And then she spat. She drew mucus from deep in her chest and flung it out towards him. It landed on his chest and hung glistening, yellow on his clean white shirt.

'Just tell me one thing,' she said, 'just one thing. The only thing I want to know. What did she say before she died?'

He took a handkerchief from his pocket and carefully wiped his shirt clean. He screwed it up and dropped it on the ground. Her gaze followed it to the floor. She bent down and picked it up. Neat red letters, embroidered on one corner. David Anthony Mitchell. She looked up at him. He smiled.

'What did she say before she died?' He repeated the words slowly, each one separate from the next. Then he put his hand in his pocket and took out his knife.

'That's for me to know and you to find out.' And he reached out and hooked one finger round the neck of her blouse and pulled it taut and with his other hand slid the knife down through the linen. She screamed then, a shriek that filled the church with its anger. He rocked backwards and forwards, laughter bursting out through his open mouth. Then he walked past her, one shoulder brushing against her arm as he moved. And he sang as he walked.

'I'm a little tea-pot
Short and stout.'

He twirled and faced her again, one hand on his hip and the other above his head, fingers slanting in a parody of elegance towards the floor. And then he was gone.

Gone, gone. The rain driving against the windows and a black emptiness where her heart once had been.

27

'So. We have a name, and an address, and an occupation. A cause for celebration, wouldn't you agree?'

They were standing just inside the Garda station's glass doors, waiting. Outside the rain washed across the main road, sheets of water drumming against the passing cars, rushing along the deep gutters and spilling over in streams that cascaded down the side roads towards Blackrock village.

'Come on, we could be here all day, let's run for it.' McLoughlin pushed through the door, holding his briefcase over his head, and turned in the same direction as the torrent of muddy water.

'Where ya going?' shouted Finney, as he followed him.

'O'Rourke's. In the village. I told you, a cause for celebration.'

'Ah, come on, boss. We don't have time.'

McLoughlin looked back at Finney standing on the footpath, the rain dripping down his forehead and staining the shoulders of his jacket black.

'What's your problem? It's lunchtime. I'm hungry.'

Finney caught up with him just as he had ordered his second pint and a plate of ham sandwiches.

'Here.' McLoughlin gestured to the stool beside him. 'What'll you have?'

'Coffee,' Finney grunted, as he pulled himself onto the seat, and began to mop his face with a paper napkin from the pile on the bar.

McLoughlin waved at the barman, and then towards the sandwiches. 'Have one,

Dave. They're the best in this part of town. Properly cooked ham, decent bread with butter not margarine, and here, try some of the mustard. It's the real stuff. Dijon. Delicious.'

Finney said nothing, his expression hostile.

They ate in silence, McLoughlin swallowing slabs of dark pink ham spread liberally with the creamy yellow mustard.

'So,' he said, as he finished his pint and wiped the froth from his top lip, 'what's your problem?'

'Look, boss, this isn't a criticism of you, but do you not think...?'

'Yes?'

'Well, this is the first break we've had so far. Up until now we've been beating our heads against a fucking brick wall. We've found nothing. No DNA, no prints, no real sightings apart from the video material. Hundreds of man-hours of questionnaires, questions, banging on doors. We've this crazy situation with the mother and the phone calls. I told you we should have brought her in as soon as we realized what was going on. All this hanging about, wild-goose-chasing all over the city after her. For what, eh? For some embarrassing hysterical scene in a fucking maternity hospital. How does that make us look? We're practically reduced to getting in the clairvoyants. And then, out of the blue, this girl walks in, and gives us our first bit of real information. And.'

'And what, Dave?'

'And instead of getting over to his place immediately, and I mean immediately, you want to go boozing.'

'Lunch, actually. Lunch.'

'Yeah, well.' Finney finished his coffee. 'You know, boss. There's a lot of talk about you these days. I've defended you. Every time.'

'Ah, gossip, the mustard in the ham sandwich of our mundane little lives.'

'You can see it like that if you like, but I'm telling you. The row you had with Finucane this morning, that's only the tip of the iceberg.'

Remember that one, McLoughlin thought. Never trust a subordinate. Ever. He stood up, put a heap of coins on the counter and picked up his briefcase.

'You've said enough. I think if anyone was to examine the conduct of this case they would find that it has been impeccably handled. I think they'd find that the more experienced officers would stand com-pletely behind me. On every count.' He opened his briefcase and took out his mobile phone. He punched in a number, and waited for a couple of seconds. Then he spoke. 'Hello, Bertie. How we doing? Any sign of life?'

There was a pause. Then 'Good. No, don't do anything. Wait for us. We'll be there in fifteen minutes. But if he should leave again, follow him and keep in touch.'

Finney looked at him angrily.

'That, dear boy, is why God invented mobile phones. So I could have my lunch while Bertie Lynch went on ahead to let me know if our suspect was at home. Now why don't you wipe that sulky look off your face? We've got work to do.'

She spread her ripped blouse on the kitchen table. It was soaked through, the dark blue linen almost black with water. When she left the church the rain had been coming down in heavy swollen drops which spread as they landed and saturated. She had been relieved that it was raining, that she had an excuse to run, that no one would look too closely at a woman clutching her clothes, her head bent low, her face wet, intent on getting home.

She hadn't stopped until she reached the front door. She was breathless, sucking air down her burning throat and into her lungs, as she fumbled in her pocket for her keys, her hands wet and trembling, the metal slipping through them so that she had to kneel and scrabble around on the top step to pick them up.

The cat had appeared beside her, mewing insistently, rubbing himself around and through her legs, falling over her feet as she finally got the door open and stumbled inside. She had caught sight of herself in the hall mirror. Mad I look, completely mad, she thought, her hair hanging in wet hanks on her shoulders, her eyes wide open, her pupils dilated. She dropped her hands and the edges of the ripped blouse fell apart. She noticed for the first time that there was a fine line of red beginning just under her collarbone, where the knife must have nicked her. She hurried into the kitchen and took the bottle of whiskey from the dresser. The cat fretted and jumped up beside her, putting wet paws on her shoulder as she unscrewed the top and poured a large shot into a glass. She drank it down in one, gagging as the alcohol scorched her throat. She poured and drank again. Warmth spread though her body. She knelt and shovelled cat food from an open tin onto a plate. The cat whimpered his thanks and purred as he chewed, delicately pushing the lumps of meat into place with his black nose.

She sat down at the kitchen table. Her breathing slowed. She picked up the blouse and began to tear it into thin strips. It tore easily, the threads already loosened by the knife. When she had finished she took the lengths of cloth and began to plait them into a piece of cord. This I would use on him, she thought. This I would use to make him suffer the way he made my daughter suffer. This I would use to end his life, the way he has ended mine. I would wrap it around his neck and twist it tight, using both hands. And I would watch as he began to realize that there was no more air making its way through his mouth into his lungs. No more air. No more life.

She got up from the table, cold suddenly washing over her. She climbed the stairs to the bathroom, slowly, stopping after every step, the muscles in her legs shaking, her heart sore under her breast, her lungs sore under her ribs. She twisted the plaited rope around her right wrist, knotting it tight. She stripped off her bra, her skirt and her pants and stood under the shower, closing her eyes and thinking of nothing but the comfort of the water, running in warm rivulets down her body.

When she had dressed she went back down to the kitchen and sat again at the table, the bottle of whiskey in front of her. Today was 28 August. Twenty-three days since she had last spoken to Mary. She had tried to hang on to that final conversation, keep it intact, keep it safe. But even now, sometimes she couldn't quite remember. Did I say goodbye first, or did she? Did she say she'd be home early or did I ask her not to be late? She kissed me, where? On which cheek, left or right? I didn't watch her go, why not? I was reading a book. I didn't look up. If I had, maybe I would have called her back, asked her to stay, begged her not to go. Why didn't I? Why did I let down my guard? I always knew that motherhood made you vulnerable, weak, easily hurt. But I had begun to forget. To relax. Not to fear. Mary was twenty. She was almost an adult. She had talked about moving out when she went back to Auckland. Getting a flat with that friend of hers. The blonde one, Louisa. Getting a part-time job. Going to college. Maybe studying medicine. Giving up the ballet. It was my fault this happened. I was too complacent. I should have been more careful. Like Billy Montgomery, she thought. A patient she had treated years ago. Suffering from what the books called paranoid schizophrenia. Acutely agoraphobic. Convinced that disaster was waiting for him every minute of the day and night. Didn't sleep at night in case he might die. Wouldn't let anyone within three feet of him in case they were carriers of a fatal infectious disease. Margaret remembered the long conversations she had had with him. She was always surprised at how reasonable he sounded. Sometimes she came away and found herself looking at the world through his eyes. In many ways he was right. Danger lurked everywhere. Nothing was safe and certain. What was the saying? 'You know not the day nor the hour.'

Poor Billy. All he wanted was security, sureness. And he got it. He killed a nurse who had been assigned to take him for short trips around the hospital grounds. When he left the building and saw the wide expanse of blue, stretching from one horizon to the other, he began to scream. When she turned to comfort him he grabbed her by the throat and strangled her. It was all over very quickly. The court found him guilty while the balance of his mind was disturbed. Sentence was imprisonment at Her Majesty's pleasure. Margaret had gone to visit him in the top-security wing of the hospital. He had looked perfectly happy as he spoke to her through the metal grille. Safe at last.

She put her hand in her pocket and put the crumpled handkerchief in front of her on the table. She ran her fingers over the embroidered capital letters. Mary had kept this handkerchief in her bag. My daddy's pocket hankie, she had called it. Now it was defiled, desecrated. She stood up and went to the dresser. She picked up the box of matches. She took the handkerchief gingerly by one corner. She lit a match and held the flame to the yellowing cotton. She blew gently on it until the flame caught. Then she dropped it into the sink and stood and watched until nothing was left but a few charred fragments.

The day passed slowly. The usual people came and went. Nellie, muttering under her breath as she mopped and cleaned, and hung washing on the line. A couple of times she heard the doorbell ring. Neighbours enquiring. Get rid of them, she told Nellie.

The hospice nurse appeared some time in the afternoon. By this time Margaret had moved out to the garden and was lying in a low chair. The nurse looked down at her and picked up the whiskey bottle, now nearly empty. 'Is this such a good thing?' she asked.

Margaret shrugged. 'It's neither good nor bad. It's just necessary. For the time being.'

The nurse put on her dark glasses and picked up her bag. 'I should tell you that your mother is going downhill rapidly. I don't think she's got much longer.'

'Do you think she knows?'

'Do you?'

It began to get cool around six in the evening. A breeze stirred the red fuchsia and the blossoms danced in step like an elegant corps de ballet. Margaret got up and went back into the house. She threw the empty bottle in the bin. I should be drunk, she thought. But there's nothing predictable about the effect of alcohol. She made some tea and carried it into her mother's room. Catherine stirred slightly as Margaret bent over her. 'Mother,' she said, 'would you like something?'

But there was no response from the tiny figure curled into the pillows.

Margaret slept too. She sank quickly, shuddering as her consciousness released her. She dreamed. She had killed someone. She didn't know who. But there was a severed head in a plastic bag. She had to get rid of it. A man came towards her. He held out his arms. She couldn't let him see the head in the bag. She wanted him so much. She was aching for him. He held out his arms again. She wanted to run to him, and she wanted to run away from him, away to hide the plastic bag. But she couldn't. Her legs were weak and soft, like melting ice cream. She looked down, and she could see her legs disappearing, dripping, running in tiny streams away from her body. Her legs wouldn't move. And he was getting closer and closer, his smile wide, his arms open.

'My legs, my legs, help me, help me.' The scream cut into her dream. She raised herself slowly. Again the scream. She rushed from her bed, running down the stairs. The scream got louder and louder. Catherine was lying, half out of the bed, her head hanging down nearly on the floor. Her mouth was open. She was gasping for breath. 'The pain,' she sobbed. 'In my chest. Crushing me. And my legs, I can't feel my legs. And I'm so cold.

Warm me, warm me, please, John? warm me.' And she began to scream again, this time like a cornered rat, high-pitched, terrified. Margaret stood and looked at her. The tears began to stream down her face. 'Mother, Mother. No, no. Please, no.'

28

'Was that your father's boat?' McLoughlin asked. 'In the Coal Harbour yard in Dun Laoghaire? The gaff rigged sloop, thirty foot or so, called *Kitty Dhubh*.'

'How did you know?' Margaret looked up at him.

'I'm friends with a few of the blokes who work there. Boat fanciers like myself. They'd heard I was involved in this case. One of the older guys said he remembered you sailing with your father years ago.'

The huge white canvas sail, patched and mended, filling with wind as they rose and fell like a merry-go-round boat, racing through the harbour mouth. Her father at the tiller, his battered felt hat jammed on his head. The bowsprit rearing up above the waves, like the elegant horn of a unicorn.

'Go on, Maggie, wave,' he shouted, as they passed the end of the West Pier, and the fishermen standing on the granite wall raised their rods in salutation.

'She's an old beauty, isn't she?' McLoughlin said, sitting down on the wrought-iron bench in the garden.

'A wreck. Falling to pieces.'

'But a terrific pedigree they tell me.'

'Take her, have her. I don't want her.'

'I couldn't. She's worth money.'

'Suit yourself. If you want her take her away, otherwise she'll be going on the scrap heap like a lot of other stuff in this house.'

They had come to see her, McLoughlin and Finney, to ask her about Jimmy Fitzsimons. Had she heard of him? Had Mary ever mentioned anyone of that name? Was there anything about him that seemed familiar?

She was in the garden by herself. She looked exhausted, her eyes sunk in deep hollows, her skin the grey of a mildewed leaf. She told them she had been up all night. It was her mother. She explained. A secondary tumour growing on her spine. Vertebral metastases, it was called. Compressing the spinal cord. Severe pain radiating down the nerves. A band of pain around the thorax. Pins and needles in the legs, coldness, leading to gradual paralysis of the lower body. Catherine had been rushed to St Luke's for radiation therapy. They wouldn't allow her home. It didn't look good.

'I really just came home to change my clothes. I'm going back into the hospital soon.'

McLoughlin made her coffee, grinding the beans, hunting through the cupboards for a jug for the milk. And he talked to her, told her about questioning Fitzsimons, that he had said he knew Mary, that they had spent from the Saturday night until the Wednesday morning together. That Mary had left. That he thought she was coming home.

'And do you believe him?'

'He seemed quite convincing.'

'But you're not going to leave it there, are you?'

'No,' Finney said. 'We're definitely not. Either way, so far he's the last person who saw her alive.'

'And why didn't he come forward before now? If he was perfectly innocent.'

'Said he was scared. That we'd assume that he killed her. The usual story.'

'So,' McLoughlin picked up the thread, 'tomorrow we're going back to his house, with a search warrant. And then we'll take him in for formal questioning. What I wanted to know was if you have any photographs of Mary's earrings and her ring, the ones that are missing. Also any pictures of her bag, or her clothes, anything that might identify them.'

Tension in her jaw, in her shoulders, in the way she abruptly left the room. The two men sat in silence in the sunny kitchen, drinking their coffee. They could hear her opening and shutting drawers, moving around from room to room upstairs.

'Are you not going to say anything to her?' Finney asked. 'About the phone calls?'

McLoughlin shrugged. 'Not today.'

'Why not?'

'Don't you think she's enough on her plate right now?'

'But they're evidence, for Christ's sake.'

'Evidence of what exactly? We don't know who made them. We certainly don't know that it was Fitzsimons. But if we need to, if we can't crack him ourselves, then we can use the transcripts to frighten him.'

'But she's been involved with him, almost colluded with him.'

'Has she? It doesn't seem that way to me, Dave. And, if we're talking about collusion, surely we've done a bit of it ourselves, haven't we?'

Finney stood up. 'I don't understand you at all. There's something weird going on in here.' And he leaned over and rapped McLoughlin's head with his knuckles.

McLoughlin poured himself another cup of coffee. He looked around the kitchen, the white-painted tongued-and-grooved walls and ceiling, the deep enamel sink, the old Aga set into the chimney breast. The black cat jumped up on his lap, staring at him, wide-eyed, kneading his trousers, purring.

He thought of the house they had left just over an hour ago. Two storeys with a slated mansard roof and dormer windows like a French country villa. Off Killiney Hill Road, a long gravel drive overgrown with rhododendrons, stone steps flanked by two carved lions and a massive front door with a heavy brass knocker in the shape of a griffin.

Mrs Fitzsimons wasn't expecting them. She was a small thin woman, in her fifties. Her blonde hair was set stiffly, wig-like in its consistency. Her skinny fingers were covered with large rings. Green and red stones twinkled cheerfully among the diamonds. She showed them into a formal sitting room, with chintz-covered armchairs and a heavy mahogany sideboard glinting with Waterford crystal.

McLoughlin told her why they had questioned her son, that he was the last person who had seen Mary Mitchell alive. Finney told her what her son had said, that he and Mary both liked fucking. He used the word, with the emphasis that Jimmy had given it. She looked away, her pale eyes filling with tears.

'Tell us about Jimmy,' McLoughlin said. 'What kind of a person is he?'

She bowed her shoulders, her hands fiddling with a balled-up tissue. 'Difficult,' she replied, 'always in trouble. He was expelled from school. I couldn't understand it. He was clever. Photographic memory, but always getting into fights with the other boys.'

'But he seems to be doing fine now, with this chauffeuring business?'

'That was my husband. He bought Jimmy the car, got him into the agency.'

'I see.'

There was silence for a moment.

'Lovely house,' McLoughlin said. 'Have you lived here for long?'

'Seven or eight years, I suppose.'

'Very nice area, Killiney. You're not from here originally?'

She shook her head, her fingers pleating the protective covers on the arms of her chair.

'You said that your husband set Jimmy up in business.'

'That's right. He's always been very good to him.'

'But you didn't refer to him as Jimmy's father.'

She stared at the swirls of colour on the carpet. She supposed, she said, that she should tell them. Jimmy was actually her eldest daughter's child. She had had him when she was fourteen. They were living in England at the time. Manchester.

'And you decided that you would bring him up as your own?'

'That's right.'

'And Jimmy's father? Did you know who he was?'

She looked up. Her gaze moved around the room, lighting for comfort on the crystal, the row of Belleek ornaments on the marble mantelpiece, the ornate brass chandelier that hung from the ceiling rose. 'I never asked,' she said.

'And does Jimmy know this?' Finney leaned forward.

'I never told him.'

A girl was leaning against their car when they left. She was fat and fair, her hair tied up in bunches behind her ears.

'Who are you?' she demanded.

'We're friends of Jimmy's,' McLoughlin replied, opening the door.

'Jimmy, Jimmy,' she began to shout, jumping up and down. 'Jimmy showed me this. Look.' And she began to sing the words and mime the actions, one hand held up, the other bent around her back. 'Listen to me. I can sing.'

'I'm a little pee-tot.
Short and stout.
Here's my hangle and here's my snout.'

He watched her in the rear-view mirror as they drove away, marching up and down, still shrieking the words out loud.

His father had always said, Be prepared. When you go into an interrogation, know as much as you can, not just about the facts of the case, but about the person. Know their family, their friends, their life. Everything. He had been good at interrogations, Pat

McLoughlin, so they all said. Some said he was the best. He never used force, even in the days when you could get away with it. He would sit in the room, and wait. For as long as it took. He would chat. Talk about the weather, the horses, the dogs. Wait for the right moment, when he could start pushing the buttons. Wait until the desire to tell became overwhelming.

Margaret came back into the kitchen. She handed him a couple of photographs, damp patches on their shiny surface from her fingers. They were head shots of Mary, and one of her standing with her bag slung over her shoulder.

'Not much good, I'd say. But you might as well take them.'

'None of the ring, no?'

She shook her head and looked at her watch, frowning. 'I've told you already. They're all I have. Now, if you don't mind, I've got to go back to the hospital.'

'You know,' he said, 'this Fitzsimons guy. Funny family background. Seems he's really his elder sister's kid. But his grandparents brought him up thinking that he was theirs.'

'So? It makes a difference?'

He shrugged. He noticed she had changed

her dress. She was wearing a long white shift. Pleated cotton, with bright red and yellow flowers embroidered around the scooped neck.

'That's pretty,' he said.

She didn't respond.

'Look, if you need anything, need any help at all, you have my number.'

She nodded. He wanted to put his arms around her, pull her small, thin body up against his bulk, kiss her neck, nibble the soft skin that pulled away from her throat.

He thought of her again that night as he sat at home on his own. The television was on in the corner with the sound turned down. It was the annual Rose of Tralee festival from Kerry. Derek Davis was standing on stage, holding a pair of high-heeled shoes while a pretty girl, her taffeta skirts hitched up, danced a jig. McLoughlin picked up the remote control and turned up the volume. A burst of applause filled the room.

'Isn't she lovely? Kathleen O'Boyle from Chicago, ladies and gentlemen, and I bet Cindy and Thomas, her parents, are so proud of her.' The camera had found them. Her father and mother were sitting close together, holding hands. Their faces were filled with love and pride. The camera zoomed into their faces, then cut back to a close-up of the girl. She was the image of her father. The same strong chin and big white American teeth. The picture changed again. Back to the mother. She was crying, the tears running unashamedly down her face. Beside her the girl's father held out a handkerchief, then tenderly and without embarrassment, dabbed at her eyes, holding her face gently by the chin. McLoughlin poured himself another glass of wine. And as he watched, he, too, began to cry. For Margaret, for Mary, for himself.

29

It was all there in the Criminal Justice Act of 1984. Section 4, page 11, *Detention of Arrested Persons in Garda Síochána Custody in Certain Circumstances.*

Subsection (3) (a) The period for which a person so arrested may be detained shall, subject to the provisions of this section, not exceed six hours from the time of his arrest.

[And]

(b) An officer of the Garda Síochána not below the rank of superintendent may direct that a person detained pursuant to subsection (2) be detained for a further period not exceeding six hours if he has reasonable grounds for believing that such further detention is necessary for the proper investigation of the offence.

And the Statutory Instrument, S.I. No 119 of 1987, *Criminal Justice Act, 1984 (Treatment of Persons in Custody in Garda Síochána Stations) Regulations, 1987* spelt it out even further. Who could do what to whom, how and why. No more picking your suspect up late on Friday evening and holding him over the weekend to make him sweat. No more beatings, unexplained injuries, undocumented visits by the doctor. None of that was allowed any longer. Everything had to be noted, timed, recorded. Charges had to be explained in clear language, rights spelt out.

McLoughlin watched them bring Jimmy Fitzsimons in. It was eleven-fifty in the morning. Wednesday, 30 August. An ordinary working day. The main street jammed with cars, the footpaths crammed with shoppers. The weather still fantastic. A bit of fog earlier on, but now it was hot and sunny.

Dave Finney and Bertie Lynch had been on Fitzsimons' doorstep at seven forty-five a.m. with a search warrant, and a technical team waiting to go in. They had searched the little mews house thoroughly, collecting hairs, fibres, prints, all the routine stuff. No sign of the girl's jewellery, clothes or bag. Then, when they were satisfied they had everything, Finney had arrested and cautioned him. The time had been noted. Eleven-oh-seven precisely.

McLoughlin walked slowly downstairs into the public area. He watched Fitzsimons as he was led in, handcuffed, through the swing doors. He looked calm, relatively untroubled. That wouldn't last. McLoughlin stood back in the shadow of a doorway where he couldn't be seen. He had noticed yesterday, when they had called to question him, what the Adamson woman had meant by his beauty. He was extraordinary to look at. Pale yellow hair. Light blue eyes, with long lashes. Smooth creamy skin. And a slim, muscular body, small waist, neat hips, long legs and a natural grace. He reminded

McLoughlin of a ballet dancer or a bullfighter. Someone who can express themselves through their gestures, the flick of their wrist, or the turn of their foot.

He stepped out into the hall and followed the small group into the sergeant's office. Sal Daly, the member in charge, was giving Fitzsimons a copy of form C.72 to read. He could hear him now, going down through the list, checking off its contents. Reason for arrest, notification to other persons, legal advice, visits, telephone calls etc. Searches, fingerprints, palm-prints, photographs and tests, meals. He went back over the most important points. Asked him again if he wanted a solicitor, did he want them to inform his parents of his whereabouts? He was surprised when Fitzsimons shook his head; Sal asked him again. He heard him.

'Are you sure you don't want a solicitor to be present? If you don't have one of your own we can arrange for a duty solicitor to be assigned to you.'

Again the shake of the head.

Next would be fingerprints and photographs, then into a cell. Not for long. And not for any particular reason. Just to shake him up a bit. Show him that they had the power, while he was in their custody, to move him from place to place, take him into one room, and then into another. Exercise the same kind of physical control that mothers have over helpless infants. Simple things, really, but they worked. Having to ask to go to the toilet. Sometimes just leaving someone for half an hour or so, after the request, could have magical effects. Interesting to watch the realization that you are no longer in control. Of course, most of the guys who came through that door in handcuffs knew all about their little games. They'd played them so many times before. But a novice like Jimmy Fitzsimons? He wouldn't be able to handle it so well, even if he had raped, tortured and murdered that poor girl. Classic bullying stuff, really. Surround him with a few guards standing over six foot, weighing over sixteen stone each, with fists the size of sledgehammers. And then wait.

He sent Finney and Lynch in first. The rules said that no more than four guards could be present during the interview and no more than two could question the arrested person. So he put a couple of heavies in as well. Just for decoration.

The morning passed slowly. It would be a

long day. Finney would be going through the routine stuff. Asking him about himself and his job. Asking him about the girl, where he met her, what they did, when he last saw her. There'd be a lot of silences. Stopping and starting. Finney would get up and walk around the room keeping eye contact, drawing him into his orbit. They'd play a few games. Guards would come in with 'messages'. They'd call him or Lynch over to the door, looking at Fitzsimons as they whispered urgently. Lynch would take copious notes. Then after two hours of this they'd stop. Offer him tea or coffee, leave him with the uniform while they all took a break.

Then they'd go back in. And start all over again.

The clock on the wall said thirteen-oh-seven. Exactly two hours since Finney had put his hand on him. McLoughlin would let him carry on by himself for a while longer. They weren't in any hurry. They had until eleven-oh-seven that night. Plenty of time.

'How's it going, Inspector?' Sergeant Daly stopped by his desk. 'Everything OK?'

'Yeah, fine. And for you?'

Daly nodded. 'Yeah, so far. Finney can be

a bit – what's the expression I'm looking for?'

'Hot-headed? Volatile?'

Daly smiled. 'Ambitious I think was the word I wanted. Something like that. But I'll keep my eye on him.'

Lunchtime. Fitzsimons was taken back to a cell. Food was given to him on a tray. He was cuffed for the short walk from the interview room. McLoughlin looked through the peephole. He was sitting on the bed. The tray was on the floor beside him. He had a blank, shocked expression on his pale pretty face. McLoughlin joined Finney and Lynch in the canteen. Egg and chips, and white sliced loaf. He buttered his bread, and stuck a corner of the crust into the yolk of the egg.

'So, what do you think?'

'He did it, all right.'

'Yeah? Why do you say that?'

'He keeps on remembering. All the time.'

'How do you know?'

'There's this expression he gets on his face, every time we mention her name. Isn't that right, Bert? His lips move. His eyes flicker from side to side. It's as if he's replaying it all over and over again.'

'But has he said anything?'

'Nothing much. Still sticking to his story. He met her a few weeks ago. She came home with him on the Saturday night, and she stayed until the Wednesday morning. Then she left. He wasn't expecting to see her again. And when he heard she was dead he got scared.'

The afternoon passed. Slowly. Around them the normal routine of the Swan's Nest station carried on. People came in and out, reporting petty crimes, getting their passport forms signed, paying traffic fines.

Three o'clock, four o'clock, five o'clock. Superintendent Finucane signed the order to extend the interview period for a further six hours. Teatime came and went. Again the same routine. Fitzsimons to a cell. Finney and Lynch to the canteen.

At eight in the evening he went and stood outside the interview room. He could hear shouting. He looked through the peephole. Finney was standing over Fitzsimons, facing the door. His face was dark red. Beneath him Fitzsimons cowered, pale, his hands screwed up in front of his face. McLoughlin knocked on the door, then opened it slowly.

The small windowless room stank. Nervous sweat, fear, anger.

'Time to take a break, I think,' he said.

He got them to set up the projector. He would use the room's blank walls as his screen. He was all ready by the time they brought Fitzsimons back into the room. He held out his hand. Fitzsimons put his into it, mechanically. He was very pale. He looked as if he had been crying.

'Shall we begin?' McLoughlin said. 'Dave, the lights, please.'

Mary's naked body was suddenly in the room with them. Huge, enlarged, sprawled across the wall. Near enough to reach out and touch. He pushed the button. The carousel of slides clicked, shuffled and moved. McLoughlin began. He described all her injuries, using the medical terms. How they had happened. What kind of force had been used. He moved on to the close-ups. Breasts, thighs, genitals, wrists, ankles, stomach. Finally face. He watched Fitz-simons in the projector's ghostly glow. He looked as if he might faint. McLoughlin switched off the projector. The room was dark. He sat back in his chair and crossed his legs.

'So,' he said, 'tell us about yourself, Jimmy.' There was silence. McLoughlin took out a cigar and fumbled in his pocket for a box of matches. He lit one slowly. The scrape of the phosphorus head along the crystals was loud in the sudden quiet. The hairs stood up on the back of his neck. The flame flared. Fitzsimons was looking at him. With apprehension. He waited. Still silence. That wasn't a problem. He could wait. He was better at it than most people. He'd had plenty of practice. Most people, ordinary people, couldn't handle the vacuum. A black hole of guilt beckoned. As they knelt, terrified, on the edge, it sucked them deep inside. He'd seen it before. The desire to fill in the empty spaces, with lies, bumbling explanations, raw lists of events, litanies of excuses. Anything to occupy the yawning gap with the sound of a voice, the semblance of human contact.

'Shall we look at the slides again, Jimmy?' He picked up the control button.

The blond head shook.

'Why? Don't you like them? Shocking, aren't they? When you see what one human being can do to another. But, of course, you know a lot about that, don't you, Jimmy? You've done it more than once.' He turned towards Finney. 'Did you tell him, Dave, about the nice girl Jenny Adamson? The photography teacher.' He turned back to

Fitzsimons. 'She had a lot to say about you, and the time you spent together. Just tell me, Jimmy, you must have had a good time with that girl. You really made a mess of her. Do you know, it took her three weeks before she could walk without pain? Three weeks. And you did that. All by yourself. No weapons, no instruments, no implements, just your hands and your feet and your fists and your prick. That was all it took to reduce her, and her a clever woman, degrees and diplomas, certificates all over the wall, to a frightened, snivelling piece of dirt on the floor in front of you. Incredible, isn't it? You don't need a gun or a knife or even a length of rope. You just need you.'

He paused and got up. He fiddled with the projector, adjusting the focus, then began to go through the slides again.

'You know, she told us you were a good photographer. Excellent, were her words. Said you could be a professional, instead of driving rich Yanks around the countryside. Your mother said pretty much the same thing. You could have been brilliant at school. A photographic memory. There's that word again. Funny how it keeps on cropping up, isn't it?'

'My mother,' Jimmy sat up. 'You spoke to

my mother?'

'Of course we did, and your little sister Molly, lovely girl. Such a shame. And you also spoke to Tina, didn't you, Dave? Your big sister Tina. Tell Jimmy, Dave, how you got on with Tina.'

'Great, fantastic. She's a gorgeous woman, your big sister Tina.'

And then he was on the floor, Fitzsimons on top of him, holding his head between his hands and banging it again and again and again, hard down on the carpet tiles. Screaming, swearing, the words falling out of his mouth like the saliva spattered across Finney's face.

They dragged him off, handcuffing him, pulling him away, the cuffs digging into his wrists. Lynch forced him back down into the chair, while McLoughlin helped Dave to his feet, wiping his face with his handkerchief.

'So that got you going, you little bastard. 'Cause that's what you are, aren't you? A dirty little bastard. Your sister's brat. And who was your father, eh? Some snot-nosed kid with acne, banging her in the bicycle shed after school, or in the back row of the pictures on Saturday afternoon? Fourteen she was when she had you. Can you imagine a fourteen-year-old? And you coming out between those fat little thighs, kind of like your little sister, isn't that right, Jimmy?'

McLoughlin flicked through the slides again, finishing on a close-up of Mary's battered face. 'Did anyone ever hit you like that, when you were a kid? Your father maybe, or should I say your grandfather? Or maybe he was both? Father and grandfather, now wouldn't that be something? What do you think, Jimmy? That little girl with her white thighs and her little tits, and that big man, and I've met him and he's big, pushing himself down on her, hurting her, like you hurt Jenny and young Mary.'

Jimmy whimpered, his face milk-white in the projector's glow. Tears welled up and spilled down. He tried to move his arms but they were pinned behind his back. He struggled, whimpering, pulling against the cuffs.

'That's right, Jimmy. Handcuffs hurt, don't they? Did you see Mary Mitchell's wrists after you took the handcuffs off her, did you? Let's look,' and he flicked again through the slides until her wrists and hands were displayed, huge, deep red weals where the metal had cut through the skin.

Jimmy sobbed and screamed. 'I want my mother. Help, help. I want someone. Please help me.'

Lynch looked at McLoughlin. He shook his head, almost imperceptibly.

'It's too late for that, Jimmy. She can't help you now. We're the only ones who can do that. You've got to tell us. What you did. How it happened. Tell us. Now.'

He handed him over to Finney. Let him take the statement. Finney wanted that. And McLoughlin felt he owed him. He went to his desk and phoned the DPP's office. Explained the situation. A statement was being taken. They would have enough to charge him. He looked at his watch. Twenty-two fifteen. Fitzsimons's detention would cease at precisely twenty-three-oh-seven. Twelve hours from the time he was arrested. But Finney knew that too. He'd make sure that everything was signed, sealed and delivered in time.

He switched off the lights as he left the office. Sal Daly was off duty. But Peter Manning, who'd taken over from him, would keep the records. Check the prisoner. Make sure the station doctor was called to look at the bruises on his wrists and Finney's cut eye. It would all be written down. The accused would be charged with false imprisonment, rape and murder. A good day's work by all accounts.

30

What would she do now? Now that her mother was dead, her daughter was dead, her father was dead.

She sat beside Catherine's hospital bed. It was early morning. She had watched the dawn come to life as her mother's life had ended, the sky lightening from black to grey to pink to pale blue. She had listened to the changing sounds outside. The night's empty silence had been filled with birdsong, with blackbirds, thrushes, sparrows, robins, the everyday accompaniment to the routines and rhythms of suburbia.

She had practised listening, shifting her awareness from the birds outside to her mother's slow, soft breaths. Sometimes she thought her breathing had stopped. But then she would breathe again, once or maybe twice. Cheyne-Stoking it was called. She remembered the term. Intermittent breathing every couple of minutes. The heart still beats, but gradually the brain is starved of oxygen. She took Catherine's wrist and felt her pulse. It fluttered and stopped, then fluttered again. She looked at her face. Her skin was waxy, her features indistinct, as if someone had drawn a hand down and across, smearing them while they were still being formed. She both was and was not the mother she had always known.

She had still been conscious when Margaret had arrived back at the hospital. They had increased her dose of morphine. She was in no pain now.

'Is that you, Margaret?' she said.

'Yes, Mother, it's me.'

'And is Daddy with you?'

'No, Mother, but he's not far away.'

Her mother turned her face towards the white wall and closed her eyes. Later she opened them suddenly and said, 'Margaret, I love you. I've always loved you.' And she began to cry, pathetic sobs shaking her wizened upper body. Margaret leaned over her, smoothing the fine hair back from her forehead, and murmuring endearments until she lapsed back into unconsciousness.

Was she sleeping? She watched the sheet over her chest. Was it moving? She held her hand in front of her nose? Could she feel the slightest feather of breath?

She wanted to ask her so many things. She knew so little, she realized now. She thought of the photograph albums. All those pictures of John, his family, his friends. And none of Catherine. She never spoke of her mother or father. She had no brothers or sisters. She had appeared, so it seemed, in John's office one day. A new secretary, a smart young woman with a shorthand notebook. And she had got him, made him fall in love with her. Married the most eligible of them all, with his own car and his own house in Monkstown.

'Why did you never talk to me, Mummy, why did you never tell me?' Margaret whispered the words into her ear. But there was no response. She remembered watching her putting on her makeup. The daily ritual. Sitting at her dressing table in her frilly nightgown, her legs crossed, one small foot in a pink satin slipper, swinging. I must have been sick, thought Margaret. Otherwise I wouldn't have been there. Usually Catherine didn't get up until Daddy and I had left the house in the mornings. But I remember. First the foundation, Elizabeth Arden, squeezed from the tube, and smoothed from the base of the neck up and over the delicate bones of her face. Then the powder from the big round box, with the fluffy puff. Then the eyes, the delicate lining of the upper lid with black, the pencilling in of the eyebrows, and the mascara on the tips of the lashes. And finally, the finishing touch, the lips, the careful outlining in the favourite colour of the day, coral, or peach, sometimes crimson. Then the filling in with broad strokes, and the bringing together of the upper and the lower lips in a narcissistic kiss to the mirror.

'Do that to me, Mummy, please,' she had asked. But Catherine had picked her up, and taken her back to her own room, closing the door firmly behind her.

She reached across the bed and took hold of her right hand. She smoothed the wrinkled skin with her fingers, and held it against her cheek. She wanted to cry but she had no tears left. All gone, she thought, as she placed Catherine's hand back down on the white sheet. She looked at her own wrist, at the strip of plaited cloth wrapped around it. One of the nurses had commented.

'It's a friendship bracelet, isn't it?' she

said. 'One of my kids has one. Her best friend gave it to her. Isn't the idea that you wear it until it drops off of its own accord? Something like that, anyway.'

She sat and watched until there were no more sighs, no more sudden gasps. Then she stood up. I will pronounce her dead, she thought. My final act as her daughter. She lifted a slack eyelid. Catherine's pupils were fixed and dilated. She picked up the frail wrist, and placed her fingers on the blue tracks of the veins. She felt no pulse against her skin. She held her pocket mirror up to the pinched nostrils. No breath clouded its cold surface.

She sat beside the bed until they came to take her away. She held the pocket mirror in front of her own face, marking the lines, the wrinkles, the cruel sagging of the skin. She had nothing more to say, nothing more to give. There will be no more of us, she thought. Mary gone. Her baby gone too. Only me. On my own.

She continued to sit on the hard upright chair as they stripped the bed of its soiled linen, mopped the floor around her feet, wiped away every trace of the woman who had died there. Then she got up, and walked to the window. The hospital was surrounded by gardens, filled with huge old trees, oak, ash, chestnut, and in one corner a grass tennis court. Two men and two women were playing a game of mixed doubles. She watched their strong young bodies as they dashed from side to side, laughing and calling out to each other. And she felt herself ageing, her muscles wasting and sagging, her bones thinning, her hair and skin losing its tone, its shine, its elasticity.

I am dead, she thought. All that is left is to bury me. And then a smell, familiar, laden with memory. Elderflower water, light and pretty but with an underlying tartness. She looked around. Mary was standing beside her. Pale, but smiling, her eyes bright and knowing.

'Don't worry, Mummy,' she said, 'you'll be all right.' And she pulled Margaret's head onto her shoulder, and stood beside her, one arm holding her close, one hand on her shoulder, the other hand stroking her cheeks, wiping the tears away as they welled up out of her eyes and trickled slowly down her face.

'Shh,' she said, 'shh, shh, shh.' And they stood, the two of them, as the sun flooded into the room, bouncing off the gleaming white walls and floor, its rays glittering on a tray of instruments on a trolley, casting a halo around Margaret's head, and filling her, just for the moment, with warmth.

PART

2

31

The taxi driver was bored. He sat, his engine idling, the radio on, watching the people trickling out of the airport terminal. Where do they all come from, he wondered, and why if they have the money to travel, do they bother coming here? Especially in the spring with the weather so unpredictable. The car in front moved off and he edged to the head of the line. Twenty to four. It had been a slow day. At this rate he'd have to stay on the road until well after rush hour. He shifted in his seat, uncomfortable, the buckle of his belt sticking into the rolls of fat that poured over it. There was the sound of the back door opening. He turned awkwardly, looking over his shoulder. A woman was leaning into the car, her face pale, her eyes hidden by dark glasses. She said, 'I've a couple of bags here. If you wouldn't mind.'

He pulled out into the traffic on the main road into the city. It was heavy as always. Moving very slowly. Must be some kind of a hold-up, he thought, further in, maybe as far as Whitehall. An accident, or some kind of Garda checkpoint. He drummed impatiently on the steering wheel, then punched the buttons on the car radio. The traffic came to a standstill. He leaned back, one hand fiddling with the headrest of the seat next to him.

'What's up?' she asked.

He shrugged. 'Who knows? It's always like this.' He looked at her in the rear-view mirror. She was sitting up very straight, looking all around. Her movements were edgy, nervous. She turned her head away from him and looked out of the window. He noticed her neck. It was long and very thin, the tendons standing out underneath the skin. She turned back towards him. He wished she'd take her glasses off so he could get a really good look at her face. When he stood beside her as he lifted her bags into the boot he had been very conscious of how small she was. Barely five foot, he reckoned. Her dark brown hair was pulled back from her forehead and gathered with a wooden clasp at the nape of her neck. When she leaned forward to settle the bags more firmly he noticed the round curve of her hips, the soft denim of her jeans pulled into her waist with a worn leather belt. He looked at the large sticker decorating one of the bags. Air New Zealand. A long way to travel with so little luggage. She thanked him for his help and smiled, her wide pale mouth opening to reveal small white teeth. And as she moved away from him, lifting her arm to pick up her shoulder bag, he had smelt something light and natural. Rose, maybe, like his daughter wore.

He put a cassette into the tape machine and pressed play. Nanci Griffiths' nasal twang filled the car. He glanced again at her in the mirror. 'Is that OK?'

'Absolutely fine.'

The car in front began to move, slowly at first, then gradually picking up speed. She had given him instructions, told him where to go. He couldn't quite work out her accent. He didn't think she was from Dublin, but she seemed to know her way around. As they passed through the city centre she commented on changes that had taken places buildings gone, buildings replaced.

'You've been here before?' he asked.

She smiled. 'Yes, a few times.'

'And the last time was?'

'Last summer.'

'Great, wasn't it? Let's hope this one will be as good.'

She didn't reply. She sank back into the seat. Her face had changed. She looked ill, the skin around her mouth loose and trembling.

When he stopped where she had asked, she didn't get out immediately. He pulled into the gravel circle in front of the tall wrought-iron gates. They were locked, a chain and padlock looped around the old ornate handle, a collection of last autumn's dead leaves still piled up against them. He turned off the engine. The music was suddenly very loud. He looked again at her. Her hands were over her face, her head was bowed. He waited. Then he got out of the car and walked away from it as far as the gates. He leaned against them, reaching up with his arms and grasping the iron bars as high up as he could, stretching his back, stiff from the hours spent sitting. When he released his grip and looked back she was standing by the boot of the car. He walked slowly over to her.

'There's something I need in here,' she said.

He opened the boot and she took a plastic container, lunchbox-sized, from one of the bags.

'You don't mind waiting, do you?' she

asked. 'I'll pay you for your time.'

He nodded, and she walked away, through a side gate in the high stone wall. He watched her picking her way along the uneven path, until she disappeared behind a row of headstones. Then he locked the taxi and began to follow her.

It was quiet behind the graveyard's high walls. The only sound was his feet on the gravel of the narrow path, which wound away from the gates leading him into the tumbled labyrinth of the graves. He was reluctant to branch off down one of the narrow grass tracks, suddenly superstitious in this place. It was cold, the spring sun not able to contend with the cold blast of a north-easterly. He zipped up his leather jacket and shoved his hands into the pockets. He began to walk quickly, every now and then jumping up to see further over the irregular horizon of crosses and angels and blocks of stone like miniature skyscrapers. And then he saw her. A flash of white from her shirt over in the far corner, just for a moment.

He turned off the path, stumbling over the rough, uncared-for ground. The sound of his breath was loud in his ears, and the grass felt damp against his legs. It was a long time since he had been in a place like this. Not since his father had been buried. He hadn't liked it then, the coffin heavy on his shoulder, and he didn't like it now. He was tempted to go back to the car, suddenly, unreasonably anxious. But then, as he turned from the end of one row into the beginning of another, he found her. Squatting by a group of graves that were separate, on their own, under a large tree. She was rocking backwards and forwards on her heels, taking handfuls of something from the plastic box and spreading it over one of the graves. A candle was burning at the base of the headstone, its flame flickering weakly in the sunlight, which dappled through the tree. The headstone was like nothing else he had ever seen. It was carved from a plain grey rock, some kind of limestone, he thought, in the shape of a seashell. Its edges were rough, and it looked in places as if it still had the accretions of limpets and other clinging sea creatures. The grave itself was covered in other rough stones, softened by mosses of a deep green. He looked again at what she was doing. She was placing shells carefully among the stones and the moss, and she was muttering under her breath as she did so. He couldn't hear what she was saying, but the sounds gave him that same sweet comforting feeling that reminded him of something, very far away, that he thought he had lost for ever. He couldn't read the dedication on the headstone so he moved forward slowly on tiptoes, but his heavy body unbalanced and he tripped.

She turned. She had taken off her glasses. She looked naked, vulnerable, as if she had just woken from a deep sleep.

'Sorry, I'm very sorry. I didn't mean to.' The words fell over themselves, tumbled from his mouth.

She looked at him silently, then returned to her task. He gazed over her bowed head and mouthed the words carved into the rocky shell.

MARY MITCHELL

1975–1995

To see a world in a grain of sand
And a heaven in a wild flower
Hold infinity in the palm of your hand
And eternity in an hour

It was about fifteen minutes later that she came back to the car. Her face was hidden again behind her dark glasses. She didn't speak, except to give him the address of her final destination. It was only as he drove down the narrow road towards the sea, past the Martello tower at Seapoint, that he realized who the girl was. He remembered. Last summer. The guards had been all over the taxi drivers. Questions, more questions, details of fares, trips, anything unusual. A couple of the lads had been taken in, given the once-over. But none of them knew anything about the girl's death. It was rough for a few weeks. And then, he remembered, they got some guy for it. He wasn't a taxi man. He had some kind of private chauffeuring outfit. A scab, in other words. It was an awful case. One of the blokes on the rank had a brother-in-law who was a guard. He said her injuries were bad, she'd had a terrible time before she was killed. Poor kid.

He got out of the car to help the woman with her bags. They'd pulled up outside a house that looked as if it had seen better days. A couple of slates off the roof, windows and doors needing painting. A pity to let it fall apart, he thought. In this lovely spot, right by the sea. It'd be worth a small fortune, these days, with the property market booming. He carried her bags up the steps to the front door. She counted out what she owed him, then added another tenner.

'Ah, here,' he said, 'that's a bit much.'

She smiled. 'No, you were very kind.'

'Listen,' he said, then he stopped.

'Yes?' She turned back to him, a bunch of keys dangling from her hand.

'If you ever need help with anything...' He pressed his card into her hand.

She watched while he drove down to the end of the cul-de-sac, turned and came back. He slowed down and saluted her, then he went on his way. She walked back down the steps and looked up at the house. Home again, she thought.

32

To market, to market to buy a fat pig,
Home again, home again, jiggety-jig.
To market, to market to buy a fat hog.
Home again, home again, jiggety-jog.

She was dreaming again. It was the same dream. She had been having it regularly now for months.

She was in a room somewhere, in a house somewhere. She didn't recognize it but she felt comfortable, relaxed, at ease. Mary was sitting across her knees, facing her. She was aged about three, a chubby little thing with strong legs, muscles under the baby fat, which drummed against Margaret's thighs. She was wearing a pair of cream-coloured dungarees. A big fat pig wearing a straw hat was embroidered on the bib in red chain stitch. She was wearing exactly the same kind of hat jammed down on her black curls. She was chanting the nursery rhyme with a syncopated rhythm. Margaret's knees were bumping her up in the air in time to it. Bump, bump, bump. Up and down she went, her curly hair and the straw hat jumping from her head in time to the little song. Margaret felt happy, so happy. She was chanting the nursery rhyme too.

To market, to market
Home again, home again
To market, to market
Home again, home again.

Then something changed. Mary was no longer on her knees. She didn't know when or how she had left. Every time she woke from the dream she tried to hold on to what had happened, but the memory left her as she opened her eyes. She could still hear her voice, her little lisping mis-pronunciations.

Jiddity-jid,
Jiddity-jod,
Jiddity-jid,
Jiddity-jod.

But she couldn't see her anywhere. She was bouncing her empty knees up and down, up and down, over and over. She could still feel Mary's weight on her thighs, but the child was gone.

She stood up. She was standing by a large plate-glass window. Outside on the vivid green grass lay the straw hat. She stepped through the glass. It shattered around her. She walked over to the hat and lifted it up. Underneath lay Mary, tiny, her mouth open, shrieking the words of the rhyme. But when Margaret bent down and picked her up she realized that it wasn't Mary. It was a china doll, her face painted in a dreadful grimace, her arms and legs in a twisted rictus, her curly hair set in stiff porcelain. Cold, hard, unyielding.

Margaret woke. She was as rigid and as cold as the doll had been. A gale was blowing outside. The wind poured in from the sea, banging against the sash windows and flicking out the hem of the curtains, like the swaying skirts of a woman waltzing. She stared at the old beige lampshade hanging above her head. The small pompoms around its base bobbled gently in the draught. Mary's room, Mary's bed, but no trace of her now on the damp pillow or in the empty cupboards and drawers, still standing open as she had left them six months ago. She had thought she would find her in their house outside Auckland. She had run from room to room, tearing back the curtains so that the bright southern sun poured in, calling her name, flinging open the door to her bedroom, sure she would be there, lying on the divan, her Walkman clamped to her head, a bottle of Coke and a half-eaten apple on the floor beside her. But nothing or no one came to meet her, nothing or no one came to comfort her. No sound except the irritated buzzing of a fly trapped against the glass of the window, no sight except her own exhausted face staring back at her from the mirror in the empty bathroom.

She got up, stiff, her legs aching. It was early, not yet seven. She walked out into the corridor. The doors to the other bedrooms were closed and the landing was dark. It was very quiet apart from the screech of the wind as it flounced around the corners of the house. She walked down the stairs, along the hall and into her mother's room. It was exactly as she had left it. She had done nothing except strip the bed of its sheets. Everything else was as it always had been. She went over and sat down on the bed. The springs creaked. The mattress sagged beneath her. She lay down, falling into the deep hollow in its centre. Her head was where Catherine's had been, her body moulding itself to the contours of her mother's. The room smelt of damp and dust. She closed her eyes but the cold nagged at her, prodding her to move. She swung her legs over the side and walked to the large window, opened the shutters and folded them back into their recesses. The sea rolled, green and yellow, dirty white breakers spending themselves on the rock. Dark clouds hung low over Howth and along the edge of the horizon wisps of rain straggled into the sea.

Rain fell in the city, rain driven by gale-force winds from the east. Winds funnelling up the Liffey, kicking up stiff little waves with white peaked caps, flicking umbrellas inside out. Rain falling so quickly and heavily that the culverts and drains couldn't cope with the volume of water, and it lay in puddles and pools.

McLoughlin's feet were already wet and it was only nine-thirty in the morning. Wet feet and a bad temper. Not the best way to begin the day, he thought bitterly, as he stood in the gents' toilet in the Four Courts. He looked down, past the white enamel urinal to the wet stain around the bottom of his trousers. It must have been a huge puddle. Took him completely by surprise as he stepped out of the car half an hour ago. But that didn't explain the temper. Another row with Janey. It had started the way they always did. A casual remark. An imagined slight. And then the stream of accusations. When he left the house she followed him onto the driveway, her dressing gown billowing around her bare legs, her voice simultaneously loud and plaintive. He'd been neglecting her, he didn't love her, he was having an affair, he was going to leave her. Go on, she screamed. Do it. See how you like it on your own. Your girlfriends won't want to know after they've spent some time putting up with you and your filthy habits, you're disgusting. No one could live with you. You bastard.

Unfortunately he'd no one to blame but himself. Somehow he'd missed their last wedding anniversary. He cringed inwardly when he thought about it. And for once there was no other woman involved. It had happened to coincide with the last Galway hooker race of the season. A blowy Saturday. A beautiful autumn day, the wind from the southwest, a steady force four to five. He was supposed to come home after the race, but it was late when they got back to the clubhouse. And then, and then. He had to stay and drink with the lads. And she'd gone to bed by the time he rolled in. She'd drunk the bottle of champagne by herself. He had no excuse. He knew that but, by Christ, she knew how to extract blood. Over and over again. Until he was sick to death of her.

He zipped up his fly and washed his hands. He stood in front of the smeared mirror and straightened his tie. The DPP v. Jimmy Fitzsimons, beginning today. Around and behind him swirled the black gowns of the barristers. For and against, pro and anti, prosecution and defence. Not that it mattered much to them which side they were on. Just a very nice lucrative game. And a chance to behave like little boys, fighting, scrapping, throwing clever insults, Scoring points. And winning. He wasn't sure where justice stood in all this. But he'd realized a long time ago that whatever happened in the Four Courts didn't have a lot to do with justice.

He looked at his watch. Time to make a move. She was waiting for him under the dome in the Round Hall, standing on her own in the centre of the vestibule. He paused at the top of the steps that led up from the toilets, and watched her. At the sight of her face butterflies danced a quadrille in the pit of his stomach. She was wearing a plain black suit, with a long narrow jacket over a short skirt. Her pale stockings shone in the dull light filtered through the glass high up in the dome. Her hair was pulled back from her face. She looked older, he thought, thinner and paler, the colour leached from her skin. He watched her, as she turned this way and that, spun around by the crowds, taking three steps in one direction then three steps back again to the same position. Her hands were clasped at waist height, her fingers locked together, twisting around each other, then releasing and clasping again. It was a characteristic gesture, he thought. When all else about her was calm her hands gave her away with their fussing and fidgeting, their constant re-assuring grasp of each other.

Her hands holding a coffee cup the day he had come to tell her that they had charged Fitzsimons. The good news, as he thought. But he hadn't known that her mother had died the day before. She was like a zombie when she answered the door. Her movements were jerky and awkward as she brought him into the kitchen and made him coffee. He had thought she would be pleased at his news, pleased at the thought of some kind of retribution, even revenge. But she stood with her back to the sink, holding the cup, then mindlessly, thoughtlessly, opened her grasp and dropped it onto the tiles as one hand reached for the other.

'And if he's found guilty,' she said, the brown liquid spreading in a steaming puddle across the cracked floor, 'what kind of sentence are we talking about?'

'Well, life is mandatory for murder.'

'And that's how long? Nominally ten years, isn't it? Then out in seven with good behaviour. Not much. Nothing in comparison with my life sentence.'

'So what's the alternative?' he asked. 'The death penalty? Would you really want that?'

She had looked up at him, her eyelids red and sore, her mouth a narrow slit.

'Yes. I would. I'm not civilized about this any more. I have no pretensions to compassion or understanding.'

Six months had passed. It had been the end of summer then, when he had knelt at her feet, a tea towel wadded in his hand soaking up the spilt coffee. It was the end of spring now, the evening sun brightening the garden despite the cold wind as he picked his way over the cracked paving stones towards the faded front door. He had phoned ahead to say that he was coming, that he wanted to run through a few points about the trial with her. She had sounded friendly, looking forward to seeing him. She had brought him something, she said, a present from New Zealand. So he stopped at a florist and got her flowers. Lilies, white and stiff, their dark orange stamens nodding in unison as he handed them over.

She walked ahead, down the hall towards

the kitchen, and he followed, noticing how her neck rose, stalk-like, from her soft cashmere sweater. There was a cardboard box in the middle of the kitchen table and she gestured to it as she knelt and pulled at cupboard doors, looking, he assumed, for a vase for the lilies, which were lying now in the stained enamel sink.

'Open it,' she said, and he tugged back the stiff cardboard tongues, tearing the box in his haste, revealing a model of a late nineteenth-century clipper ship.

'Hey, that's beautiful. The *Thermopylae*, I do believe. Do you know that she was one of the fastest tea-clippers ever built? Capable of fantastic speeds. Once she made a run of three hundred and eighty miles in one day. Incredible for the time.'

He held the model up to the light, turning it this way and that, admiring its lines, commenting on the exactness of the rigging, the accuracy of the scale. He began to talk to her of his desire, his dream. To sail around the world, braving Cape Horn and the Roaring Forties, while she bustled around behind him, producing glasses, a bottle of whiskey, a tray of ice and a jug of water. He poured for both of them, then sat down at the table, the model in one hand, the glass in the other.

'So tell me,' she said, 'the trial. How long will it last? How many witnesses will be called? Who is representing us, and who the defence?'

He looked from the boat's white sails to her face, grey with tiredness. He explained. Who and what, how and why. She stood with a large blue vase in her hands, half filled with lilies. Their scent curled into the still air, as the water rose up their hollow stems. And again, her hands opened as if involuntarily, and flowers and shards of pottery littered the floor, while the sound of the breakage echoed through the silent house. She knelt quickly and began to gather up the pieces, careless, cutting the pad of her thumb so that drops of blood threaded through the water on the tiles. He had tried to help, squatting beside her, offering his handkerchief to staunch the bleeding, but she had pushed him away.

He watched her, as she stood, as always on her own. He was sure there must have been someone who could have come with her. A neighbour, an old friend, like that nice Anne Brady. Someone. But she stood by herself, while around her pushed and shoved the usual Four Courts throng.

He noticed a group of journalists standing near the main entrance. One of them, a thin young man with sandy-coloured hair and glasses, detached himself from the group and headed towards her. McLoughlin stepped forward quickly and got to her just before he did. He took her by the arm, positioning himself neatly between them. He looked at the young man and shook his head vehemently, then led her over to a bench against the wall, just by the entrance to Court Number Two. They sat down together.

'Sorry about that,' he said.

'What?' She looked puzzled.

'That guy. Better stay out of his way.'

He had wanted to meet her to make sure that she would get a seat in the court. He explained to her that as the victim's mother she had no formal role in the business of the trial. Her status was exactly the same as the most casual observer. She would be well advised to get to the court early every morning if she wanted to keep her place. Particularly as the case proceeded and got more and more publicity. But he needed to warn her that the court officials dealt rigorously with outbursts, regardless of who they came from.

She looked at him blankly. 'Who do you take me for?' she said, her voice harsh and angry.

He shrugged his shoulders and stood. She didn't realize what could happen behind those two glass doors. The ancient ritual of trial by jury. Trial it was aptly called. And it didn't just try the accused or the guilty. He knew that only too well, and soon she would too.

33

He had never got used to being watched all the time. It had begun that first day. When the two guards arrived at his house. He had just come back from the church in Monkstown. That had been fun. It had given him plenty to think about over the following days and months. But he hadn't expected the guards to show up on his doorstep so soon. He'd tried to fob them off, but they'd started watching him immediately. And he didn't like it. And he liked it even less when they brought him in for questioning, and put him in that room, with the blank walls.

Nothing to look at but the chequered carpet tiles, beige and brown, the red fire extinguisher in the corner, the two strips of fluorescent lighting. No one to talk to but them, all over you, gnawing at you, sucking out everything you know. And watching you all the time. Through the little pane of glass in the door, and later on the peephole in the cell. They all wanted to have a look. He could hear their footsteps coming down the corridor, and then there'd be silence for a moment, before they slid back the metal. Silence, then talk and laughter receding back down the corridor. And silence again. And after they charged him he tried to keep calm but he couldn't bear the way they checked him every fifteen minutes. He timed them on his watch. He knew it was because they thought he was a suicide risk. And they were almost right. He'd have tried it. Just to give them something to worry about. Not because he wanted to die. Fuck them, he didn't.

They still watched him here in Mountjoy. Spied on him. Listened to his conversations. Searched his cell. Kept him away from the other inmates. Said it was for his own protection. But he didn't believe that. And he felt as if he was caught all the time, like

337

the moth in the flame of the candle, or the corpse in the flash from the camera. He had never felt like that before. Before he had always been the watcher. The thing in the dark who can see everything, but can't be seen. Like the black cat. Only noticed when its yellow eyes are lit up by the headlights of a passing car. And then only for an instant, before the blackness reasserts itself.

But it was never really black in here. Always shades of murky grey or green. Lights on somewhere right through the night. Even if you put your head under the blankets you still couldn't get away from them.

He had never thought about getting caught. Not really, not seriously. Of course he wasn't stupid. He'd taken lots of pre-cautions. Like the condoms he'd worn when he was with Mary. When he had to, when there was a chance that his semen might have stayed in her body. Not for when she took him in her mouth, though. It wasn't necessary then. It was a big sacrifice wearing the condom. He'd told her. The sensation just wasn't the same. But, he reasoned, he was getting so many other feelings that he shouldn't complain. He should be prepared to miss out on the odd one.

The one mistake he'd made was her body

being found so quickly. He'd really thought that he had that one sussed too. He'd used a wheelbarrow to carry her from the boot of the car along the path. That hadn't been too difficult. And he'd made a second trip with the concrete blocks. He should have been able to see enough by the light of the moon to know exactly where he was putting her. But he'd misjudged it. Fuck that old man and his dog. It had really been a surprise when he turned on the radio and heard the news. He'd thought that it would be just another unsolved mystery, another strange disappearance. After all, there had been so many over the past few years. Girls who went out and didn't come back. He could kick himself for being so sloppy.

And if he'd been more careful he'd have had time to try it out on someone else. He already had a couple of possibilities lined up. One was a girl who worked in one of the hotels that was on his regular route. A sweet-looking little thing. Skinny, needy. And she'd even written to him since he was in prison. Terrible spelling, dreadful handwriting on pale pink paper. She wanted to come and see him. But he wouldn't let her. This place was too disgusting for a little girl like her. The only person he'd let visit was his mother. Serve her right. Let her see what she'd done to him, what her tender loving care had driven him to.

But, really, what he wanted most of all in the world was Margaret. Since that first day when Mary had taken the plastic photo album out of her bag and shown him the photographs – Margaret as a baby in a frilly white dress with booties laced around her chubby little legs, Margaret as a little girl, holding her daddy's hand as they stood outside the house, Margaret as a teenager, wearing a short skirt, her hair hanging in her eyes and a cigarette hanging from her mouth, Margaret with Mary, an exhausted young mother, her face thin and wretched, and the one he liked the most, Margaret on the beach. He'd been silent as he leafed through the pages.

'Pretty, isn't she?' Mary had said, as she lay on the back seat of the car, her feet sticking out through the open window, her hands behind her head.

He didn't answer. His mouth was dry.

'But not as pretty as me,' and she reached over to snatch the little book, but he held on to it, pushing her hands away. He had his own collection of photographs too. Not that he could get at them now, but he had his

340

memories, and the pictures he had torn from the newspapers that made their way into the prison. There'd been a feature article in the *Sunday Independent* a couple of weeks ago, about women who had died violently, and they had published a photograph that made his heart pound. The caption read 'Mary Mitchell, murdered last August, with her mother Dr Margaret Mitchell'. He hadn't see that one before. It was a mid-shot, showing from the waist upwards. It must have been taken in New Zealand, because they were both wearing bathing suits. They were looking at each other and smiling. He was struck by how alike they looked. It wasn't in the colouring, or the features. It must be in the expression, he concluded. Those indefinable combinations of movements of the muscles under the skin that produce a particular look. He'd never noticed it before.

Certainly not the last time he'd seen her. In the church. He was sorry he hadn't grabbed her when he had the opportunity. If he'd known what was going to happen, that the guards were waiting for him, that he wouldn't have time to plan what he was going to do next. If he'd hit her hard, just once, or held the knife to her neck instead of slashing her blouse. He had thought at the time that it was a bit melodramatic, but it had worked. The memory of her had been nearly enough to sustain him all these months. She had been so sure of herself, so confident. And then when the knife slid through the material of her blouse the colour had run out of her face like bleach dripping down a bloody handkerchief. It had been wonderful.

But to be caught because of that fucking English girl. And she was the reason he didn't get bail. He was sure of it. Although they told him, after they'd charged him with Mary's murder, that she wasn't going to co-operate in taking a case against him. She was too traumatized. He mimed the word, turning his face into a tragic pierrot. Silly cow. If he'd known what she was going to do he might have considered going a bit further with her. Just a wee bit further. Or, there again, he might have considered taking it all the way. Then she would have been his first, Mary would have been his second, and the mother his third. And then, and then.

But, instead, he was here. Fucking Mount-joy. And today was the first day of his trial. Oh, joy unconfined. They'd be coming for him soon. And he'd be outside. Breathing real fresh air. He couldn't wait.

He stood up in the narrow cell, and looked at as much of himself as he could see in his tiny scrap of mirror. His mother had brought him a suit to wear. It was a nice one. Charcoal grey wool. Three-piece. And one of his favourite shirts. Pale lemon. He'd worn it often enough so it was nice and soft around the collar. And his tie was grey and lemon too. Heavy silk. Embossed. An intricate design of spirals and circles. Funny to think that it had been a present from Mary. She'd picked it out all by herself. She always used to say that she didn't have a clue about men's things because she didn't have a father. He imagined her flirting with the assistants in Brown Thomas. All gawky legs and curls. Little Miss Innocent.

He paced backwards and forwards a couple of times. Ten feet from the small window high up in the wall to the metal door. Ten medium paces or seven long strides. Fifteen steps if he carefully put the heel of one foot bang up against the toes of the other. Anything to keep himself amused. There were two bunks in the cell, but he'd been on his own for most of the time. For some reason, the other inmates didn't like men like him. Accused of sexual crimes. He couldn't see the logic himself. It seemed pretty hypocritical. After all, how many of the men inside had used their physical strength to get what they wanted? How many men had pushed it just that bit too far, made it happen when it didn't seem as if it would? Wasn't that what being a man was all about? Denying nature? Refusing to accept limits? Using your imagination to change situations?

Any minute now they'd be here. He supposed they'd handcuff him. Then he'd walk down the landing, ignoring all the shouts and screams and abuse from the others. Out into the chilly spring morning. Damp and fresh. The buds on the chestnuts and the cherries swelling. And they'd drive in the police van out of the high spiked gate, turning right up the North Circular Road, then left down Phibsborough Road, past the neat red-brick Corporation houses, onto Constitution Hill, with King's Inns just visible over the high grey wall, across North King Street into Church Street, close to the river now, and then left along Chancery Street and into the back of the Four Courts. There'd be a crowd of reporters and TV people all around the van when he passed. They'd be holding up their cameras to try to

get a shot of him. He didn't mind. He'd
nothing to feel ashamed about. And when
he got out of the van there'd be a few more
waiting, circling, hunting in packs. He
wouldn't put something over his head. It
looked really silly, he always thought.
Undignified. No, he'd want to stand
straight, show off what kind of a guy he was.
And the best thing of all would be that when
he went into the court room he was
absolutely certain that she would be there.
Close. Probably less than ten feet away from
him. Breathing the same air, in and out, in
and out. And the guards would be decent.
They'd take off his cuffs. They'd buy him a
newspaper. And he'd sit there on the bench,
looking just like anyone else. And he'd be
able to look at her as much as he wanted. To
his heart's content.

34

The golden harp hung, silent, high on the
cream wall. Above the judge's raised oak
bench. Above the rows of seats in the body of
the court. Above the empty jury enclosure.

Above the polished wooden bench where the accused would sit. Above the people crowded into the aisles, chatting, gossiping, greeting friends, turning around to look, to gawk, to stare.

Margaret stood just inside the door, McLoughlin at her side. Around them in a protective semicircle stood the other guards who had been involved in the investigation. Some of them she knew. Like good-looking young Finney, with his shiny black hair and dimples, Brian Conroy, with his rumpled jeans and leather jacket, and skinny, freckled Bert Lynch. The faces of the others slid into a blur of hair and noses, teeth and chins, none of whom she would ever recognize away from this place.

McLoughlin had introduced her to the prosecution team. The senior counsel had barely glanced at her as she took his hand. His white wig and black gown gave him a certain dignity, which she was sure was missing when he was dressed like any other middle-aged, middle-class man. Like surgeons, Margaret thought, whose green scrubs, testimony to their skill and knowledge, gave them an aura of power unmatched by any number of expensive suits. She remembered girls she had known in medical school who had fallen in love with men old enough to be their fathers, seduced by the eyes that gazed at them over the tops of their masks, beguiled by the hands, delicate inside their rubber gloves, that cut, stitched, probed. She had never succumbed herself. But she remembered, once, coming across a couple in one of the cubicles just off the main theatre. She hadn't seen the girl's face. It was buried underneath the man's gown. His eyes were closed, his body thrown back against a trolley, a mouthful of gold fillings exposed as he grunted his pleasure. One of the top heart surgeons in the country, getting his reward after another triumphant triple bypass.

McLoughlin began to explain the geography of the court room, who sat where and why, but she brushed his explanations away. She looked around her, warily. Wondering. She had been here, before, a long time ago. In another life, it seemed. It was smaller than she remembered, and less formal. The atmosphere was curious. Casual, almost everyday, but with a strong undercurrent of tension. Like the pools of cold water in a warm lake, she thought, that wait for the unsuspecting swimmer.

'Where is he now?' she asked.

347

'He?'

'He.'

'In the cell in the basement, probably. But he'll be here soon. How do you feel?'

She didn't reply. She stepped forward. 'I'm going to sit down,' she said, moving away from them.

McLoughlin watched her seat herself in the first row of the second of the two blocks of seats that stretched from the bottom of the judge's podium to the door at the back. Already most of the public benches were full. He looked from the judge's empty chair to the registrar and court stenographer who sat below him, and from them to the instructing solicitors for the state and the accused who sat side by side, facing the court, at floor level. Files were piled haphazardly on the polished desk in front of them, and on the benches where soon the senior counsels would take their place.

A steady drone of conversation drifted up to the large square skylight overhead. Any minute now. Margaret's hands were sweating, but her mouth was dry. Strange and contradictory are the ways of the body, she thought. The sweat is caused by increased activity in the capillaries close to the skin, the result of an accelerated heart-rate because of the amount of adrenaline in the bloodstream. And the dry mouth comes from the same increased hormone levels, which shut off the routine functions of the body, like growth, reproduction and digestion. No wonder she could feel her breakfast, frugal as it had been, lying in her stomach, unchanged.

A flicker of movement to her right. A change in the level of noise in the room. The hairs on her arms prickled. Cold, so cold. Her body contracted inside its shield of clothes. She turned her head, slowly. He was standing just inside the door, flanked by two guards. Close, so close. He was looking straight at her. His face was alight with a smile, an expression of recognition. She reached down for the briefcase at her feet. She rested it on her lap and put her thumbs against the locks. They snapped open. She put her right hand inside. She took out a piece of dark blue material, plaited into a short rope. She put the bag back down on the floor. She wound her hands around the rope of linen, testing its strength, stroking it with her fingertips. Then she looked at him again. They had led him to his seat. A guard had taken off his handcuffs. He was sitting now, at right angles to her, twelve maybe fifteen feet away. He looked relaxed, comfortable. His skin was pale, but his hair shone in the light, which fell, soft and diffuse, through the glass above.

A small figure appeared from the back of the court. A girl who pushed and shoved her way through the crowd of guards in the aisle. She was wearing a red velvet dress with flounces and long white socks pulled up over her bulky calf muscles. Her feet were shoved into patent-leather slip-ons. She was holding a small bunch of flowers in one plump hand, Limp white daisies and crushed yellow dandelions. As she bustled towards him she was making a noise, a kittenish mewing sound. She hurled herself over the wooden front of the row, throwing her arms around his neck and covering his face with loud kisses. He pulled her arms from him, pushed her away. Then he stood up and leaned over, kissing the tips of his fingers and planting them on her flushed cheeks. A middle-aged woman, her expression bleak, hurried towards them. She took the girl by the arm and dragged her away. As she turned round, Margaret saw her features, heavy eyelids, puffy cheeks, wet open mouth. The girl began to cry, noisily, her anguish silencing the room. The woman

350

pulled her by the arm, rushing her past where Margaret was sitting. She could have reached out to touch them, the girl sobbing loudly, and the woman, her blonde hair neatly permed, and her expression set in the concrete of unrelieved misery.

Jimmy looked again towards Margaret. A moment of panic showed, as he chewed the inside of his cheek, his face distorted, his chin trembling. Then she watched him as he sat down slowly, pushing himself into the straight back of the seat, calming himself, the skin of his face settling in its usual way over the bones of his forehead, his cheeks, his chin and the cartilage of his nose.

McLoughlin watched from his position beside the door. He could see the dark shine of Margaret's sleek head, and her small hard shoulders. He noticed the way the muscles in her upper back shifted and tensed underneath the fine wool of her jacket. He watched them as she bent to lift her bag from the floor. He saw how her arms were rigid as she snapped open the locks. Then he waited to see what she would do next. Nothing obvious, he knew that. There would be no outbursts of emotion, no torrents of sobbing, no spitting or abuse. Not from her. He saw how Fitzsimons looked at her. But he couldn't, from where he was standing, see her face. He wondered what expression she had as she sat, so close to him, nothing between them but fifteen feet of light blue carpet.

The noise level dropped suddenly as the door to the Round Hall was closed and the tipstaff preceded the judge into the court. It should seem anachronistic, McLoughlin thought, even silly, the gowned figure, shuffling forward, rod in one hand, mumbling in a muffled voice, 'All rise.' But he found himself standing straight, feet together, shoulders thrown back, resisting the desire to bring his right hand up to his shoulder in the kind of smart salute he had been taught in Templemore. He couldn't remember how many trials he had observed, in how many he had been an active participant, but they never failed to move him in a way he found hard to define. This was what it was all about. The prosecution of justice. He could be, and he was, as cynical as the next man, but he knew when it came to it that the law and rule of law was all anyone had to hang on to. Without the judge, the pompous well-fed barristers in their wigs and gowns, the whole creaking, tedious bureaucracy, it was a short tumbril ride to the punishment beatings, the vigilantes, the blood-covered baseball bats.

The judge settled himself on the bench, and leaned forward to say a few words to the registrar. Then he cleared his throat and called for the jury.

This was the moment of real mystery, thought McLoughlin. Take twelve people, with no training in the law, no guaranteed level of education or intelligence. Give them the power to assign guilt or innocence, and watch what happens. Somehow or other these twelve people take on the mantle of the court. They are transformed by the responsibility placed upon them. They become greater than the sum of their parts. He watched as the jury-keeper opened a small door in the wall to the right of the judge, and they shuffled into their places. Eight men and four women. Most of them were aged, he reckoned, between twenty and thirty. The defence solicitor had done his best. He had limited powers of challenge, but within those limits he had managed to pick a jury which, on balance, looked as if it might favour the accused. But who could ever tell?

The registrar called the jury roll, number first, followed by name. McLoughlin looked towards Jimmy. He was still standing, straight, expectant, a sombre but responsive expression on his face. The registrar read the charges in a rapid monotone...

'James Fitzsimons. Count number one. You are charged that on the thirteenth day of August nineteen ninety-five, in the Dublin Metropolitan district, at a place unknown, you did murder Mary Mitchell, contrary to section four of the Criminal Justice Act, nineteen ninety-four. How do you plead, guilty or not guilty?'

Without hesitation came the answer. 'Not guilty.'

'Count number two. You are charged that on the fifth day of August nineteen ninety-five at twenty-two Canal Lane, Dublin 2, you did falsely imprison Mary Mitchell, contrary to section 2(1) of the Criminal Law Jurisdiction Act. How do you plead, guilty or not guilty?'

Again the answer. 'Not guilty.'

'Count number three. You are charged that between the fifth day of August and the thirteenth day of August you did rape Mary Mitchell, contrary to section two of the Criminal Law (Rape) Act, nineteen eighty-one. How do you plead, guilty or not guilty?'

The same response. 'Not guilty.'

The judge leaned forward, his jowls beagle-like beneath the yellowing wig. 'And who is appearing for the defendant?'

There was silence for a moment. Then a tall thin figure, wigged and gowned, pushed his way quickly to his place on the front bench. He stood still for a moment, waiting for the silence, which came quickly, then bowed his head slowly. When he spoke his voice was clear and strong. 'May it please your lordship, I appear on behalf of the defendant, instructed by Mr Simon Mc-Ginley. And my apologies for my lateness, which was unavoidable.'

McLoughlin smiled at the unnecessary theatricality of it all. All this bowing and scraping. More game-playing, more dressing-up. More playing to the gallery. And then without warning he saw Margaret rise to her feet and push past the other people in the same row. She turned towards the door behind him and he saw her face. Anger was scrawled across it. He tried to stop her, but she brushed him out of the way. He followed her into the Round Hall, quiet now, like a school playground after classes have begun, but she had disappeared outside, through the glass door that led onto the quays. He quickened his step, ignoring the uniformed attendant, and hurried out under the building's huge Portland stone porch. He crossed over to the river and looked up towards O'Connell Street, then down in the direction of Heuston Station. He ran back over the road, dodging through the heavy traffic and up Chancery Place, left and on to Chancery Street, past the Bridewell and left again on to Church Street. It had begun to rain, a soft, drenching drizzle. Water dripped down his forehead and into his eyes. Fuck the woman, he thought, holding his jacket closed and feeling yet again the wet of his socks and shoes. He stopped at the iron railings that bounded the playground outside Church Street Corporation flats. The, miserable concrete rectangle was deserted. Washing sagged on lines strung between metal poles. A burnt-out car was falling to pieces beside a row of swings, their seats lashed together with a thick piece of chain. Two women walked past him, pushing an old-fashioned pram. They looked suspiciously in his direction, and as he turned towards them one of the women shouted, 'What you fuckin' lookin' at, mister?'

'Not you, you fat ugly cow,' he muttered under his breath, as he hurried back down the street and onto the quays. Perhaps, after all, she might have returned to the trial. She probably just needed a breath of fresh air. He'd probably overreacted. As always. Wherever she was concerned. The rain dripped down his neck and seeped through the seams on his shoulders. He felt cold, miserable and foolish.

35

I must begin at the beginning. That is what I must do. But what is the beginning? Is it the day that I was born, or the day that he was born? Did it start when my father stopped outside a house in Merrion Square and took my hand and ran my fingers across the engraved surface of a shining brass plate, tracing the name and the letters that followed it? That will be you, he said, when you grow up. And I smiled at my reflection, butter yellow, against the grimy brick. Or maybe it began when I sat next to a boy called Joe Macken, our first day in pre-med physics, assigned alphabetically to our seats, and I lent him a biro because his had leaked

357

all over his pocket. And three years later he invited me to his twenty-first birthday party. Was that what set the clockwork in motion? Wheels grinding, gears meshing, chance and coincidence colliding? Or maybe the beginning was quite simply my willingness, my desire, my sudden surprising need to be loved?

Margaret stood in front of a high wide mirror, fluorescent light carving grooves under her eyes and around her mouth. Behind her the cubicle doors were open, ten identical lavatories reflected along the wall. She had stumbled from the Four Courts up the quays in the rain, and eventually hailed a taxi. She had told the driver to bring her to the airport. There was no reason for her choice of destination, just an overwhelming desire to be alone, to be in a place that held no memories, that did not resonate with desire or sorrow.

Water had soaked through her shoes, and mud had splashed up her legs. Her hair was plastered to her scalp. She had taken it out of its wooden slide and shaken it loose to encourage it to dry. The skin in her face felt taut. Rainwater had leached out its natural oils and left behind a husk, creased and crinkled, cross-hatched like a dry riverbed.

She turned on the tap and held her hands under the warm flow. The tops of her fingers, from the first joint to the tips of her nails, were dead white. She turned them over and held them up in front of her face. The skin was soft and wrinkled, like something, she thought, that you'd find when you lifted up a large stone. A small slug-like creature, soft and wet, its body transparent so you could see the workings of its internal organs. She remembered standing, shivering, her hair wet and dripping down her back, a small towel wrapped around her shoulder. Behind her, way out in the sea, her father, one arm waving as he trod water. 'Come back in, Maggie, it's lovely.' But she stood and shivered, her feet and hands an identical pale blue, her finger- and toenails yellow, her little nipples scratching against the elasticated material of her bathing suit, and her teeth banging together.

She drank the hot whiskey she had ordered in one large gulp and asked for another. The airport bar was empty. She sat by the big window that looked onto the runway. Should it be called the runaway? she thought, as she lifted the steaming glass, her hand not quite steady. She had to think about it now. She had to turn her attention back to what had happened this morning. I am so stupid, she chastised herself. How could I not have realized that he, given his job, his life, could be involved somehow or another with Mary's case?

He? Why did she still refer to him as 'he'? At least give him his proper title. Mary's father. Mary's real father, not the fictional, made-up version. Not the 'David Anthony Mitchell, marine biologist. Born in London, orphaned at the age of seven. Brought up in a Barnardo's home'. The man she had fixed so firmly in her memory that she believed, as much as Mary, as much as everyone else, that he had once existed. She remembered. She had sat down one morning when she was eight months pregnant, with a pen and a piece of paper, and she had drawn up his dimensions. Like an architect designing a building. Name, date of birth, place of birth. Height, weight, colour of hair and eyes. Likes and dislikes. Education and occupation. Where and how they had met. She had practised and rehearsed his vital statistics until they came automatically, like the words of a nursery rhyme or the ten times table. And how surprised and relieved she was that everyone else believed them too. She had torn a photograph from a magazine of a man who fitted the description and she had gone to a photographer and asked him to make her copies. She had sent one to her parents. Mary had spotted it amongst the clutter on the mantelpiece in Catherine's room.

'Look, Mummy,' she had said, picking it up, 'it's our picture of Daddy. Doesn't he look nice?'

She had had six copies made. One was in her office, three were scattered around her house, and there was one more. It was missing. Mary had always kept it in her bag, and her bag was gone.

Poor David Anthony Mitchell. She had bought some books and clothes in a second-hand shop in Portobello. William Blake's *Songs of Innocence and Experience*, a couple of dog-eared Charles Dickenses, *A Christmas Carol* and *David Copperfield*. Some old orange Penguins. Graham Greene and Kingsley Amis. Virginia Woolf's *Orlando* in a handsome Hogarth Press first edition, and a few old books on birds and butterflies, fish and insects. She had carefully printed his name on the flyleaf of the books, and had his name, embroidered, boarding-school style, on ten old handkerchiefs. There was a microscope at home in Mary's bedroom that she told her had belonged to her father.

Just think, she had said, when you put your eye against the glass, his eye would have been there too. Years ago. When he was about your age. The lies had come easily. She raised her glass to the memory of the man she had created, saluting him in the shadowy reflection that the rain-spattered window gave back to her. But now she could delay no longer. She had to deal with the real man, not the convenient figment of her imagination. She waved her hand at the barman. I will wait for another drink and then I will think about him.

She stirred the black cloves, like tiny bones, around in the sugary whiskey, pressing the slice of lemon against the glass to extract as much of its tartness as she could. Now it was time to bring him out into the light of day. Name him. Christian name, Patrick, surname, Holland. Not heard the name out loud for twenty years until McLoughlin had said it in the kitchen last night, and the sound of it had caused her hands to lose their grip, the vase to fall to the floor. Not seen for the same number of years until today when she recognized his tall, angular body as he hurried to his place at the front bench. Not heard his voice until he announced himself to the court as the senior counsel defending the killer of his daughter, her daughter, Mary.

Now I will indulge, she thought as she drank again from the warm glass. Starting with the twenty-first birthday party. The one Joe Macken had invited her to. Just before Christmas 1972. His family had a large farm somewhere in Co. Laois. They thought, he said, that when he qualified he would go home to take over his uncle's rural practice. But they were in for a surprise. Joe wanted to be a plastic surgeon and live far away in the heat and the light. The New World. As far as possible from the mud and the damp and the smell of wet dogs. Come with me, Margaret, he said. It'll be fun. But she just laughed and kept him at bay with jokes and silly games. He was a nice boy, handsome, with a wide smile and a long nose. But he was just a boy.

He had arranged that she would get a lift to the party. His cousin, a barrister in Dublin, was coming down with his wife. They would pick her up, drive her safely in their nice warm car. Then she would stay the night, and they would drive her back again the next day, after breakfast. It was all arranged. No, she protested. I'll get the train. But he insisted. Kept on phoning her at home to confirm the arrangements. You'll like Patrick, he said. He's a bit older than us, and he seems a bit formal to begin with. But he's got a great sense of humour. And his wife, Crea, is a sweetie.

But when the car pulled up outside the house, it contained only one person. A man with curly hair, falling down over his collar, who explained that his young son had whooping cough and his wife had decided to forgo the pleasures of the party to look after the child.

She pulled her black velvet cloak around her as she sat in the passenger seat beside him. The atmosphere in the car was brittle and tense. He looked as if he was carrying the aftershocks of a row in the stiffness in his jaw and neck and the way he accelerated the car in the confines of the narrow sea road. She remembered wishing, as he drove up the hill, that she could get out and find her own way to the party. She had made a few polite attempts at conversation, but eventually she gave up. He fiddled with the radio and found music. Kathleen Ferrier singing. Her strong dark contralto sliding over the notes. The sorrow of Orpheus losing his love to the underworld.

'You like it,' he said.

'What?'

'The music. You're humming.'

'Oh, I'm sorry. I didn't realize.'

'No, that's all right. At least you can hum in tune.'

'It's one of my father's favourites. He's always playing it at home.'

'I see.'

They didn't speak again until he swung in through the gates to the house. His headlights played over rabbits nibbling the front lawn like the plaster bookends she'd had as a child.

'How about one to take home for the pot?' he asked, and turned the car onto the grass in pursuit.

'Stop,' she said, 'they're not doing you any harm.'

'What?' He looked at her, as if for the first time.

'I mean it. Stop. I don't think it's funny.'

He pulled up abruptly, and she got out, slamming the door and tripping on the soft ground in her haste.

She didn't see him again until much later. She had danced and drunk and picked at the food. She had fended off Joe, more than once, and now she was standing at the back of the ballroom leaning against the doors, which folded open into the conservatory, watching as the dancers shuffled in circles to the amplified beat of a local band. Her legs were tired, her high heels uncomfortable. Around her, lips sought lips, arms encircled bare shoulders, hips and thighs pressed against each other. She moved back into the dark of the old glasshouse, and lay down on a sagging chair, looking up at the stars, which hung as low as fairy lights swagged across the winter sky. She turned her cheek into the hardness of the splintered cane and closed her eyes. She slept. For how long she didn't know, but when she woke, when her eyes accustomed themselves to the gloom, she saw that someone else was there, a bottle at his feet on the tiled floor. He leaned forward into the glow of a candle, and she saw clearly for the first time how beautiful he was. His face was long and pale, his eyes dark blue underneath thick eyelashes. They sat in silence. He offered her wine. She accepted. They drank together. Then some time later he stood and held out his hand. She took it, feeling the hardness of the muscles lying just under the surface of the smooth skin, and the long slender fingers which slipped through hers.

The band was playing waltzes. He swung

366

her around the room.

'You dance too,' he said, their feet moving perfectly in time. 'Your father again?'

One, two, three; two, two, three, three, two, three. Wet Sunday afternoons, the gramophone tittuping Victor Sylvester in strict tempo, her head reaching just above her father's waist, her nose rubbing against the leather buttons on his fawn cardigan.

Her head rested against his shoulder. She could smell the spicy scent of his skin and feel the black grosgrain of his lapels under her cheek. He swung her out and around and he laughed. And, as he pulled her in close again, she felt him hard against her.

He drove her home in the dead of night, the back wheels of the car slewing on the frosty road. Above, the pole star and the Little Bear, the Plough and the Great Bear hung like giant eyes watching, matched by the eyes of night creatures lit up in hedgerows as they passed.

They sat side by side in the dark. Not speaking, not moving. She breathed in and out, conscious of his breath slipping through her nostrils and into her lungs, gliding into her bloodstream, changing her body into a reflection of his own. He took her hand as he said goodbye, and kissed it.

She stood by the sea wall, smelling the thick black mud that lay just beneath the sand. There was a spring tide that night, the sea in retreat. She heard a rustle under the weed, which draped the rocks with its ornamental bobbles and spread between them like strands of thick glossy hair. A rat ran out, moonlight silvering its dull grey back. It stopped and sat up on its haunches. It gazed calmly at Margaret, holding out its dainty little paws. And then it was joined by another, and another. As her eyes searched through the contours of rock, weed and sand she saw that it was a shifting mass of lithe grey bodies, long tails rippling, scrabbling claws and sharp little teeth. She turned away and looked at the row of houses, curtains pulled, shutters fastened, safe and secure, unknowing.

It was morning when she finally slept, the grey winter light falling across her bed. And when she woke much later she could barely remember what had happened. But it was there to see when she looked in the mirror. Don't be ridiculous, she said to herself. Silly fairy-tale stuff. But he was in her eyes, her mouth, on her cheek, in the tilt of her head. And there was nothing she could do to get rid of him.

36

'What a shame, boss. All set for a lovely long day in court. Best suit and tie, new haircut, shoes polished. Learned your evidence off by heart. And what happens? The stupid fucking accused starts to have some kind of a fit. He gets carted off to hospital. Judge adjourns till tomorrow, and where does that leave us?'

'Having a bloody great time, Bertie. Now, shut up, drink your beer, and I'll open you another.'

It was all very strange, McLoughlin thought. He'd just got back into Court Number Two, when Fitzsimons stood up in his seat, his face white, and began to scream and shout. None of it made any sense. Just a babble of sound and noise. And then he threw himself down on the floor and began to writhe and shake. Instantly there were guards all over him, calls for a doctor, then an ambulance and he was off to the Mater. So that was that. As Bertie said, no more court for the day.

They had wandered out onto the quays, then into the Legal Eagle for a pint. Lunchtime. No point in going all the way back to Swan's Nest. He phoned in. Nothing doing there. He phoned home. The answering machine was on. He had thought he might offer to take Janey for lunch, but she'd obviously made other arrangements, and when he tried his mother's nursing home they told him she was out at her musical appreciation class. So that just left the boat.

It was a fifteen-minute drive down the quays to Poolbeg. He'd asked for volunteers, and he got three. The usual suspects. Always game for a bit of adventure. Finney, Conroy and Lynch. They hadn't worked together since the Mitchell case. Conroy and Lynch were both in Store Street. They knew as much about drugs now as your average pharmacologist. Finney had been transferred to Community Relations, based in Harcourt Square. There was talk of him being sent to Cork to replace Tony Heffernan, who'd left the force after his marriage break-up. McLoughlin felt a shiver of apprehension whenever he heard people talk about Tony. The split had been a disaster. Breege had roused herself from her bed and her television and phoned everyone from the Commissioner down. She'd got the solicitor from hell, who immediately put an attachment on his salary and summoned the Protestant widow to the family court as a witness to his adultery. The two boys had taken Breege's side and refused for months to see their father anywhere except in Mc-Donald's. Finally it had got too much for him, and he took early retirement. There were some who said he was lucky to get it. McLoughlin felt a sudden wave of guilt wash over him. He hadn't been to see him, or even phoned him since he left the force. He realized he wasn't even sure where he was living or what he was doing.

He pulled another six-pack of Heineken out of the tiny fridge in the boat's cabin, and handed them around.

'Anyone hear anything recently about Tony Heffernan?' he asked.

'Like what?' said Finney, snapping open the ring-pull on the can.

'Like what he's doing for a crust?'

'Yeah, I heard,' said Lynch. 'He's working for a security company. Training their new recruits. Jesus, I don't envy him.'

There was silence for a moment as they all thought about it.

'Come on, lads.' McLoughlin pulled a bundle of life-jackets out of a locker and handed one to each of them. 'We'll never get to Dun Laoghaire at this rate.'

The rain had eased by the time they cleared the mouth of the Liffey, and a weak and watery sun was beginning to raise a few wisps of steam from the boat's sodden deck. The vibrations from the diesel engine tickled his feet as he stood at the wheel, plotting their course, first east out into the bay, then south towards the twin encircling arms of Dun Laoghaire harbour. Usually he'd have raised the mainsail and the jib by now, but with this rookie crew it wasn't really worth it. There'd be so much huffing and puffing and complaining, as their soft winter hands came into contact with the heavy halyards, that it would spoil the whole trip. Better to motor today. Enjoy the sea, the bit of sun, the anticipation of the summer's sailing ahead. It was at times like this, when he was on the boat, that he felt he had everything that he had ever wanted, that he had ever needed. But those feelings were increasingly rare and elusive. Too often now the world followed him snapping at his heels, dragging at his coat, forcing him to pay attention.

'So what did you make of it?'

'What?' He looked up. Finney was standing on the roof of the cabin, his back to the sun, his face in shadow. He jumped down beside him, and took hold of the wheel.

'Can I have a go?'

'Sure thing.' McLoughlin stepped back and opened another can of lager.

'You were saying?'

'Yeah. Why did she go off like that, your Dr Mitchell?'

'She's not my Dr Mitchell.'

'No?' Finney looked at him and grinned. 'Gone off her, have you?'

'Shut up, for God's sake, and watch your course.'

He picked up the binoculars and scanned the coast. Beautiful from the sea, the jumble of houses, the brown smear of sand across Sandymount and the smooth undulations of the mountains behind.

'Here, listen to this.' McLoughlin struck a pose, feet wide apart, one hand on his heart, the other open wide towards the city.

'Part elegant and partly slum,
Skies cleaned by rain,
Plum-blue hills for a background.
Dublin, of course,

The only city that has lodged,
Sadly in my bones.'

Finney looked at him blankly.

'"A Melancholy Love", by Sheila Wing-field. Do you not know it?'

'You're a real romantic, aren't you?' Finney grinned, his dimples deepening. 'I bet you'd like to bring her, your good lady doctor, out here for a spin.'

'Don't you ever give up?'

'So where's she been for the last few months? Did she go back to New Zealand?'

'Yeah, she sure did. A long way away.'

'And were you in touch with her at all?'

'I had to phone her a couple of times, and I wrote to her every couple of months, just to keep her up to date with what was happening. Only fair, really, after what she went through.'

And I wrote her a lot of letters which I didn't send, couldn't send, he thought. Sitting up late at night at the kitchen table, pissed, thinking about her, wishing I'd done something about it while she was here. I even drove down to the house and parked outside and thought about her. And went to the yard to see what was happening to her father's boat. She was right, she was telling

374

the truth. She'd told them to dump her, unless I showed up to take her away. So what could I do? I hired a trailer and put her in the back garden. Janey was absolutely delighted.

'How we doing, skipper?' Finney yelled, as he turned the wheel and set course for Dun Laoghaire. The boat rolled and plunged, taking the wind on her side. McLoughlin adjusted the engine, listening to the change of sound, as the screw took on the heavier weather. Soon the Martello tower at Seapoint was in sight. McLoughlin put the binoculars to his eyes again, and focused on the row of houses that faced the sea. Margaret's house looked deserted, neglected, the façade a dull, dirty grey, in comparison with the fresh creams, pinks and ochres of the houses on either side. An old woman walked along the footpath towards Margaret's gate. McLoughlin found her with the glasses, and followed her, catching her as she wiped her nose with the back of her hand. She looked familiar. Then he realized. It was Nellie, the cleaning lady. She pushed in through the gate and walked up the steps, fishing in her basket for keys before letting herself into the house.

'What you see, boss? Anything interesting?'

He took down the glasses, wrapping the straps around them and putting them away in their case.

'Nothing at all. Not a creature stirring. Now, how we doing, lads? Better than a day in court, eh?'

Conroy turned towards him, his face pale green.

'Don't know about that. I feel like shite,' he said, as he leaned out over the bulwark, retching into the sea.

McLoughlin made him tea and tucked him up on a bunk, wrapping him in a sleeping bag. 'Don't worry, Brian, we'll go back by taxi. I can leave the boat in the Coal Harbour for a couple of days. No problem.'

It was just as well, really. Somehow they ended up visiting all of the six pubs between the Coal Harbour and York Road. McKenna's behind St Michael's Hospital for brandies. O'Loughlin's in George's Street for hot whiskeys, and Ryan's, Smyth's, the Cumberland Inn and Murphy's for pints, pints and more pints. He did remember at some stage eating spring rolls and chips with curry sauce from a Chinese takeaway, and he remembered a bit more clearly Conroy finally getting sick out of the taxi. But mostly he remembered that he made the driver take the sea road through Monkstown, and he needed the last remnants of his self-control not to get out of the car as they approached her house, not to bang on her door, not to force his way in, not to fling himself at her, not to tell her that he wanted her more than anything else in the world. Not to make a total fool of himself.

37

She had thought at first, as she waited by the side gate outside the Four Courts in the late afternoon, that she would have to follow him by car. She assumed, why, she wasn't sure, that he would go straight home when he finished for the day. Wherever home was now. Twenty years ago he had lived with his wife and son in a large house in Foxrock, set back from the road behind a high privet hedge. Mock Tudor, a mixture of red brick and dark beams. She had laughed at his choice. Teased him about its predictability. If I had a house of my own, she had said, I'd build a modern one, lots of glass and concrete, interior and exterior mixed together.

Like Frank Lloyd Wright. And all the furniture would be simple and unadorned. Chrome, steel, leather. No family portraits and especially no family photographs. She had said to him. Then.

He had taken her to his house. During that last summer before she got pregnant. The family were away, staying with his wife's parents in Connemara. A case had brought him back to Dublin. Preparation for a murder trial. Or so he had told them. She had met him at Heuston Station, a hot day, dust and litter lying in the gutters and a stink from the Liffey, dark green at low tide. She had borrowed her mother's old Mini.

'Where to?' she had asked, her foot hovering over the accelerator. He had given her directions, precisely.

'Turn here, turn there, right, left,' and she had obeyed with mock servility.

'Do you really mean here?' she asked, as he pointed her in through the high gates.

'Of course,' he replied. 'I have to get a few things. Come with me and I'll show you around.'

They had ended up staying. She had played cook and maid and mistress of the house. They had used the child's attic bedroom. The last night, when he had fallen asleep, his head buried in his son's Womble pillow, she had got up and walked down to the floor below. She had opened the door to the big bedroom, the one with the bay window that faced the front garden. Moonlight laid squares of light across the pale pink carpet. She sat down on the big bed. She lay back against the pillows stacked neatly beneath the pink bedspread. On the bedside table nearest the door were a clock, a radio, a phone and a notepad and pencil. On the other side was a stack of books. She turned her head sideways to look at the authors. Margaret Drabble, Doris Lessing, Jacky Gillott, John McGahern, Dr Spock's *Babies and Child Care* and Tolstoy, *Anna Karenina*. Her gaze moved beyond the books to a photograph. A couple dressed for their wedding. Kissing. Her face turned up to him. Their hands joined.

She would have followed him to that house again, or wherever he lived now. She was prepared. The taxi driver who had brought her from the airport to the cemetery, who had given her his card, had parked where she could see the car park. They had sat and watched. Seen the Mercedes and the Volvos, the Saabs and the BMWs pull slowly out onto Chancery Place, and prowl down onto the quays. But he had left on foot, buttoning his charcoal grey overcoat against the wind, which was spinning down the river from the east. She had paid off the driver, Andy was his name, and he had looked at her through the thick lenses of his glasses and told her to take care. She had smiled and thanked him and set off quickly, following the tall, slightly stooped figure.

Her footsteps trod in his as surely as if they had been walking on sand. The route was familiar. Along the quays on the north side as far as the Halfpenny Bridge. Dodge between the cars without waiting for the lights to change. Onto the bridge, pausing to look at the way the wind plucked at the dirty river water. Remember the meeting, the second time, nearly a year after the party. Under the bracket where the gas lamp had once hung, casting its steady phosphorescent glow in the gloom of an Edwardian night. Midway between north and south. She had been rushing to a clinic in the Rotunda Hospital. He had been coming from court. It had been cold, threatening rain. They had shaken hands and he had said, 'We must meet.'

'Yes, why don't we?'

'How about tomorrow, early evening?'

'Why not. Say, six o'clock?'

'Great. Where?'

'What about Conway's, across from the Rotunda?'

As simple as that.

She watched him reach down and put some coins on a piece of cardboard in front of a girl sitting cross-legged, a baby in her lap. She saw him speak to her, then walk on. Under Merchant's Arch, under the looming mass of the Central Bank and across Dame Street. She knew now where he was going. She followed more slowly, stopping to gaze into shop windows, checking how she looked, how she might seem to him after so many years. A young couple stood in the middle of Grafton Street. They were kissing open-mouthed like goldfish. Their eyes were closed. She had never kissed him like that in public, not giving a damn who saw them. Always hidden, always a secret. But people must have known. She had said that to him. Asked him.

'Doesn't she, your "wife"?' She hesitated before she said the word. Putting inverted commas around it.

'No,' he said. 'She doesn't.'

'But how can she not? I'd know, if it was me. I'd sense it in you, when I touched you.

When we...' She stopped then. His look told her all she needed to know. Be careful, it said. Don't presume too much.

The windows in the street were filled with impossibly thin mannequins, their arms and legs unnaturally bent and twisted. They reminded her of Mary, with their putty-coloured bodies and their hip bones protruding. Her own face swam up as she passed a display of black knitted dresses. She had never thought the two of them were alike, but others did. Must be the mannerisms, the gestures, the speech patterns, she always said. The learned behaviour. Not the parts that come to you whether you want them or not, like the shape of your nose or the gap between your front teeth, the colour of your hair or your height, your build. They came from him. She always said that, told Mary. You're very like your father. Much more like him than me. Physically that is. And she had heard Mary passing this on to her friends.

'Mummy says I'm just like my daddy. Just like him. She says she's always amazed when she looks at me, when I'm sleeping. I'm the dead spit.'

'Dead spit, what's that?'

'You know, like peas in a pod.'

She had brought Mary here to the Shelbourne Bar, one day not long after they had arrived. They had come into town to get out of the house, away from Catherine's complaints. They had walked around the shop trying on clothes. Margaret had wanted to buy Mary a dress, but they had nearly fallen out over styles and colours. Eventually Margaret had handed her some money and said, 'Here. Buy what you want. Meet me in an hour.'

'Where?'

'Um.' She thought for a moment. 'I know, the Shelbourne. Up to Stephen's Green. Turn left, big hotel. Go in through the revolving door, past reception. The bar's at the back.'

'Not one of the sad dumps you used to go to when you were a penniless student?'

'No, Smarty-pants. Now get lost.'

And Mary had liked it. They had sat at the marble bar and drunk gin and tonics with slices of lime, and helped themselves to handfuls of peanuts. Mary had pulled faces at herself in the mirror behind the row of spirits bottles, which were ranged in order of height, like soldiers on parade. She had pulled open her carrier bags to show off the skimpy tops and tight jeans she had bought, and 'Look at this, isn't it just gorgeous?' a deep red suede skirt. And Margaret had wondered, just for a moment, if she should tell her the truth. But the impulse had passed. There was no point, really. Not now. It would only upset her, upset everyone.

He was sitting on the far side of the bar, side on to the door. Two men were with him and a woman. Young, very blonde, wearing a fitted red jacket with a long gold chain looped around her neck. Margaret didn't recognize them. She pulled herself up on a high stool. If he had turned in her direction he might have seen her, but the room was dark, her face as she sat with her back to the light from the lobby, in shadow. She ordered a drink. She watched his hands. She remembered his fingers, long and narrow, the nails clipped short. They hovered now over a stainless-steel bowl of peanuts; then picked them out delicately one by one. He lifted a pint of Guinness, his skin pale against the black liquid. He turned to take the first sip, and licked the froth from his top lip.

'How can you drink that stuff!' Her voice, younger, happier.

'What stuff?'

'That stuff.'

'You mean the black stuff!'

384

They were in the bar of the Angler's Rest Hotel, Pontoon, Co. Mayo. The third Sunday in September 1974. The day of the All Ireland football final. Dublin playing Galway. A perfect autumn day. The sun still shining, but somewhere a prickling of the nape of the neck which says, watch out, winter's coming.

'Here,' he handed her his pint, 'have a taste.'

She slipped her mouth over the place on the glass where his had been.

'Ugh!' The bitterness hit her tongue. He took the glass from her and kissed her, sweetening her with his saliva. The afternoon slipped by. The sun moved from window to window across the bar. Cigarette smoke turned the light the shifting grey of the lake outside. The television in the corner flickered its black and white story. Dublin scored fourteen points and beat Galway. She stood and cheered and he caught her round the waist and guided her up the stairs to their room.

When she was pregnant even the smell of Guinness made her sick. And she remembered, years later, a party in Takapuna. Someone had got hold of a case of bottled stout.

'Come on, you Irish,' they all said, 'show us how it's done.' And she had drunk for politeness, then gone to the toilet and put her finger down her throat.

He called the barman over and ordered another drink. There was laughter and jokes, voices harmonizing. His a rich bass, the younger man a golden tenor, the girl's a light soprano. He slapped a handful of silver on the marble counter top, and a tenpence piece spun on its edge towards her. He reached for it, stretching out as he slid over. Then he looked up, in the direction of the silhouetted woman, expecting more laughter.

She could see it in his face. He was going to flirt with her. She knew his way of crinkling up his eyes, like a small boy. He was just about to say something. Then he stopped. Silence. Awareness. Confusion.

'Hallo,' she said.

'Hallo,' he replied.

The coin spun off the bar and hit the tiled floor. It spiralled into a corner and collapsed on its face.

'Forgive me,' she said. 'I didn't want to interrupt you. But I need to talk to you.'

He came and stood beside her. She tried to stand, but the muscles in her calves had collapsed. He took her right hand. It fitted, as always, snugly into his palm. He said nothing, just stood and looked, his eyes moving across her face like a mother gazing at her firstborn. The others watched, curious.

'I don't know what to say.' He ran his thumb over hers.

'Say nothing.'

'Go and sit down. Over there.' He waved his hand towards an empty corner. 'I'll join you.'

'No, not here. Can you come to meet me? Later tonight. At my parents' house in Monkstown.'

'Are they still...?' The question hung.

'No, they're both dead.'

'I'm not sure.'

'It's very important. It has to do with–' She paused, and took a sip of her drink. 'It has to do with our daughter.'

'What?' The word came out of him with a nervous half-laugh.

'Please. Don't say anything else. Here.' She handed him a piece of paper. 'In case you don't remember. Address and phone number. Please. It's very important.'

She left him then. Looking after her. Folding and unfolding the paper in his hand. Wondering as she had had to wonder. How could this happen? Why now? With no warning.

It was just getting dark as she left the hotel. It had begun to rain again. Margaret pulled her collar up around her face, but she didn't feel cold any longer. She had stood beside him and he had warmed her, filled her with bright light. So it had been, always. So it was still.

38

'I don't believe it.'

'Don't believe it, or don't believe me?'

'It, you, any of it. The whole thing is crazy.'

The room was dark. It was cold for April, and she had gathered apple logs from the back of the tool shed and lit a fire, which hissed and spat as the resin rose bubbling to the surface and ran down the wood like liquid honey.

It was late when he arrived. She had been surprised by the heavy knock on the front door. There had been no sound of a car in the narrow road, nothing but the whoosh and whistle of wind and sea, and the occasional spatter of rain flung like a handful of shingle against the front windows.

She had carried on with her task. Systematically, relentlessly, clearing the house of all its possessions. The hall was filled with plastic bags, labelled. Ten, with Catherine's clothes, bags, shoes, hats, were for the Simon shop. Another five, stuffed with sheets, towels and blankets, were for the Vincent de Paul. Tomorrow night after she came home from the trial she would start on the books, newspapers and magazines, carefully packing them into the stack of cardboard boxes that were waiting in the kitchen. They would go to Oxfam. And the furniture and pictures, like the house, would be auctioned. When she left here, when the trial was, over, she would take nothing with her and leave nothing behind.

He came into the house with a wary expression. For once he seemed ill at ease. She hadn't remembered him like that. She felt that it should have given her solace but it just made her feel faintly sick, the way she had in those early months of pregnancy when even familiar smells made her mouth fill with bile, and unexpected movements, the lurching of a bus around a sharp corner, covered her forehead and the palms of her hands with a clammy sweat.

She gave him a drink. Scotch, no ice and a drop of water, and they sat on either side of the fire in her mother's old armchairs, their covers faded, and fraying. Like a parody, she thought, of the happy couple sharing the events of their busy day.

She didn't speak immediately. She sipped from her glass and watched the fire. It was glowing an even red. She prodded it with the poker and a flame shot to the surface, like the flattened head of a cobra, turning this way and that, and then sinking back down into its coils.

When she told him about Mary, he didn't respond. She had been careful what she said. She knew his barrister's mind. She'd had arguments with him before, where she'd seen how he could use his attention to detail, his ability to pick on the tiniest scrap of information and turn it to his advantage. But this time he said nothing.

And then. 'I don't believe it.'

She shrugged her shoulders. 'Well, I can't prove it to you. The physical evidence isn't available any longer. You'll just have to take my word for it.'

'And why should I do that?'

She looked at him, anger beginning to

gather itself somewhere in the pit of her stomach. 'Why should I lie to you about something as important as this? I never lied to you before.'

He turned towards her, the firelight catching the wrinkles around his eyes and winking in the grey spangled through his black hair. 'Didn't you?'

It had been here in this house that she had told him she was pregnant. October 1974, the weekend before Hallowe'en. It was her intern year. She had been living in a flat in Pembroke Road. She'd got a phone call from her father. She was out of breath and slightly dizzy by the time she'd run down three flights of stairs to stand in the cold, dirty hall, holding the greasy black receiver to her ear, her gaze wandering over the numbers scribbled in blunt pencil on the tattered wallpaper.

'I'm taking your mother to Paris for the weekend. You will come and stay in the house while we're away, won't you? You know how anxious she gets. You know how she frets. She's convinced that the minute we're on the Monkstown Road some dreadful thing will happen to all her precious furniture.'

They had left a fridgeful of food but she didn't feel like eating. Patrick was to come and see her on the Saturday afternoon.

'It'll be fine,' he said. 'I have to take James to rugby at three, so I'll be with you by three-fifteen, three-thirty at the absolute latest, and I don't have to pick him up until five.'

But he didn't arrive. And he didn't phone. She went to bed with a book and fell asleep almost immediately. A deep sleep as if she was drugged, filled with images, bright colours and strange shapes. She could feel herself reaching out, trying to find, to understand, to get, to do. Struggling but not succeeding. When she woke hours later her legs and arms were so heavy and stiff that she lay for a while, moulded to the bed, until the sound of the phone dragged her upright. He was full of whispered apologies. James had fallen and twisted his ankle. He'd had to spend the whole afternoon in the casualty department in St Michael's in Dun Laoghaire. He hadn't been able to get to a phone, but he'd come tomorrow, definitely without fail. Crea was going to a birthday party with the boy and wouldn't be home until late. And he hung up, quickly, without saying goodbye.

The next day they lay in her narrow bed.

The autumn sun was warm through the window. He pulled back the sheet to look at her. He kissed her nipples. She pulled away.

'What is it, my love?'

'They're just very sensitive, very tender.'

He kissed them again, licking the dark areola, nibbling at them until they stood up, tight like overripe raspberries. She gazed around at the faded flowery wallpaper. She looked over his shoulder at the lampshade, dusty, covered in horses' heads. When she was little she had given them names, Beauty and Silver, Cascade and Dancer, Topsy and Polly, culled from books set in English villages where girls called Bunty and Charlotte ate egg and cress sandwiches that Cook had packed in a wicker hamper.

'Hey,' he said, 'what's wrong? You're not with me.'

'I am, I am,' she protested, sitting up and pulling him into her, wrapping her legs around his waist and sliding her wetness up and down on him until his eyes lost focus and words no longer came out of his mouth.

Afterwards he slept, his head heavy on her breast, his stubble pressing into her soft skin, making it itch. Then she, too, slept and woke, her face crushed against the bones of his shoulder blades, her right arm slung over him, her hand between his thighs. She remembered that she moved away, and lay on her back, and he moved with her, slipping his arm underneath her shoulders and cradling her to him, so that now her face rested on his breast, one small brown nipple within reach of her tongue. And then she told him, and when she had finished she kissed him gently, squeezing the soft flesh with her fingers so that his nipple popped into her mouth, and she teased and tickled it with her lips. And waited for his response.

Did he say anything? She couldn't remember the words, but she remembered that he moved, shifted his body slowly, deliberately. Foot, ankle, knee, thigh, hip, waist, rib, arm, shoulder, neck and head. Away.

He got out of bed and began to dress. He didn't look at her. His movements were methodical, systematic. He lifted each item of clothing carefully from the neat pile on her old rocking chair.

'You shouldn't have done that,' he said.

'What? I don't understand. Done what?' She sat up, the sheet falling away from her. She stretched out her arms and plucked at his shirt-tails.

'You shouldn't have lied to me. You told me, I thought we had an understanding.

That this would never happen.'

She remembered the taste of the tears as they slipped down her face. They dropped onto her hands, faster, faster. 'It was a mistake. I don't know how. I didn't plan it. But now that it has happened, I feel it, the baby, our baby, growing inside me.'

Still he didn't look at her. His zip made a crisp, sharp sound as he pulled it up, tucking his shirt neatly inside his trousers. He picked up his leather belt and slid it carefully through the keepers in his waistband. He pulled it tight. He picked up his wallet and his watch from the dressing table. She remembered she had begun to beg then. She had forgotten the words she used, but she could taste the vomit in her mouth and smell the fear from her own body. She got out of bed, and stood in front of the door. She remembered she tried to stop him, but he pushed her out of the way, his tweed jacket brushing her skin as he passed. His anger surrounded him, protecting him. She couldn't understand what had happened. It was as if, suddenly, she was blind or deaf or dumb. The world as she used to know it no longer had any meaning.

'Stay,' she said. 'Stay, just for a few minutes. We can talk about this. Decide what we're going to do. Please, stay.'

What was it he had said, as he turned back, his car keys jingling in his hand, the front door already open behind him?

'I've always been very straight with you. You know how I feel about my child, my responsibilities. I really have nothing more to say.'

'But you've always said you loved me.'

She was standing so close to him now that she reached out her hand and held it gently against his cheek. He lifted his hand and took hers. He pulled it away and let it go. It dropped down at her side. He slammed the door behind him as he left.

'That's the Kish light, isn't it?'

'That's right. Flashes twice, white, every thirty seconds.'

'And the Baily to the north?'

'Flashes once, white, every twenty seconds.'

'And Dun Laoghaire, West Pier?'

'Three green flashes every seven point five seconds.'

'The East Pier?'

'Flashes white, twice, every fifteen seconds.'

'And the Poolbeg?'

'Occulted, red, twice, every twenty seconds.'

'What?'

She picked up the bottle of whiskey and topped up her glass, gesturing towards his. 'It means it's a constant red light, but it darkens, it "occults", twice every twenty seconds.'

'I've never heard the word used that way before.'

'Haven't you? Well,' she raised her glass in mock salute, 'you know me. Wonderful at crossword puzzles and Trivial Pursuit. A mine of useless information.'

She had stood at the window, the darkness pressing against the glass, her father's arm around her, the smell of hair oil and tobacco clinging to his tweed waistcoat.

'Now, Maggie, let's go round the bay, starting with the Baily to the north.' The gold chain hanging from his pocket watch dug into her ear as he bent forward to point out the lights. Leaning back against him she listened to the slow and steady beat of his heart.

'Daddy?'

'Yes, my pet?'

'Who do you love the best in the world?'

'You, my pet.'

'For ever and ever?'

'Forever and ever, amen.'

'But that's not useless. Imagine,' Patrick sipped his whiskey, 'imagine you'd been shipwrecked, spent days, weeks in a lifeboat, floating, out of sight of land, living on a seagull who happened to drop dead beside you and handfuls of rainwater you scooped up from the bilges of your little boat and then one night you suddenly saw all these different flashing lights, you'd know,' and he pointed his glass at her, 'exactly where you were, and you'd summon up all your strength and get out your paddle and row like mad. But I'd just think I'd gone crazy and I'd give up completely, probably decide to end it all. Throw myself head first into the cold sea.'

'Hardly likely. Self-sacrifice was never a problem for you.'

'Hold on a minute. Fair's fair. I offered you help.'

Help. A phone call, a suggestion of a place to go, 'where you can stay until it's all over and you can have it adopted'.

'And you rejected my offer. And you told me you were going to get rid of it. If you remember because I certainly do. You screamed down the phone at me. I offered you money, I offered you support. And you hung up.'

He picked up the bottle from the hearth and helped himself. She noticed his hands in the firelight, the scattering of brown marks across their backs. She held out her own hands in the faint light from the street. The same kind of discoloration, the same awkward clotting of melanin, the harbinger of old age, senility, death.

'So. Why didn't you?'

She shook her head, turning away.

'Or perhaps you did. Flushed that baby down the sluice and then you got pregnant again, and now for some strange twisted vengeful reason you're trying to get me to believe that she, that poor dead girl, is mine.'

'What?' She took a step towards him.

He leaned back in his chair and looked steadily at her. 'This is rubbish, all of it.'

'What?' She took another step closer.

'If this was true, this crazy story you're telling me, you'd have told the guards. You'd have stood up in court this morning and told the judge. You'd have done something.'

'What?' Again the same word, said with the same disbelieving, rising tone. She looked down at him. He looked up at her, calmly. He raised his glass and drank, and as he did she knocked it from his mouth, the skin on her knuckles tearing as they banged against the heavy crystal. The smell of whiskey in the room. And a scream that came from somewhere as she hit him hard across the cheekbones, once, then twice, then three times. And pulled him from his chair, tearing open his shirt to drag her fingers through the soft skin of his chest, drawing blood in deep gashes with her fingernails. 'Here,' she shouted out her rage and sorrow, 'before you sneer at me any more look at these. Look at what came from your body as surely as it came from mine.'

She pulled a pile of photographs from the desk and flung them at him. He closed his hands into two fists. She picked them from his knees and his lap, scrabbling in front of him on the dusty carpet, and grabbed hold of his hair.

'Look at these, you bastard. Look.' And she rubbed his face against the shiny prints, as the tears spilled down her cheeks, and her breath shuddered out in gasping sobs.

He sat, his head bowed, his eyes downcast. Then he bent and gathered up the pictures, smoothing out their creases, and straightening their crumpled edges. He piled them together like playing cards, and like playing cards he shuffled them, laying them out one by one on the floor in front of him. Over and over again. The dark blue eyes, the smiling face, the long and slender arms and legs, the black curls, the gestures, the expressions. Matched them up, assigned them, recognized them, compared and contrasted them. Stood and crossed to the window. Looked at his reflection in the dark glass. Looked again at the girl, whose image was everywhere. Knelt beside the woman who lay curled in a tight ball in front of the flames. And said, 'What do you want from me?'

Waited for the whispered reply.

'I want you to be her father. I want you to do the right thing.'

Sat again in the armchair until the only sounds in the room were the hiss and crackle of the fire and the rain against the window pane.

39

I want you to be her father. I want you to do the right thing.

He sat at his desk, the room dark. Around him the house breathed quietly. The faintest tinkle of water dribbling into the storage tank in the attic, the hum of the central heating boiler, the tick-tick-tick of the electricity meter in the cupboard under the stairs. Upstairs, above his head, his wife lay sleeping. He knew how she would be lying. On her right side, her arms around the pillow, her legs drawn up to her breasts. Her blonde hair would fall across her cheek, and when she moved, her body would give off the faintest scent. Joy, wasn't it? Wasn't that what it was called? He should know. He had given her bottles and bottles of the stuff over the years. Birthdays, Christmas, anniversaries. Bought at duty-free counters, as he rushed for a plane, snatched from Brown Thomas's on Christmas Eve, already gift-wrapped. And now it clung to all the tiny cracks and crevices in her skin, replacing the natural smells that should have marked her.

He switched on the lamp on the desk. He put his hands down in the yellow light that spilled across the dark wood. He turned them over and looked at his palms, at the deep lines that scored the pink skin. He could still remember the feel of Margaret's small hand in his when he had asked her to dance all those years ago. Soft, but strength and power in the grip. The same strength and power that radiated through her body as she twisted and turned in front of him, controlling every step and every movement. There had been a mark across her cheek. A deep indentation from the cane chair on which she had fallen asleep. He remembered he had wanted to smooth it out with his fingers, run his tongue along it, then pull her head back and kiss her throat. But he had done nothing. Except waltz with her, then drive her home, unable to speak for the longing that choked his vocal cords and made him aware of every single part of his body as it rubbed and chafed against his clothes.

Longing. What did the word mean? He had longed for her. To see her, to speak to her, to hear her name, to touch her. But he had done nothing. It frightened him, this feeling. It was new and unfamiliar. He had never before wanted something that could damage his life. Everything until then had been simple and straightforward. School, university, the Bar, marriage, fatherhood. A continuous, seamless progression that would lead, he knew, to success. But this? What was this?

He stood up and walked to the door. He opened it and stepped out into the dark hall. He walked across the polished floor to the dining room. His path was diagonal rather than straight. Avoiding the board that creaked loudly. A lesson learned early in his marriage. He felt his way to the sideboard and picked up a bottle of brandy and a glass. He carried them back with him, once again his feet taking the familiar well-trod path.

He unlocked the filing cabinet and pulled out three heavy bundles of papers. He sat down at the desk. He poured brandy into the glass and drank. He spread the papers in front of him and began to read.

She had said to him, earlier that night, 'How can you defend someone like that? How can you help someone who has done what he has done?'

And he had started to give the standard answer, the response that every barrister gives when they are asked the question.

'Everyone is entitled to a defence. Everyone is presumed innocent until proven guilty. I don't make that judgement. Nor can you. Only the court can decide. And until that happens this man is innocent. And he has the same rights as you or I.'

But the words had failed to come. He knew. As much as she knew. But barristers weren't supposed to know in that way. They were only supposed to know the facts of the case, and the law that they could apply to them. It was their business to know the law inside out. All its inconsistencies, all its failings. And to know how to apply the law to protect their clients. And guilt or innocence didn't enter into it.

He had met Jimmy Fitzsimons how many times? On two, possibly three occasions. He had sat across the table from him, in a small and miserable room in the prison, close enough to smell the caul of cigarette smoke that wrapped itself around every inmate. He had asked him the details that he needed to know. He had listened to the story that he told. If he had wanted he could have read between the lines, filled in all the gaps, but that wasn't his job. He had been more interested in the way the guards had behaved towards his client. He had read Jimmy's statement, marking its weaknesses, its inconsistencies, noting times, planning the defence. But Jimmy had wanted to talk about the girl. He had begun to volunteer information that wasn't necessary. He had wanted to describe her, to discuss her, to make her real. Until Patrick had stopped him. Had ended the discussion, left the room.

Now he went back over all the statements, read again the pathologist's report, and finally opened the album of photographs that the guards had made ready for the trial. He had looked at these pictures before, a number of times. Looked at parts of the girl's body, assessed the extent of the bruising, the lacerations, the burns and bite marks. Looked at them as evidence. Of a crime or an intense and passionate sexual relationship? Now he spread them out again on the desk, looking this time at her face, her features, her colouring. He put his hand in his jacket pocket and laid two other photographs down beside them. In one she wore a pale pink leotard. Standing at the barre. A perfect arabesque. Her head held high. Her neck long and straight. Her hair caught up in a tight knot, all except for a couple of stray springing curls. In the other she sat cross-legged on a large cushion, her head resting on one hand, looking up into the lens of the camera, a fire flickering behind her, laughing.

How to compare her with the broken thing that lay across his desk? He read again the description of her injuries, and matched them with the close-ups. 'Burns to the inside of her right thigh,' he read, and he picked up the photograph. There were marks across the pale skin. Like a dotted line. A birthmark, perhaps. Three small red circles in a row, and between them, joining them into one red, raw mass were the burns.

'It's your Orion's Belt, that's what it is, isn't it?'

'My what?'

'You know, the constellation. Orion the Hunter, with the three stars lined up to make his belt. In the winter sky. Really easy to see.'

Lying in his younger brother's brass bed, in his flat in Mountjoy Square. The first time they slept together. The night they met for a drink. A year after the party. Waiting for her in Conway's. Looking at his watch. They had agreed on six o'clock. He ordered a drink, and sat down in a corner facing the door. The television was on. The angelus bell rang. The picture was a Renaissance Madonna and child. Raphael, he thought. He drank and waited. He looked at his watch. Ten minutes passed. He should go. It would be better this way. Then she was there. In front of him. Wearing a long brown coat, silver buttons, military-style, and a black beret, which she pulled off her head, shaking out her hair, while all around men watched.

They stayed until closing time. 'I don't want to go home,' she said, as they walked along Parnell Street, a bitter wind snatching at her long scarf. He opened his own coat and drew her inside, feeling her mouth open, sucking him into her.

He took her to Hugh's. The attic floor of a restored Georgian house. Ivy green ceiling and walls. Faded Turkish carpets. An old record player open on the table. 'Look,' she said, pulling the black disc from its cover. 'Listen.' Kathleen Ferrier sang again. Again the story of Orpheus and his doomed love for Eurydice. He stood her in the middle of the room and took off her coat. He pulled the fine black sweater over her head. He unzipped her long pleated skirt and let it drop in concertinaed folds around her ankles. He knelt and pulled the suede boots from her feet. Then he stood again and slipped her breasts free of their white bra. And ran his hands down her waist, unscrolling the rest of her underwear so she stood, small and delicate, in front of him.

He remembered some time in the early morning. Light from the windows turned everything a dusky grey. She pushed back the bedclothes. 'So I can look at you,' she said. Then she began to kiss him. From his mouth, down the rest of his body until she got to the marks on his leg.

They stayed together for the weekend. Somehow he made an excuse. Phoned home. Lied. He couldn't leave her. Until the Sunday evening. They said goodbye at the taxi rank opposite the Gresham Hotel. They had held hands as they walked down Parnell Street, but as they turned into O'Connell Street he had slipped his fingers from hers, moved away from her, walked just that bit faster. Looked away so he couldn't see the expression on her face. He had stood in front of the bathroom mirror, here in this house, until the steam from the shower obscured his reflection. Looked at himself through eyes that were filled with her. And as he lifted the sponge to wash all he could smell was her body, and all he could feel as he wrapped the towel around him was her touch.

The girl was his child. There was no doubt. He poured more brandy and drank again. Then he angled the lamp so it shone on the row of framed photographs on the black marble mantelpiece. James, the elder. Conor, the baby. James was twenty-six. A barrister too. Just beginning. Conor was twenty-one. Born at the end of July 1975. Conceived, he knew, a couple of weeks after Mary. He stood up. He walked over to the mantelpiece and one by one he picked up and put down the row of pictures. From babyhood to adulthood, they were all there. Both boys had his black curls, blue eyes, pale skin, height. Both boys had the little gap between their two front teeth. His gap. The gap he had noticed in the photograph that showed the extent of the damage done to Mary's jaw and teeth by the beating she had received.

He went back, to the desk and looked at the picture closely. Then he crossed to the CD player on the shelf in the corner, hunted through the stack beside it, slotted one into the drawer and pressed Play.

The voice filled the room.

true verdict give according to the evidence.

The members of the jury had sworn the oath. The jury-keeper had led them into the court. They had seated themselves in the raised box at right angles to the judge. From now until the end of the trial all that was important in the world would take place in the invisible triangle marked out between the jury, the judge and the accused.

David Douglas, the prosecuting counsel, stood. His plump right hand grasped the edge of his black gown. McLoughlin watched from his customary place standing by the door at the back. The prosecuting counsel faced the jury. He swayed slightly, from side to side. Behind him, at the end of the front row of benches that were at right angles to the rest of the court, sat Jimmy. His face was pale. He had been given a shot of Valium, and had slept around the clock. The prison doctor said he was as right as rain. No reason at all why the trial couldn't continue. Better if his sister, 'you know, the handicapped kid, is kept out of the way. She seems to upset him.'

Douglas began to speak. He explained to the jury what would happen, how evidence would be presented and examined. McLoughlin looked over the heads in front of him for Margaret. Her head was bowed, concentrating on the notebook on her knee. She had arrived, early to take her place in the front row. He had noticed that she was very pale. There were shadows under her eyes and, deep grooves on either side of her mouth, furrows ploughed, he thought, by loss and longing. But she had dressed with her usual care. She was wearing dark wool trousers, with a matching waistcoat and a white shirt underneath. McLoughlin looked at the row of journalists, whispering, giggling. He watched them watching her. He could imagine the headlines, 'Anguished Mother in Trial Vigil', and the like. Perhaps he should suggest that coming here every day might not be for the best. That it might cause her too much pain. But there again, if it had been his daughter he wouldn't have been able to sit at home and read about it a day late in the newspapers or watch the potted reports on the nine o'clock news.

Douglas continued. 'This,' he said, 'is a tragic case. You will hear evidence in the course of this trial which will upset you and cause you distress. You will be asked to share the last few painful days in the life of a young woman called Mary Mitchell. And you will be asked to decide the guilt or innocence of this young man, seated here, behind me, who is accused of murder. And I must remind you of something that you will hear over and over again in the course of this trial. The law presumes the innocence of the accused, until the prosecution has demonstrated beyond reasonable doubt, let me repeat that, beyond reasonable doubt, that the person is guilty. And it is up to you, the jury, and no one else to decide on the facts of the case.'

McLoughlin shifted from foot to foot. His head was aching and he felt desperately sick from last night's excesses, but at least today his feet weren't wet. The weather had changed again. Outside the sun shone in a clear blue sky, washed clean by yesterday's downpour. He closed his eyes and listened as the prosecuting counsel began to set the scene, to tell the jury the story of the crime. He was creating, McLoughlin knew, nothing less than a complete, self-contained world in which the guilt or innocence of the accused would be decided. From now on there would be nothing more or less than this reality, shaped from a mass of circumstances, coincidence and random events by the prosecution and the defence. It was no longer a question of establishing the truth of what had happened. Truth in these circumstances would be a bonus. Instead, the court would determine the details of this world it was creating, and the evidence that it would allow itself to see or to use. He looked up at the skylight and back down again to the panelled doors which led out of the court. The one to the left of the judge led up the private staircase to his chambers. The one to his right to the jury room. Behind McLoughlin, glass doors opened onto the Round Hall. He closed his eyes and imagined. A cube made of stone and plaster, sealed, floating. A time and space machine. And inside would be brought to life those eight days, six months ago, when Mary Mitchell died.

'Let us go back,' Douglas said, standing with one polished shoe up on the bench in front of him, 'to Sunday, the thirteenth of August nineteen ninety-five. You may remember it, you may not. I can tell you,' and he glanced down at his notes, 'that it was a hot day, like so many days in that extraordinary summer. A man called Barney Morrison was walking his Springer spaniel along the bank of the Grand Canal, just past the bridge at Hazel Hatch. This was a favourite walk of his, especially early in the morning between seven thirty and eight, when he could let the dog have a ramble and a swim. He was throwing a stick for the dog, a piece of elder I do believe, throwing it into the water and the dog was jumping in and swimming out for the stick. But this time when he threw the stick the dog didn't come back. So Mr Morrison went over to the bank to see what the dog was up to. He called him and he called him, and eventually the dog came, and he had something in his teeth. And when Mr Morrison managed to prise the dog's mouth open he found that it was a piece of black plastic sack, and a lock of black hair. And when he looked over the bank where the dog had been swimming, he found wrapped in plastic the body of Mary Mitchell, caught in the submerged branches of an ash tree.

'Now.' He stopped and drank from his cut-glass tumbler. 'Let us go back to the previous Sunday, the sixth of August, the Sunday of the bank holiday weekend. A woman phones the Garda station in Dun Laoghaire. She says that her daughter is missing. She spends the next week in agony until she is told at twelve noon a week later that a body has been found. And it was the body of her daughter, Mary. Let me tell you something about this young woman.'

McLoughlin looked around the court. The barrister's voice rose and fell. Words like beautiful, talented, innocent hung in the air, like bright points of light. He looked at the faces of the jury, rapt now, caught by the simple power of the prosecutor's narrative. He looked at the face of the accused. He had the expression which all in his position hold, fixed, in place. Impassive, unresponsive, as if unconcerned, his hands clasped in front of him, his shoulders erect. He looked at the faces of the court officials. The jury-keeper's arms were folded across his navy blue sweater, obscuring the green harp embroidered over his left breast. The registrar sat equally still, his papers a neat pile in front of him, with the stenographer beside him, her eyes fixed on whoever was speaking, her body twisted away from the computer keyboard across which her hands travelled with complete certainty.

'I will not,' continued the prosecutor, 'describe in detail, at this time, the injuries this young woman received. Expert witnesses will give evidence as to their nature, and you will see photographs which will demonstrate to you unequivocally the pain that she suffered, both physical and psycho-

417

logical, and the manner of the injuries which caused her death. But I will say that the prosecution case asserts and intends to prove beyond reasonable doubt that this was a murder which was executed with great attention to detail. This was not a crime of passion. This was not manslaughter. This was murder. It is the prosecution's contention that young, pretty, talented, innocent Mary Mitchell was imprisoned against her will, was raped, then brutally beaten about the head in such a way that there can be no doubt as to the intention of the accused. He intended to murder her.'

His voice had risen, slowly and steadily. It filled the room, blocking out every other stray, distracting thought. He paused again, and shuffled through his papers and extracted a single sheet from the pile. He put on his half-glasses and peered for some moments at what was written on it. He took off his glasses again and twirled them in his fingers as he continued.

'Let me define murder for you.' He paused, cleared his throat and let his gaze travel along the front row of the jury. *"Where a person kills another unlawfully, the killing shall not be murder unless the accused intended to kill, or cause serious injury to, some*

418

person, whether the person is actually killed or not."' He paused again. There was silence. And he continued, 'and furthermore "*The accused person shall be presumed to have intended the natural and probable consequences of his conduct.*"

'You hear that, do you?' He looked up at the jury, as if questioning each and every one of its twelve members. 'The accused person shall be presumed to have intended the natural and probable consequences of his conduct. In other words, if I hit a man over the head with a hammer I can be pretty certain what will happen to him, and if I smash my fist into the temple of a young woman, smaller and slighter than I am, after having starved her, beaten her, raped her vaginally and anally, burned her thighs and genitals with cigarette ends, slashed her breasts with a knife, I think I can also be fairly sure what the consequence of those actions will be. And if, having done these things to her I don't put her in my car and drive her to a hospital to get medical attention for her, to stop the bleeding of the ruptured blood vessels in her brain, then I think I can also be fairly sure of the consequence of my actions. Because if the accused, Mr Fitzsimons, had taken that

419

course of action Mary Mitchell might now be alive and well, and not lying in a quiet corner of Mount Jerome cemetery.

'And now,' he paused and sipped from his glass again, 'before the prosecution begins to call its witnesses may I remind the jury again of the presumption of innocence. The accused is innocent until the prosecution has proved its case beyond reasonable doubt. And finally, may I point out to you that there is no obligation on the accused to give evidence, no obligation on the accused to give any explanation whatsoever of his actions. He can and may remain silent if he so wishes, and no inference whatsoever may be read into this silence. He is innocent until proven guilty.'

He sat. The courtroom stirred and buzzed. Like the bee-loud glade, thought McLoughlin, as he stretched and eased out his legs. Or the intermission in a very long film, *Gone With the Wind* or *Lawrence of Arabia*. Time for people to go to the toilet or have a smoke. Although there were more people coming into this trial than leaving it. Throughout the prosecution's opening statement a steady stream of women, wigs and gowns framing and emphasizing their youth, had entered and lounged discreetly against the wall, listening intently to the way in which their learned friend, the senior counsel, had framed his opening remarks. Learning through observation, highly commendable, thought McLoughlin. Ambition leaping the gender divide or whatever they called it these days.

The prosecution's junior counsel, a small woman, dark hair hidden nun-like beneath her wig, stood and called the first witness. McLoughlin stretched again, folding his arms at the elbows behind his head, and twisting it from side to side. This was where it began, the establishing of what was called the chain of evidence. Each link attached inextricably to the next. He had often thought that a jigsaw puzzle was a better metaphor for what happened in court. The prosecution calls their witnesses so that each piece dovetails snugly with the next piece. No jagged edges, no rough sides, no gaping holes. And eventually the picture is clear and unmistakable. A crime has been committed. These are the details and this is the person or persons who did it. It was quite different from the process of detection. That was more like one of those 3D pictures. At first when you look at it you can see nothing but a blurred mass of colours and shapes. So you look and you look. You hold it this way and that. You narrow your eyes. You close them and open them again. And suddenly the solution is there. In front of you. Clear as day. Standing out from the background. And you can't understand how you haven't been able to see it all along.

The first four witnesses were the kids with whom Mary had spent that Saturday evening. Each in turn stated their name and took the oath, their light middle-class accents lost in the court room. One of them, the boy, fiddled with the microphone, making it howl. The registrar leaned over to adjust it again, and it fell over, bouncing across the floor. Everyone laughed with nervous relief. They each described that night. Who they'd met, what they'd said. They talked about Mary. She was fine. She was grand. She was in good form. She was drinking Malibu and pineapple. Then she left. Did she seem apprehensive, anxious, worried, frightened? Each in turn said no, she didn't. And in each instance the defence counsel declined to cross-examine.

An old man shuffled to the stand. He stated his name. He took the oath, the Bible shaking in his right hand. The junior counsel asked him to describe what he was doing on the morning of Sunday, 13 August. He began hesitantly, but soon his voice was strong and clear. McLoughlin watched the way the old man's eyes sparkled and his cheeks flushed as he told his story. The words fell out of him with practised ease. How many pints had been bought for him at his local as he spun out the drama? How many times had his children and grand-children put up with his sputum-filled cough, just to hear the story again and again? Ah go on, Granda, tell us again. What did she look like? Did she smell? Was she green?

He was excused from the box. Again, no questions from the defence. He shuffled back to his seat, but as he passed Margaret he stopped and wordlessly placed one gnarled hand on her shoulder. McLoughlin could see her recoil, remembering as he remembered the sight of the girl lying in the mortuary, the marks of the dog's teeth visible in her white forehead.

I hope she's feeling strong, he thought. It's going to get worse. It would be photographs next. Not that she would see them. But they would be shown to the judge, the jury, the defence and prosecution. There was an album, already prepared. He had watched Gerry Scully, one of the technical team, develop and print them, then order and label them, pushing them under their plastic covers the way you would with wedding or confirmation pictures. They were being handed round now. Senior counsel was taking Gerry through his evidence defining in tedious detail when and how the photographs had been taken, from what angle and what distance. There were fifteen prints in the album. The barrister dealt with them in order, asking Gerry to explain and describe each one. McLoughlin watched the faces of the jury as they turned the pages. He could see how their initial shock was quickly replaced by a controlled curiosity. They would get used to the colours and the shapes. They would objectify the girl and the parts of her body. They would listen to the descriptions of her injuries without nausea. She was the victim, but she would cease to exist as a real person. If she had survived, had been able to sit in the witness box and describe what had happened to her, her evidence would have been the most powerful single force in the trial. But because she could not speak for herself she could be created in whatever image the prosecution or defence wanted. He had seen it so many times before. The real Mary

Mitchell would not come to life in this court room. A surrogate would be fashioned, a double, a doppelgänger, and this would inhabit the reports and the records, the memories of all who would sit here, listening, day after day until the case had ended.

41

Margaret watched the judge as he flicked through the album. Seated above the court, maroon velvet drapes behind him, the oak bench in front of him. His face was professionally expressionless. She looked at the jury. They were not so practised in the art of composure. She could see what they were seeing from the paling of the skin, the hand rushing to the mouth, the eyebrows tightening in concentration. And she looked at Patrick. He was sitting swivelled round, the album resting on the seat beside him, one arm trailing along the back of the seat, one hand drumming idly on the wood.

Garda Gerry Scully, giving evidence, spoke of angles, distance, lenses used. It was almost as if he and the senior counsel were members of a camera club. He described the scene on the canal bank, His first photographs were taken before Mary's body had been lifted out of the water. They showed, he explained, what was subsequently identified as the deceased's head. He explained that her neck was wedged between the roots of a tree, which was growing out of the side of the canal. Margaret could imagine. The roots of the tree cradling her between them, catching her just beneath the ears and holding her up. Like one of the Arthur Rackham illustrations in the copy of *Peter Pan* she'd had when she was small. Trees with long fingers and wraith-like bodies. Eyes that stared from knot-holes and wisps of leaves trailing like straggling hair to the ground. When Mary had been little in New Zealand there was a series of books about two tree children called Hutu and Kawa, named after the pohutukawa, huge and graceful, growing on cliff tops, with its beautiful bright red flowers. She had loved them, the way her mother loved the Arthur Rackham pictures. And somehow Margaret liked the idea that it was a tree that had caught her, stopped her from falling to the mud and the dirt of the canal bottom. Kept her away from the thick black ooze.

Douglas moved him on to the next series of pictures. These had been taken after the water in the canal had been lowered by two feet. They showed exactly how she was lying in her shroud of black plastic, the two concrete blocks attached to her by lengths of thick blue rope. One was tied round her neck, the other round her waist. There were close-ups of the blocks and their attachments. And more close-ups of the marks on her face.

'Now,' said Douglas, 'explain these to us.'

These, Scully said, had been taken when the body had been removed from the water. It had been laid out on the path that ran along beside the canal.

'Here you can see clearly the kind of heavy tape that was used to bind the plastic bags together, and again the concrete blocks and the ropes.'

'Finally,' said Douglas, 'the last set of photographs, taken where?'

'In the morgue, prior to the post-mortem,' replied Scully.

'And what do they show?'

'Bruising to her face, upper body, and thighs. They also show, particularly in the photograph labelled number twelve, that her hair has been cut.'

'And the one labelled number thirteen, what does that show us?'

'That her pubic hair appears to have been trimmed. It also shows a number of injuries, burns I believe they are, my lord, to her thighs.'

'Quite, Garda Scully.' Douglas looked again at him over the top of his glasses. 'And finally photograph number fourteen?'

'The area of her breasts and upper diaphragm, my lord. Lacerations and bruising, as you can see.'

Margaret looked at Patrick again. He was flicking quickly through the pages. He glanced up and around him for a moment then turned back to the splashes of colour in front of him. He had seen, she knew, many photographs like these. He had told her how, in the beginning, his stomach had turned when he had read and seen the evidence of crimes that men he was defending were alleged to have committed.

'So, what do you do?' she had asked him. 'What do you do if you know they are guilty?'

'Well,' he replied carefully, 'it depends on what you mean by know.'

'Ah, come on, don't get all philosophical with me.'

'No, I'm not. What I mean is that your clients tell you their side of the story. You don't make decisions as to their guilt or innocence. Only the jury can do that. Of course you have to act on whatever it is they tell you. So if they tell you something prejudicial to their case you can't hide it.'

'But,' she said, 'they don't.'

'No, they don't. And, anyway, there's far too much presumption of guilt. Just because the guards have arrested someone, brought them in, questioned them, made sure they're denied bail, and the whole world sees this bloke with a coat over his head, handcuffed to some great lump of a policeman, they automatically assume that he's guilty. You know, Margaret, everyone is–'

'Yeah, yeah, entitled to a defence.'

'But it is so. They are. And it's my job to defend them to the utmost. Come and watch. Come and see what I do.'

So she had sat here in this same courtroom – was it on the same seat? She wasn't sure. But she remembered the trial. The defendant was accused of murdering his wife. He had confessed to the killing, but he was pleading not guilty to murder. His defence was that he had been provoked and he had lashed out without thought or intention. She had gazed at him, trying to decide if that was true. He was small and pale. He looked malnourished, as if he had spent his whole life eating white bread and chips. When the prosecuting counsel described how his wife had died, how she had been bludgeoned to death with a heavy wrench in her kitchen, he had cried. His sobs washed around the courtroom, pitiful, painful to hear. And it had seemed a foregone conclusion that he would be found guilty. Until Patrick began to lay out the defence. She remembered the way he had done it. Witness after witness called to describe the dead woman. A bully, a nag, selfish, vain, aggressive, mean with money, sexually voracious. Margaret sat and listened. And watched the jury. Nine men and three women.

And listened to the way he dissected the evidence. Took it apart, meticulously. No murder weapon had ever been found. There was blood on the shoes of the accused, and on his trousers. But, said Patrick, he found her. He touched her. He knelt beside her to try to help her. Of course he would have blood on his clothes. And there were witnesses to say that he had been seen leaving home at his usual time to go to his job as a bus conductor. And more witnesses to say that he had seemed perfectly normal during the day.

'And what of the confession?' she remembered him saying to the jury. 'Look at him, his size, his demeanour. Think of how he would feel, grief-stricken for his wife. Suffering. Terrified by his surroundings. Intimidated.'

And that was the conclusion the jury came to. She waited in the Round Hall for the verdict. She watched Patrick, walking backwards and forwards, his black gown flowing around him. She heard his laugh as he joked with his peers. From time to time he looked in her direction. Once he came and sat beside her, as if by chance, casually, his thigh pressing for a moment against hers, and slipped a piece of cardboard into her hand. The top of a cigarette packet with the words 'I love you' printed in black ink.

And she said to him afterwards, 'But is there no one to speak up for the victim? For the dead woman? No one to take her side, to challenge all those witnesses?' And he looked at her as if she didn't understand anything at all and explained that there wasn't, that the victim had no place in the trial.

She shifted uneasily on the hard bench. People had crammed into the public seats filling up every available space. McLoughlin had warned her that this would happen. Once the trial began to be reported, curiosity would be excited. She would need to arrive earlier and earlier every day to make sure she got her seat. She crossed and uncrossed her legs, using her elbows to move the man pushed up against her right-hand side a fraction further away. She could smell him. He was sucking extra strong mints, but they couldn't completely hide the underlying taint of stale sweat and dirty hair.

'Dr James Greenaway,' the senior counsel called. Margaret watched as the forensic pathologist loped up to take the stand. One gangly arm reached round to smooth in place his long wisps of hair. He dispensed with the oath in double-quick time and perched on the chair, looking like a hare about to leap from the path of a greyhound.

'Dr Greenaway, could you describe to me,' Douglas began, 'the scene on the bank of the Grand Canal on Monday the fourteenth August last?'

Greenaway began. He could have been talking about a picnic, an outing, an occasion of great happiness. He described the weather, the sun, the heat, the water, the wildlife. His melodic voice rose and fell, cushioning, softening the impact of his words. He began to describe Mary's injuries, beginning with her head. He talked about what he had seen as he looked at her from the canal bank, and afterwards, when, under his instructions, she had been moved. Rigor mortis had not set in so this was not the difficulty it might have been. He differentiated between the damage that had been done to her before she was placed in the water and after. He commented on the work of small rodents, rats and water voles, the marks caused by the dog. Douglas moved on to the post-mortem. He described his observation of the exterior surface of the body, the marks around the wrists, caused by what appeared to be handcuffs, which had been removed before she was put in the plastic bags. There were similar marks around her ankles. Could he say whether or not the handcuffs had been on the body when she had died? Difficult to say, probably not he thought, as the scabs that had formed were a number of days old.

'Explain to us the nature of the marks here in photograph number thirteen,'

'Ah yes.' Greenaway put on his glasses. 'There is what seems to be an extensive burning of the skin, probably by a cigarette end. The deceased appeared to have a series of moles in a line on the inside of her right thigh and it looks as if the cigarette was applied to the skin between these marks, almost like those join-the-dots pictures that children have.'

'I see. And photograph fourteen?'

'Slashes made with a very sharp knife or blade around the nipples on both breasts.' He peered at the photograph for a few seconds. 'Very sharp. Almost scalpel-like, these incisions.'

'And do you have any suggestion as to what kind of a knife was used?'

'Possibly a Stanley knife, or a carpet knife, something of that order.'

'Any other marks on the body you should draw our attention to?'

'A number of bite marks on the upper breast, stomach, inner thighs, buttocks.'

The senior counsel pressed him to move on to the results of the post-mortem.

'Ah, yes, may I, my lord?' Greenaway gestured to his notebook, addressing the judge, Margaret noted, as the guards had, rather than David Douglas. The pathologist flicked through it, humming softly under his breath.

'Death,' he said, 'was caused by an intercranial haemorrhage, as a result of the laceration of the middle meningeal artery.'

'And what was this caused by?'

'Injuries were consistent with a blow, probably from a fist, to the left temple.' Greenaway rubbed his fingers against the side of his skull.

'And would death have been instantaneous?'

'No.' Dr Greenaway looked straight at the judge as he answered.

Not at all, thought Margaret, remembering the diagrams, the descriptions in her textbooks. There would have been a temporary loss of consciousness at the time of the blow, followed by a period of normal consciousness, possibly for one to two hours. Then gradual loss of consciousness again, with death resulting from increased intracranial pressure. The Glasgow scale of consciousness, she remembered, is the standard measurement. They call it the 'talk and die' phenomenon.

McLoughlin had told her. 'It's not going to be easy for you,' he had said. 'What you have to understand is that as far as the law is concerned nothing exists unless it is said in that courtroom. Practically every single piece of evidence, except for the very occasional exception, must be stated, described, explained, accounted for by word. And you will have to sit there and listen. Everything that happens every day is going to cause you a lot of pain – the description of, your daughter's injuries, the manner of her death, everything will be spelt out, syllable by syllable. If Fitzsimons had pleaded guilty, and we did think he would to begin with, he'd have saved us all a lot of bother, but now that he's using Patrick Holland, God knows what will happen. Because Holland is the worst or the best, depending on where you're standing. He's methodical, relentless, completely ruthless.'

The senior counsel was speaking again. 'Let's move on, Dr Greenaway, to her other injuries.' Margaret willed her ears to close. The man next to her was making notes. She looked at his lined pad, a leaking biro smearing words across the page. She watched the jury. They were all staring, mesmerized, at James Greenaway's description. She looked at Patrick. He, too, was making notes, staring down at his pad. Finally she looked at Jimmy Fitzsimons, He was pale. From time to time he ran his tongue over his bottom lip and bit deep into his thumbnail. She wanted to stand up and rush to the doctor and put her hand over his mouth. Leave her alone, she wanted to shout. Don't do this to her. This body that you describe in such beautiful, careful, fastidious detail doesn't exist any longer. There are no longer any tissues. No longer any flesh, any blood. There are just my memories of her. Please, please, leave them alone.

But the process of revelation was relentless. The doctor was now describing the nature of the injuries to her vagina and anus.

'Evidence of semen?' asked Douglas.

'Actually no. But skin was found under her fingernails which matched that of the accused.'

Margaret swallowed hard. As the prosecuting counsel sat down, Patrick stood up. He waited until the room was once again in complete silence. He looked around him. Then he began.

'Now, Dr Greenaway, of course we all know your expertise in these matters, and of course we would not deign to question any of your findings.' A titter of laughter rose up from the group of journalists. 'However, Dr Greenaway, there is something in your report which I don't think the prosecution has seen fit to bring into court. Perhaps you

437

would like to describe to the members of the jury your findings in relation to the condition of Ms Mitchell's cervix, which,' and he turned smartly to his right to address the jury, 'for the benefit of those of you with a less than encyclopaedic knowledge of the anatomy of a woman, is the neck or entrance to the womb.'

Dr Greenaway hesitated. 'From my examination,' he began, 'I would say that the deceased had been pregnant at some time in the recent past.'

'And, Dr Greenaway, how do you know this?'

'There are physical changes,' he said. 'The cervix is slit-like after pregnancy. The skin around the nipples, the areola as it's called, changes colour, darkens, as does the skin of the vulva.'

'So, can you tell us if that child was carried to full term?'

'I cannot,' he said. 'Practically speaking there are no signs, in any woman, to show this, apart from changes to the skin of the lower abdomen, "stretch marks" as they're commonly called. There were none of these on the body of the deceased, but they do not occur in every pregnancy, so that of itself doesn't tell us much.'

'You said "had been" pregnant, Dr Green-away, so she was not pregnant at the time of her death?'

'Definitely not.'

'And, Dr Greenaway, do you know if Mary Mitchell had any children?'

Again the hesitation. Then the answer. 'I don't. Not within my ambit, I'm afraid, my lord.'

Patrick turned again to face the jury. 'Well, I do know and I can state quite categorically that Ms Mitchell had not given birth to any living child.' He paused, and then spoke clearly and slowly. 'Any living child at all.'

Greenaway stepped down from the stand. Patrick slumped in his seat. A hiss of interest spread around the room. Margaret looked at Jimmy, at the way he had relaxed back into his bench, the way his eyes shone as he looked across the room at the jury. She could almost hear the tune he was humming. She dropped her gaze to the knot of cotton around her wrist. Still there, frayed, but still there.

42

It was winter. It was London. Twenty-one years ago. Sun trickled through the small square frosted window and laid its weak light across Margaret's bare wrists and hands. She was lying on a trolley, a faded surgical gown, tied criss-cross around her waist, barely covering her knees. She was very cold. She had waited with the ten other women in a large dark room. They sat on either side of a long mahogany table, some leafing through old copies of *Cosmopolitan* and *Woman's Own*, others gazing idly into space. Net curtains shielded them from the view of passers-by, although there was nothing to distinguish the red-brick house from any other on this suburban street. No one spoke. When her name was called she was taken into the anteroom, told to undress and handed the gown and a paper hat. 'For your hair, dear. Stuff it all in like a good girl, will you?' Now she lay still, her eyes fixed on a patch of damp that stained the ceiling in an irregular spidery shape. A swing door led into the operating theatre. Familiar sounds filtered through to her. The clang of stainless steel on stainless steel. The beep of an electronic sensor and the chatter of the team.

'...so it's up to you next Saturday, Jim.'

'Well, if you think I'm going to have a barbecue in this weather, you've got to be kidding.'

'It's not a barbecue, not really, but there'll be fireworks, won't there? And food and drink? And music. Sarah, you bring your banjo and I'll bring the guitar.'

Guy Fawkes Night.

Remember, remember the fifth of November, Gunpowder, treason and plot.

Remember, remember the first of November, the day that you told your father you were pregnant.

Her parents had come back from Paris late on Monday evening. She had waited for them. The house was clean and warm. She had bought flowers, bunches of freesias, clear, strong yellow and deep pink. Their gentle sweet scent seeped from room to room. Her father had brought her a present. It was a print from the Louvre.

'*La Gioconda,*' he said grandly. 'I know it's a bit of cliché, but really, Maggie, she is so beautiful when you actually get to see her. We had to wait until the guided tours had moved out of the way, but I fell in love, instantly. And the way Leonardo has painted her, you feel that you could reach out and put your arms around her waist.'

'Rubbish.' Catherine stood up abruptly. 'Romantic rubbish. I'm going to have a bath and go straight to bed. And will someone please bring me a cup of tea. I haven't had a decent one for days.'

They had sat in the kitchen drinking first the tea, then Calvados, which he had brought from a small wine shop, 'just near that famous café, you know the one where Jean-Paul Sartre and Simone de Beauvoir used to spend all their time.' He sniffed the golden liquid. 'Delicious, this stuff, isn't it? My favourite, reminds me of picking wind-fall apples in my granny's orchard.' She had watched him with love. At last she felt safe. Her pain, which had coagulated and hardened into a thick crust, began to melt. It would be all right. He would understand. He would hold out his arms, and, wrap them around her and take her fear and make it vanish.

Outside it was a cold night. Later there would be fog, which would soften the trees' jagged outlines and hug the shore like a mohair shawl. But now the stars stood out from the sky, the shape of the constellations revealed, and ice crystals were beginning to form on the short winter grass, the bare granite walls, the last red rose in the garden, defining its petals with a clear white line. A stray cat had slunk along the back wall above the railway. The light from the kitchen window fanned out into the black. He jumped down onto the path and trotted confidently towards the house. Sometimes the door would be open and he could sneak in to snatch a piece of meat or lick the butter in its dish leaving fine hair-like markings on its smooth surface. Sometimes he could find a place to curl up and sleep, in a basket of clothes from the washing line, or the shelf at the top of the broom cupboard. Tonight the door was closed. He jumped up against it and pushed but it didn't budge. He picked his way delicately through the flower bed that ran along the wall beneath the window, then climbed up through the branches of a small hebe. From there it was just a step onto the window sill. He sat on the ledge, settling himself into the warmth

443

of his winter coat. But there were noises, loud, from inside. Voices, angry. The cat's yellow eyes widened. He sat up, and then, as the noises grew and grew, he leaped out over the bushes and back into the safety of the darkness. He prowled around the side of the house, slipping through the bars of the wrought-iron gate. The lid of the dustbin might be loose, and he could nudge it with his head and hunt for whatever scraps of food might be there. But just as he reached the bin the front door opened. A blast of light and noise, footsteps slipping on the gravel, and the loud clang of the front gate. He shrank back beneath the hedge and waited until the door closed, the light went off and the footsteps outside on the path slowly faded.

She woke early next morning. She turned her head slowly to look at the man lying with his head on the greasy pillow beside her. What was his name? Freddy, Teddy, Eddy? He had bad skin. Acne scars etched deeply into his cheeks and as he turned away from her she could see that they ran across his shoulders too. She hadn't cared last night. All she'd wanted was someone to put his arms around her, to tell her that he wanted her. It didn't matter that she'd never

444

met him before, that he was the cousin of a guy in the year below her, that all he talked about was rugby.

She had got off the bus at Greene's bookshop and stumbled into the Lincoln Inn. It was packed as always. She pushed her way through the solid mass of bodies crammed up against the bar, men with barrel chests and thick wrists where heavy gold watches nestled in among the black hair. In a corner at the back she found a group of students she vaguely knew. They were surprised to see her, and even more surprised when she bought a drink and stood with them. She knew what they were thinking. Snooty bitch, slumming tonight. She drank quickly, brandy and ginger ale, then staggered down the steep stairs to the tiny ladies' toilet where she vomited until her knees sagged. Then she drank more and more. Finally at closing time there were just the two of them left in the deserted bar as the lights flicked on and off and a tired barman swept cigarette butts from under their feet.

She didn't remember much of what had happened next. They had walked, she was sure of that, to his flat, They had drunk more before he pulled her clothes off and

445

fell on top of her. Now she just wanted to get out, quickly, before he woke. She had phone calls to make, arrangements to take care of. She crawled carefully out from under the blankets. Her clothes were scattered over the dingy carpet. She dressed and found her bag. She didn't look at the figure in the bed as she quietly opened the door and left.

It had all been very easy. They had asked her if she was sure of her decision, discussed in a desultory way what her options might be. She didn't cry any more. She had been certain, but now as she lay on the narrow metal trolley, certainty left her, dribbled away like water seeping through sand. She felt acutely aware of everything around her, the sticky plastic mattress under her bare thighs, the bulky sanitary towel they'd told her to place between her legs. Outside, beyond the glass, a blackbird was singing one of its incessantly happy tunes. She could imagine it, high up in the branches of a leafless cherry tree, the sun shining on its glossy back, its head turned slightly to one side, and its song lifting up over the roofs, catching the attention of every other blackbird in the neighbourhood. She got up and went to the window. She tried to open it, but its old brass handle wouldn't budge. Her fingers came away stained with green, the same colour as the gown she was wearing.

The door from the theatre swung open.

'Your turn now,' the nurse said, pulling her mask down and smiling. Margaret's heart began to beat quickly. 'Are you feeling all right? You look a bit flushed.'

Of course I'm not feeling all right, Margaret thought. I'm feeling worse than I've ever felt before. She got back up on the trolley and allowed herself to be wheeled into the operating theatre. No one spoke. She tried to detach herself, look at it from a medical point of view. She had no principled view on abortion. I am a practical person, she had always said when the subject came up. People make decisions based on what's right for them at the time. And that was what she had done. She had looked at the situation and made a practical decision. Patrick had rejected her. Her father had rejected her. She couldn't tell her mother. She would never be able to work and support herself as a doctor with a tiny baby. It was all very simple, very straightforward.

The nurse bent over and picked up her left hand. She smoothed down the skin.

'Tiny veins,' she said, sighing, 'oh dear.'

She slapped Margaret's skin, as she slid the needle into her left wrist.

The anaesthetist stood beside her. He was wearing square black-rimmed glasses. She could see herself reflected in the lenses, her face swollen, egg-shaped. She looked at the tube in his hand. Ten mls of sodium thiopentone, she thought. For such a short and simple procedure. To put me out. Then he'll probably follow it up with scopalomine, maybe atropine. Then he'll put the laryngoscope into my mouth, pull down my tongue, so he can see my vocal cords, and intubate me. Or maybe he won't bother. Ten minutes or so? Hardly worth it.

The doctor leaned forward towards the i/v, which was now hanging from her wrist. He was humming. The Beatles. 'Will you still need me, will you still feed me, when I'm sixty-four.'

'No,' she said. She sat up, pushing him out of the way. She pulled the needle out. Blood spurted onto the floor. She put the thumb of her right hand firmly over it and pressed hard. She swung her legs over the side of the trolley.

'No,' she said again. 'I don't want this.' She walked out of the theatre, back the way she had come, grabbing her clothes from the chair where she had left them, past the woman lying waiting, past the others sitting, tense, frightened. There had to be another way, something else she could do.

The blackbird was still singing as she walked out of the clinic. Shafts of sunlight angling between the November clouds brightened up the dreary road. She craned her head and shielded her eyes as she searched for the bird. Finally she found him, high in the tree, orange beak open and his song, lilting up and down the scale. She sat down on a concrete bench beside a bus stop. I will listen, she thought, I will listen and I will wait.

43

'I will rise now until two-thirty this afternoon.'

Judge Hanratty stood and all stood with him. He gathered together his papers and followed the tipstaff out through the oak door. Patrick stood too, and stretched, easing out his long back. Around him continued the business of the court. The comings and goings, relating to this case and to others that would be held next week, next month, next year. There was laughter and loud talk as the crowd flooded through the doors to the Round Hall, leaving behind, like cockle shells at low tide, a couple of figures still seated on the hard wooden seats.

Margaret sat still. Her head was bowed. One of the guards had sat down beside her, and was speaking urgently to her, putting out his hand to touch her shoulder. But she got up, quickly, and left the room, her movements stiff and automatic.

Patrick had watched her today whenever he could. Watched her face, a perfect oval, alert, responsive, alive. Remembered how he had felt about her before. Felt all morning that he was still in that room in front of that fire. Listening as she told him what she wanted from him. What she wanted him to do. Tried to understand her. And began to see the world from her point of view. Listened to her as she talked about Mary. Felt her love and her grief in equal amounts.

He had wondered, from time to time over the years, if they would ever meet again. And when he had dropped the handful of coins on the polished counter, reached to grab the errant ten-pence piece, sliding his hand along the marble, and looked up to see who was watching, his first reaction had not been surprise or shock. It had been relief that now he could stop waiting.

He had watched her last night in front of the fire. The way she curled herself into that old armchair, her legs in smooth velvet leggings, a soft sweater falling from her shoulders, her hands fluttering like birds' wings, always moving, stroking her hair, fiddling with the fire, playing with a twist of silver on one small wrist, and a bracelet made of plaited material on the other. When she leaned into the fire's amber glow he could see the lines around her eyes and mouth, the strands of grey in her hair. They were new. But when she stood and stretched and walked about the room she seemed the same woman she had been twenty years ago.

There had been others since her. But he had never loved them. After she left he dreamed about her. Often. It was a dangerous dream and his awakening was always swift and brutal. Once Crea woke too, just at that moment. He turned his body away from her and buried his face in the pillow. Struggling to gain control. She didn't ask.

He didn't tell her.

Last night the room had been quiet. Neither had spoken. The open curtains stirred gently in a draught from the window. Outside in the hall the grandfather clock ticked. And then came the sound of scratching from the other side of the door. She uncurled herself from the chair and padded across the worn carpet. He could hear her voice low and soothing, and when she came back a large black cat kept pace, rubbing himself against her legs, jumping up beside her onto the arm of the chair.

'So,' his voice sounded unnaturally loud, 'what did you do next? Where did you go?'

She picked up another piece of apple wood and placed it carefully on the fire. She prodded it with the poker, holding the hot metal against it until a small curl of smoke twisted and turned and the air was filled with the crisp smell of burning.

'You're asking me now, but didn't you wonder at the time where I was, if I was all right?'

'Of course I wondered.'

'But you didn't do anything about it.'

'I asked Joe Macken, and he said he'd heard that you'd gone to England and got a great job there.'

'But you knew that. You knew where I'd gone.'

'Yes, I knew that, because you told me that was what you were going to do, but I thought you'd come back afterwards. And when you didn't I asked Joe again and he told me you'd got married.'

'And he heard it from my father, I presume.'

'That's right. He'd rung here, and your father had been most forthcoming, he said. Joe was pretty upset about it.'

'Joe was upset?'

'Well, you know the way Joe felt about you.'

'The way Joe felt about me.' She prodded the fire again. 'So that was that. I was conveniently out of the way.'

He looked at her, the lines deepening between his eyebrows and around his mouth. 'Bitterness doesn't suit you.'

'What?' Incredulity almost made her laugh.

'You're behaving as if I was the only one with a choice to make. What about your choice?'

'What choice?'

'You know, Margaret. I did wonder why you left, took yourself off like that. You could have stayed and made things very difficult for me. But now I realize. You didn't leave Dublin because of me. You left because of your father. It was his disapproval you couldn't face, his rejection you couldn't deal with. Not mine. Wasn't it?'

She wanted to deny it, but even as she opened her mouth to speak, tears came slipping silently from her eyes.

'My mother didn't tell me he was dead until after his funeral. She wrote to me and sent the letter sea mail. I couldn't believe it. I used to think about him a lot. And I couldn't believe that he could have died and I didn't know. Mary was twelve when it happened, and she was going through a phase where she had this little routine. She'd get up before me in the morning and bring me tea in bed. And this particular morning she brought me the tea and the post. And I remember when I read the letter I actually dropped the mug right there, scalding hot, all over me and the sheets and the mattress. And I didn't feel a thing. I just sat there, reading and rereading the letter and crying. And do you know he never ever referred once to what had happened between us. I created this fiction, the husband, and the accident that left me a widow and all that, and he just played right along with it.'

'And did you ever see him again?'

'After that dreadful night, you mean? No, never. I spoke to him on the phone. He was quite kind in some ways. He sent me money. At first I wouldn't take it, I used to send it back, but he opened a bank account for me so finally, I caved in.'

'But didn't your mother think it was odd?'

She sighed, a long shuddering sound, her back heaving.

'My mother, I'm afraid, tried very hard never to think about anything that wasn't directly to do with her. And, for some reason, that included me.'

'So, what did you do that day, after you didn't go through with the abortion?'

Sitting in the winter sun, listening to the blackbird. Hungry, thirsty. Nothing to eat since the night before because of the anaesthetic. Feeling sick. Light-headed. Lifting my eyes up to the blue of the sky. A milk float comes down the road. Its electric motor purrs, the bottles shake and rattle. It stops at the clinic. The milkman lifts a crate and walks around to the back. I get up and follow him. Down steps to the basement. Into a kitchen. It's warm. They are all there.

The receptionist. The doctors, the nurses. Sitting at a long table. Having breakfast. Plates of rashers, scrambled eggs, hot buttered toast. The smell of fresh coffee. The receptionist pulls out a chair. I sit. They give me food. I eat. They ask me questions in that disinterested English way. I tell them what, who, why.

'A doctor, fully qualified?'

I nod. They talk quietly for a few moments. Then. 'We're looking for an extra pair of hands here, we're swamped with work. Night duty, weekends.'

Gave me a room, in the little mews behind the house. And when the shape of the baby began to burst through my clothes, they put me to work in the office. They were friendly, kind, proud of me in a funny kind of way.

He looked at her, at the droop of her head. 'So you survived it?'

Routine was the answer. Get up at the same time every morning. Go to bed at the same time every night. Structure the day around meals. Keep busy. Take hot baths. Go for a walk whenever possible. Put one foot in front of the other and keep your eyes firmly fixed on the ground. If you can't sleep take a pill. Don't drink alcohol. Be wary of intense feelings. Don't daydream.

Don't desire. Don't want or need.

The black cat rubbed its head against her hand and purred loudly. She cupped his large triangular face in her hands and smoothed down the shining pelt above his gleaming gold eyes.

'Why New Zealand?'

'It's a long way away.'

'You'd a job? A place to live?'

'Not much of a job to begin with. Out in the middle of what they call the bush. But it was a beginning.'

Loneliness eating you up. The baby waking at three, at four, at five. Screams that sounded like pain, like fear, so loud from that small round mouth. What to do. How to stop them. Hold her to your breast. She clings on, sucking. Milk gushes into her mouth. Fast, too fast. She gags and chokes. Milk dribbles out of her mouth and down your breast. She cries and sucks. Air fills her stomach. It hurts. She pulls away. Twisting, kicking. Her body contorts. She doubles up with pain, screaming louder. You hold her up against your body, rubbing her back. Banging her back. Stop. Be careful. Not too hard. She's so small. You could hurt her. Still she cries. You're so tired. The light from the single bulb is too bright. Outside it's

457

quiet. The stars in the sky look different, upside down. The night is full of strange noises, animals and insects. Nothing smells the same. At last she's sleeping. You tiptoe over to her cradle. You bend over carefully, slowly. You put her down. But instantly, as soon as she leaves the warmth of your body, she begins to cry. Again. And again. And again. And now you're crying too. Please, someone, help me.

'And did she ask about her father?'

She sat back and looked at him. 'She had a father. Created by me, for me. And he satisfied her, he was enough for her.'

'Was he?'

Sitting on the verandah at the back of the house. A summer's night. The cicadas chirruping, an enormous choir, ceaseless, until you didn't hear them any more. Mary, aged five. Holding the telescope awkwardly up to her eye.

'Can't see, Mummy.'

'Here.' She fiddled with the focus and held one hand over Mary's little face. 'Look. What's up there?'

'Lots of twinkle, twinkle little stars.'

'And can you see three twinkles in a row?'

'Mmm.'

'And what's that called?'

''Rion's Belt, like the ones on my leg and on my daddy's leg too.'

'That's right, my little love.' Burying her face in the child's curls. Holding her small, warm body close. Rocking her until she was asleep. Carrying her inside and tucking her into bed. Putting her favourite teddy under the sheet beside her. Switching off the overhead light and leaving the night-light, shaped like a white cat, glowing. Standing at the window. Wanting, thinking, longing.

'But you've done well, haven't you?'

She poured more whiskey into her glass.

'Yes, I have. I'm considered something of an expert there on women and their mental health. I've written a number of books. I write a regular column in the *New Zealand Herald* and I've made three television series on the subject.'

'I thought you wanted to specialize in surgery. Joe always said you were streets ahead of everyone else in your year.'

She shrugged, and held out her small hands towards the fire. 'Another thing I lost when I had Mary.'

'And now she's dead.'

'She looked up at him. 'I don't care about any of that now. And I haven't for a long time. Surgery's the grand opera of medicine. It's full of monster egos, packed with prima donnas and divas. No, what I care about is making someone pay for Mary's death.'

'You mean you want justice.'

'You'd know more about justice than I would.'

'You think so?'

'Well, you tell me.'

'What you're talking about is revenge. Retribution. Something that will make you feel better. But the law isn't concerned with that. The law doesn't feel. Barristers slog it out like prizefighters. Looking for the holes in the case, the inconsistencies in the evidence. Analysing the text, finding the comma missing or the full stop in the wrong place.'

'Don't you approve?'

'Approval or disapproval doesn't come into it. It is just the way it is.'

He leaned forward and pulled the poker from the embers. He scrutinized its glowing tip.

'I used to love playing with the poker when I was a kid. Seeing how long it would take for the heat to travel up the rod. I nearly set fire to the house once. It had got so hot that I couldn't hold it. I dropped it onto the hearthrug and immediately it began to burn. I stamped on the flames but when my mother found out what had happened, there was no pocket money for weeks. I didn't think it was fair. I hadn't meant to burn the rug.'

'But the law assumes that we all intend the consequences of our actions.'

He smiled. 'Who taught you that?'

'So.' She took the poker from his hand and pushed it into the back of the hearth. 'Am I going to get justice?'

44

It was the handcuffs that he hated more than anything else. After all, he had heard the judge say, time after time, that he was innocent until proven guilty. So why the need for them? He had said as much to the guards. The big fat one, who farted the stench of rancid Guinness, just raised an eyebrow at him and said nothing. The younger of the two, who always gave him his copy of the *Star* to read, was more forthcoming. 'It's the regulations, Jimmy. Nothing we can do about it. In the interests of public safety.'

Fuck public safety. He hated it most when he was walking across the Round Hall back to the courtroom after the lunch break. They gave him his meals in the rat-hole of a cell in the basement. Chips, beans, sausages swimming in their own grease, eggs fried hours ago and kept lukewarm in the oven, stewed tea with long-life milk. He hated long-life milk. It left a scum all over his mouth and even though he carried his toothbrush with him and a small tube of toothpaste he could still feel it clinging in the little spaces between his teeth and coating his tongue.

They let his mother come in and sit with him while he was eating. He wished she'd stay away. They had nothing to say to each other. And she kept on watching him, looking at his hands as he speared chips with his fork and at his mouth as he shovelled in the food, and then sitting back in her chair, a mug of tea going cold on the table in front of her. The break for lunch was far too long. Over an hour. Sometimes an hour and a half. He'd finish eating in less than thirty minutes and then there was nothing to do but sit in the Round Hall and watch what was happening. It would have been all right if it hadn't been for the cuffs. Without them he could have pretended that he was just any other casual observer. It was funny sometimes, people's responses. Especially women. They would look at his face first, in that sneaky way that women have. Not openly admitting interest or attraction. And he'd see them thinking, not bad, or quite nice, or whatever. Then they'd slide their eyes down his body, to see what the rest of him was like. The way that men do. And then they'd spot the cuffs, and instantly they'd jerk back up to his face again. As if to say, 'I don't believe it, he couldn't have.' He'd see them, watch them do a double-take. Like a comedian on the telly. Sometimes he'd smile at them then. His biggest, best, poor-little-boy grin. And as they walked away he would see them whisper to their friends, turning back for another look and now, because they were suddenly in a position of power and superiority, they'd stare openly, without any sense of shame.

The only compensation for all this was that a couple of times he'd managed to get quite close to her. Not close enough to smell her, but near enough to see that she was looking tired and worried and very un-happy. Yesterday they'd passed each other on the steps which led from the Round Hall towards the Law Library. Their feet had stepped onto the first step at exactly the same moment. She was wearing a short black skirt, and long black boots, laced up the front. Unfortunately, the fat guard was, between them. She didn't see him immediately. She looked as if she was on another planet. He'd noticed that expression on her face before. Glazed and indifferent. She had to move slightly out of the way to let them pass. The guard said, 'Excuse me,' to her and she turned, swivelled just a little bit towards him. She had that mechanical 'you're excused but don't bother me any more' smile on her face, but when she saw him so close her face changed completely. She went red for a moment, and then white. The way she had that day in the church in Monkstown. He was about to stop. He thought he'd speak to her, but suddenly the guard recognized her too, and pulled him away, hard, dragging him by the handcuffs, the metal digging into his wrist-bone, catching it, pinching the skin. And he looked at him, nasty stare, which said, 'Don't even think about it, not for a moment.' The pig.

He should never have made that statement. He couldn't understand what had happened to him that day. Why had he been so scared? Why had he let that cop bully him? Get under his skin that way. It was so stupid. They had offered him a solicitor and he had turned the offer down. They had said they'd get his mother or his father or anyone else he wanted. And he'd said no. He was easy meat after that.

He told his barrister what had happened. After he'd talked to the other guys in Mountjoy. They'd said, you're crazy. They've fuck-all evidence against you. Fight it. He was a funny guy, that barrister. He never looked him in the eye when they met. He always stood and paced around behind him, asking the same questions over and over again.

'You did know the girl, didn't you?'

'How well did you know her?'

'For how long did you know her?'

'What did you feel about her?'

'What did she feel about you?'

'What did you do together?'

'Did she enjoy it?'

'Did you enjoy it?'

'Did you ever fight, have rows?'

'Did you ever hit her?'

'How did she respond?'

'And you saw her last, when?'

'Where was it?'

'When was it?'

'And how was she, when she left you?'

'What did she say to you?'

'What did you say to her?'

'You didn't go to the guards when you heard she was missing?'

'You didn't hear she was missing?'

'You were sick. Flu, fever, weak, couldn't get out of bed.'

'And when you recovered?'

'You still didn't know she was missing. You don't read newspapers, or watch TV?'

'And what happened to you in the Garda station?'

'Threats, inducements? Were you scared?'

'What time did you finish giving your statement?'

'Are you sure?'

Over and over again, repeated and repeated.

'Will you get me out of here?' he asked, him once.

The barrister didn't answer. 'Lunchtime, I think,' he said, and he left the room.

The pathologist had interested him. He liked the way he described Mary, went through the medical evidence, painted a picture with his words. Probably a better picture than the photographs the cops had taken. He'd caught a glimpse of them when the barrister had left the album open on his desk. He didn't think much of the framing of the images, and the cheap colour. His photographs were much better. Not, of course, that he'd been able to take any on the canal bank. A pity, really. Black and white would have been best. A big white flash and the body lying on the grass. Blacks and shades of grey, contrasts with the white of her skin. And it had been so interesting when the pathologist had said that she'd been pregnant. He could tell that everyone was shocked. Except for him. She'd told him all about that. And that she'd had an abortion. Got rid of it. Didn't tell her mother. He didn't approve of abortion. It was wrong. To kill something so weak and helpless. Who knows what might have happened to him and to Molly if abortion had been legal here? Swept away, both of them, flushed down the sink.

He stretched, lifting his cuffed arm, pulling at his wrist and the wrist of the guard he was locked to. It was nearly time to go back in for the afternoon session. The Round Hall was busy now, full of people. Standing in groups, the talk and chatter rising like steam to the dome above. It must be raining outside. People were shaking water from their coats, closing umbrellas. A couple of women had just come in together. He recognized them. Journalists. There was one in particular that he liked the look of. A girl with dark hair and a big mouth. She was a giggler. She sat at the end of the bench chatting to everyone who came in. Even the guards seemed to like her. She had very long legs and she often wore tiny skirts or tight leggings. He'd caught her looking at him more than once. He'd like to put his hands around her throat and squeeze until her eyes began to pop, and then he'd fuck her till she screamed through his fingers. She was standing just in front of him. She had one hip stuck out. He watched the way her bottom moved underneath the clinging black material of her skirt. She turned towards him, laughing, chatting. Her tongue slid out and licked gently from one side to the other. He thought of a lizard sitting on a rock in the sun, flicking insects deep down into its long throat. One day, one day. Soon.

45

McLoughlin finished his second pint and picked up his cigar. He tapped the tip carefully on the rim of the heavy glass ashtray, already overflowing with cigarette butts and screwed-up crisp packets. Half an inch of ash dropped off, spilling across the table's chipped black veneer. He leaned back into the lumpy upholstery and puffed hard. Lunchtime. He'd love another drink. Preferably a large vodka. He could quite easily spend the rest of the day with a glass in one hand and a cigar in the other, and to hell with the world.

This afternoon the head of the forensics lab would be on the stand. Hairs, fibres, dust, body fluids. Christ. In some ways it was even worse than pathology. At least there you still had some semblance of the human being, some shape, some form. Forensics was all about reducing everything to the nasty leftovers, the detritus, the rubbish. There'd be a lot of talk about fluff under the mattress and in the cracks in the

469

floorboards, bits and bobs found down the plughole and beneath the lino. And she'd have to sit there and listen to it all, keeping her face still and unmoved. Not giving anything away.

He had asked her to have lunch with him. She had refused. She wasn't rude. Just very remote, her face set and closed, her hands gripping her bag, her shoulders hunched. He knew that it was crazy the way he'd allowed himself to become so fascinated by her. Sad was the word to describe it, he thought. Sad in the sense that kids nowadays use. Pathetic, ludicrous, laughable. All those silly fantasies. Meals he'd cook her, wine he'd pour for her, places they'd visit. A total heap of crap.

Finney stood beside his table, his anorak slung over his shoulders. He looked pale, hollows under his eyes, and McLoughlin noticed he'd cut himself shaving. The remains of a piece of bloody tissue were still stuck to his neck. McLoughlin dropped the end of his cigar on the floor and ground his foot down onto it. He stood up and pulled himself out from behind the table. Not for the first time he noticed that he seemed to take up more space than usual. Fucking middle age. He straightened up and self-consciously sucked in his belly.

'Come on, boss. We'll be late.' Finney held open the door for him, giving him a shove in the small of his back to propel him on his way.

'Watch it.' He glared back at the younger man.

'OK, OK.' Finney held up his hands in mock surrender. 'It's just I know you. I could see that look in your eye. That "wouldn't it be nice to stay here all afternoon?" look.'

'Cheeky little fucker, aren't you?' McLoughlin grabbed his head in an arm lock and dragged him across Chancery Place, dodging in and out of the heavy stream of traffic, which poured across the bridge from the south side.

'Hey, let go. Sorry, I didn't mean it.' Finney banged ineffectually on McLoughlin's back; laughter shaking his shoulders. 'Stop. Please. I give in. I promise.'

McLoughlin dropped his arm, suddenly, and Finney reeled back, overbalancing and nearly collapsing on the footpath.

'Come on,' called McLoughlin over his shoulder, 'you're going to be late.'

They caught up with Margaret just as she walked up the steps and in through the double doors that led into the Round Hall. She stopped suddenly in front of them. McLoughlin looked past her. Fitzsimons was seated on a bench by the door to Court Number Two, his legs splayed out in front of him, his head flung back against the wall.

'Hey, Billy,' McLoughlin called out.

The guard looked up from his paper. McLoughlin jerked his head towards Margaret. The guard stood, pulling Fitzsimons up from his seat.

'Time to go,' he said, and pushed him in the direction of the court. Margaret walked on quickly, heading towards the sign for the ladies' toilet.

The afternoon proceeded as McLoughlin had predicted. Dr Pat O'Malley, head of the lab, was his usual phlegmatic self. As always he kept any speculation, any supposition, out of his voice and his answers. He was an empiricist first and foremost. Measure it, quantify it, analyse it. Then report on exactly what you have observed. He could say that the samples of hair found in the accused's house matched the hair of the victim. He could say that the fibres found matched clothes similar to the ones she had been wearing when she was last seen. But as her actual clothes had not been found it was impossible to say that they were an actual match. However, they had done tests on fibres taken from other clothes that the deceased had worn in the two months before her death and they had matched exactly fibres found in the accused's house and his car.

The questions moved on to body samples. Skin and tissue. It was all very clear-cut, very easy to define. No fuzzy boundaries for Dr O'Malley, thought McLoughlin. And so it should be. God forbid that we should find ourselves in the situation like in Britain where half their forensics seem to be corrupted or tainted, whether by design or misfortune. We have to believe absolutely in the power of scientific analysis, or else we're finished, he thought.

Margaret felt sick. She could taste the oxtail soup she had eaten for lunch, curdled now, bitter. She put her hand in her jacket pocket and felt the smooth surface of a small photograph. She had found it today in the inside pocket of her bag. It was passport size, one and a half inches by two. She took it out and rested it on her lap. It was one of a sheaf that Mary had got before they left New Zealand. For her new maroon Irish passport. She had put them on the kitchen table, four strips, half of them taken with Louisa. The two of them laughing, clowning, pulling faces. And then one strip, mock serious.

'Mugshots,' Mary said. 'Which one looks most Irish, would you say, Ma?' She had torn off two and gone to the post office to send away the forms, and Margaret had picked her favourite of the other two and slipped it into her bag. And forgotten all about it. Until lunchtime. Sitting in the gloom in Conway's, eating lukewarm soup. And her hand had slipped as she lifted a spoonful to her mouth, and thick liquid, Franciscan brown, had dropped onto her skirt, and begun to set and congeal. She had fumbled in her bag, looking for a tissue and found instead the photo. She cupped it in the palm of one hand, folding the other protectively over it. Mary peeked out at her through her fingers, so pretty, so happy. Or so she had seemed.

But she hadn't told her she was pregnant. She hadn't told her she was going to have an abortion. She had told Louisa. And it was Louisa who had gone with her to the clinic, who had waited and brought her back to her home. Who had lied to Margaret that she was 'Fine, just fine. She's got a bad period.

You know the way she gets, so she's going to stay here with me for the night. She'll be home sometime tomorrow. OK?' More lies, more deception. How can I blame her? she thought. When I started it.

She had sat in Conway's, the soup growing cold, and a pain in her chest, like a heavy stone on her heart. What had they talked about, herself and Patrick, the first time they met here? Politics maybe, books they had read, films they had seen. She remembered that she was wearing a long brown pleated skirt, with a pair of dark brown suede boots. And she had waited across the road in the Rotunda's lighted doorway until she saw him go into the pub. And then counted to a hundred before sauntering casually through the door. She had been so nervous to begin with, her words tumbling from her mouth. And he had been nervous too. She was surprised. She hadn't expected it.

They had stayed drinking until closing time. Then he had gone to use the phone, borrowing, she remembered, twopences for the box. She didn't ask who or why. They had walked down Parnell Street and he had kissed her, pushing her into a dark doorway and wrapping his heavy navy blue overcoat around her.

'I don't want to go home,' she said.

He pulled away for a moment, then he took her hand. They walked quickly past the Parnell monument, and across O'Connell Street, towards Gardiner Street. That night the place had been all but deserted, barely a straggler to be seen in the gloom. She leaned into his body, struggling to match his stride. She had lost her gloves somewhere, and she slipped her right hand into his coat pocket, feeling a bunch of keys, a handkerchief and some loose change. He turned left, up the hill towards Mountjoy Square, pulling her with him. He stopped at the first house on the right, and fumbled with the lock. Outside it was dark, cold, misty. Inside was a perfect Georgian hall, black and white chequered tiles, walls the colour of faded ox blood, and a huge gilt mirror. They stood together, looking at their reflection. Then, still looking in the mirror, he took her face between his hands and kissed her again, first on the forehead, then on the bridge of her nose, then on each cheek and finally on her mouth.

He used another key at the top of three flights of stairs to open a small door, which opened again onto attic stairs. High up in the eaves, three perfect rooms. Wallpaper striped a dark ivy green and cream covered the walls, and the ceiling was painted with the same ivy colour. Faded Indian rugs covered the floorboards. A tapestry quilt in rich reds, yellows and blues was strewn across a shining brass bed. Bookshelves ranged across one wall. In the other a small marble fireplace, laid with turf, and beside it on the floor a record player. Records were piled in two high stacks on another shelf. He knelt and shuffled through the sleeves.

'Listen.' he said.

Kathleen Ferrier, again. Loud crackles from the dusty surface.

'Hum it again, the way you did in the car,' he asked.

That had been Friday night. They had stayed there in those rooms until Sunday. She had phoned in sick to the hospital, and made some excuse to her father. She put her head under the pillows when he spoke to his wife, and tried not to hear that he called her darling, then opened her arms to him again as he climbed back into bed beside her.

'This place, it's so lovely,' she said.

'It belongs to Hugh, my younger brother. He's away at the moment.'

'And do you often bring girls here?' she

asked, suddenly, furiously jealous.

He just smiled, and ran steaming water into the huge old bath in the green tiled bathroom.

He cooked her meals. Breakfast. Rashers and eggs, sausages and black pudding. And fresh coffee. Fillet steak for supper. Biscuits with cocoa at midnight. And when he slept she lay with the bedside lamp still burning and watched him. The smooth pallor of his skin, his long black lashes lying on his cheek. The way his hair curled down over his forehead. And she pulled back the sheet to look at his body. The thick black hair covering his chest, the shape of a bat's wing. Tapering into a thin black line, which she traced with her finger, from his navel to the top of his pubic bone, where it spread out again, thicker, more springy, coils of hair that tickled her nose as she bent to kiss him.

They said goodbye on O'Connell Street. They didn't touch, not here, out in the open. He pulled away as she tried to take his hand.

'I'll phone you,' he said, but she didn't believe him.

None of it had changed much. The house in Mountjoy Square was still there. It was empty. About to be demolished, the barman in Hill 16, just around the corner on Gardiner Street, told her, when he recognized her, poured her a drink, said he was delighted to see her again after all these years. And when she tried her keys they still worked, and the rooms on the top floor were just as she remembered. Except smaller, more cramped. She'd gone to all their favourite places that dreadful day last summer, after McLoughlin had come to see her and told her about Mary's pregnancy. He'd been so clumsy. Read to her from the pathologist's report. Stumbled over the unfamiliar words. Left her distraught, needing to be comforted, to talk to the only person who could share her grief. So she had traced their time together. Gone first to her old flat in Pembroke Road. Her former landlady's daughter was living there now. She didn't remember Margaret, but she let her in, to climb up the stairs to the room on the top floor that looked across Wellington Road to the mountains. And from there to every other place she could remember that they'd spent time together. Talking to Patrick as she walked through the crowded streets, telling him how she needed him, that she couldn't bear the pain any longer, that she couldn't do this by herself. And waiting for an answer. But there hadn't been one. Until now.

She looked up, away from the photograph. An attendant was setting up a video screen. David Douglas was saying something about introducing video evidence. The young guard in the witness stand was explaining. Evidence taken from a television rental shop in George's Street. Douglas pressed the button. It was Mary. She was looking straight at the camera. She was dancing, her mouth open, singing. She was smiling as she spun around on the footpath. The guard pointed to the numbers flicking at the top right of the screen. Date and time, he said. Behind her, cars and buses passed. Douglas took out the tape and inserted another one. Again he pressed the button. Mary again. Not as clear, taken from further away. The guard explained. Security camera at the traffic lights at the junction of Dame Street and Trinity Street. She was standing, waiting. Looking left, then right, then left again.

'Hold hands, Mummy. This is the way to do it. No, Mummy, don't run across the road. It's dangerous. Teacher says. It's not allowed.'

Another tape. Security video. Again, the

guard explained. From a camera inside the lobby of the Central Bank. She was standing on the steps outside the door. She had her back to the camera, but she was instantly identifiable. Curly hair, long legs, short skirt, skinny arms. A big bag slung over her shoulder. She looked at her watch. Then she began to hop. Up and down, down and up the marble steps. Playing the game. How many can you jump in one?

'Come on, Mummy, you can do better than that. Don't be such a scaredy pants. You won't fall.'

The time code on the tape said 23.15. She looked up. She waved, and ran. Jumped down the stairs and out of sight.

The final tape. The traffic lights outside the Bank of Ireland in College Green. A car was stopped. Two people were sitting in the front. A young woman and a man. She was leaning over him. She was kissing him on the mouth. She sat back. It was Mary. The man was laughing.

'So, Garda Byrne, can you tell the court. Can you identify the occupants of the car?'

'I can, my lord.'

'And they are?'

'The young woman is the deceased, Miss Mary Mitchell, and the man is the accused,

Mr Jimmy Fitzsimons.'

The pain in her heart was worse now. A hand, turned into a fist, squeezing and squeezing. Squeezing the life out of her.

46

It rained again that night, and the wind blew from the east, dragging the sea up and over the wall, flinging it onto the road where it lay in puddles, which shimmered, black and orange, under the street lights. There had been a message for her when she got home. Scrawled in Nellie's hand, with the stub of a pencil, on the back of an envelope. The estate agent had been to visit with a prospective buyer. They wanted to make an offer.

She sat in front of the fire, too tired to do any more packing. The photographs were in a neat pile at her feet where Patrick had left them. She picked them up and sifted through them again. A couple were missing. One in particular she noticed. Mary on her eighteenth birthday. Wearing a party hat and a big grin. She had been born in July. Irish summer. New Zealand winter. In the photograph she was sitting on the floor, in front of the fire. Her legs were crossed, her head was resting on one hand. She was, Margaret remembered, a bit tipsy. There was to be a party, but they had drunk champagne together, on their own before all her friends arrived. Then she had left them to it. Stayed out of the way, gone to bed, read a book. Fallen asleep and woken hours later, the sound of music still pumping down the corridor to her room. She had got up warily, stepping across sleeping bodies, empty bottles and cans. Mary was lying on the sofa in the sitting room. She was crying. Margaret sat down beside her and stroked her hair.

'What is it?'

'I feel sad.'

'Why?'

'I don't know. I just do. I wish.'

'Wish what?'

'Wish I had a father. Wish he was here.'

She had lain down on the sofa beside her, pulling her head onto her breast, murmuring words of love and comfort until Mary had fallen asleep, her breath coming out of her mouth in soft, alcohol-scented puffs.

She had been so certain for so many years

that she had been right. There was only one course of action open to her and she had taken it. She had been proud of her resolution, her hard work, her consistency. Nothing had been too much for her to do on her own. She had asked for help from no one. But now she no longer knew. She tried to trace back through her actions over the years. She had gone wrong somewhere. What had been her greatest sin? She supposed now that it was pride. She had been so proud of her success, her perfection, her ability to survive. But she had mistaken arrogance for strength.

She got up stiffly. She walked down the hall, down the steps into the kitchen. She switched on the light. Her thin face and thinner body looked back at her from the reflection in the window. She sat down at the table and stared out into the darkness.

Out in the darkness a car was parked, facing the sea. Music seeped faintly from it. Frank Sinatra swooping up and down the scale. McLoughlin sat behind the wheel, his coat collar turned up around his face. He reached forward and lit a match, holding the end of a cigar into the flame until it began to glow. He puffed hard, then let the smoke out in a long stream. Still his after-dinner treat. Not that he had had much of a dinner tonight. He had cooked it, as usual, at home on his own. Pasta with a tomato and anchovy sauce and a salad. But somehow his appetite had dulled, and he had scraped most of it into the bin. He had wondered should he keep it for Janey, but there didn't seem to be much point. When he thought about it, he hadn't actually spoken to her, face to face, for days. They left messages for each other on the answering machine and on scraps of paper anchored to the kitchen table with the salt cellar. I'll be late. Don't wait up. I'll be late. Don't cook. Don't forget to feed the cat. Your mother phoned. Nothing important but ring her when you've a minute.

He sometimes wondered if she had someone else. He'd tried the thought out for size, the odd time, waiting at traffic lights, standing in the queue in the canteen, sitting here now, wondering if she'd get home before him. He'd tried out the idea before, but it had never seemed to fit. Because he supposed he had been the unfaithful one, inconstant, unreliable. Always, it seemed, looking for something else. Even in Rome on their honeymoon. The day they had gone to the Spanish Steps and drunk strawberry milkshakes, *frulati* they were called. They'd sat too long in the sun at a little café near the Borghese Museum and Janey had felt sick, her pale skin reddening, the freckles on her bare arms standing out like crumbs of crusty bread.

'I'll go back to the hotel. You stay here.' She had insisted. She didn't want to spoil the day. He had walked with her, then kissed her goodbye at the iron door that led from the street. The nausea he could see had taken hold. Her face was as white as a St David's lily. She waved him away, before turning quickly and running into the little lobby. And what was he to do? Except wander the streets, looking at the sights and the people, stopping in bars for cold drinks, until nightfall.

'Per favore. Uno gin e tonic?'

'Certamente, signore, gin-tonic.'

Until he reached the Trevi Fountain, turned a corner and without ceremony it was there, in front of him, dolphins spouting, Poseidon with his trident, figures from a million postcards. Close enough to touch. And he remembered the scene from *La Dolce Vita*. Anita Ekberg in the water, her dress stuck to her like the skin of a ripe mango, and all the photographers scrambling to get the best shot.

He sat on the low wall and threw coins, Irish pennies, and watched them spiralling down to add to the pile. There was a girl beside him doing the same thing. An English girl staying in the student hostel near by. A long tattered dress, light brown hair straggling down her back, arms and legs the colour of shiny bright autumn conkers. He had looked at her, and wanted her. Why? He didn't know. He hadn't done anything about it that time, but he had looked and wondered.

He leaned forward and reached into the glove compartment. He pulled out a bottle. He unscrewed the top and swallowed. He choked as the whiskey caught in his throat. It was time to talk to Janey. Properly, seriously, about the future. But now he heard above Sinatra's plaint the sound of a car, slowly, passing him, and stopping. Right outside Margaret's house. He held his wrist up into the pale glow of the streetlight. One a.m. He twisted round to look at the tall figure getting out. A man, carefully pushing open the creaking gate. Taking the front steps two at a time. Waiting for the door to open. Then ducking into the wedge of yellow light that poured out into the night.

He sat and waited. Half an hour, forty-five minutes, an hour. He got out. A gust of wind blew water in his face. He took his handkerchief from his trouser pocket and wiped his eyes. He crossed the road and walked past all the other houses. He opened the gate quietly. He walked up the path, careful not to trip on the uneven slabs. The curtains in the sitting room were open. He took hold of the iron banister and walked up the steps. When he reached the top, he paused and leaned out as far as he could towards the window. He craned his neck to see inside. He could hear two voices. One light and high, the other deeper. A glow came from the room. Red and yellow. Shifting and changing. He put one leg over the railing, then the other, and holding on tight with his arms stretched behind him he leaned forward as far as he could. Two bodies dark against the fire. The steady ripple of conversation. The high and the low threaded through each other, punctuated with a gentle beading of laughter.

His arms ached. He pulled himself back. He tiptoed down the steps again. He felt sick.

47

'You're sure, aren't you, Dave? The statement, there's no problem with it, because you know, it all really stands or falls around the statement. Everything else is circumstantial. Finger-pointing at best. The forensics are fairly useless. So, we found evidence of her in his house. So what? He doesn't deny that he knew her. So, we found skin under her fingernails? Again, so what? They had a sexual relationship. People do all kinds of things when they're at it. The skin, even the bruises and bites, mean fuck-all without the statement. You did observe all the procedures, didn't you, Dave?'

They were sitting in Bewley's in Westmoreland Street. It was coming up to nine o'clock. Finney was due in court at ten. McLoughlin had stood in the queue and ordered sausages, black and white pudding, rashers, hash browns and two rounds of toast. But he had barely been able to eat any of it. Last night's whiskey had coated his mouth and turned his stomach into a sludge of bile.

'What's wrong?' Finney paused, his laden fork midway between his plate and his mouth. 'Not hungry?'

McLoughlin shrugged and pushed the plate out of his line of sight.

'Well, I'll eat it, then.' He leaned over and helped himself, mopping up the grease with a piece of brown bread.

'You're OK about all of this, Dave?'

Finney gulped down a mouthful of tea and gazed calmly at him. 'What's your problem? I've told you. And, anyway, you know the DPP wouldn't have gone ahead with the charges if they were dubious about any of it.' He buttered another piece of bread, and smeared it with marmalade. 'You don't look so good today. What were you up to last night?'

He didn't tell him. How he had sat outside her house, drinking from the bottle. Waiting. How he had been going to wait until whoever he was had gone, and then he was going to knock on her door and tell her. But he hadn't. He'd fallen asleep instead, and woken with a stiff neck and foul headache and a uniformed guard from the Blackrock station banging on the window.

They walked up the river together. It was

another cold day, the sky a nervous and uncertain blue, wisps of dark cloud skipping from horizon to horizon. Monkstown had been yellow this morning, full of forsythia, thrusting its new growth, laden with astringent flowers, over the tops of granite walls, and pushing through dull privet hedges. And laburnum, golden pendants sweeping down onto the footpaths, shedding their petals in a gleaming shower. But the city here was grey and green, slick and shiny, even the river water giving off a metallic sheen.

The court seemed more crowded today than before. More journalists, more casual observers. Margaret was squeezed into her usual place. He paused to ask her how she was, noticing the dark shadows, under her eyes, but although she smiled politely, he could see that she was completely distracted, her attention somewhere else altogether. He took his place as usual at the back of the room, and waited for the prosecuting counsel to call Finney to the stand. It would be all right. He had checked everything that had happened that night in the station, taken care of the details.

But now he could see it beginning to unravel. In front of his eyes.

Dave Finney walked up to the stand. He stated his name and rank and took the oath. He began to lay out the evidence. He testified that they had called to Fitzsimons' house for the second time on Wednesday, 30 August at 7.45 a.m. They had a search warrant. It took four hours for the technical team to complete their job. Fitzsimons was present the whole time. At 11.07 a.m. the accused was arrested and cautioned. He was then driven to Swan's Nest for questioning. They arrived at the station at 11.50 a.m. They questioned the accused until 17.07, including an hour's meal break. Superintendent Finucane renewed the detention order. They continued questioning the accused. At 22.05 he indicated that he was prepared to make a statement. He did not finish his statement until 23.45.

Douglas took him through it slowly, carefully. 'And, Sergeant Finney, your legal detention of Mr Fitzsimons expired at exactly 23.07. Am I right?'

'Yes, my lord.'

'But the accused continued with his statement until twenty-three forty-five until, as I understand it, he was happy with what he had said, he had read it over and he had signed it. Is this so?'

'Yes, my lord.'

'And, Sergeant Finney, he was aware that his time of detention had come to an end, that he was free to go, but he chose, voluntarily, to finish making his statement, is that correct?'

There was a moment's silence. 'Yes, my lord.'

'So now, Sergeant Finney, if you would be so good as to read the statement that the accused made on the thirtieth of August, nineteen ninety-five.'

And that was where it all started to go wrong. Holland, suddenly on his feet, objecting, asking for the jury to be removed, stating that the inculpatory statement had been obtained when his client was illegally detained. That his client had not been cautioned again, that he had not been told of his rights, that it appeared that Sergeant Finney had at best been economical with the truth and at worst had perjured himself, that his client Mr Fitzsimons had been placed in an appalling position that night, six months ago. Ignorant of the law, never having been in a Garda station before, harassed, threatened, offered inducements, bullied, blackmailed, threatened and finally, the greatest crime, lied to by this officer.

And not only that, not only what had taken place within Swan's Nest station, that night, but there was the whole question of the search that had taken place in the morning.

'I would like to enquire of Sergeant Finney, my lord, exactly what was the nature of the request that Mr Fitzsimons remain present during this search. Let me put it to you that Mr Fitzsimons was not free to leave the premises, was not free to go, for example, to leave the country, leave the county, even leave the city. That in effect his detention began at precisely seven forty-five a.m. when the guards arrived on his doorstep, and that it expired at precisely seven forty-five p.m., and not as the officer has stated at eleven seven p.m. Therefore, my lord,' Holland said, his voice booming around the packed courtroom, 'it would be my respectful submission that this statement should be ruled inadmissible and on that basis I would apply to have these charges against my client dismissed on the grounds of denial of my client's rights to liberty, which are upheld by our constitution.'

McLoughlin looked at Finney. His face was pale, his expression a mixture of anger, guilt and confusion. He looked from Finney to Fitzsimons. A gleam of understanding was illuminating his face. He looked for Margaret, seated in her usual place. She turned slightly towards him, gazing around the room, from policeman to accused, from judge to the row of journalists seated at right angles to her. Then she turned and looked back, over her shoulder, at him. She looked at him, then through him, and turned away from him again.

The two barristers were still arguing, discussing, debating. Citing cases to be consulted. A game of legalistic ping-pong, he thought, and who would be the most nimble, the most fleet of foot, the most able to hang on by the fingernails to the tiny crevices where advantage, not truth, could be found.

He turned on his heel and walked out into the Round Hall. He was sick of it all. Too much involvement. Too close to them all. Suffocated by the misery and the pain, the tiny nuances of all these lives, which filled his nostrils with their identifying stench.

He walked down the steps, out into the lobby, and opened the door. Outside, the air was fresh and surprisingly clean. A flock of seagulls swooped low over the river, shrieking loudly, moving as one, dipping down towards the green water, then back up again, their wings flashing white against the grey of the building, climbing higher and higher into the sky, then wheeling, still together, over the bridge and away. He leaned against a pillar, pushing his back up against the stone. He was tired.

Behind him a stream of people came from the court. Words and phrases floated his way.

'Incredible, isn't it?'

'Bloody guards, I thought they'd given up on all those heavy-gang tactics.'

'Game-playing, that's what it is. Just a way of barristers making more money.'

'Statements, always dodgy.'

'Don't need corroboration, not in a case like that.'

'Guilty as sin, you just have to look at him.'

To hell with the whole fucking lot, he thought, and he turned and walked away, his hands in his pockets, his head down, and a hollow in his stomach.

A pair of tights, discarded, lay in a tangled heap on the dirty white tiles. Cold water dripped into a stained wash basin. A ventilator high up on the cobwebbed wall whirred fitfully, its white plastic louvres flicking erratically open and shut. Margaret stood in front of the smeared mirror. It was very quiet down here in the basement below the Round Hall. The ladies' toilet was a decrepit comparison to the splendid formality of the rest of the building.

She opened her bag and took out her hairbrush. She undid her hair from its clasp, and pulled the brush methodically through the dark strands. Then she smoothed her hair back from her forehead and fastened it again at the nape of her neck.

There was the sound of water gushing from a cistern and the cubicle door behind her opened. Margaret watched in the mirror as a woman approached. She stood at the basin and held her hands under the tap. She carefully soaped her fingers, rubbing between them, and massaging her palms together. Then she held them under the tap again, the large diamond ring on her left hand scraping against the enamel. She turned away and dried her hands thoroughly on the damp roller towel. Then she turned back to the mirror. She opened her handbag and took out a lipstick. She pulled off its gold-coloured cap, and wound up its red, shining point. She leaned forward towards the mirror, shaping first her full upper lip with one careful movement, then wiping more colour across the lower one. She took a tissue out of her bag and blotted her mouth carefully. Then she put away the lipstick and the tissue. She stood back and looked at herself in the mirror, turning slightly from left to right to check her reflection. Jimmy's bright blue eyes looked back at her. She smoothed down her tight black sweater over her heavy breasts, and straightened her short skirt. The Lycra in her stockings gleamed, stretching tight over her hard, fat legs. She ran her hands through her tousled blonde hair, pouting at herself in the glass. Then she opened her mouth wide again and stepped forward, baring her teeth, running her tongue over them. She looked for the first time in Margaret's direction.

'He didn't do it, you know,' she said.

Margaret said nothing.

'He didn't. Really. The police framed him. They couldn't find the real killer so they stuck it on our Jimmy. It's complete rubbish. He wouldn't hurt anyone. He's a real sweetheart. Your daughter must have been going out with someone else. And that's the person they should have been looking for, instead of intimidating our little boy. Keeping him in prison for all those months. Someone's going to have to pay for this, you know.'

Margaret looked at her in the mirror, the fleshy face, the heavy body. She gave off a strong smell of perfume. Musky, clinging. Margaret's gorge rose. She backed away from the basin, and took three long strides into the toilet. She sank down on her haunches, grasping the seat as a stream of thin grey liquid poured from her, filling her mouth with its bitter burning. Tears poured from her eyes as she vomited until nothing more would come. She thought of that woman as a girl, her girl's body grotesque with her pregnancy, her girl's body split apart by the baby who forced his way out. Had she loved him with a mother's love, the way Margaret had loved Mary? Instantly, completely, totally committed to this tiny little person, so new yet so familiar?

She sank down on the dirty floor, oblivious to the stains on the tiles. She could see the woman's feet, still in front of the mirror. She was wearing very high black shoes, which distorted her insteps, crushing them into shape. Margaret wiped her mouth with toilet paper and rested her head on her knees. She watched the black shoes, standing with the weight thrown first to one side then the other. Then they moved, one after the other, out of sight.

Margaret was cold now. She could feel the chill of the tiles through her skirt. She got up slowly, stiffly. She went out to the basin again, and rinsed her face and her mouth, careless of the water running down the front of her blouse. She put her hand in her bag and felt for the photograph of Mary. She took it out and gently kissed the smooth surface. Her daughter smiled back at her, reassuring her. This was the Mary she knew, the Mary who liked making scones and fairy cakes. The Mary who loved *Anne of Green Gables* and *The Wizard of Oz*. The Mary who could sing her way right through *The Sound of Music*. The Mary who could do sixteen *fouettés* and was trying for thirty-two.

'Hold on, my love, it's nearly over,' she whispered. But there was no reply.

48

For the first few days after he was let out of prison he couldn't sleep. It wasn't possible, not at all, to lie down and close his eyes, shut out all the wonderful sights, colours, shapes, smells, tastes and sounds. Why would anyone choose oblivion, darkness, when the world was so beautiful, so rich, so exciting?

It had been raining that afternoon when he had walked from the Four Courts, but he had crossed from the shelter of the building to the footpath by the river and stood with his head back, and the raindrops sliding down his face. He had put out his tongue and tasted the water, bitter and cold, held out his hands and watched it collect in the cracks and crevices of his palms. And he felt so powerful. Now he could do anything. He had looked around for her. He wanted her to share in his triumph. But she was gone, driven away by the guards. Never mind. There was plenty of time. But the next day when he went out to Monkstown the house was empty. There was an estate agent's board in the front garden, with the words 'sale agreed' stuck diagonally across it. He had nearly cried with disappointment. He had gone through the side gate to the garden and peered through all the windows. And although the house looked empty he forced the lock on the back door and went in.

She had left nothing for him, except a pile of old newspapers in the kitchen and a couple of black plastic bags in the hall. He upended them and sifted through the contents. Nothing of interest. Rags, torn sheets, an old blanket with moth holes decorating it. There were dirty marks on all the walls, squares and rectangles, signifying absence and loss. He went up the stairs, slowly, running his hand along the banister, imagining that her hand was underneath his. In the small bedroom at the back of the house a lavender bag was hanging from a wire coat-hanger. It was tied on with a length of narrow pink ribbon, which he undid carefully, picking at the tiny knot with clumsy fingers. The lavender was encased in a piece of flimsy faded material. He held it to his nose and breathed deeply. But the smell only brought the daughter back to his memory. She had liked it, he remembered. There was that unusual bush of white lavender she had found that first day. But he didn't want to think about any of that now except to learn from his mistakes. He had been so careless before, so much the amateur. If he had learned anything from his time in prison it was the value of planning and cunning.

He wandered into the other, bigger bedroom upstairs. Here, a mattress and a couple of old pillows lay on the dusty floor. He sat down, with his back to the wall, and closed his eyes. He fell sideways and rolled onto his stomach. He buried his face in the pillow, and breathed deeply. It smelt stale and musty, but there was a hint of something, warm, living, deep down in the feathers. He rolled over on the mattress, and gazed up at the ceiling. He slipped his hand down into his trousers. Touch me, there and there and there, he whispered, keeping her face just where he wanted it. Right above him.

He had looked straight at her at the moment when the judge had said he was free to go. Straight at her, not at anyone else. It was a wonderful moment. And he thought about it again and again and again. He wished that he could have had it on tape. He could have played it to her, the night that he phoned her in New Zealand, a week after she'd got back. His phone call must have been the last thing she was expecting. He thought that maybe she might have changed her phone number, that it wouldn't still be the one he'd found in Mary's address book, but she answered the phone herself, after just two rings. It was late there. About eleven o'clock, he calculated. She must have been in bed. Hallo, she said. Then again, Hallo. He didn't speak. He lay back on his bed, looking at his photographs of her. Hallo, hallo, again and again. She was beginning to sound nervous. He blew her a kiss. Then she hung up. When he tried the number again, a few minutes later, it was engaged. Silly woman, he thought. Phone off the hook. He supposed that she would get the number changed, but if New Zealand was anything like Ireland it would take a few days. He'd have a couple more scores before then, he was sure. And he could write to her too. There were a few things he wanted to send her. He would have to get out his negatives, print up a few good ones and put them in the post.

He was surprised at how quickly life went back to its normal routine. His mother, the stupid cunt, had wanted him to move back home. She'd made him come and stay for a couple of nights after the trial was over. She'd had a celebration party. Not that there were many people at it. They'd invited Patrick Holland, but he declined the invitation. Didn't give any explanation, just sent a note saying he couldn't make it. Molly was there, as sweet and loving as ever. She'd been waiting for him in her usual place, sitting on the front steps, and she was bursting to tell him her news. I'm going to a new school, she said. And I have a friend. His name is Peter and he's got black hair, and he has a dog called Fluffy. She was behaving, he noticed, with a certain sense of decorum. A new self-awareness. At first he wasn't sure he liked it, that she didn't fling herself onto his knee and cover his faces with kisses. There was something pricking at him, niggling. Jealousy, maybe, and for a moment he wanted to reach out and hurt her, make her realize that his love wasn't unconditional. But he stopped himself. It wouldn't be fair to do that to Molly. She wasn't capable of understanding. Not like the others.

Tina had been there, too, with her fat husband Bill. Jimmy had sat on the sofa, a beer in his hand, and watched the two of them. Tina was sitting in an armchair, her legs crossed, her skirt halfway up her thighs, and Bill was perched on the arm. He had his hand around her, his fat fingers gripping her shoulder, Jimmy knew he was just waiting for the moment when he could slide his hand down and grab her big tits and squeeze them. Jimmy wanted to do that too. Squeeze them so hard that his fingers would leave black marks that would take days to fade.

And work was fine. Eventually. It took a while. To begin with there was a lot of talk, about him, not to him, but then people began to forget and soon the bookings started coming in again. It should be good through the summer. Lots of trips to Dromoland and Ashford Castle. Plenty of parties of rich Yanks coming over to play golf at Mount Juliet and the K Club. And he'd even had a couple of ageing rock stars hire him for a week at a time. That was fun. Those guys knew how to live. And they weren't snobs. They always included the hired help. But none of it had been as good as those few weeks last summer. The only time in his life when he really knew what it was all about. He was so excited all the time. He didn't want to sleep or to eat. He just wanted to be and to do. He'd been looking around to see what to do next. But he had to

be careful. He'd seen that fucker McLoughlin a few times. Bumped into him, casually,
in town. Not enough to constitute harass-
ment, but it made him a wee bit worried.
He'd toyed with the idea of going to New
Zealand. He'd even gone into a travel agent
to find out about planes, and prices and
timetables. But he wasn't going to make any
hasty decisions. Planning and cunning. That
was what he needed to remember.

He looked at his watch. It was eleven-
fifteen. Saturday night. The girl in the agency
had been very specific in her instructions.

'Jimmy,' she said, 'listen, this is a good job.
They've offered big bucks. They want you
for the next ten days. Beginning late on
Saturday night. It's an around Ireland trip.
Just the two of them. You're to pick up the
wife from outside Bloom's Hotel at eleven
fifteen and take her to Wexford, where she's
meeting her husband. They're staying the
night there with some friends. Then next
day you're to carry on with them to Cork.
She'll give you all your instructions when
she meets you. They're paying top rates.
And a bit extra. So be on your best
behaviour. OK? The name? Let's see. Mr
and Mrs Blake. OK?'

He had driven in from the canal, along

507

Leeson Street, the road slick and shiny. Then spun around the Green and along-South King Street. The crowd from the Gaiety was spilling out in front of the traffic. The usual happy Saturday-night bunch, women who looked like his mother, costume jewellery and smudged lipstick. He blew his horn at a couple who were wandering down the white line. The man turned around and gave him two fingers. He was tempted to put his foot down and show him. But he contented himself with rolling down the window and shouting. When he pulled up in Anglesea Street, though, it was quiet, only the muffled boom of a nearby disco to tell that it was the weekend.

He reached into the glove compartment and took out Molly's shell. Funny, really, how things work out. He'd been so angry with Molly when he discovered she'd taken it from the car, but it had been just as well. When the cops searched his house and the car all they found were hairs and fibres. He could have said that Mary had given him the shell, but that just might have raised more questions about where her bag had got to, and he didn't want that. He'd had to bribe Molly with an extra large box of chocolates to give it back when he came home. He held it to his ear and listened. The song of the sea whispered to him.

He looked at his watch again. Eleven-twenty. Come on, come on. He fiddled with the radio, switching from station to station. He wanted to get going. He liked the idea of driving through the dark with a woman he didn't know. He looked in his rear-view mirror. A woman was approaching the car. She was small and slight, her face in darkness shrouded by a long, light shawl, which was looped about her head. She stopped and he got out and went around to the passenger side. She turned to face him. His heart leaped in his chest and blood surged through his eardrums, blocking out all the other night-time sounds.

'Hallo, Jimmy,' she said. 'Open the door.'

49

So it has come to this.

McLoughlin sat in his kitchen by himself. He had opened a bottle of wine and drunk most of it. The remains of his dinner were congealing on his plate. Pork chops, mashed potato, and a salad. He had picked at it, then left it. He began to scrape the meat onto the cat's dish on the floor, and then he remembered. There was no cat any longer. He had gone when Janey went three weeks ago.

He had never got around to having that conversation with her. He thought back over those days and weeks, looking for the tell-tale signs, the clues, the gestures. But he could remember very little of anything other than the case, the dead girl, her mother and the trial. He picked up the bottle and poured the end of it into his glass. Drink was part of it, a big part of it if the truth was to be told. God knows what it had done to the structure of his brain. One thing, however, stuck in his throat. She hadn't even told him to his face. He'd come home that terrible night after Fitzsimons had been released and there was a note. Just a fucking note. Written on a piece of lined paper torn from a spiral pad. It was lying open on the kitchen table, not even in an envelope. He'd sat down and picked it up, carefully pulling off the jagged scraps of paper along the top, and piling them into a little heap as he read. Two lines of Janey's neat sloping writing. He tore it, first in half, then half again, and laid the pieces down on the table. He spent the next half-hour matching them up, Sellotaping them back into place. Then he pinned the patchwork paper up on the noticeboard, alongside all her flyers about evening classes and morning courses and weekend workshops. He'd walked around the house and looked to see what she'd taken. Not much. Her clothes, of course, and her books. Her old LPs. A few photographs. Not, he noticed, the one on the mantelpiece, the one taken on the pier. She'd lit the fire in the sitting room before she went. He sat down in front of it and warmed his hands, and in spite of himself he began to cry. He slept that night in the same place, curled up on the hearthrug with a couple of blankets wrapped around him.

Later, he noticed other things she'd taken. The lawn-mower, for instance, and some, but not all of the tools in the toolbox. The electric drill and the box of bits, and a wood sander. She didn't say in her note where she was going and he realized that he didn't know who to ask. A week later he got a letter from a solicitor, informing him that she wanted a legal separation. He kept waiting for the phone to ring. But it didn't. So after a few more days he made his way to the women's centre where she'd spent so much time.

'McLoughlin, Jane McLoughlin?' The woman behind the desk shook her head, her long bead earrings writhing sympathetically. 'Doesn't ring a bell.'

'Well,' McLoughlin paused for a moment, 'perhaps she was using her maiden name, Reynolds. Jane Reynolds.'

'No,' she replied, with another vigorous head-shake. 'Don't know anyone by that name. What does she look like?'

'She's–' McLoughlin stopped. He couldn't describe her. The twenty-five-year-old Janey or even the thirty-five-year-old, yes, definitely, but the woman as she was now? He turned away, slowly. 'It doesn't matter. I've probably got the wrong place.'

Funny, he thought. Here he was. A guard. Supposed to be able to find people, observe them, know what was going on, investigate their inner secrets, the dark and nasty things they keep under the stones of their everyday lives, and when it came to it he hadn't even noticed what his own wife was doing. And now she was gone, he couldn't even find her.

The house was cold. A layer of dust covered all the hard surfaces. Sometimes when he sat down on the sofa he felt as if a puff of fine grey filament was floating out of the upholstery, hanging in the air for a moment then falling all over him. Like a picture in a children's fairy story. Grey shards of cobweb drifting, then settling, holding him immobile, in place. Fixed. He tried to analyse what was happening, work out what was going on. He knew he hadn't loved her for years. He'd spent most of them tormenting her, careless of her feelings, her desires. So he should be pleased that she was no longer here to annoy him, to shout at him, to get in his way. Christ, he groaned. Don't tell me you're suffering remorse, not that disgustingly hypocritical bullshit that you've seen so many others come out with when it gets too late. But it wasn't that. He didn't want her back. He had no illusions about his ability to live with her. It was just, it made him see what a waste it had all been. What had he been doing for all those years? He sat now in the evenings on the sofa by the unlit fire or at the table in the kitchen, always with a glass in his hand, and he didn't know how he was going to put in the time.

And then there was Margaret. Another humiliation. He had walked with her out of the Four Courts, taken her by the arm and led her to the car. That day, the same day. He had driven her back to the house in Monkstown. He had followed her into the house, wanting to talk to her, to tell her how sorry he was. She walked ahead of him down the steps to the kitchen. He waited until he heard the sound of water gushing from the tap into the kettle. Then he went into the sitting room. Two battered armchairs were placed on either side of the fireplace. An empty whiskey bottle stood, with two glasses, on the hearth. He bent down and picked them up. Both were smeared with dusty fingerprints. There was a pile of photographs on the floor. He squatted down to look at them. They were of the girl. He put down the glasses and picked them up, flicking through them, surreptitiously. And found some others. Of boys, of young men, handsome, happy. With dark curly hair and blue eyes. Taken on a playing field, a tennis court, sunburnt legs and arms and broad smiles.

'I'll take those.' She came towards him, her hand outstretched. She took the pictures from him, and put them up on the mantelpiece.

'Look,' he began.

'Yes?'

'I–' He stopped. 'What can I say?'

'What can you say?' She put out her hand and rested her index finger lightly on his chest. His fingers closed over hers. He stroked the soft skin. She stepped back quickly.

She didn't offer him tea or coffee or a drink. He walked out into the hallway. She opened the front door, He stood, looking at her, then he bent to kiss her cheek. But somehow she had moved away, and his mouth just brushed the corner of her ear. He stepped back, suddenly flushing, and then he turned and walked out of the door and down the steps. When he got to his car he looked back. She had closed the door behind him.

It still made him blush to think of it. And it made him feel even more lonely and even worse about Janey. There was one evening a week or so ago when he decided to look for her again. This time he tried the group of pubs around Dame Street, the places she told him she went with her new-found women friends. It was quite late, around ten o'clock, when he pushed open the door into the Foggy Dew. He stood in the middle of the floor and looked around him. Groups of people in threes and fours hugged the seats along the dingy walls. The talk was low and intense. Faces lifted towards him, scanned his dress, his demeanour, then dropped away. He walked to the bar and ordered a drink. A pint and a Black Bush. Ceilidh music droned from the big old radio on the shelf behind the bar, He pulled himself onto a stool and took a cigar from his breast pocket. The barman proffered a light.

'All regulars in here?' he asked.

'That's right.'

He twisted around on his stool.

'Not much of a crowd for a pub in the city centre.'

'Yeah, that's what the new owners think. We're closing next week. Refurbishment.'

'So where'll they all go?'

The barman shrugged. 'Plenty of other places round here.'

McLoughlin took a swallow from his pint, wiping the froth from his top lip with the back of his hand. He picked up his drinks and moved over to a table in the corner, sitting down beside a group of women. They all looked alike. Short hair, earrings, baggy trousers and thick sweaters. He tried to eavesdrop on their conversation but they seemed to be speaking a language unlike his own. The women looked like Janey had become: their hair was short and naturally grey, their bodies solid, stocky. They all wore silver rings, heavy, simple, the kind that could double as a weapon. He remembered Janey's engagement ring. It had belonged to his grandmother. Seed pearls and amethyst. Victorian. Very pretty. She'd stopped wearing it about ten years ago. She said her fingers had swollen and the worn gold of the band cut into them. He wondered where it was. He must look in the chest of drawers. See if her jewellery box was still there. The wooden one he'd given her the first Christmas they were married. Walnut, handmade, lined with green baize, with little compartments for rings, earrings, bracelets. You'd better give me something to put in it, she'd said. Of course I will, my love, he'd replied. But of course he didn't.

He moved from pub to pub. Each one was like a parallel universe, he thought. All these people whose sensibilities and customs were so different from his own. He stared at the alcohol in front of him, the gleaming dungeon-black of the Guinness, golden hops and barley transformed by fire, and the glistening silk of the whiskey. As he swilled it around his mouth it reminded him of Janey's wet softness. Once it had given him so much pleasure.

A girl sat down in front of him. She was very young, with a ring in her nose. Her hair was cropped short, very black and shiny. Her leather jacket swung open as she leaned across the table to pick up a box of matches. Underneath she was wearing a skimpy vest top, tie-dyed in brilliant greens. Her nipples peeked through the cotton, small and round, the size of peanuts. She smiled at him, showing pretty teeth, and crossed her legs, her tiny skirt riding up her narrow thighs.

'Do you want a drink?' he asked, conscious suddenly of his words slurring. She drank brandy with Coke. Doubles at a time.

'How about it?' she asked, holding out her hand.

He followed her outside, and filled her hand with money. She stopped in a doorway and drew him in. He reached to kiss her, but she pulled away, dropping down, kneeling in front of him, her small fingers fumbling with his zip, her little girl's mouth teasing him, drawing him out. He closed his eyes, scarcely able to stand as the pleasure roared through him. Afterwards she spat in the gutter and walked away.

He fell from the doorway and followed in

her footsteps. The streets were filled with people. They all seemed to have somewhere to go, to be with someone. He walked down the road, heading towards the river. Light poured from doors and through windows smeared with condensation. A band was playing, country music. Tears filled his eyes as he stopped to listen to the aching choke of a harmonica. He pushed his way in through a half-open door, stepping over a couple who were lying on the footpath, their legs splayed out over the cobbles, their arms wrapped around each other. He squeezed his way up to the counter. It was nearly closing time. Panic filled him as he watched the big hand on the round wooden clock high on the wall creeping up to and past the number eleven. He banged on the bar, waving at the barman, who seemed to have stopped serving and was lounging at the far end, a cigarette in his hand.

'Hey, over here. A pint. Please.'

The barman looked at him, eyes narrowed through the smoke. He waited for a couple of seconds then moved reluctantly towards the taps. Slowly, carefully, he put a glass under a spigot and began to pour. McLoughlin felt relief flooding through him as the stout flooded into the glass. He pulled himself in closer to the bar, making space with his elbows between the jostling bodies and shoved his left hand deep into his trouser pocket, looking for money. Flesh pressed in all around him. The curve of a buttock against his, the softness of a breast against his back, the heavy thrust of a beer drinker's gut against his ribs. He closed his eyes and leaned back into the warmth, his fingers curling around the comfort of the glass. And then he felt it, unmistakable, a hand touching him, feeling his balls, tracing the line of his penis through the soft wool of his trousers. For a moment he did nothing. He stood, looking at his own flushed face in the mirror behind the bar. The hand moved gently, slowly, then suddenly, pain, excruciating, shooting down his thighs, up into his groin, and out into his belly as the hand twisted and turned, grasping the soft loose flesh of his scrotum and pinching the hard spheres of his testicles. Vomit rose up into his mouth. He dropped the pint glass. It fell and rolled, the creamy liquid pouring across the bar, drenching, soaking, flooding. He screamed once, loudly, then staggered back, crashing through the people around him and finally as the hand released him, falling onto the filthy floor, lying, sobbing, surrounded by shoes, boots, butts, crisp packets, rubbish.

Someone, he didn't know who, helped him to his feet and led him outside where he sank onto a low window sill, gasping out his thanks. And then he saw him. Lounging against a lamp-post on the other side of the narrow street. The light shone down on his blond hair. He was smiling, a broad smirk of triumph carving his face in two. He walked slowly towards where McLoughlin was sitting, his hands tucked into the pockets of his jeans. 'Naughty, naughty,' he said, then turned and sauntered away.

McLoughlin took his handkerchief from his pocket and wiped the tears from his eyes. He blew his nose. Cold seeped into him. His jacket and shirt were sodden. He felt in his pocket for his wallet and car keys. His hands shook as he did up the buttons of his jacket. He got to his feet and began to walk carefully back towards Dame Street and his car.

He hadn't been out socializing since that night. A couple of the lads had phoned him but he'd said he had flu. The doctor gave him a cert. Told him to take it easy, pre-scribed tranquilizers, warned him about taking them with drink. He'd flushed the green and black capsules down the loo. There would be an inquiry into the Mitchell case. He wasn't sure which way it would go. The judge had been extremely critical of their conduct. 'Mendacious,' he had called it. Said it 'grievously undermined the integrity and the legality of the criminal process'. Said that 'irreparable harm had been done which militated against the accused's right to a fair trial now or at a future date'. Even if he was exonerated, he didn't think he'd have much of a future in the force. But did he care any longer? It was, after all, just a job. Nothing more.

He stood up and went out onto the terrace. The concrete slabs were slippery under his feet. Green algae had grown on them over the winter. They needed to be treated, like his boat. This summer he had planned to go to France, maybe even the Mediterranean. He would sneak past the Gates of Hercules at Gibraltar and meander, rust-red sails against the navy-blue sea, as far as Menorca. The little island. He would lose weight, get fit and strong, cleanse his mind and his body. Lick salt from his lips as he swam, pushing his arms and his legs together like a frog. It was all ahead of him. If he could just free himself from everything that had happened, the corroding sense of guilt that followed him around every day, sneaking up on him when he let his guard down.

He remembered last summer, the beautiful summer, when it had all begun. If he could only go back to the beginning again. He'd do it all differently. He knew he would.

50

'How long will it take?'

'About a week, perhaps ten days.'

'Without water?'

'Without water.'

'And with water?'

'Much longer, a month. Possibly a month and a half. Once 60 per cent of body weight is lost it is inevitable.'

'But you won't do it, will you?'

'Why not?'

'Let me touch your hair. The way I used to. Let me feel it against my skin, slippery and soft, making me shiver.'

She turned her head and let it drift over Patrick's bare chest. Backwards and forwards, the fine strands falling across his nipples, gleaming like a bird's wing.

'Yes, that's it. Do it again.' He arched back, the firelight turning his pale skin the colour of Victorian gold. 'Kiss me, kiss me now.'

'No,' she said, 'not yet.'

He had come to see her. The night before the trial ended. She wasn't expecting him. And she called out, asking who it was, before she opened the door. As he stepped inside he pulled her to him. He took her head between his hands and kissed her. First on the forehead, then on the bridge of her nose, then on each cheek and finally on the mouth. She opened her lips and his tongue slid in, meeting hers, in that familiar way. Then she stepped back, and took him by the hand, leading him into the firelight.

They sat side by side in the old armchairs. He began to talk. Memories poured from him. He took hold of her left hand, and held it tightly, running his fingers over hers, from time to time kissing her palm, or rubbing its soft skin against his cheeks and his chin. 'I had forgotten,' he said, 'how much I loved you.' And he stood her again in the middle of the room, and began to undress her, dragging her clothes from her body.

When she was naked he knelt down, his head against her belly, his arms tight around her hips. Then he pulled her onto the floor and cradled her to him, feeling her softness through the layers of his clothes, breathing in the smell of her skin, from the creases in her neck, the hollow of her armpit, the bend of her elbow, the dark softness of her hair.

'Let me,' she said, and she rolled him onto his back, tugging at his shirt and tie, his belt and trousers, until he too was without clothes. She lay beside him, resting on one hip, and touched him, running her hand down his chest, over his stomach, gently, carefully.

'Do you remember?' she asked. 'The picture in the gallery.'

'Of course,' he replied, turning his head to look at her. 'The beautiful bare-breasted lady. Robert Fagan's wife, wasn't she?'

'Would I still remind you of her?'

He raised himself up on one arm and touched her nipple, then bent to take it in his mouth, pushing her down flat on the hard floor, gathering with one hand both her wrists behind her head. Then with the other hand he opened her to him, feeling her wetness slipping down his fingers, pausing to lift them to his nose, touch them with his tongue, before pushing himself deep inside her, until she opened up her mouth to let out all her pain and her body rose up to meet him. He kissed her then, nipping her top lip with his teeth, so the taste of her blood filled his mouth, and then he let go of her hands so her arms could fold around him and her legs slide up his back until she rolled him over and braced herself against the floor, crouching above him while he reached up to kiss her, to lick her, to bite her, his fingers leaving their red imprints across her white skin.

'My love, did you ever love anyone the way you loved me?'

She didn't answer. She pulled herself off him and knelt, her hair falling forward, her mouth sliding up and down his silkiness until there was nothing else but the sounds and the smell and the sweetest pleasure.

She thought about him now as she sat in the back seat of Jimmy's big car, how he hadn't believed her when she told him what she wanted to do. How he had looked at her and laughed. Nervously.

'Think about it,' she said. 'Think about what he did to her.'

And he had thought about it. She had watched him in court, the way his gaze rested on Jimmy's face. Drifted from his files and his piles of books, constantly, inexorably, back to the bright golden hair, the pretty blue eyes and the soft red mouth. A puzzled gaze, some of the sureness of the barrister knocked off. And he had said to her, 'I should be inured to this. I thought I couldn't be shocked or frightened or horrified by anything. But, suddenly, I am.' She had seen how Jimmy came up to him after the judge announced that he was dismissing the charges. She had seen how he took him by the hand, and put one arm around his shoulders, thanking him, congratulating him. And she saw the look of revulsion on Patrick's face, how he moved away quickly.

She had said to him, that first night he came to see her. 'You have breathed the same air as that thing that calls itself a human being. You have sat in the same room with him and talked about the weather and football and the price of a pint. But don't you see, can't you see, that he is a monster? How do you think he killed our daughter? He didn't just beat her to death with his fists. First of all he turned her into an object, a shapeless, inhuman creature. That is what he did. And that is how he was able to kill her. And that is what I will do to him.'

They were stopped now at traffic lights. The suburb of Tallaght lay all around them, the houses the colour of diluted orange squash in the light that poured from the surrounding criss-cross of roads. To the right was the white glow from the glass dome over the shopping centre. She had been there with Mary, one bright summer's evening, to see a film. She couldn't remember what it was, but she could still feel the greasy slick of popcorn on her fingers, and Mary's breath on her cheek as she whispered a running commentary in her ear, making her laugh, until a man sitting in front had turned round and told them off, sternly.

She shifted on the leather seat. It creaked beneath her. It was very quiet inside the car apart from the heavy breath of the engine idling, and the muffled pulse of the traffic. She looked up at the rear-view mirror, and at Jimmy's eyes which flicked constantly from the road to her face.

'Of course you know where we're going, don't you?'

He shrugged.

'Well, then, where would you like us to be going?'

He turned round to look at her, one hand

drooping over the seat. He touched her knee, lightly.

'Clever, aren't you? How did you find out about it?'

The lights changed to green and the stream of traffic moved off. Slowly at first, then gathering speed along the wide straight road. Three cars behind them on the inside lane, McLoughlin straightened up, half lifting himself from his seat to get a better view of the black Mercedes. And its passengers. The man in front with the fine blond hair, and the woman in the back, the shape of her head and shoulders unmistakable, even through the disguising shroud of her long shawl.

McLoughlin had been sitting on the steps outside the Central Bank when she walked past. There was quite a crowd in the city that night. Tourists, visitors, people out to enjoy themselves. He had looked at the woman below him on the footpath. He couldn't see her colouring, or even her features. But he had known her immediately from her size and her shape, the carriage of her head, and the way she moved. He had got up and followed her, seen her turn to her left and walk down Anglesea Street towards Bloom's Hotel. No, he had wanted to shout. Don't go there. Watch out. But he had pulled back, and waited. And seen him get out of the car and open the back door for her. And seen her get in, willingly, voluntarily, of her own accord.

It had become a habit. Watching Jimmy. It was something to keep him busy, out of the pub, and away from the bottles of whiskey, while his bosses decided what to do with him. 'Patrolling' he called it. He had been careful after that incident, that night when he was so drunk, not to get near enough to be seen. But close enough all the same, to observe what Jimmy was doing, where he was going, who he was meeting. To keep a record. Sure that sooner or later something would give. That he would burst open like a rotting apple, and reveal all the putrescence beneath that pristine exterior.

But he had never expected this. That he would see Margaret getting into the car, driving off with him in the dark, heading out towards Tallaght, and now on the road to Blessington. The last person on earth he had thought would show up, on that warm summer's night, in the middle of Dublin.

The guards had never known where Jimmy

had taken Mary, where he had killed her. He had said in his statement that she had died in his house. That he hadn't meant to kill her, that it was an accident. But she had bled from her nose and her mouth and they had found no traces of blood. They had asked Margaret if she could think of anywhere Mary might have gone with him, but she had been unable to help them. Until she went back to New Zealand, after Jimmy had been charged, and before the trial, and Louisa showed her the photographs that Mary had sent her. Taken outside a pretty stone cottage. She was sitting on a low wall, her head thrown to one side in an exaggerated film-star pose. Pink sedum, white sea campion, tiny magenta cranesbill and purple aubrietia tumbled around her. Behind was the cottage and above it, like a finger pointing skywards, a huge brick chimney.

She questioned Louisa. Did Mary say where it was, who lived there? Louisa was kind. She gave her the letter that had come with the pictures.

'Here,' she said. 'Maybe it'll help. Maybe the police would like it.'

But it didn't help. It told her where the cottage was, but it also told her a lot more. Details that made Margaret feel ill, her mouth filling with saliva as she read of her daughter's feelings for the man who killed her. Of her desire for him, of her need for him, and her wish to be an adult, to be free of her mother.

It was darker now. They had left the main road, and were climbing higher into the hills. Jimmy leaned back again and tapped his fingers on the upholstery.

'Did you recognize the car?' he asked.

She turned away from the window. 'What?'

'The car, you've seen it before.'

'Have I?'

'Don't you remember?'

'No.'

'A couple of nights before Mary died. She wanted to see you. She was crying for you. So I drove her down to the house. You were standing outside on the front step in the moonlight. She wanted to wave, but I would have had to untie her hands.'

She looked out into the dark again. Mary's face looked back at her, Mary's body pressed against her side, Mary's voice whispered in her ear.

She had sat up in front of the fire. Patrick had lain beside her. With one finger he traced the silvery lines across her stomach.

'Like snails' tracks, aren't they?'

Written on my body, she thought. Her birth and her death. In the shape of my breasts and my belly, inside and out. Marked by her.

He got more wood for the fire and built it up so it reddened her skin. He brought whiskey and glasses from the kitchen and a rug from somewhere. He wrapped it around her and pulled her down beside him, cradling her in his arms like a small child. He watched her, the way her face softened and crumpled, her eyelids fluttering as she began to dream. They had slept together so rarely. That first weekend in Hugh's flat, the time she stayed in his house, the weekend in Mayo. He didn't think she knew how much he had wanted her, wanted to lie beside her, turning as she turned, breathing as she breathed, dreaming as she dreamed, in unison, unconscious, unaware and wakening beside her, his eyes opening as hers opened. Carefully he reached for his wallet which he had placed with his car keys on the hearth. He had taken one of the photographs of Mary, and slipped it into the inside pocket, where he kept pictures of James and Conor. He pulled them all out now and spread them on the floor. My children, he thought, as he wrapped his arms more tightly around Margaret.

It hadn't been difficult to find the house. Mary had said in the letter that it was above a lake and beside a quarry. Margaret had bought an Ordnance Survey map of Dublin and Wicklow on her way through the airport the day she came back for the trial. She had sat at the kitchen table that night and spread the map out in front of her. And there it was. Ballyknockan, across the lake from Blessington, twenty miles or so from Dublin. A cluster of stone buildings and a stack you could see for miles.

She had borrowed the next door neighbour's car and driven out, across the causeway, the lake cold and unwelcoming, and up through the village. The cottage was screened from view by a stand of pines. An iron five-barred gate stood open and beyond it a winding, narrow track. In front of the house was a concrete terrace surrounded by low walls. And in a pot beside the door a large grey bush. She bent to pull the dried remains of last summer's flowers. Lavender, white lavender. She peered through the small windows, noting the huge hearth and the turf ashes blown in a brown drift across the flagged floor. She walked round to the back and found three outhouses, solid beehives of dressed granite, each with a large padlock on its heavy wooden door.

Was this the place where Mary had died? She wasn't sure until she got the jack from the boot of the car and smashed in one of the small panes of glass. Then, as she put her head carefully over the jagged sill, she smelt the stale smell, saw the iron ring on the wall and the straggling brown marks, finger-shaped, hieroglyphics waiting for her Rosetta stone.

After she had wiped the vomit from her mouth and sat for a while in the shelter of the pine trees, she went back to peer in through the windows of the other sheds. The second contained what seemed to be garden equipment, a long-handled fork, a spade and a hoe, in the corner a wheelbarrow, and beside it a pile of concrete blocks and a length of blue nylon rope. The window of the third was covered from the inside with a heavy black blind. She pulled at the padlock, and banged on the door but with no effect. She would have to wait.

The barman in the pub by the lake roused himself from his game of pool to boil the kettle for a hot whiskey. His friend looked on. Then, fat belly falling over the table, he leaned forward to pot another red. The glass was smeared but she drank without complaint and ordered another.

'And what will you and your friend have?' she asked.

Time passed. Beams of sunshine glanced through the dirty windows, lighting up an unwashed floor, stained cushion covers, the layer of fine ash from last night's fire.

'So, tell me,' she asked, 'who owns that nice little cottage up by the quarry?'

The barman stepped back from the table and paused while he considered the game. He walked around to the other side, massaging the end of the cue with a cube of chalk.

'They're Germans, aren't they, Mick? Or are they Dutch?'

His friend lounged against the bar, half empty pint glass in his hand.

'No, they're definitely Germans. They don't speak much English. The Dutch are better at the languages.'

'So have they been here recently?'

'Not now. They used to come over every year for a couple of weeks in the summer. They had daughters, gorgeous-looking girls.

They did a lot of windsurfing and water-skiing. They'd a boat on the lake. But something happened. Didn't the old man have a heart attack or a stroke?'

'Did he? You'd know. I wouldn't have a clue. Too many new people out here now. Not the way it used to be.'

'Would it be for sale, the, house, do you think?'

He shrugged. 'Couldn't say, but I'm pretty certain they sold the boat last year.'

What was it Mary said in her letter to Louisa? That the cottage belonged to a family from Frankfurt. That Jimmy had a special arrangement, with them, to collect them from the airport. That they'd given him a key, so he could keep an eye on the place, but he hadn't heard from them in a while. That it was great. He could go there any time he wanted, and it was really out of the way.

It was very dark away from the main road. Even now at midsummer, when the light still clung after the sun had dropped behind the hills. No moon, no star to steer us by, McLoughlin thought, as the rest of the traffic drifted away, filtering into the housing estates on either side of the dual carriageway, until there was just the one pair of red lights in front. He kept his distance, as the road narrowed to a single lane, the street lights ended, and countryside replaced suburbia. Pine trees on one side, tall dark shapes planted right up against the wooden forestry fence, and on the other, open fields where groups of cattle stood, jaws rhythmically chewing, eyes shining, as his headlights played across them. He tried to imagine what was happening inside the car in front, but somehow he couldn't. He needed a drink very badly. Just the one, to settle his nerves, and calm him, so he could think. He slowed down, and pulled into the side of the road. He reached over and felt around in the glove compartment, his fingers finding a torch, a couple of maps, a forgotten packet of half Coronas. He slammed it shut with a disgusted click, then leaned down to grope in the gap underneath the front seat. Nothing, but a couple of biros and an old notebook, the pages curled and grimy. He got out of the car, and hurried around to the boot. Inside was a sports bag. Left there after some weekend trip or other. To play squash or badminton with the lads, he probably said to Janey. An excuse, they both knew, to get away, to Galway or Cork, for some fun without her. He rummaged inside it, pulling out a pair of runners, thick socks, tracksuit trousers, a shirt that still smelt of alcohol and stale sweat, and underneath them all, the smooth bliss of a bottle. Vodka, three-quarters full.

He got back into the car and carefully unscrewed the cap, lifting it to his mouth to swallow a great, burning gulp. He coughed as he replaced the top, wedged the bottle between his thighs, and started the car again, speeding now to catch up. It was a while before their lights appeared like two glittering red eyes, a quarter of a mile or so in front. As a reward he lifted the bottle again to his lips, and for the first time in ages he felt almost happy. She was here. Once more. He thought he'd never have the chance to talk to her again, to apologize to her for what had happened. But maybe now everything would be different. His foot pressed down on the accelerator, and he drank again from the bottle. Then slowed abruptly as he swung onto the tree-lined main street that ran through the little seventeenth-century town of Blessington. A crowd of people were standing around outside the pub, some still with glasses in their hands. A lot of shouting, laughter, then someone burst into song. A football chant.

'Olé, olé, olé, olé,
Olé, olé.'

Taken up by the others, in unison, one loud voice breaking up the night's silence. Nice to see people enjoying themselves, McLoughlin thought, the vodka beginning to smooth away the troubled edges of his anger and tension. He wound down his window, leaned out to wave and shout encouragement. He was tempted for a moment to stop and join them, offer around his bottle, sing their silly song, forget about the car that once again had disappeared from view. But the thought lingered, just for that moment, as long as it took to drive through the town, and leave behind the brightness of its street lights and windows. And look again for the lights of their car, the two beacons that were drawing him on.

But where were they? The only lights now were coming from behind, dazzling his eyes in the rear-view mirror, then passing him out, or coming towards him on the other side of the road, figures in silhouette as they shot by. And up ahead was a junction. Straight on was the road to Baltinglass; to the left the bridge across the lake, to the Poulaphuca reservoir, and the villages of

Valleymount and Ballyknockan on the far side. He stopped again, and again drank from the bottle. He wiped his mouth with the back of his hand, trying to think, to work out which way they would have gone. He got out of the car and walked, first ten paces down towards the lake, then back to the crossroads and ten paces in the other direction. A sign was what he wanted. Something to show him where to go. But there was nothing. Only the sound of his shoes scuffing over loose stones, and further away the insistent yapping of a dog. And another, and another, a chain of sound. Signalling what? The passing of a car? Someone calling out for help? He listened again, spinning around to try to pinpoint the direction. Then he got back into the car and turned towards the bridge, the water ahead like a spreading pool of black ink, the darkness closing in around him.

Darkness too, in the laneway that Jimmy had turned into. Only the lights of the car cutting through the black, the yellow beams bouncing over the pot holes. Quiet, hushed. No sound when he switched off the engine but his breath coming from his mouth in short gasps. He got out of the car first and came around to her door. He held it open for her, and as she stood beside him he lifted his arm and let it graze her breast. His face was in shadow, but she could see the outline of his open mouth and smell his excitement. He took her hand. It was cold and limp. He fumbled with the keys and unlocked the low front door. He stood aside to let her in.

They had sat in front of the fire, Patrick and Margaret, that night wrapped in blankets, drinking whiskey and talking.

'This reminds me,' she said, 'of what it was like all those years ago.'

'All those years ago.' Patrick turned her face towards his own. He kissed her gently and pulled her head onto his shoulder, 'Have you ever done anything like this with anyone else?'

'Have you?' she asked, her voice soft.

'Tell me what you want,' he said.

'I want him to be punished. Really punished. The way he punished Mary.'

'But the state will punish him.'

'Will it? How? With a prison sentence which will last barely seven years? That's no punishment. No, I want to do it. On her behalf. And I want you to help me.'

'How?'

542

'I want you to do your job to your utmost. And then I want you to deliver him to me.'

'And will that make you happy?'

'Nothing will make me happy. Ever again.'

'Tell me again what you want.' And he pulled her down beside him, wrapping his body around hers, lulling her with his warmth, until eventually he slept, and she lay awake, staring at the shadows cast by the firelight on the ceiling, until the sun began to creep back into the room.

She didn't look behind her as she walked into the cottage in front of Jimmy. She knew what would happen. They had agreed it all.

'What will you use?' she had asked Patrick.

'I have just the thing. A heavy rubber cosh. It was given to me, as a joke really, by an old client. But I know how to use it. You learn a lot playing rugby.'

She waited until there was silence. Then she turned round. Jimmy was lying on the floor. Patrick was bending over him, handcuffing his hands behind his back. Margaret picked up the set of keys that had dropped like a silver blossom beside him. She knelt down and checked his pulse.

'OK?'

'He's fine.'

Together they dragged him out through the back door. It had been easy for Patrick to push it in, the jamb rotted by the winter wet, to wait in the dark until he heard the sound of the car, then to take his place in readiness. Margaret took a small torch from her bag and tried each of the keys in turn until the padlock on the outhouse clicked open. She stepped inside and shone the light around her. Over the marks on the wall, the marks on the cement floor, the iron ring with the length of chain hanging from it. They didn't speak as they dragged Jimmy inside. Patrick held the light while Margaret threaded the length of chain through the loop in the cuffs and padlocked it tightly around the ring. Jimmy bled against the wall, his head drooping. Margaret handed Patrick the keys. Then she sat down, cross-legged, and waited.

The barking of the dogs, drawing him on around the margin of the lake. White cottages scattered here and there like handfuls of sugar lumps. Soft smudges of light behind curtains. A child's bicycle leaning against a hedge. A car up ahead, but too small. McLoughlin drank again, and rubbed his eyes, tired now. Exhausted from the days spent watching, waiting, wondering. He wanted to sleep, to rest his head on Margaret's shoulder. To see in the dark the outline of her jaw and her mouth. To hear her voice. To stop her before she got hurt, before she ended up like her daughter. Ahead was another junction, a sharp bend to the right. He tried to slow down, to turn in time, but his back wheels skidded, and he slid sideways, feeling the lurch of a ditch opening up beneath him. Then silence as the engine stalled and stopped. Shit. He banged his hands down violently on the steering wheel, then got out of the car, and walked around to the other side to assess the damage. He leant against the passenger door and pushed, feeling the car move beneath the weight of his shoulder. He got back into the driver's seat, put the car into gear and turned the key in the ignition. He revved the engine and slowly, carefully, he began to move forward, the tyres gripping the long grass of the verge, until he was free. And on the road again. Tired, clinging on to the bottle for support. And saw a signpost. Black letters on a dirty white background. He craned his neck to read it. Ballyknockan. His headlights showed him small stone houses, a narrow main street, curving down to the lake, then branching off, up towards the dark undulating curves of the Wicklow hills. Which way to go? He stepped on the brakes, and again the car stalled. He leaned back in the seat, his head lolling. His eyelids closed, just for a moment. He struggled to open them. Again, as if he had lost all control of his body, they slid shut. He tried again, but the effort was too much. He shifted his legs and the bottle rolled down onto the floor, resting beside his left foot. He leaned back. He slept.

She wanted to know, she told Patrick, everything that had happened to Mary during those eight days of her imprisonment. He had argued with her, pleaded with her. Pointed out that she would be giving satisfaction to Jimmy.

'You know what he wants is to draw you into it with him. Don't you. Don't let him do it.'

But there was no give in her. So now she waited in the dark, until Patrick came in, the torch in one hand, a wad of photographs in the other. He sat down beside her. He handed her the light and the pictures. Some were in black and white, some in colour. He watched her face as she flicked through them. Soon her skin bore the same pallor as her daughter's had in death.

'Wait for me outside,' she said.

'How long will you be?'

'Not long.'

Pain, pounding through Jimmy's neck, up the back of his head, down into his temples. Pain in his shoulders, his wrists, something cutting into his skin, dragging at his arms. He tries to move, but he cannot. He tries to pull himself upright, but he cannot get his balance. He kicks out with his feet, but there is nothing. He opens his eyes. Someone is there. A shadow. Holding a torch that shines in his eyes. He wants to put up his hand, to shield them from the light, but he can't move his arms. He struggles, and cries out. Help me, please, he says. But there is no answer.

The figure moves. The light moves. He sees who it is. Then he remembers. She turns the light towards herself. She has something in her hands. She holds them up, one by one. She begins to speak. Do you know what these are? she says. And then she begins to tear them, the soft photographic paper slowly surrendering its images.

He tries again to move his hands. And he realizes. He feels with his fingers the shape of the metal. And he knows what it is. He tugs and tries to grab hold of the chain. But it is pulled too tight. Already his shoulders are beginning to ache. And there is a sudden pressure on his bladder.

She moves again, easing herself out on the hard floor. Her white skirt spreads around her. He can smell a sweet scent. Lavender, is it? She stands up and comes over to him. She has something in her hands. A roll of grey sticky tape. No, he says, please, don't, but quickly, she has strapped the tape across his mouth, and around the back of his head. And around and around and around, until only his pale blue eyes are visible. And then she has stepped back. Back to her place against the wall. And she has begun to speak.

I asked you once, she says, what my daughter said to you before she died. You wouldn't tell me. You laughed at me, you humiliated me. In the church that day. Do you remember? You thought you were so clever. Getting me to come and meet you. But you didn't realize, did you, what the consequences of your actions were going to be. And now I don't need you to tell me. I know for myself what she said, and how she said it. Because I know her, and I will always know her. As she really was. And now it is my turn, on her behalf, to tell you a few things. First of all I am going to tell you how you will die. Are you listening?

She watched the shock in his bright blue eyes as she explained to him what it would be like to die of hunger and thirst. The slowness of it all, the torment as every cell in his body loses its precious moisture, the madness that would gradually creep over him as his brain wastes. He doesn't believe me, she thought. He thinks that at the last minute I will take off his gag, undo his handcuffs, take pity on him. He thinks I'm a civilized person, compassionate, understanding, someone who believes in the rule of law and justice. He never knew with whom he was dealing. He didn't realize what his actions would do to me. The effect they would have. The damage they would wreak. And now it's too late.

She stood up and looked down at him. At the golden hair, at the pale skin, at the slender body. At the dark patch spreading from his crotch. Then she switched off the torch. She stepped outside, closed the door, and fastened the padlock to the bolt. Patrick was waiting. She nodded to him. He was holding a piece of board, some masonry nails and a lump hammer. He began to close off the broken window. The thud of metal on wood rang out in the quiet night. The last human sound he'll ever hear, she thought.

They drove slowly away from the cottage along the eastern side of the lake, the hills dark smudges above them. Patrick was in front in his car. She was behind in Jimmy's Mercedes. When they came to the causeway that led to Blessington they drove halfway across and stopped and got out. They stood in the dark, side by side, looking down at the blackness of the surface. He held out his hand. She took the piece of plaited cloth from her wrist and gave it to him. He tied it around the keys, to the cottage, to the outhouses, to the handcuffs. He took a step forward, then lifted his arm and flung them out as far as he could. There was a small splash and a tiny echo as the water rushed up to claim its prize. He took her hand and kissed it, then turned it over and kissed the palm.

McLoughlin woke. He had slipped sideways, and now he was lying with his head on the passenger seat, his body twisted awkwardly. Beams of light played across the windscreen, and over the car's grimy ceiling. He sat up slowly, rubbing his neck. It was stiff and painful. And he saw the first car as it passed him by. And the face of the man driving it. And then the second car, Jimmy's car. And saw that Margaret was alone, seated behind the wheel. He twisted around in his seat, reaching for the door handle, nausea making him weak. He breathed in the sweet fresh country air. Then he swung his body around and got out, his eyes burning, gritty, his mouth stale and dry. He stretched both arms above him, feeling the muscles in his back shift and his vertebrae creak in protest. Then he dropped his arms, straightening up, and watched the red points of light, disappearing now as the road dipped and curved away in the distance. And he remembered that night, when he had sat outside her house and heard the voices and seen the shadows against the firelight. He remembered when he had told her about the trial, and she had cut her hand on the vase. And he remembered the way she had rushed from the courtroom. That first day. All those months ago.

He wiped his mouth with the back of his hand and got back into the driver's seat. And drove up the hill, in the direction from which she had come. Through the five-barred gate, along the potholed lane, to the low white cottage. He took the torch from the glove compartment, got out of the car and stood and listened. Silence. He tried the front door, but it did not yield to his touch. He walked around to, the back, peering in through the darkened windows. He saw the dim shape of the outhouses, revealed in the golden beam of torch light, fanning out in front of him. The heavy padlocks on the doors, and the one with the piece of wood where the pane of glass should have been. And then he heard a sound. A rustle, a movement, something scraping on concrete. He put his ear to the door and listened. Again the sound. He fished around in his pocket and brought out a large bunch of keys, then held the padlock in the beam of light, trying each one in turn until at last the metal hook was released. He pushed open the door, and saw, as he cast his torch across the darkness, Jimmy's face looking up at him, contorted beneath the sticky tape, his body twisted by the cuffs. And McLoughlin saw, too, the photographs spread around him. And felt again the shame and guilt eating into him, burning through his conscience like battery acid. As he thought of the way the girl had looked as she lay in the morgue.

He squatted down on the concrete floor. Jimmy tried to move, twisting from side to side as best he could. His eyes filled with tears as he gazed at him above the mask of tape. McLoughlin picked up the photographs and looked at them in turn. And saw the process of transformation. The girl as she had been at the beginning. Her thick curls, her unmarked face and body. And then the expressions on her face. Her cropped hair, her eyes wide with fear and panic. Her body marked. Curled against the wall, her spine turned towards the camera, each of her vertebrae isolated through her fine white skin. Like an anatomical drawing in a textbook. And then he saw, suddenly, the resemblance. The man in the car. The man in court. His thin, handsome face beneath his barrister's wig. His black hair, cut so that the curls were close to his head. Long legs and arms. Long fingers. He flicked through the prints again. Faster this time. Not looking at the details, just at the overall impression. No doubt about it now. The relationship was as plain as the nose on his face.

McLoughlin leaned back against the wall. He began to laugh, an hysterical chuckle that ended as quickly as it had come. He looked, at Jimmy, at the hope that sprang into his eyes. Then he looked down at the photographs again, sorting through them, putting them in front of him in a neat pile. Corners and edges aligned. He picked them up, slipped them into his pocket and took out a crumpled white handkerchief.

'You'd have to hand it to her, wouldn't you, Jimmy? Always one step ahead. Of both of us. But she made a bit of a mistake here, didn't she? Leaving those pictures around. Her fingerprints, I'm sure, all over them.' He leaned towards him again, as Jimmy strained his face up to him. 'And all over that stuff on your face too. I bet she didn't think of that, did she?' And he carefully wiped down and over the shiny grey tape, feeling the contours of Jimmy's bones, smoothing the creases around his nose and mouth.

'Now, how's that? Better?' He stood up and turned and stepped over the threshold into the quiet night. And closed the door, and fastened the padlock, wiping it and the bolt and the edges of the door clean. And walked away without a backward glance. And got into the car, resting his head on the steering wheel, the tears pouring down his cheeks, and the sobs of grief bursting from his throat.

They drove slowly, carefully. Along the T42 to Brittas, left on the L199 towards Willbrook. The suburbs drowsed on one side of the road, the hills on the other. Patrick watched the headlights of her car, following an even distance behind. He thought of her sitting by herself, her hands on the wheel where Jimmy's hands had been. He wanted to stop, to bury his face in the soft folds of skin on her belly, to breathe in her smell, catch her taste on his tongue again. To talk to her endlessly. Tell her how much he loved her now, had always loved her. How sorry he was that he had abandoned her when she needed him. How he had pushed those memories away for years, flinching at first when he thought of her, until a thick layer of scar tissue cauterized his emotions. Until that night in the house by the sea when she had pared back the skin, and exposed once again the raw nerves of his feelings. And made him see that he would have to do the one thing she asked of him. No matter what the consequences. For Mary. To make up for all the years of silence. And now he wanted to know more. About Mary, about Margaret. About their life together. He couldn't believe, somehow, that it would all end here, on this bumpy road in the dark. But he couldn't stop now. He had to keep on driving, watching her in his mirror through Sandyford, past Leopardstown racecourse, until he turned right at Torquay Road, towards home.

He followed the rest of her route in his mind's eye. Down Newtownpark Avenue, the lights of the Howth Road a shining necklace across the bay. Left along Stradbrook Road, turning back through Monkstown and into Dun Laoghaire. The first boat left at six-fifteen. She'd make it with plenty of time to spare. She'd leave the car, as they had agreed, in the car park on the seafront, past where the old swimming baths used to be. Then she'd walk down to the terminal to wait. She'd bought a return ticket when she travelled from London yesterday, so she wouldn't have to speak to anyone. And halfway across the Irish Sea she'd go up on deck and drop the car keys over the side. When she got to Holyhead she'd take the train to London, then go straight to Heathrow to catch her flight back to New Zealand. She'd be there on the other side of the world in thirty-six hours, and he'd be in Sicily, on holiday, with Crea.

She watched the tail lights of his car, red and comforting. She could dimly see the back of his head. And then the orange indicator began to blink as he turned off to the right. He would drive along the quiet hedge-lined roads, past all the big houses wrapped in their layers of silent respectability. He would park the car beside the tennis court, then slip in through the kitchen door. His black Labrador would bang her tail on the hall floor as he passed, and he would bend down and dig his fingers into the soft indentations behind her ears. Then he would walk slowly and carefully up the wide panelled staircase into that bedroom, the one with the pink carpet and the pink bedspread and the photograph on the table.

She wanted to go with him but she kept on by herself. A strip of pale gold lay along the dark horizon. She held the little photograph of Mary in her left hand. All for you, my baby, she thought. All for you.

The publishers hope that this book has given you enjoyable reading. Large Print Books are especially designed to be as easy to see and hold as possible. If you wish a complete list of our books please ask at your local library or write directly to:

Magna Large Print Books
Magna House, Long Preston,
Skipton, North Yorkshire.
BD23 4ND